He pulled her closer to him, and she seemed to fit perfectly in his arms. And then he deepened the embrace, parting her lips to taste of her sweetness.

But at his bold invasion, reason returned. This was Jack Logan! With all her might, she shoved against his chest. Jack was caught unaware by her sudden move and let her go.

She found herself free and glared up at him, her arms akimbo. "You're a horrible, terrible man!"

He grinned down at her. He thought she'd never looked prettier. "I've been called worse," he said.

"I'm sure you have!" she countered.

His grin grew lopsided. "And you, my dear, are one stubborn, hard-headed female. I feel sorry for your poor father. I don't know how he's going to handle you once I get you back to him. I wish him luck, because he's going to need it!"

"We can't get to San Rafael soon enough to suit me!"

"My sentiments exactly. It will be a pleasure to be rid of you!"

# THE LADY & THE TEXAN

## BOBBI SMITH

LEISURE BOOKS    NEW YORK CITY

*This book is dedicated to Debbie Pickel Smith, a true friend and a great supporter of romance! Thanks, Deb!*

A LEISURE BOOK®

November 1997

Published by

Dorchester Publishing Co., Inc.
276 Fifth Avenue
New York, NY 10001

ISBN 0-8439-4319-X

# ACKNOWLEDGMENTS

I'd like to thank the bunch of booksellers who work out of Anderson Merchandisers in Amarillo, Texas. Their support has been phenomenal. Thank you—Bill Lardie, Mike Garner, Deborah McKirdy, Carla Watland, Robert Hill, Pat Brown, Scott Weisenberger, Ann Mangin, Kim Vorpahl, Linda Clark, Jennifer Espiritu, Alena Pifer, Kristen Shannon, Colleen Sommerville, Paula Cariker, Staci Newton, Jim Mueller, Tony Arnone, Mike Dowling, Ron Karis, Tim Creghan, Charlie Southern, Marilyn Deering, Vera Coberly and Sid Thomas.

And two friends I missed at Annie's Book Stop in Florissant, MO—Nena Horack and Melissa Chenault.

# THE LADY & THE TEXAN

# *Prologue*

San Rafael, Texas 1878

*Elizabeth was in his arms, kissing him.*

*"I've missed you," she whispered.*

*"I'd almost given up hope that you would come to me."*

*Just the scent of her perfume aroused him. Already the fire was burning within him to be one with her.*

*They fell together on the bed, their clothing shed in a heated frenzy as they strained against each other. He moved over her and thrust deep within her. She met him in that feverish mating, clawing at his back, urging him to take her harder and faster. Her wildness was unlike anything he'd ever experienced before, and it pushed him to the limit.*

*"Do you want me, Jack? Really want me?"*

*"You know I do."*

*"How do I know you want me? I want more of you, Jack... More—"*

Her taunting urged him on. He quickened his pace, driving into her, wanting to please her. But Elizabeth was the one in control, and she took him to ecstasy and beyond.

She lay on top of him, smiling in triumph. As he gazed adoringly up at her, her passion-sated expression began to change. Jack knew a sudden apprehension as her gaze turned cold and was filled with blood-lust.

*"Elizabeth...?"*

*"You're a fool, Jack Logan... a fool!"* She gave a maniacal laugh as she moved from the bed to stand over him. She lifted her hand and Jack saw only the gleam of the knife before she struck.

Searing agony tore through his body as she stabbed him again and again. She was smiling.

He began to scream...

Jack Logan was thrashing wildly about as he awoke with a start. He threw himself from the bed and stood in the middle of the cheap rented room, shaking from the power of the nightmare. He stared sightlessly around as he relived the horror in his mind. When at last he had calmed enough to realize that nothing had happened, that it had only been another dream he drew a ragged breath and staggered back to the bed. He sat down on the edge and blindly grabbed for the whiskey bottle on the night table nearby.

He lifted it to his lips, eager to find forgetfulness. He muttered a vile curse when he found it was empty.

In a fit of frustration and rage, he threw the offending bottle across the room. He groped around in the darkness to find a match and lit the single lamp on the table. Staggering to his feet, he pulled on his clothes and stormed out of the room. He needed escape from the demons that haunted him.

Jack made his way downstairs to the saloon. It was late, well past midnight, but a few patrons were still there drinking and playing poker. He ignored the others and made his way straight to the bar.

"Whiskey," he ordered tersely, rubbing a hand over his face. He looked worse than a saddle bum, and he didn't care. It was nobody's business but his own what he did. All he wanted to do was drink . . . and forget.

Charley, the barkeep, took out a glass and started to pour him a single shot. Jack leaned across the bar and snatched the bottle out of his hand.

"I want the whole thing, not just one."

"Let's see the color of your money, Jack," Charley said.

"Here." Jack all but threw the money at him. Granted, he only had a few dollars left to his name, but he'd worry about that in the morning. Right now, he just wanted to get through the night.

Charley picked up the money and moved away. Talk had it that this man had once been a Ranger. He had to admit that sober, he would have made a formidable foe, for he wore his guns as if they were a part of him. He wondered what demons were driving him to destroy himself with liquor.

Jack poured himself a full glass of whiskey and downed it. He enjoyed its fiery bite, knowing that he would soon feel its ease. He spied a secluded table near the back and made his way there to finish what he'd started. He had a meeting with an old friend scheduled for early the next day, but right now that didn't matter. All that mattered was erasing the memories that threatened to destroy his very soul.

The knock at the door jarred Jack awake, and he sat up groggily in bed.

"Jack?" a voice called out as the knocking continued.

"Yeah, yeah. . . . Just a minute." His words were slurred and his voice gruff.

It was daylight, and Jack wondered where he was and why he was there. He got up and made his way unsteadily to the door. In irritation, he threw it wide to find himself face-to-face with Dan Taylor, the man he was supposed to have met downstairs half an hour before.

" 'Morning, Jack. Looks like you had yourself one helluva night. No wonder you're running late," Dan Taylor greeted him.

"Dan . . . Damn, it's good to see you." Jack shook his hand as he tried to compose himself. "I'm sorry I overslept. Give me a minute and I'll be down."

"I'll be waiting."

Dan went back down to the bar where he'd already been waiting for Jack for the better part of an hour. It was deserted since it was so early, and he was glad. When they talked, he wanted some privacy.

Jack's appearance had shocked Dan. The Jack Logan he'd known when he'd commanded him during

12

the war had been a brave young man, a man he would trust with his life. He wondered about this one.

Dan had known that Jack had come to Texas after the war and had joined the Rangers. He'd heard recently that Jack had been involved in a particularly deadly incident in the town of Del Fuego. He had quit the Rangers afterward and had been hiring himself out as a gunman ever since. That was why, when word came to him that Jack was in Corona, a town nearby, he'd sent a message requesting a meeting in San Rafael this morning. He had a job that needed to be done by someone he could trust implicitly.

"Sorry," Jack said as he joined him a few minutes later.

"Sit down." Dan gestured toward the chair opposite him. He noticed that Jack had taken the time to splash water on his face and change his shirt, but that had barely improved his appearance. "You look like hell. What's happened to you?"

Jack grimaced inwardly at Dan's bluntness. "Nothing."

" 'Nothing'?" he said pointedly. "You've changed."

"I made a mistake, and I learned from it. I'm not quite so trusting any more, that's all."

"Then why the whiskey?"

"I like the taste," he stonewalled, not wanting to talk about the past.

Dan looked him over with an openly critical expression. "The Jack I knew was a man of conviction and honor. I need that man now. I need someone I can

13

trust and rely on. That's why I sent for you. Was I wrong?''

Jack heard the doubt in his tone, and it stung.

"No," he answered tersely, suddenly caring that he did not look his best. He owed this man his very life, and he would not let him down. He would do whatever Dan wanted, no questions asked. "I'm fine. What do you need?"

Dan studied him long and hard, and then nodded abruptly. "I need you to go to Philadelphia. I'd make the trip myself, but I can't leave right now. My brother and I own Taylor Stage and Freight Line, and we've had some trouble—two robberies in the last few months. I have to stay here and keep an eye on things. That's why I need you."

Jack nodded. "What's in Philadelphia?"

"Not what, who—my daughter Amanda. I need you to bring her back."

"Your daughter?" This was the last thing in the world he'd expected. He'd thought Dan needed a hired gun. He'd certainly be more comfortable riding on a stage as shotgun than traveling back East to escort a little girl home.

"Yes. That's why I need someone I can trust. My wife passed away some years ago and Amanda's been living with her maternal grandmother. Circumstances are such now that she needs to come home."

Jack was silent for a moment as he digested this information. After Elizabeth, he wanted nothing to do with females of any age. He wanted to say no right then and there, but he couldn't. During the war, Dan had saved his life. He owed him. "If you need me to go, I'll do it."

He sounded less than enthusiastic, so Dan quickly offered, "I'll pay all your expenses, plus five hundred more when you get back."

Jack was impressed by the money, but he would have done the job without it. He was about to agree, when Dan went on.

"I do have one requirement."

"What's that?" He frowned.

"I'm entrusting my daughter to your care. I want to know that I can count on you to stay sober while you're with her. Will you give me your word?"

Jack could have groaned out loud, but he knew it was a legitimate request. He hadn't been the most up-standing citizen lately. "I agree."

"Good. Here's all the information." Dan took a packet out of his inside jacket pocket and handed it over. "I appreciate your doing this."

"You saved my life, Dan. Picking up one little girl in Philadelphia is hardly as important as what you did for me. I'm glad to help you."

"I've already written to my mother-in-law and told her that someone would be coming for Amanda. There is one thing, though, Jack." He sounded uneasy.

"What's that?"

"Amanda—"

"Yes?"

"Well, she's not a little girl anymore. She's nine-teen now. I'm sure her grandmother will see that she has a suitable traveling companion to accompany you on the trip back."

Jack stared at his friend and knew he could say nothing more. He had already committed himself. But in truth, if there were two things in the world that he didn't want to do right now, they were stay sober and be with women. And he'd just given his word that he would do both.

The old adage was true—paybacks were hell.

Texas Ranger Jim Eskin took a drink of his whiskey and smiled to himself as he sat at the bar in a saloon in San Antonio.

"You look mighty happy," the barkeep said as he wiped the bar before him.

"It's been a real fine day."

"Oh? What happened?"

"I brought in The Gila Kid today. He won't be robbing or shooting anybody for a long time to come."

"You deserve a drink on the house for that," the bartender offered, reaching for the bottle of whiskey to refill his glass. "It ain't every day a mean one like The Gila Kid is locked up."

"Thanks for the offer, but no more for me tonight. I have to be up and out of here early in the morning."

"Well, the offer stands for next time you're in town."

"I appreciate it."

Jim finished his drink, then set his empty glass aside and left the saloon. It was a moonless night and the streets were deserted. Jim's mood was relaxed as he started down the quiet side street that led to his hotel. But just as he crossed the entrance to a particularly

16

dark alley, an uneasy feeling came over him. It was a sixth sense he had that had saved his life many times—the ability to feel someone watching him. It served him well this time, but not well enough. Jim knew there was danger, but he couldn't prevent it. He started to turn back, but before he could, two shots rang out. Jim collapsed, bleeding and grievously wounded.

The sound of muted, triumphant laughter came from the depths of the alley.

Hank Sheldon emerged from the darkness and walked toward the fallen Ranger. He nudged him with the toe of his boot, and when Jim didn't move, he smiled. "Three down and one to go."

"We're showin' them sons of bitches!" Willy Sheldon, Hank's younger brother, crowed. "Them Rangers are gonna die for what they done to us."

"All we gotta do now is find Jack Logan. Once he's dead, our revenge is complete."

"I'm gonna enjoy watchin' Logan die," Willy said with bloodthirsty eagerness as they disappeared into the night.

"So am I," Hank agreed in a deadly voice as he remembered how their little brother, Kyle, had been killed in a shoot-out with four Rangers several years before. They'd lost that fight and had been sent to prison, but they'd broken out now. So far, they'd killed three of the four who'd taken them in. Only Jack Logan remained. "So am I."

Captain Steve Laughlin of the Texas Rangers quietly entered the semi-darkened room. "Jim?"

"Steve . . . You're here," Jim Eskin whispered. The Sheldons' bullets had done their damage, and he had been hovering near death when some of the townspeople had found him that night lying in a pool of blood in the alley. He had fought desperately to live so he could tell Steve what he knew about the shooting and the Sheldons.

"I came as soon as I got word. God, Jim, what happened?" Steve came to his bedside and gazed down at his friend. He clasped his hand in a firm grip, wanting to share his strength with him. They had worked together for years, and Steve knew Jim was one of the best.

"It was the Sheldons—" he managed in desperate tones. "I didn't see them, they shot from down the alley, but I heard them when they came to check on me. One of them said, 'Three down and one to go.' I heard them, Steve. . . . I heard them." There was a frantic look in his eyes as he drew a strangled breath and tried to summon enough strength to continue. "You gotta warn Jack. . . . They're out to get the four of us who sent them up. . . . Jack's the only one left."

"Joe and Vic—"

Jim nodded slowly as he closed his eyes for a moment.

It all made sense to Steve now. Joe Reynolds and Vic Everly had been shot down in cold blood earlier that month in West Texas. There had been no witnesses to their deaths, no clues to their killers. Until this moment, Steve had been at a loss to explain the murders, but now he understood. The Sheldons had broken out of jail some six weeks before, and they were back for their revenge.

"Find Jack. . . . Tell him they're gunning for him. . . . Tell him he's next."

"I haven't heard from him in months."

"Corona—" Jim whispered, his strength ebbing from the exertion of talking. "He was in Corona last I heard, drinking and working as a gun for hire."

"I'll get word to him right away," Steve promised.

"Thanks." Jim collapsed weakly on the bed, his breathing strained. "I beat them, you know. They thought I was dead." He looked up at Steve and almost managed to smile in spite of his pain.

"I'll make sure Jack finds out," Steve promised. "You get well."

"I aim to."

Steve was proud of Jim. He had once again proven himself to be exactly the kind of man the Rangers wanted. He was brave, courageous, determined and loyal. His injuries were grave. His recovery would be slow, but he would ride with the Rangers again.

Steve bade him good-bye and left. As he stepped out into the daylight, he was ready to ride. He would track down his old friend Jack and warn him that the Sheldons were gunning for him. Then he would go after the Sheldons himself. They had killed two of his friends and had wounded Jim. He wanted to make sure they never hurt anyone again.

# *Chapter One*

*Philadelphia*

Jack Logan was not in the best mood as he stared out
the window of his hired carriage. He'd thought things
would go smoothly once he reached Philadelphia.
He'd thought it would be a simple matter to go to
Margaret Randall's home, give her Dan's letter of introduction and then escort Amanda Taylor back to
Texas. That done, he would have fulfilled his promise
to Dan, and he could get back to doing some serious
drinking. But the way things were going, he wondered.
It seemed he was on a wild goose chase, and the wild
goose he was looking for was one Miss Amanda Taylor.

Oh, he had made it to Margaret Randall's home all
right. Dan's mother-in-law had been expecting him,
and, after reading Dan's letter of introduction, she'd
greeted him warmly. She'd then informed him that

Amanda was not there, but was spending the night at a friend's home. Mrs. Randall had given him the address, and he'd started off to find her.

It seemed, however, that the young woman had lied to her grandmother. Amanda was not at her friend Bethany Wycliffe's home. The butler at the Wycliffes' had told him that the two young women could be found at the address he now sought. He'd offered no further information, and Jack had noticed that he'd been a bit nervous about telling him what little he had. Jack had been curious about the servant's reluctance— until now, as the carriage drew to a stop and the driver called out.

"This is the address you gave me, sir."

Jack descended from the vehicle and re-checked the numbers just to make sure. He shook his head in disbelief as he realized he was at the correct address. He had no idea what sweet, young, innocent Miss Amanda Taylor was doing in this part of town, but he intended to find out. This was no place for a lady.

It was still light out, and for that Jack was thankful. When night fell, this street would be a dark and dangerous place. There was a bar on every corner and scurrilous-looking people milling about. Not that that bothered Jack; he was used to dealing with unsavory characters. Hell, he'd been one until Dan had asked him to do this job. But he could see no reason why Dan's daughter would be associating with them.

The particular address the butler had given him was for a bar called The Palace. There was a crowd gathered in front of it, and he wondered why as he reached up to pay the driver. He started to walk away, judged the look of the crowd, then had second thoughts.

"Wait for me, and I'll make it worth your while," he called back.

The driver's eyes brightened at the promise. "Yes, sir. I'll stay right here."

"I shouldn't be long."

As Jack moved off toward the bar, he could hear shouts and loud noises coming from inside and wondered what he'd gotten himself into. This was supposed to have been a simple trip, but so far nothing about it was turning out simple. He couldn't imagine what was going on, and he girded himself for the worst—whatever that was.

And it was the worst.

The sight that greeted him when he reached the bar's doors and looked inside left him stunned. Six wild-eyed, axe-wielding women were systematically smashing every table, glass and bottle of liquor in the place.

"Down with demon liquor!" Their high-pitched, condemning shouts echoed through the male sanctuary.

"Liquor is a bane on mankind!" another woman yelled as she wielded her axe with enthusiasm, sending a group of startled patrons running.

Jack mourned the loss of the liquor as that particular female destroyed the half-full bottle of fine bourbon the men had left behind when they'd abandoned their table. For the first time since he'd left Texas, he regretted giving Dan Taylor his word that he wouldn't drink. Right now, a straight bourbon would have made all this seem a lot easier to deal with.

"Damn it! What the hell is going on here?" the bartender bellowed, outraged by the hostile invasion. "What do you women think you're doing?"

"Do not use vile language in our presence, sir! We are here to save souls!" the women of the temperance movement responded as they continued their attack.

Jack pulled the tintype Dan had given him out of his pocket and glanced down at it. If one of these battleaxes was Amanda Taylor, he had to get her out of there fast before she got herself into real trouble. The bartender didn't look like the forgiving type.

As he studied Amanda Taylor's picture, he heard more glass being shattered and thought of all the whiskey being destroyed. As much as he wanted a drink, a promise was still a promise. Jack hadn't promised Dan he wouldn't cuss, though, and he muttered a curse under his breath. Forcing himself to focus on the picture of the female he sought, he tried to reconcile this dark-haired, dark-eyed, angelic beauty with the fire-breathing hellions who were wreaking chaos in the saloon.

"Quit wasting my good stuff!" the bartender shouted.

The woman standing near him raised her weapon threateningly.

"There is no good liquor!" she returned indignantly as she smashed another bottle.

"Ladies!" he shouted again, trying to be heard over the din.

When they ignored him, he stayed behind the bar

to protect his most expensive stock. He snatched up the whiskey that had been on the counter and was about to store it away when a tall, raven-haired Valkyrie confronted him.

"Put that bottle down and step back! I don't want to hurt you!" she ordered as she took aim at the bar. "We're here to destroy this terrible evil! This blight upon our land!"

He saw the fierce determination in her righteous expression and stumbled backward out of harm's way just as she brought her axe down with unerring accuracy. She destroyed the half-full bottle of whiskey he'd put back on the bar, leaving him staring at the remains, horrified.

"You swing that axe again and I'm sending for the law!" he snarled.

She did.

And he did.

"You men!" he called out to his patrons, who were standing around in shock. He dodged more flying glass and the spray of wasted whiskey as he continued, "Call the constable! Get some help in here! I want these women arrested and put in jail!"

Several of the men needed no further encouragement. They bolted for the door, eager to go for help.

Jack stepped farther inside the saloon to get out of their way as he took one last look at the picture. He recognized Amanda now. She was the hellcat attacking the bar. He jammed the picture back into his pocket, ready to do what had to be done. If the other men were going for the law, he had to make his move now. The last thing he wanted to do was bail Miss Amanda Taylor out of jail.

"Damn it, woman! I've had enough! Stop it! Right now!" The bartender lost his temper. He advanced on the young woman who was destroying his liquor, intent on doing her bodily harm.

Jack saw the fury in the man's face and knew Miss Amanda was in big trouble. He strode forward, ready to disarm and overpower the woman he'd crossed half a continent to find. He was going to fulfill his promise to Dan. He was going to see Amanda safely home, in spite of herself. True, she was armed and might prove dangerous if he wasn't careful, but he'd dealt with worse than her before and survived.

"She's mine," Jack stated arrogantly. "I'll handle her."

His tone was so deadly and so serious that the bartender stopped his advance. He looked between them and was more than happy to let him handle the axe-wielding maniac. "I want all of them arrested! I want them to pay for the damage they've caused! I want—"

"Will you pay for the damage you've caused in the lives of the countless women and children who were victimized by the evils of drink?" one of the other women cried.

Jack paid no attention to the others. He was single-minded as he stalked his prey. He scowled blackly as he watched Amanda lift the axe again and aim for what looked like the last full bottle of whiskey in the bar. He wasn't about to let it go the way of the others. In one deft move, Jack saved the liquor from certain extinction by snaring her around the waist and jerking her back against him. He twisted the weapon out of her grip.

"What are you doing! Unhand me, you fiend!" Amanda cried out in alarm as she found herself pinned against a hard male body in an unyielding grip. She'd been concentrating so hard on breaking whiskey bottles that she hadn't paid attention to what was going on around her. She didn't know who this man was, and she had no intention of suffering his abuse. "Let me go!"

"Shut up, you little fool!" he ground out. He tossed her axe aside in disgust and started toward the door, dragging her along with him.

"How dare you!" She was fighting tooth and nail to free herself, but it proved impossible. Fear filled her. His hold on her was iron, his strength overpowering.

Jack had been irritated to start with, and his exasperation grew as she continued to struggle, hampering his attempt to get her out of the bar before the law came. Time was of the essence, so he gave up the effort to treat her like a lady and did the simplest, most effective thing. He picked her up and tossed her over his shoulder like a sack of grain. She went still, and he smiled grimly. He might have knocked the wind out of her, but at least he'd shut her up for a little while.

The other women were so busy wrecking The Palace that they didn't react immediately to the sight of Amanda being carried bodily away by the tall stranger. By the time they realized what had happened, Jack was already disappearing out the door with her.

"Wait!"

"Amanda!"

They rushed to follow, emerging from the saloon just in time to see him put Amanda in a waiting hired carriage, yell something up to the driver and climb in after her. The other women ran toward them, fearing something terrible was going to happen to Amanda.

"Go!" Jack shouted to the driver as he slammed the door behind him.

The temperance ladies had almost reached the carriage when the vehicle rumbled off. They would have given chase, but the police arrived right then and complete pandemonium broke out.

Jack was feeling quite satisfied with himself as he sat back on the carriage seat. Dan would be pleased that he'd gotten his daughter out of there just in time. He started to relax, believing the worst was over. He had finally found her. Now, all he had to do was get her home to West Texas.

Leaning back, Jack folded his arms over his chest. He glanced across the carriage at Dan's daughter and tried not to smile. She was a pretty young woman, but he wondered if his friend knew what a spitfire she was. It would be interesting to see what kind of sparks flew once he got her home to her daddy and he found out what she'd been doing in Philadelphia.

Amanda could feel her kidnapper's gaze upon her and was terrified. She had to escape this man! She'd never seen him before in her life and could only imagine what he wanted with her. She studied him from beneath lowered lashes as she huddled on the opposite side of the coach. He was a big man, and he was obviously strong. How else could he have carried her from the bar with so little effort? His very presence dominated the carriage, and she knew he was a man to be reckoned with.

Had she been more calm, Amanda might have noticed that her captor was wearing a Stetson, a rather uncommon sight in Philadelphia. Right then, though, she was not being logical. She was struggling not to panic. She had to keep her nerve. This was no time to turn into a sniveling coward.

Amanda began to tremble as she realized how helpless she'd been against this man once he'd taken her axe away from her. But afraid or not, she had to save herself. Nobody else was going to do it! She might be unarmed, but she could use her wits and outsmart him—whoever he was.

Without a thought, she made a grab for the carriage door. If she moved quickly enough, she could throw herself from the vehicle. She might get a few bumps and bruises, but nothing she wouldn't get over, and at least she'd be free of him. She threw the door wide, ready to reclaim her freedom at whatever cost.

Jack had just begun to relax when Amanda suddenly opened the door and tried to jump out. With no thought of anything but saving her, he reacted instinctively. He grabbed Amanda just in time and hauled her back onto his lap in a bone-jarring move.

"Idiot!" he snarled, thinking how close she'd come to possibly killing herself.

"You animal!" Amanda was not used to being thwarted. She swung out at him with all her might.

She was no weakling. Her slap was hard and caught him fully on the cheek.

Moments before, Jack's mood had almost been light-hearted, but not anymore. He was furious. He crushed her against him. When she would have swung at him again, he caught her wrist in an almost bruising grip.

"Are you trying to kill yourself?"

"Let me out of this carriage! How dare you take me against my will?" she demanded, her eyes ablaze with anger. "Do you know what they do to kidnappers? You could be hanged! You could be shot! You have no right—"

"I have every right!" Jack growled in a tone that would have cowed any man.

But Amanda was not any man, and she was past being afraid. "I've never seen you before in my life! You just walked right into that bar and abducted me! There were witnesses! You're going to be arrested and—"

"Your father gave me the right," he said, cutting her off.

"My father?" She went suddenly still, blinking as she really looked at him for the first time. Under other circumstances, she might have found him attractive, but at that moment she saw only the fury in his glittering, dark-eyed gaze and in the hard set of his jaw. Her tone was cautious as she spoke again. "What's my father got to do with this? How do you know my father?"

"My name's Logan, Jack Logan. Your father sent me here to bring you home."

"My papa sent *you*, after me?" Amanda scoffed, finding that difficult to believe. Her father would never have sent such a barbaric man after her, and he certainly wouldn't have approved of such uncouth actions. "I don't believe you," she said indignantly. "If my father had wanted me home, he would have come for me himself."

Jack shrugged indifferently. "It doesn't matter to me whether you believe me or not. Your father asked me to escort you home, and since I owed him, I said yes."

"You're lying."

Jack shot her an ugly look. He didn't take well to being called a liar. "I've been a lot of things in my life, but I've never been a liar. I've got a letter from him right here that explains everything."

"Why didn't he come himself?" She still didn't trust this Jack Logan.

He was growing even more exasperated with her mule-headedness. "All your father told me was that he couldn't leave the stage line right now and that he wanted you back home."

When she wriggled against him trying to free herself, Jack suddenly realized that he was holding her far too tightly. He'd been too irritated with her to notice before, but her breasts were pressed against his chest and her hips were snug in his lap. Immediately, he let her go.

The sudden release, coupled with the jolting of the carriage almost sent Amanda sprawling. She quickly took advantage of her freedom, though, and shifted to the other seat.

Jack ignored her difficulties as he dug Dan's letter out of his pocket and handed it to her. She snatched it from him, still skeptical of his honesty. When she recognized her father's handwriting, though, she knew he'd been telling the truth, and she was stunned.

"Papa did send you." There was amazement in her tone.

She didn't say any more, but ripped open the missive and began to read it to herself.

*Daughter,*

*I have been notified by your grandmother and by the school that you have been suspended for your "unusual" activities. The news distresses me greatly, and I fear your actions bring shame upon our family name. I would make the trip myself to retrieve you if I could, but the situation is such that I cannot leave the stage line for even a few weeks.*

*I am sending in my stead Jack Logan. He is a friend of many years and an ex-Ranger. I trust him completely and know that he will keep you safe on your trip back home.*

*Needless to say, I am greatly disappointed at this turn of events. I had set great store on your getting the same fine education your mother had. It pains me sorely to know that you have failed in this endeavor.*

*We will speak of this more upon your return.*

*Your father*

Amanda fought back tears as she carefully refolded the letter. It seemed she had let her father down yet another time. She wondered vaguely if the day would ever come when she would do something that would please him. Her father had been disappointed in her from the day she was born for he'd wanted a son, not a daughter. She forced a smile, refusing to let Jack Logan see her distress.

"Do you believe me now?" Jack asked, seeing that she'd finished reading.

"Yes. I believe you." She took a minute to put the missive back in the envelope.

"And?"

"What if I say I won't go back with you?" Amanda looked at him challengingly. She had known that her father would be upset by the news of her suspension, but she'd thought she'd be able to continue living in the East. She wanted to keep working with the woman's suffrage movement. Never in her wildest imaginings had she thought that her father would actually force her to return to Texas.

"I'd say you don't have a choice," Jack said tightly. He would never have guessed that locating Amanda and taking her back to her father would be such an ordeal. But she was turning out to be one contrary female.

His dictatorial tone stung, and Amanda lifted her head to give him a cool, disdainful look. "I am perfectly capable of taking care of myself, thank you. If I choose to stay here, I will. I have much work to do. There's the suffrage movement and the—"

"Little lady"—Jack was deliberately condescending as he spoke—"you are an unmarried female. As such, you are bound to do as you're told. Your father wants you home, and that's the end of it. It would be best if we just got you back to your grandmother's house so you can start packing."

Amanda glared at the arrogant male who was trying to tell her what to do. He was a prime example of just why women needed the franchise! Women were intelligent and perfectly capable of taking care of themselves. They didn't need men! They were men's equals in every way....

She paused at that thought and realized that this Jack Logan had bested her in one area. He was physically stronger than she was. She supposed she had to give him credit for that, but otherwise she refused to give him credit for anything.

"Mr. Logan—" she began calmly.

"Yes, Miss Taylor?" His tone was mocking as he regarded her across the carriage.

"If I go back to Texas with you, and I do mean 'if', it will be because I have chosen to go, not because you've forced me. I will not be bullied—"

"Miss Taylor," Jack interrupted her. "I don't care how you come to your decision to go home. I'm just here to make sure you do it and that you get back to your daddy all safe and sound."

Amanda gave a defiant lift of her chin as she glowered at him from across the carriage.

Jack managed a wry smile at her seeming capitulation, but he wasn't amused. If Dan had warned him about what a hellcat his daughter was, he might have had second thoughts about agreeing to take on the job.

He might have just stayed drunk in a nice quiet saloon somewhere in West Texas. Surely, that would be preferable to babysitting this wildcat, but it was too late now. He'd made a promise to his friend, and he was going to keep it—with or without Amanda's cooperation. And right now, watching her as she scowled at him, he wasn't sure which way it was going to be.

"How did you know where to find me?" Amanda finally asked after a long period of silence. She'd told her grandmother that she was going to be at a friend's house, yet somehow he'd managed to track her down at the saloon.

"It wasn't easy, considering you lied to your grandmother about where you were going to be and what you were going to be doing tonight."

"I didn't *lie* to her!" she protested, thinking 'lie' was an awfully strong word for just not telling the whole truth.

"She thought you were spending the night at your friend Bethany's house. I'd say that was stretching the truth more than just a little bit. I mean, I think your friend is probably being taken off to jail right now," he drawled. "And she'll probably be there a while . . . maybe until morning. How do you think your grandmother would have felt about having to go downtown to bail you out?"

"Grandmother doesn't approve of my interest in the women's movement, so I thought I would save an argument between us by just not telling her everything." Amanda tried to make the reason for her omission sound noble.

Jack gave an expressive shrug of his shoulders.

"Call it what you like. The fact is, it took a while to find you."

The thought that he'd had trouble gave Amanda a small sense of satisfaction, and a slight smile played about her lips. "How did you manage to do it?"

"Bethany's servant gave me the information I needed."

A sudden wave of guilt washed over Amanda as she thought of her friend, who was probably locked up in jail right now and was no doubt worrying about her. Bethany probably thought something terrible had happened to her, but there was no way to get a message to her.

Jack saw the change in her expression and knew what she was thinking. "I wouldn't worry too much about her or your other friends. You all knew what you were getting into once you entered the place with your axes."

She gave him a fierce, defensive look. "I'll have to go see her tomorrow. I want to make sure she's all right and let her know that I'm safe."

"There won't be time. You'll have to send her a note."

"What do you mean, there won't be time?"

"We're sailing for Galveston tomorrow afternoon."

"That's ridiculous! I won't do it!"

"You will."

"My grandmother will never go along with this!"

"She already has. We met earlier today. I told her what I had come to do. She was in complete agreement."

"You are so—" Amanda was seething at his high-handedness. "You have the audacity to—"

He cut her off. "To what? Carry out your father's expressed wishes?" Jack's smile was confident. "He made it clear to me that he wants you back home as quickly as I can get you there. I don't intend to disappoint him. We're leaving tomorrow."

"But I won't even have time to say good-bye to anyone." She gave a slow shake of her head. She should have realized that her father would react this way.

"You have until noon tomorrow. That's when we'll be leaving for the docks."

Amanda fell silent. She was going home. It looked as if there was no way out of it.

For a moment, she considered running away that night, but thoughts of her father forced her back to reason. She loved him. If he wanted her to come home, she would. Perhaps after they'd had a chance to talk, he'd understand why she'd gotten involved with the suffragists. And then, if he did come to understand, he wouldn't stand in the way of her returning to resume her work. That was the hope she clung to as the carriage drew to a stop before her grandmother's impressive, three-story brick home.

Amanda was suddenly nervous at the prospect of facing her grandmother, especially if Jack Logan was with her. She had not deliberately lied to her about her whereabouts, but as unscrupulous as Logan seemed to be, he just might tell all to her grandmother, and that was one confrontation she wanted to avoid on this, their last night together. She prepared to get out of the carriage as quickly as she could, hoping to dismiss Logan with a quick, but firm, good-bye.

"Well, we're here. Thank you so much for your help. I'll see you—"

Jack moved to block her exit from the carriage. "Allow me to escort you inside."

Amanda wanted to scream. Instead, she gritted her teeth and managed a tight smile as she sat back to await his descent. "Of course."

"It wouldn't be proper for me to just drop you off," he drawled as he climbed out of the carriage and turned to help her down.

Amanda met his gaze and saw the knowing look in his eyes. She wanted him gone. He had already proven he was no gentleman. Why was he putting on an act now? She wondered if he'd ever done anything "proper" in his life.

Resigned to suffering his company for at least a few more minutes, she put her hand in his to allow him to help her down. His grip was warm and strong, and she suppressed a shiver at the contact. Certainly her reaction was just because she found him so totally irritating, and not because she thought him handsome or attractive or anything. She pulled free of his touch as soon as she was on the ground and swept proudly away from him, her head held high.

"Grandmother . . . I'm back," she called out as she entered the house.

"Amanda . . . Did that nice Mr. Logan come in with you?" Margaret Randall called from her parlor.

"Oh, yes. Mr. Logan's right here."

Margaret emerged from her sitting room to greet them. "Thank you so much for seeing my granddaughter home, Mr. Logan. You are truly a gentle-man.''

"It was my pleasure, ma'am," Jack answered. He smiled as he glanced at Amanda.

Amanda was hard put not to glare at him hatefully in return. She wondered how her grandmother could be so fooled by him. *Talk about not lying to her grandmother!* She just hoped he'd leave, and soon.

"And how was Bethany tonight, dear?" Margaret asked.

Thinking quickly, she made sure she didn't lie as she answered, "Bethany was disappointed at the way things turned out. We had great plans for the evening, and she was distressed when I had to leave early with Mr. Logan."

Jack couldn't help himself. He could tell how carefully Amanda was phrasing her words, and he wanted to put her in her place. "Yes, it was difficult dragging Amanda away from her friends as I did." He saw the angry challenge in her eyes and smiled easily as he went on. "But there was little time to spare—"

Margaret nodded sadly. "I'm upset, too. I can hardly bear the thought of Amanda leaving me so soon. We have so little time left together."

"And I still have to pack," Amanda added quickly, wanting him to be on his way. "Mr. Logan, thank you again for escorting me home."

"Shall I meet you here at the house tomorrow or shall we rendezvous at the dock?"

"The dock," she answered before her grandmother could say anything.

For a moment, Jack thought she might be be trying

to get rid of him quickly just so she could find a way to avoid returning to Texas. But he knew he couldn't stay there all night keeping an eye on her. Mrs. Randall knew Amanda was supposed to go with him by her father's orders, and he would rely on her influence to see that her wayward granddaughter showed up on time the following day. He left the sailing information with them and arranged exactly where to meet.

"Good night, ladies." He looked straight at Amanda as he added, "I look forward to seeing you tomorrow."

"Good night, Mr. Logan," Margaret said.

"Yes, good night," Amanda said, all too happy to close the door behind him.

She almost sagged back against the closed portal in relief and sighed out loud when he was gone. However, with her grandmother standing there, she had to act as if absolutely nothing unusual had happened that night.

Getting Logan to leave had been hard, but now came the really difficult part. Amanda had to face her grandmother and say good-bye. She followed her into the parlor and sat down next to her on the sofa.

# *Chapter Two*

Amanda could see the disapproval mirrored in her grandmother's expression now that they were alone and she knew a sinking feeling in her heart. Margaret Randall was a society matron, a woman of high standards who expected all those around her to live up to her expectations. In her grandmother's opinion, Amanda had failed miserably.

Not that she hadn't tried to please her. Amanda had wanted to make her proud. She'd studied hard and made good grades. She'd minded her manners and achieved a certain social polish that had satisfied her grandmother, at first. But once she'd heard Susan B. Anthony speak at a suffrage rally, Amanda had been so inspired that nothing else had mattered except working with the women who were trying to get the right to vote.

''This episode of yours has proven quite upsetting to your father and me, Amanda,'' Margaret began, broaching the subject that could no longer be avoided. "Being expelled from school is just the latest in a series of things you've done that have caused us concern." She gave a disgusted shake of her head.

"I had hoped that when Papa found out, he would understand and let me stay here and keep up my work with the suffragists."

"No! I will not stand for you associating with those women any longer!"

"*Those women,* as you call them, are trying to make life better for us," she began, making sure that her tone was courteous and respectful. She wanted to explain to her grandmother once more the freedoms that would be theirs if they were given the franchise. As it was now, women were almost fully under the control of men, and that had to be changed.

"This attitude of yours is precisely the reason why I believe your father is correct in demanding you return home."

"Yes, ma'am." Amanda was disheartened as she realized her grandmother would never change. Margaret Randall thought the world a fine, orderly place. It saddened Amanda that a lot of the resistance to the suffragists' efforts came from other women.

"Enough about that now. We have more important things to consider. I have arranged for a proper hired companion to accompany you on your journey."

"I'll be fine, Grandmother. I can take care of myself. I don't need a chaperone."

Margaret grew indignant as she dictated, "You are Amanda Randall Taylor of the Philadelphia Randalls. You are an unattached young woman. You cannot and will not travel alone across this country with a man who is not your husband or a relative!''

Amanda remained quiet, knowing better than to argue with her grandmother when she used that tone.

"Her name is Miss Eileen Hammond, and she will be arriving here in the morning to meet you and get acquainted before you sail."

"She can be ready to travel that quickly?"

Margaret met Amanda's gaze squarely. "Your father wrote a few weeks ago that he would be sending someone to escort you home. I interviewed Miss Hammond then, and she agreed to take the job."

"I see." Amanda was shocked that her grandmother had known all this time that she was being sent back home and had said nothing to her.

"Miss Hammond is a lovely lady. I'm sure the two of you will get along famously."

"Yes, Grandmother."

Margaret studied her headstrong granddaughter and saw the look of sadness in her eyes. Amanda was a beautiful girl—smart, capable and a quick learner, just as her mother Marissa had been. But unlike Marissa, there was a wildness about Amanda, an untamed quality that had defied all her attempts at civilizing. True, Margaret had learned how to control the wild streak most of the time, but now, with all this suffragist madness and being expelled from school . . . Well, it was more than Margaret could handle.

"It's not easy for me to let you go back to your father."

"I know. I'm going to miss you very much."

Margaret grew teary-eyed as she embraced Amanda.

"I love you, Amanda. I hope you know that, and I'm going to miss you, too."

They embraced warmly.

"Well, we'd better go upstairs and see to your packing. We don't have much time." She rang for the servants as she contemplated all they had to do before noon the following day.

Miss Eileen Hammond arrived at the Randall home right on schedule the next morning. When Amanda met the petite older woman for the first time, she knew Eileen Hammond was her grandmother's idea of the perfect chaperone. "Tiny, but mighty" was the phrase that came to mind as Amanda was introduced to her. Barely five feet tall, Eileen had silver hair and a sharp-eyed gaze that Amanda was sure missed nothing. As upset as her grandmother was with her, Amanda had been afraid that she might be stuck with a chaperone with a sour personality. The twinkle in Miss Hammond's blue eyes had relieved her of that fear, and although Amanda wasn't looking forward to the trip, at least her companion promised to be a friendly, good-natured one.

"Good-bye, Grandmother," Amanda said as she hugged her one last time in the foyer. Their bags had already been loaded on the carriage, and Miss Hammond was waiting for her outside.

"My darling—" Margaret's voice was tear-choked. "Be careful, and write to me as soon as you get home to your father, so I know that you're safe."

"I will. I promise." Tears burned in her eyes as she pressed a kiss to her grandmother's cheek. She loved her with all her heart and hated to leave her.

"Good. You are the light of my life, Amanda. I'm going to miss you more than you'll ever know."

"I'll miss you, too, Grandmother. Take care of yourself."

They embraced one last time, and then Margaret touched her granddaughter's cheek in a gentle caress.

"I told Miss Hammond to keep an extra sharp eye on you and keep you out of trouble, since I won't be along to do it. She's assured me that you're in good hands."

They shared a loving smile, and then there could be no delaying any longer. Amanda hurried outside to the waiting carriage. Her tears fell unheeded as the driver helped her inside and closed the door after her.

Miss Hammond had already taken her seat, and as Amanda settled in next to her, she gave her hand a reassuring pat. "It will be all right, my dear."

"I'm going to miss her," she said softly as she waved to her grandmother from the carriage window.

The driver climbed aboard and took up the reins, urging his team onward.

Amanda watched until her grandmother had disappeared from sight and then turned away from the window and sat back. She drew a deep breath and finally faced the reality of the day—she was going home to Texas.

"Are you excited about the trip, Miss Amanda?" Eileen asked. She was thrilled to be making the journey, having never been farther west than her native Pennsylvania. She imagined that the young woman she was accompanying would be glad to see her father again.

Amanda hesitated before answering, unsure of her real emotions. "It will be good to see my father," she said honestly. "But I'm not looking forward to the actual trip."

"You're not? Why? The ship we're sailing on is quite modern from what I understand. It should be most comfortable."

"Oh, I'm not worried about the accommodations, and if it were just the two of us making the trip, I'm sure we'd have a fine time together. But this Jack Logan who's escorting us . . . Well, he is not my idea of the perfect traveling companion."

"Oh, really? Your grandmother spoke highly of him this morning. He sounded rather nice from her description." Eileen wondered what had transpired between the two to make Amanda dislike him so.

"I found him to be high-handed and arrogant. The less time I spend with him, the better."

"Maybe we can just stay in the cabin for most of the trip and try to avoid him," Eileen suggested, thinking he must be quite awful for Miss Amanda to react this way.

"I would like nothing better, but I doubt we can get away with it. I have the feeling he's going to want to keep an eye on me every minute."

"Well, if you truly dislike him so much, maybe one of us could pretend to be seasick," Eileen suggested with an impish grin. "He might believe that and leave us alone."

"I like the way you think." Amanda laughed for

the first time that day. She decided that she and Eileen Hammond were going to get along famously.

The carriage drew to a stop at the dock where the ship was moored.

"We must be a few minutes early. I don't see Mr. Logan anywhere," Amanda said looking out the window. It was then that she spied Bethany waving at her a short distance away. "Miss Hammond, my friend Bethany's here!"

"Go. Visit with your friend and say your good-byes," Eileen suggested. "I'll stay right here with the carriage."

"Thank you."

Throwing the carriage door open, Amanda climbed down and rushed to greet her friend.

"You got my note!"

Bethany's expression was sad as she hurried to join Amanda. She couldn't believe the events of the past twenty-four hours.

"Amanda! Tell me it's not true! You can't be leaving! Not today! You just can't!"

"I'm afraid I am," she replied, giving her friend a hug. She had sent a letter to Bethany late the evening before explaining all that had happened and hoping her friend would receive it in time. She had desperately wanted to see her one more time before she had to sail.

"This is terrible! What's happened? Your father wants you to come back home? Why?"

"When he found out that I'd been expelled, he was very angry." She looked up just then to see Jack coming toward her from across the dock. "Father sent

Brutus there to bring me back.'' She nodded in Jack's direction.

Bethany glanced that way and saw a tall, good-looking man walking toward them. ''Brutus? Is that his real name?''

''No, but it suits him. His real name is Jack Logan.''

''He's the one who dragged you out of The Palace last night, isn't he?''

''Yes. He thought he was saving me, but I would rather have stayed there with you and been arrested. I didn't need him to rescue me like some knight in shining armor saving a damsel in distress. We were doing just fine at the bar.''

''Yes, we were—until the police came.''

''What happened after we left? We drove off just as they arrived.''

''They took us all down to the jail and would only release us to a male family member.''

''Didn't that infuriate and humiliate you?''

''Absolutely, but I don't think they'll be forgetting us any time soon. At least, I know those in the bar will remember us.''

They shared a smile at the memory of the wild night just past.

''I bet it wasn't easy for you to face your grandmother after what happened,'' Bethany went on.

''I was careful not to tell her about the temperance protest, and thank heaven, Logan didn't either.''

''That was lucky.'' She glanced at him with renewed respect. ''Maybe this Logan fellow isn't as bad as you think.''

''Ha! He's arrogant and obnoxious! You should

have seen the way he manhandled me! I can't wait to get away from him.''

"Well, if he had said something to your grand-mother, you would have had a whole lot more explaining to do.''

"I know. I guess I was lucky that way, but it wouldn't really have made any difference in the long run. I still have to sail for home today.''

"What am I going to do without you?''

"Don't worry. I've got it all figured out. When I get home, I'll tell my father that I'm needed back here. I promise you, Bethany, I'll return as fast as I can.''

"I hope so. I need you! With your enthusiasm and courage, the women's movement can't fail.''

Jack had gotten close enough to hear their conversation. His smile was condescending as he remarked, "So that's what you call this trouble you're involved in . . . the women's movement? You two aren't women. You're just babies. That scene at The Palace last night was a game to you.''

"Babies? We're nineteen years old!'' Amanda countered.

"And this is no game. We were serious last night, and we're serious about getting the right to vote!'' Bethany insisted.

"Of course, you are,'' he agreed too easily, "and your papas still pay for everything and cater to your every whim.''

Bethany shot him a disparaging look. "Our papas may give us some things, but they don't give us what we really need and want.''

"And that is?''

"Equality with men. Women are not chattel," Bethany declared.

"That's right," Amanda added. "We can take care of ourselves. We don't need men to protect us."

Jack eyed them both. "I've known some females who could take care of themselves, but you aren't two of them."

"Why you—" Amanda began, seething at his condescending attitude.

"Miss Amanda, our bags are already on board," Eileen called out from where she stood by the carriage. She had seen the tall, dark-haired, very good-looking man walk up to Amanda and her friend, and she'd wondered if he was the infamous Jack Logan. She hadn't been able to hear the particulars of their conversation, but judging from the way Amanda stiffened at his approach, Eileen felt reasonably certain that it was he. Just watching them, she could tell they struck sparks off each other, and she smiled to herself, thinking this could be a most interesting journey.

"Thank you, Miss Hammond." Amanda was glad for the interruption. The last thing she wanted to do was waste time arguing with Jack Logan.

"*Our* bags?" Jack asked, glancing at Eileen and wondering who she was.

"My grandmother hired Miss Eileen Hammond to travel with me as my companion and chaperone."

"You felt you needed a companion? I thought you were any man's equal," he taunted.

"I am, but since I was traveling with *you,* my grandmother insisted."

"A very wise woman, your grandmother." He

grinned wickedly as he looked around. "She didn't come down to see you off?"

"No. We said our good-byes at home."

"Then let's go on board. It's almost time to sail."

"Let me tell Bethany good-bye and I'll be ready."

Amanda expected him to move away and give her a moment of privacy with her friend. When he didn't, she threw him a cold look. "Is there a reason why you feel the need to hover over me?"

"I want to make certain that everything goes as planned."

"I am not going to run away."

"That's right. You're not." His tone and expression were confident.

"If I had wanted to, I would have," she retorted, angered by his boldness. "As I told you last night, if I travel with you today, it's because I've made the decision to do so, and not for any other reason."

The boat's whistle blew just then, and Amanda knew she could delay no longer. It was time to board. She quickly hugged Bethany.

"It's men like him who make us want to fight for the right to vote," Bethany whispered to her.

"I know," Amanda agreed with a grimace. "And to think that I have to travel all the way to West Texas with him."

"Good luck," Bethany encouraged her.

"Thanks. I think I may need it."

They moved apart, smiling, but sad.

"You'll be back?"

"As soon as I can. Promise me you'll keep in touch and let me know what's happening?"

"I will, and I'll be waiting eagerly for your return."

With that, Amanda allowed Jack to escort her to where Eileen stood. She made the introductions and then moved up the ramp with them. Standing at the rail, she waved one last time to her friend.

"Shall we go below and look at our cabin?" she suggested to Eileen, wanting to escape Logan's presence as quickly as she could.

"Of course," he agreed smoothly. "Allow me to show you the way."

Amanda took one last look at Philadelphia, then turned away, ready to return to the life she'd left behind so long ago.

"Luke! Someone's riding in," Cody Jameson Majors called out to her husband from where she stood on the front porch of their small ranch house.

Luke had been working some of their horses in a corral by the stable. At her call, he hurried to her side. They didn't get much company, and he hoped that, whoever their visitor was, he was bringing good news. As Luke reached his beautiful wife, he stole a quick kiss.

"I missed you, woman."

"You were only down at the stables for an hour." She laughed, thrilled by his ardor.

"It seemed longer," he said with an easy grin. In the time they'd been married, his love for her had deepened. He hadn't thought it possible to care this much for someone, but he knew now that Cody was his life. Without her, he only existed.

"Can you make out who it is yet?" she asked, shading her eyes as she tried to get a good look at the rider. "It's not your father or your brother."

"I can't tell either." He waited another minute, then realized who the man was. "Damn."

"What?" She looked at him worriedly.

"It's Steve Laughlin, the Ranger captain."

"You think something's wrong?"

"He's not here on a social call."

They stepped down from the small porch and went to greet Steve as he reined in at their hitching post.

"Cody, Luke." He tipped his hat as he dismounted. "I'm glad you're here."

"It's good to see you, Steve. How have you been?"

"I'm doing fine, but there's been some trouble."

"We figured that when we saw you riding in. Come on inside out of the heat," Cody invited him. "Have a cool drink and relax for a minute."

"Thanks, Cody, don't mind if I do." He smiled at the woman he knew to be one of the best bounty hunters in the state. She and Luke had helped the Rangers bring down the El Diablo gang, and bounty hunting didn't get any deadlier than that.

Once they'd settled in around the kitchen table and had had a drink, Luke could wait no longer to find out the reason for Steve's visit.

"What's happened? Is there trouble in town?"

"No, nothing like that. I'm here because I'm trying to find Jack Logan."

"You don't know where Jack is? Has something happened to him?"

"Not that I know of, and I want to keep it that way.

That's why I'm looking for him. Have you seen him lately?''

"No. We haven't seen him since right after El Diablo was brought in. Why?''

"Well . . . Jack's changed.''

"How?'' Cody knew Jack was rock-solid, a man she could trust with her life. This news surprised her.

"The only thing I can figure is that all the treachery with El Diablo got to him. He quit the Rangers.''

"He what?'' Now it was Luke's turn to be shocked. He'd known Jack since they were boys back in Georgia before the war. After the war, Luke had ridden west and become a gunfighter, while Jack had come to Texas and become a Ranger. The Rangers had been Jack's life. It was hard to believe that he'd abandoned it.

Steve nodded in affirmation. "He up and quit. Took to drinking and hiring out his gun. I haven't run into him in months, but I've got to find him now. It's a matter of life and death.''

"Whose?''

"His.''

At their startled looks, he quickly explained how the Sheldons had broken out of jail, killed two of the four Rangers who'd locked them up several years before and wounded another. "Jim Eskin heard them talking after they'd shot him. They're after Jack next. They don't intend to stop until they've killed all the men responsible for shooting their little brother and putting them away in jail.''

"Where have you looked for Jack so far? Have you talked to his sister in Galveston?''

"I checked with her first after I left Jim in San Antonio. It seemed the most logical place to go, but she hadn't heard from him in months either. Jim had told me that he'd run into Jack in Corona not too long ago, so I checked there before coming here to you. He'd been there, but no one in Corona could say where he'd gone. He'd led a very solitary existence. One day he'd been there, drinking non-stop in the saloon, and the next day, he'd disappeared.

"What kind of bounty are you offering on the Sheldons?" Cody asked with interest.

"No!" Luke spoke up immediately when he recognized the gleam in his wife's eyes.

She gave him a look that would have made any other man cringe. But not Luke. He knew her too well.

"I was just asking out of curiosity."

"Five thousand dollars apiece," Steve answered.

Cody nodded, understanding why the bounty was so high. "They're that deadly."

"They're that deadly," he repeated for emphasis. "We want them back where they belong—behind bars—and after murdering my Rangers, I want to see them hang."

"I'll see what I can do," Cody said thoughtfully.

"Cody—" Luke gave her a thunderous look, but she only smiled sweetly and ignored him.

"Now, about Jack," Steve went on. "You haven't heard anything from him? Nothing that would give me a clue where to look next?"

"No, I wish we had," Luke answered. "I'll ask around and see what I can find out. If we turn up

54

anything, we'll send word to you through Ranger Headquarters.''

"I'd appreciate it." He stood up to go.

"You won't stay for dinner?" Cody offered.

"As much as I'd like to, I'm worried about Jack. I've got to find him as quickly as I can. I don't want to take the chance of his ending up dead like Reynolds and Everly.''

They walked Steve to his horse and watched as he rode back toward town.

"Luke—" Cody turned to her husband, smiling slightly as a plan began to take form in her mind.

"Cody, don't start. We've got a ranch to run and horses to tend. There's no time for bounty hunting.''

"But, sweetheart, didn't you hear how much he said they were paying for them?''

"I heard, but I don't want you putting yourself in that kind of danger again.''

"I wouldn't be in danger. I'd have you and Stalking Ghost watching over me.''

He was adamant. "You'd still be tracking cold-blooded killers. You remember how deadly the El Diablo gang was.'' Even now, there were nights when he woke up in a cold sweat after dreaming of what might have happened to her while she was working under-cover with the gang.

"I remember exactly how deadly they were, and that's all the more reason why we should do this,'' Cody told him, wanting to see the murderers behind bars. "The Sheldons are killers. What did Steve just tell us—that they had already killed two Rangers and seriously wounded a third? The only one left is Jack.

You know what kind of men these are. They're not going to stop until they've killed Jack, too—unless we stop them first. We've got to do this.''

"No, Cody." Luke was firm. "This is Ranger business. Let the Rangers handle it."

She grew frustrated, for she recognized the look in her husband's eyes and the tone of his voice. Somehow, she had to find a way to convince him to go along with her idea, but she knew she wouldn't win him over by arguing. She had to be more subtle. She smiled to herself at the thought.

It was later, at bedtime, when they lay together in the warm haven of their love, that Cody made her second attempt at convincing Luke.

"You know, if I'd thought like you a while ago, I would never have answered Jack's telegram to bring in the infamous Luke Majors. I'd heard stories that Luke Majors was a deadly gunfighter, and I'd heard how terrible the El Diablo gang was. If I'd played it safe, I would never have met you or fallen in love with you or married you."

"That was different."

"Why? I didn't know you then. All I knew was that Jack was worried some bounty hunter with an itchy trigger finger was going to bring you back dead instead of alive, and he wanted you alive. He believed in you when no one else did. How can you turn your back on him now?"

Luke lay in the dark with his wife in his arms, silently cursing the way she'd outsmarted him. She was right. He owed Jack a lot. If their going after the Sheldons would save his life, he'd do it.

Cody had been curled up against him, but she shifted to brace herself above him. She looked down at him in the darkness. "I love you, Luke Majors. If anything had happened to you, I would have missed this . . . Our life together . . . Our love." She punctuated those words with a passionate kiss. "We have to help Jack. We have to find the Sheldons before they find him."

Luke's arms came around his wife, and he held her to his heart. "I love you, Cody."

"I know. I love you, too, but how would we feel if we heard in a week or two that Jack had been gunned down by the gang?"

"I'm afraid something will happen to you," he said in a low, emotional voice. "I don't want to risk losing you."

"You won't. Don't you remember? I'm Cody Jameson. I'm the best bounty hunter in Texas."

"You're Cody Majors, my dear," he said huskily as he wrapped his arms around her and rolled to bring her beneath him. "And you're right . . . You are the best." His lips sought the sweetness of her throat.

"I work hard at being the best."

"Perhaps you need some practice tonight to stay sharp?" His tone was rich and deep and filled with love.

"Practice does make perfect."

Luke and Cody came together in a union of perfect marital bliss. They loved with their hearts, their bodies and their souls. Each caress was meant to show the depths of their adoration for each other. Each kiss expressed the sweetness of their devotion. Ecstasy was

57

theirs. Pure rapture. They loved and were loved.

Later, their desire spent, they lay together, enjoying the beauty of being in each other's arms.

"Are you sure you want to do this?" Luke asked as he ran his hands over her silken curves. He never tired of loving her, even after all this time of being married.

"We have to. Your father and brother will take care of things here for us, if we tell them why we have to leave."

He nodded slowly, knowing she was right. "All right, my love. When do we start?"

"Tomorrow!" she said excitedly. She had already formulated a plan to use in tracking down the killers.

"Why do I get the feeling that you knew I would eventually come around to your way of thinking?" he asked with a quirky smile.

"Just call it female intuition." Cody kissed him again. "We need to get word to Steve that we're going after them. Then we can start making inquiries. My father's sources are always reliable. We'll need to talk to Jim Eskin, too. I want to know everything he can remember about how the Rangers tracked the Sheldons down the first time. I want to know all the circumstances surrounding their arrests and the brother's death."

Luke could feel the tension building within her. "Whoa, sweetheart. . . . Slow down a little," he said as he nuzzled her neck. "That's in the morning. We still have a lot of tonight left."

"Yes, we do," she said in a sultry voice as she drew

him to her for a kiss. "You won't be sorry for trusting my judgment, Luke."

"I've never been sorry for trusting you, Cody. I love you."

# Chapter Three

"If you need anything, I'm in the next stateroom down the hall. Dinner is at six. I'll be back for you then. If you need anything before then, just let me know," Jack told Amanda and Miss Hammond as he escorted them to their cabin.

"We won't be needing a thing. Thank you." Amanda smiled sweetly at him and quickly disappeared inside with Eileen, shutting the cabin door firmly behind them.

Jack smiled at the closed door. It looked as if the worst was over. He'd gotten Amanda on the ship, and they were on their way to Galveston. The rest should be easy.

Jack let himself into his own cabin, intent on relaxing for a while. He'd had a few tense moments that morning wondering whether Amanda would show up or not. As wild as she was, he wouldn't have put it past her to try to slip away from him. She'd made it quite obvious what she thought about going home to Texas.

Now that they were settled on board, though, Jack could let down his guard somewhat. Except for stops at a few ports between here and Galveston, there would be no way for her to get into any real trouble during the trip. He hoped she would keep to herself in the cabin with her companion. He was looking forward to delivering her safe and sound to Dan and then having a drink at the nearest saloon. It was a worthy goal.

Amanda was amazed that the cabin Jack had taken for them was so comfortable. She had expected a spartan room with little in the way of amenities. To her surprise, the cabin had not only a small sitting room with a bunk that Eileen could use, but also a tiny bedroom opening off it for her own private use. Both women were delighted with the arrangements, and they quickly settled in.

"Miss Amanda?"

Amanda had been resting in her own bed when she heard the call, and she rose to see what was wrong. Eileen sounded strange.

"What is it, Miss Hammond?" she asked as she emerged from her room. "Oh—" The sight of the older woman's green face told her immediately what was wrong.

"I don't think I'm meant to travel by sea," she said weakly, trying to maintain some sense of dignity as she clutched the sides of her bed.

"How bad is it?" Amanda asked, going to her side.

"It's bad," she managed, fighting for control over her churning stomach and reeling senses.

"The only thing I know about seasickness is that it's best if you don't move." Amanda got a cool, damp cloth and pressed it to Eileen's brow.

The boat swayed just then. Eileen moaned aloud at the motion, then managed a woeful laugh. "I'd love to stay still . . . if only the ship would let me."

Amanda made her as comfortable as she could.

"There isn't much more we can do for seasickness, other than tough it out until we're on land again."

"I'm sorry." Eileen truly was sorry. She knew that Margaret Randall had wanted her to keep careful watch over her granddaughter, and now it looked as if it was going to be the other way around for a while. "How many days until we reach Galveston?"

"Too many," Amanda said sympathetically. "Can I get you anything? Anything at all?"

Eileen managed a wan smile. "No. The thought of anything to eat or drink just makes my stomach worse. I'll just lie here and be miserable all by myself."

Amanda tucked the blankets more closely around her. "Just call if you need me. I'll be right here."

Eileen closed her eyes and sighed wearily. It was going to be a long voyage.

As the time neared for them to go to dinner, Amanda was tempted to skip the meal so she could keep watch over Eileen. But the chaperone encouraged her to go.

"I know I said one of us could fake seasickness, but I hadn't planned on this. Still, you shouldn't skip a meal on my account. Go ahead and have your dinner.

I'll be right here waiting for you when you're done, and it will give you an excuse to hurry back.''

Reluctantly, Amanda agreed, promising to return as quickly as she could.

Amanda changed from her rather rumpled day dress into a fashionable, deep blue gown more suitable for the atmosphere of the ship's dining room. It was demurely cut at the bodice, yet form-fitting, emphasizing her perfect figure. She smoothed her hair up into a sleek, sophisticated style that she knew her grandmother liked on her. She was ready to go when Jack knocked at the door precisely at six o'clock.

Jack stared at Amanda when she opened the door. He had been so busy being her adversary that he hadn't thought of her as a beautiful woman, but as he gazed at her now, he realized she was lovely. The discovery irritated him, and he frowned.

''Are you ready? Where's Miss Hammond?''

''She won't be joining us this evening,'' Amanda informed him as she quickly stepped from the cabin and closed the door behind her. ''She's indisposed.''

''What's wrong? Is there anything I can do?''

''Not unless you can speed up this ship and get us to Galveston within the hour,'' she suggested. ''She was stricken with seasickness almost as soon as we left port.''

''Perhaps the seas will calm once we're farther out.''

''I hope so. I'd hate to think that she'll be forced to stay in the cabin the entire time.''

They made their way to the main dining room. It was an elegant salon with long tables set with heavy china. There were several alcoves where travelers could dine in privacy if they chose. Crystal wine glasses were held in racks that hung over the tables, affording easy access to the diners and safety for the glassware in case of rough seas.

"Do you have a preference as to where we sit?" Jack asked.

She was surprised by his courtesy, and she had to admit that she was surprised, too, by his appearance that night. He looked handsome in the dark suit he wore. She thought he could have passed for a gentleman—if you didn't know him—but her experiences with him had taught her otherwise. She was sure that he was a self-centered brute who cared only about his own interests. She supposed there might be more to him, but she doubted it and didn't care to waste any time finding out.

"Let's sit at the main table," she answered, not wanting to spend any time alone with him if she could avoid it.

Jack held a chair out for her, and she gave him a weak smile as she slid into it. He sat down beside her and the uniformed waiter immediately approached to give them menus.

"Yes, sir. Can I bring you or your lovely companion anything to drink tonight?"

It irked Amanda that he was speaking only to Jack.

"I'd like a cup of hot tea, please," she said, perfectly capable of selecting her own beverage.

"Sir?" he repeated, deliberately ignoring her order.

Jack sensed the tension in Amanda and knew exactly why she was angry. Still, it was a man's world.

She was going to have to learn to live with it or she was going to be a very frustrated woman.

"Nothing for me, thanks, but Miss Taylor will have hot tea."

"Fine, sir."

Jack heard her sharp intake of breath as the waiter hurried off to get her beverage.

"How dare he ignore me that way? There's no reason I couldn't order for myself!"

Jack saw the flush of indignation that stained her cheeks. "You're not going to change the world in one day or the way things are done on this ship, so you may as well just enjoy your tea when it comes."

"But he wouldn't even look at me. It was as if I didn't exist."

"Believe me, you exist. I've seen you in action. I'm just glad you don't have an axe right now."

She glanced at him angrily. "You're right. If I had one, I would be tempted to use it."

At the thought of her smashing whiskey bottles in The Palace, he had to ask, "Whatever possessed you to pick that particular bar?"

"Bethany and I had heard about it from a woman whose husband used to drink at The Palace all night and then go home and beat her. She died from one of his beatings two weeks ago."

"Do you really think causing all that damage to the bar made any difference?"

"You think staying quiet and doing nothing is more effective?"

"There are other ways to make yourself heard besides taking an axe to liquor bottles."

"Not for women. We've been held down and ignored by men for too long."

"Not all women have been," he said, his tone serious as he remembered another woman who had been as deadly to reckon with as any man he'd ever known.

"How can you say that when we are practically chattel?"

"When I was a Ranger, I ran into a number of women who were men's equals."

At his mention of the Rangers, Amanda asked, "My father mentioned in his letter that you were an ex-Ranger. Why did you leave the Rangers? They're the best, aren't they?"

"They are the best, and that's why I quit. I was wounded a little over a year ago, and I didn't feel that I was up to doing my job to the best of my ability any more."

"What happened?"

"Let's just say I had a momentary lapse in judgment. It won't happen again."

"So, how do you know my father? He's never mentioned you that I can remember."

"He was my commanding officer during the war."

"That was a long time ago."

"Yes. It was." Jack rarely allowed himself to think of his life back then. His youth had been an idyllic time, growing up at Riverwood Plantation surrounded by a loving family. But then the war had come and the life he'd known had been destroyed forever. After the war, he'd come to Texas with what was left of his family—his mother, sister and brother-in-law. They'd settled in Galveston, and he'd joined up with the

Rangers in the early seventies. Being a Ranger was the only life he'd wanted until last year . . . and El Diablo. . . .

"Well, I'm sure he'll be pleased with the fine job you've done getting me home."

"We're not there yet," he drawled sarcastically.

"I get the distinct feeling you don't trust me."

"I don't trust any woman. I'll keep a careful eye on you until I deliver you to your father."

"Even if I give you my word that I'll behave myself on the rest of the trip home?"

"I doubt your word's worth anything. I've learned the hard way that women say one thing and do another. They're not always what they seem."

Amanda heard the flatness in his voice and glanced at him then. The expression in his eyes was so cold and so devoid of emotion that she shivered in spite of herself. She wondered what had happened to him to make him so hard and unfeeling. Whatever it was, it had turned him into a very dangerous man. She was glad she was not his enemy.

The waiter returned with her tea and was ready to take their order. Jack asked Amanda what she wanted, then told the waiter. Amanda managed not to say anything.

The rest of the evening passed quietly. When it was time to return to the cabin, Amanda had Jack order some tea and a few biscuits to take to Eileen. She wasn't sure if her companion would be up to eating, but she wanted to have something for her, just in case. Jack bade her good night at her cabin and waited to hear that she'd locked the door before he went on to his own quarters.


Amanda found Miss Hammond asleep when she returned to the stateroom, and so she let the older woman rest. After undressing for bed, she brushed out her hair and lay down, ready for a good night's sleep.

The sound of a woman's terrified cry jarred Amanda from her rest. Thinking it was Miss Hammond and that something was seriously wrong, she rushed to the outer sitting room. To her surprise, the older woman was awake, too, and sitting up in bed looking horrified.

"Was that you?" Eileen asked as Amanda came running.

"No. I'm fine. I thought it was you."

They heard the woman cry out again then and realized it was coming from the cabin next door.

"She sounds scared to death."

There was a muted crash, and the unknown woman screamed, "Don't, Micah! Don't hit me again!"

"Shut up, woman, or I'll give you something to really cry about!" the abusive man shouted back.

"I've got to do something to help her!" Amanda told Eileen in an urgent, hushed whisper.

"But Miss Amanda . . . You might get hurt. . . . He sounds so mean—"

"I don't care. I can't just sit here and listen to him beat her." Amanda ran back to her room and grabbed her dressing gown. Throwing it on, she tied it about her waist and ran from their cabin.

Eileen was inspired by Amanda's fearlessness, and she ignored her own queasiness as she got up to follow. She would not let her charge face this unknown, vicious man alone. Tugging on her own wrapper, she went out into the hall.

Amanda hurried to the next cabin and pounded on the door. She wondered if anyone inside could hear her, for the woman was sobbing loudly. She knocked again as she heard the sound of another dull thud. She wasn't sure what it was and she didn't want to speculate, for her imagination was conjuring up heartrending images she didn't even want to consider.

"Open up!" Amanda cried, pounding on the door as hard as she could with both fists.

"Who is it?" the man demanded through the door.

"I'm here to speak to your wife. She sounds like she needs help," Amanda said bravely.

"She don't need no damn help! Go the hell away and leave us alone!"

Amanda heard the fury in his tone, but she was too angry to care. "I'm not going away until she tells me to leave herself."

There was the sound of angry voices from inside the room, but neither Amanda nor Eileen could make out what was being said. Then there was another crash and finally the woman spoke. Her words were mumbled, her voice unsteady but understandable.

"I don't need help. Go away."

Amanda stood before the door, frustrated and furious. She was about to say something more when she looked down the passageway to see Jack coming out of his cabin. He was wearing only his pants and was tugging on his shirt as he strode angrily toward her.

"What is it? Are you all right?" he demanded. His

gaze raked over Amanda. The silken fabric of her dressing gown did little to disguise the soft fullness of her breasts and the curve of her hips, and his body tightened in response. He silently cursed his reaction to the sight of her so meagerly clad.

"We heard things crashing and a woman crying in there," she explained quickly. "The man was hitting her—"

Jack heard the angry voices through the door and realized what she'd been trying to do. He knocked. "Is everything all right?"

"Everything's fine. Go away," the man ordered.

Jack looked from Amanda to Eileen and then nodded toward their stateroom. "You two need to go back inside."

"But—" Amanda started to protest.

He cut her off. "There's nothing you can do here, and you shouldn't be standing out in public dressed like that. Get back inside your stateroom."

The look he gave her was bold, and Amanda suddenly realized just how little she was wearing. She started back to her cabin, but hesitated to go in until Eileen was with her.

Eileen remained to speak with Jack. She looked up at him and put her hand on his arm as she spoke.

"It was terrible," she told him. "We could hear the woman screaming at him not to hit her any more. . . ."

Jack stared down at the little woman who was looking at him much as his mother used to do. He knew he could not just walk away from this. He patted her hand. "I'll do what I can."

She smiled at him angelically. "I knew you

would,'' she said softly as she moved away.

Something stirred deep within Jack's soul. The look Miss Hammond had given him was one of complete and utter faith in the goodness of him and his intentions. He found himself knocking solidly and loudly on the closed door before him. "Mister? I want to talk to your wife."

"Leave us alone!"

"I'm not leaving until I talk to her."

"We don't need no damned interfering from you!"

"If she tells me she's fine, I'll go, and then we can all get some sleep. But I'm not leaving this spot until I hear from her. What's it going to be?"

There was silence, then she spoke.

"I'm fine. Go away."

Jack glanced over to where Amanda and Eileen stood. He knew there was little more he could do.

"Ma'am. If you need anything, say so now."

"No."

Jack remained in the passageway a moment longer just to make sure all was quiet again. Then he moved to speak with Amanda and Miss Hammond.

"It should be all right now. I don't think he'll do anything more to her tonight."

"Thank you, Jack," Eileen told him, giving him a gentle smile.

They slipped back inside their room.

Jack returned to his own cabin, wondering as he went if Amanda could manage to keep herself out of trouble for the rest of the night.

Jack lay back on his bed and turned out the lamp. As he stared sightlessly into the darkness, an image of

Amanda, her hair down around her shoulders, wearing only her silken robe, drifted before him. He gave a growl of irritation and rolled over, seeking sleep. He wanted nothing to do with that hellion.

She was walking trouble.

She was Dan's daughter.

Sleep was long in coming.

Jack could have used a drink.

Jack was up early. Actually, if he wanted to be honest about it, he never got to sleep. Not that it mattered. He was used to going without sleep when he was sober. He shaved, washed and dressed, then went up on deck to watch the sunrise. The ocean was calm, and the day would be clear and bright. Breakfast was to be served at eight, so he went below to check on Amanda and Eileen. He met Amanda in the passageway on her way up to find him.

"I knocked at your cabin, but when you didn't answer, I figured you were already up on deck."

"How's Miss Hammond feeling this morning?" he asked, almost sorry that she wasn't joining them. The feeling puzzled him.

"She's a little better, but I doubt she'll leave the cabin today."

Jack led the way to the dining room, and they ate in relative silence. During the meal, Amanda noticed a couple who came in and sat at the far end of the table away from everyone. The woman seemed intent on keeping one side of her face averted from everyone's view, and she wondered if this was the woman she'd heard crying last night.

Jack noticed Amanda's interest in the couple and hoped that she wouldn't say anything. The lady was wearing a wedding band, so even if she was the woman who'd been beaten, she was the man's wife. Legally, he could do with her as he pleased.

They started to go up on deck after eating, and Amanda deliberately slipped away from Jack, so she could get a good look at the woman's face. She was horrified when she saw the bruises and swelling there. Jack had continued on up the companionway, unaware that Amanda was lagging behind. She waited until the man had left the other woman for a moment, then went to her, wanting to help.

"Ma'am?" Amanda said softly. She wasn't surprised when the woman jumped nervously.

"What do you want?" Her tone was sharp and suspicious.

"My name's Amanda. I believe I'm staying in the cabin next to yours. I'm the one who heard you crying last night."

"I don't know what you're talking about," she said firmly.

"If your husband is beating you, you don't have to put up with it."

"Go away. . . . Mind your own business." She was panicking.

"You can leave him. Save yourself. I'll help you if you want me to."

"Who are you?" interrupted a harsh male voice. "And what the hell are you doing talking to my wife?"

Amanda tensed and turned to look at the man she

73

hated already. "I was trying to help her," she announced with dignity and moral superiority.

"My wife doesn't need your help. Becky's just fine. Why don't you shut up and go on your way?"

He was a small, wiry man with a meanness in his eyes that told Amanda all she needed to know.

"I happen to think that she does need my help," Amanda replied.

"No, I don't. Micah, I didn't say nothing to her. She just came butting in and started talking to me like she knew me or something. I told her I didn't want anything to do with her, but she wouldn't go away. She wouldn't leave me alone."

The look in Micah's eyes grew even more ugly. He grabbed his wife by the arm and pulled her away from Amanda. "Let's go on back to our cabin."

"Wait! Becky—" Amanda felt helpless and enraged at how easily the other woman gave in to him. "Don't go with him. Life can be better than this."

"What do you know about my life?" Becky challenged. "Leave me alone. You don't know nothing about me. I don't want your help. I don't need it!"

Amanda took her other arm, wanting to stop the bully from dragging her off. Micah turned on her, and for the first time in her life, she saw true evil mirrored in someone's eyes.

"You're tempting me to give you a taste of what she got last night, bitch."

"Stay away from her!" Jack's commanding voice cut across the distance between them.

Micah looked up to see a tall, powerful-looking man coming toward them. He tensed and squared off.

"You should control your woman better, mister. She's got no business messing with what's mine."

Jack gave Amanda a look that sent her rushing to his side. "I can control my woman without brute force. An intelligent man doesn't need to use violence."

Micah was seething and look as if he was tempted to fight, but he backed down. "Let's go, Becky." He shoved her ahead of him, and they quickly disappeared down the passageway.

Amanda looked up at Jack, her expression furious. "Aren't you going to do anything?"

"Don't you think you did enough?"

"What are you talking about? I was trying to help her!" She was frustrated.

"The only thing you did was set her up for another beating. Who do you think he's going to take his anger out on? Men like him beat women because it makes them feel powerful. The only way it will stop is if she leaves him, but she's got to do that herself. You can't do it for her, and neither can I."

"There has to be something I can do—"

"You're a bleeding heart. You have no idea what harm you may have caused by interfering. What do you know about being beaten by a drunk? What do you know about suffering? Let me give you a piece of advice, Amanda. Be careful, because a lot of things in life are not what they appear to be."

"Why, you . . ." She was seething.

"I leave you to your thoughts, my dear, but stay away from them. There's no telling what a man like that will do."

"But you said yourself that he might beat her again!" She couldn't bear the thought of the other woman suffering.

"And maybe she damn well deserves it! Some women do, you know!" With that he walked away, leaving her staring after him, furious.

Amanda couldn't believe that he really meant what he'd just said, and in that moment, she despised Jack Logan almost as much as she did the man named Micah.

It was going to be a long trip back to West Texas.

# *Chapter Four*

Amanda's mood was dark as she sat in her cabin later that day. Eileen was napping, so she finally had time alone to think.

The memory of Jack's words returned, and she grew angry again. How dare he say that some women deserved what they got! No one ever deserved to be treated cruelly. Husbands were supposed to love and cherish their wives. Her father had certainly adored her mother. Though her mother had been dead for over eight years now, she could still remember the tender moments she'd witnessed between them. Her Uncle Asa treated women well, too. Some years back he had married a widow named Mona who had a son by her first marriage. He had always treated her with affection and good nature.

Thoughts of the abused Becky stayed with her, though, and Amanda realized that a part of what Jack had said was true. No one could help her if she didn't do what was necessary to help herself. As long as she stayed with a man like Micah and then perversely defended him against righteous attacks, there would be no changing her life. It saddened Amanda to think of anyone being involved in such a relationship.

Still, Amanda wondered what had happened to Jack in his past to make him feel the way he did about women. As soon as she started thinking about him, she got mad at herself and pushed all thoughts of him aside. Jack Logan was an irritating man, and she didn't like him. No, she didn't like him at all. Since they'd been together, he'd manhandled her and outwitted her at every turn. Not that she had deliberately tried to put anything over on him, but he seemed to be one step ahead of her at all times.

Amanda couldn't wait to get home so she would be rid of his annoying presence, but it was going to take a while to get to San Rafael. She was stuck, and if she was resenting his presence already, on board the ship, it was only going to get worse in the even closer confines of the train from Galveston to San Antonio and then the long days on the stage during the final leg to San Rafael.

Her grandmother had always tried to teach her that she could catch more flies with honey than with vinegar. She supposed she could try to make friends with Jack, just so they could travel in peace, but somehow, she didn't think he wanted to be friends. He seemed quite pleased with the idea of getting her home as fast as he could, so he could get away from her. She would have to settle for peaceful co-existence and hope he'd cooperate.

The knock came at the door, interrupting Amanda's thoughts, and she realized it was time to brave Jack's company again at dinner. Girding herself, determined to be agreeable, she quietly made her way to answer the door, leaving Eileen to her rest.

"How's Miss Hammond?" he asked as she emerged from the stateroom alone.

"She fell asleep, so I thought it best to let her rest. She's feeling somewhat better, but she still isn't back to normal. I'll bring her something to eat from dinner just in case she wakes up hungry later."

He nodded and led the way toward the entrance of the dining room. He was not looking forward to the evening meal if the couple from that morning showed up. Jack knew the man had been ready to fight, and he was in no mood for further confrontation. When they entered the room, he was greatly relieved to see that the pair was not among the crowd at dinner. He requested a table in a more private area, and they were given one off to the side in one of the alcoves.

"There was no trouble in the cabin next to yours this afternoon?"

"No. It was quiet."

"Good. Maybe he'll control himself for the rest of the voyage."

"I'd like to think so."

"So would I," he agreed.

Amanda was surprised by his remark. "The way you sounded earlier, I had the impression that what he was doing didn't bother you a whole lot."

"Your impression was wrong. It did bother me, but people have to help themselves. We could have helped her to get away, but if she went back to him in two or three hours, what would be the point? He'd only be angrier than he was before at her show of independence."

"Have you had experience with this kind of thing? Your parents or someone else you knew?"

"No!" he answered a little too sharply. "My family was very loving. Idyllic really, at least until the war came and our whole way of life was destroyed. My father and brothers were perfect gentlemen."

She was saved from asking what had happened to him by the waiter's approach. She saved her outrage over being ignored again by the waiter for another time.

Tonight, she just wanted to relax and enjoy the meal. It had been a long three days, with all that had happened. She needed some peace and quiet. She needed to get ready to face her father.

"What? No fury over being a woman scorned?" Jack taunted after he'd placed their orders and the waiter had left them.

"As you said earlier, I'm not going to alter the way this ship is run overnight."

"This certainly is a change of heart for you. I thought you made it a point to stand up against injustice to women, no matter what the odds."

She cast him a sharp glance to see if he was mocking her. She was surprised to see a look of almost understanding in his eyes. She actually found herself smiling at him, and that bothered her. "Tonight, I just wanted to relax for a while. I could have made a scene, but as you said earlier, it wouldn't make a difference."

Jack returned her smile. "One lesson my father taught me early in life was to pick my fights with care. He told me to make sure the battle was worth the effort, and once I decided that it was, then I should give everything I had to win."

"A wise man, your father."

"Yes, he was." Jack tried not to think much about the old days. It made living now seem harder when he remembered how warm and loving his family had been.

"You know all about me and my father, but what about you? Where's your family? You said 'were' when you referred to your father and brothers. Are they all dead?"

His jaw tightened as he answered, "Yes. The only family I have left is my sister and her family."

"I'm sorry."

"Things change. People die. It's the way of the world." He sounded hard and cold.

Amanda remembered the look she'd seen in his eyes the other day and began to understand. "But you survived."

"Thanks to your father. He saved my life about a month before the war ended."

"He did? What happened? That was so long ago, you must have been very young."

"I was, but my father and brothers and all my friends had gone off to fight, so I was going, too—no matter what my mother and my sister said. I joined up with your father's company. We were in the midst of a fierce battle and had almost been overrun when your father saw a soldier taking aim at me. He yelled a warning to me just in time and then shot the man before he could kill me. I owe him my life.''

''And that's why you agreed to come after me?''

''That's right.''

''Well, I'm glad my father didn't call in your debt on something more deadly and dangerous,'' she said with a laugh.

''You think going into that bar didn't take courage?'' He grinned at her. ''Given the choice again, I think I'd rather face a dozen Yankees than six axe-wielding women.''

''You handled yourself quite admirably considering the circumstances. I could have hurt you if I'd seen you coming.''

''Maybe, maybe not.'' He tried not to smile.

Their meal came then, and they ate companionably. Their conversation turned to general topics, and the evening passed quietly.

Jack was relieved when he parted from Amanda at her cabin after they'd finished eating. It irritated him that he'd found her company almost enjoyable this night. Certainly, she was a beautiful woman, and she was intelligent, too. But he wanted nothing to do with females. Pleasant though having dinner with Amanda might have been, he would distance himself from her and keep that distance until he could leave her in her father's capable hands. There would be no softening of his feelings toward her. She was trouble, and he would have to remember to treat her that way.

Jack lay in his bed later that night, tossing and turning and trying to sleep. He hadn't been with a woman since Elizabeth, and that was fine with him. He liked it that way. He knew how deceitful women were, what liars and connivers, and he had no intention of allowing himself to fall into that trap ever again. He had thought himself in love once, and it had nearly cost him his life. It would never happen again. Love was a highly overrated emotion. Attractive though Amanda Taylor might be, he would not allow himself to feel anything for her other than a fleeting physical desire—one that he would make certain to keep under control.

Amanda entered the cabin to find Eileen still resting, and she was glad. Sleep would help the older woman get her strength back.

When Amanda retired herself, she fell asleep right away. Her night was fitful, filled with dreams of axes and whiskey bottles, Texas and her father—and Jack. She awakened after dreaming of Jack, and she lay there for some time, thinking about him. It was bad enough that she had to put up with him during the day. It was truly annoying that he was even taking over her dreams.

The following morning, Eileen awoke before Amanda. She was feeling much improved and actually was looking forward to having breakfast.

"The sea must be much calmer," Eileen told Amanda when the young woman joined her in the outer sitting room. "I almost feel like my old self again, and it's about time, too. Your grandmother wanted me keeping watch over you, not you nursing me for the whole trip."

Amanda smiled at her. "Well, at least we've learned that if you're going to travel great distances, it's better for you if you go by railroad, uncomfortable though it might be."

"I've been wondering how I would get back home. Going this way on the return trip surely doesn't seem like a good idea."

They were dressed and ready to go to breakfast when Jack came for them.

"Good morning," Eileen said as she answered the door, smiling happily up at him.

Jack was surprised to find her looking so well. "You're better?"

"Much, and we're both ready to eat."

Jack was annoyed when he found himself looking past Miss Hammond into the cabin for some sign of Amanda. When Amanda did appear, wearing a pale blue daygown and her hair pinned up in a tumble of curls, he had to remind himself of his vow the night before. He would not allow himself to feel anything for her. He was her hired escort; that was all their relationship would ever be. Still, as she swept past him out the cabin door, the delicate scent of her perfume sent a shaft of awareness through him. It was a delicate scent of honeysuckle and other soft blossoms, and it reminded him of the serenity that was lost to him forever. He stiffened and carefully distanced himself from her.

After breakfast, Jack couldn't wait to get away from them, even though the conversation had been entertaining and he'd found himself growing quite fond of Miss Hammond. As they made their way from the dining room, he asked, "Do you have plans for the day now that Miss Hammond is back among the living?''

''Nothing out of the ordinary.''

''Shall we plan then to have dinner? I'll come for you around six?''

''You aren't going to have lunch?''

''No,'' he answered. ''I've a few things I need to do, but I'll see you both later this evening.''

Amanda found that she was irritated by the thought that she wouldn't see him all day, and that was ridiculous, because she didn't even like him. It would be better if he was off doing whatever it was he was going to be doing.

''That will be fine,'' she said coolly.

''I'll see you then.''

''He's a very nice man,'' Miss Hammond said sweetly as she watched Jack stride away. She was quite smitten with him. She knew a gentleman when she saw one, and Jack Logan was as fine as they came. ''How is it that you find him so overbearing?''

''It's a long story.''

''We have all day. Shall we go to the ladies' salon? We'll have a change of scenery there, and then you can tell me how you met.''

Amanda and Eileen made their way to the spacious, plushly furnished room and sat together on a comfortable sofa.

''So tell me all about Jack Logan. I think it fascinating that we're having such different reactions to him.''

''You really are that fond of him?'' Amanda looked at her curiously.

"I think he's very handsome, don't you?" Eileen asked.

"I try not to think about him at all, if I can help it. I can't wait to get back home to my father so Jack can go on his merry way."

"Why? It seems he's been nothing but courteous to you."

"But you weren't there that first night—" Amanda stopped, wondering if she should tell Miss Hammond everything.

"What happened that first night?"

"I may as well tell you the truth, since I doubt you can get word back to my grandmother any time soon."

"Amanda, if you tell me something in confidence, I will hold it in confidence. I would never betray you that way."

"Thank you. You see, that first night when Jack came to my grandmother's to get me, I was spending the night at a friend's house."

"Yes—" Eileen prodded when Amanda hesitated.

"Well, I suppose I should rephrase that. I had intended to eventually spend the night at my friend's house, but before that Bethany and I were involved in a protest of sorts."

"A protest?" Eileen was puzzled.

"You see, the whole reason my father wants me to come home to Texas is because I got involved in the women's movement and I was expelled from school. The night that Jack found me, Bethany and I had joined four other women who were temperance marchers, and we were smashing up a bar."

"You were what?"

"We took axes and went into a bar called The Palace and smashed up all the whiskey we could find."

Eileen laughed in pure delight. "I can't believe you did that! You say your grandmother doesn't know?"

"No. I didn't lie to her. I just didn't tell her the whole truth."

"I see. And our Jack? How did he get involved in all this?"

"My father hired him to escort me home. He went first to my grandmother's. When she told him I was spending the night with a friend, he went to her house to find me. A servant there told him we were at The Palace and he followed me there."

"Mr. Logan is a determined young man," Eileen said with approval.

Amanda grimaced at her observation. "He caught up with us just as we were attacking the place. What's so maddening is that I wanted to stay with my friends, and he just walked right in the bar, took my axe away from me and hauled me out of there. It was so humiliating! He threw me over his shoulder. At the time, I didn't have any idea who he was. I thought he was some kind of kidnapper. I fought him and tried to escape from him until he showed me my father's letter. Then I told him that I wouldn't go back to Texas with him, and he kindly reminded me that I was an unmarried female and I had to do as I was told."

"And that didn't sit well with your desire to be your own woman, I take it."

"Exactly." Amanda looked at her companion with renewed respect. "Do you know a lot about the suffragist movement?"

She nodded. "I've been following it for some time. A few years ago, I attended a speech given by Elizabeth Cady Stanton. She is a wonderful speaker, a very intelligent woman. I agree with their ultimate goal of equality, but I don't know that I'll see it in my lifetime. Society is a difficult thing to change, and there is a lot of resistance to our having the right to vote."

"I know," Amanda admitted tiredly. "We've been marching and lecturing and trying to get the word out so other women will join in and help us. Sometimes, though, other women are our biggest problem."

"I understand completely," Eileen said. "But whatever you do, don't give up. I may never have the right to vote, but I bet you will."

"I hope so. I certainly am as good as any man. I was thinking about that just the other day. When I was young, I could ride as fast and shoot as straight as the boys I played with. I made excellent grades in mathematics and science at school, so I know I'm as smart as any man. The only way a man is superior to a woman is in brute strength," she concluded.

"That's very true, my dear, and usually that's a wonderful thing, for a man will protect what's his with his power. But then there are men like that Micah. Just look at how he uses his strength. Instead of protecting his wife with his might, he batters her with it. It's men like him who remind us of the need for our own independence."

"If only we could convince his wife to save herself. You know, I didn't tell you this earlier, but the reason we went to The Palace in the first place was because one of the regular patrons of the bar had gotten drunk and had beaten his wife to death a short time before.''

The thought quieted them both as they shared a look of mutual understanding. Then Eileen spoke up to lighten their somber mood.

''So Jack carried you out of the bar and took you home to your grandmother, but he didn't say a word to her about your activities?''

''No, and I was glad for that, but by then, it really didn't matter, for I was already going home. What more could my grandmother have said?''

''What happened to the ladies who stayed behind at the bar?''

''As it turned out, the police came just as Jack was taking me away, and all my friends were arrested.''

''Thank heaven Jack showed up when he did!''

''I would have preferred to go with my friends,'' Amanda said with loyal dignity.

''Really? Jack probably thought he was doing you a favor. I believe he wanted to get you out of there to save you, your grandmother and your father from embarrassment. He was, after all, hired to bring you home and he was just doing his job.''

''You're making him out to be a hero when he was high-handed and very arrogant.''

''He's a man,'' Eileen responded.

''I don't like him. He's too domineering.''

''Your father told him to bring you home safe and sound. He's just trying to do his job, and so far you've led him a merry dance. Think about it.''

Amanda did, remembering the bar scene, the ride home and her attempted escape from the carriage, and her run-in with the couple in the cabin next to theirs.

She tried not to smile, but couldn't hold it back. "I have, haven't I?"

"Yes, dear, you have." Eileen patted her hand as she smiled, too. "But I suppose he's man enough to keep up with you."

Amanda didn't respond, but she knew Eileen was right. Of all the men she'd known, Jack was the only one she hadn't been able to outsmart or outmaneuver. She found nothing endearing in that, though, and still couldn't wait to get home and be free of him.

Jack made his way to the crowded saloon that was the men's haven on the ship. Those gathered there were smoking and drinking and generally having a good time. Jack would have greatly enjoyed a whiskey right then, but he joined in a poker game instead. As he played, he discovered that he was a bit sharper at keeping track of his cards playing sober, and he was pleased.

As the hours passed, Jack found himself glancing toward the door every time he heard a woman's voice as she passed by the entrance to this male haven. He didn't know why he thought it might be Amanda or why he was so interested in seeing her. It was his job to make sure she was safe, and she was. He didn't have to do another thing except deliver her to her father in San Rafael. And he would do that soon. Thank heaven.

Jack had been playing cards for some time when he caught sight of the man named Micah as he entered the saloon. Jack had no use for him, and he was irritated when the bully joined in the poker game.

"Afternoon, gentlemen," Micah said as he sat down, a smug, confident look on his face. "We playing for high stakes?"

"As high as you want them," another player said, although up until that time it had been a comfortable game with no great losses among the players.

Micah began to drink and play with a vengeance. He bet large amounts that drove several of the other men from the game. He eyed Jack across the green-topped poker table as if he planned to teach him a lesson. Jack had interfered in his business and had insulted him publicly, and Micah likely wasn't a man who forgave insults. He'd already punished his wife for trying to stand up to him.

"You ready to play some serious poker?" Micah asked, his beady, black-eyed gaze riveted on Jack.

Jack looked up at him, his expression passive. He understood men like Micah, and he didn't like or respect them. He thought about leaving right then, but decided it would feel good to best him at least once at the tables. Micah was drinking heavily and would grow careless over time. When he did, Jack would make his move and see that he paid for his weakness. "I always take poker games seriously."

They began to play in earnest then, the stakes running high. Jack won one, then lost one. The other men at the table were enjoying the added excitement, and several men gathered around just to watch.

Betting ran hot and heavy and two men dropped out, but Jack, Micah and one other stayed.

Micah ordered another drink and downed it without pause. He forced the pot higher, apparently wanting to prove that he was the best man at the table. When the third player matched his wager and called, he was ready.

"A pair of aces," the man said, laying down his hand.

"I've got two pair," Micah announced with a triumphant smile as he, too, showed his hand. He started to rake in the pot. His gaze locked on Jack, wanting to see defeat in his expression and misery at the knowledge that he'd lost so much. Micah was startled when Jack just smiled.

"The pot's mine," Jack announced. "I've got a full house." He spread his cards out for all to see—three sevens and a pair of fours.

Micah was furious, but he couldn't show it there. Outwardly, he had to be a good loser. "Nice hand."

"Thanks," Jack replied with an easy smile. He pocketed his winnings. "If you gentlemen will excuse me, I think I've played enough poker for today."

"But I want a chance to win my money back—" Micah sputtered as Jack stood to leave the table.

"Maybe later. I hate to tempt fate, and my luck's played out quite profitably this afternoon. Gentlemen." He walked away from them to stand at the bar.

Micah continued to play and to drink. Jack knew the other man was angry, and he didn't care. It gave him a certain satisfaction to have taken his money. He couldn't do anything else to him, but he could do that. His smile was one of grim satisfaction.

It was late afternoon when Micah made his way unsteadily from the saloon. His mood had only grown uglier as the day progressed—not that he'd lost any more, but just the thought of having lost to Jack gnawed at him. He headed back to his cabin expecting to find Becky there. He'd told her to stay in their stateroom, and she'd damned well better be there. There would be hell to pay if she wasn't, and maybe even if she was. He smiled drunkenly as he started down the companionway. When he reached their door, he had trouble fitting the key into the lock, so he knocked and waited for Becky to answer and let him in.

"Becky, open the door," he demanded gruffly when she didn't respond right away.

He pounded again. When silence was his answer, his temper raged. The woman should be rushing to do as he'd bid! Where the hell was she? In an absolute fury, he managed to unlock the door. He threw it open with such force that it slammed violently back against the wall.

Micah stepped inside and stared at the empty cabin. Becky was not there, and that made him even more furious. She was his wife, and she was supposed to do exactly what he told her to do.

"Where are you, woman?" he bellowed, thinking she might have been in the small water closet, but when he opened that door, he found it empty, too.

It was only then that he noticed some of her things were gone from the room. Frowning, he opened her trunk and discovered that her clothing and jewelry and some of his money were missing.

"What the hell!" he shouted. In a rage, he tore the place apart, then realized that the ship had made a short stop in some port early that afternoon while he'd been up in the saloon. She must have left the ship then. She was gone. She had fled from him.

He left the cabin and sought out one of the stewards. The man informed him that Becky had indeed left the boat when they were in port. Micah demanded that the ship return so he could go after her, but he was humiliated even further when he was summarily and coldly rebuffed. They would not be docking again for another two days. Only then would he be able to leave the ship.

Barely in control, Micah returned to his cabin. He dug through his trunk and took out his silver flask. Sitting down heavily on the edge of his bed, he took a deep drink, his eyes aglow with the power of his anger. He imagined what he would do to Becky when he found her—and he would find her. He had no doubt about that. He would teach her once and for all that she couldn't defy him.

He heard the sound of muted female voices coming from the cabin next door and remembered how that woman had interfered in his business . . . in his marriage. He took another deep drink and then snarled in rage as he stood up. It was her damned fault that Becky had left the ship. Becky would never have dreamed of leaving him before she'd butted in.

Micah staggered from the cabin. He was going to teach that arrogant bitch a lesson, too. He knew Jack was still in the saloon, so there would be no one to stop him. When he got done with her, she would never stick her nose in somebody else's affairs again.

# *Chapter Five*

Micah knocked on Amanda's stateroom door, controlling his fury as he did so, not wanting to give away the power of his anger.

Eileen answered his knock right away, thinking it was Jack coming to take them to dinner.

"Yes, sir? Can I help you?" she asked in her most dignified manner. She was surprised to find herself face-to-face with the evil man from the cabin next door and thought that, perhaps, he was just so drunk that he'd gone to the wrong cabin.

"Damn right you can!" he snarled, pushing his way past her and into their room. It didn't matter to him that she was old enough to be his mother. He'd hated his mother. "Where is she?"

"She's not here," Eileen lied calmly, wanting him out of there. She hoped Amanda had sense enough to overhear what they were saying and stay in her room.

Micah turned on her and slapped her full force. Eileen cried out in pain.

Amanda was dressing for dinner when she heard the commotion. She couldn't imagine what had happened and rushed out to see what was wrong. The sight that greeted her stopped her cold in her tracks. She found herself staring at the man she despised.

"You!" she said in disgust, her stomach roiling at the sight of him, drunk before her. "Get out of our cabin! You have no business here." She started to go to Eileen.

He gave a savage laugh and advanced on her. He had only one thing on his mind. "You're wrong, you bitch! I've got business with you. You're the one who caused it all. It's your fault."

"Get out!" Amanda backed away. She could see that he was beyond reason, and she knew what violence he could wreak. She looked around, desperate for something she could use to defend herself. She wished for her axe or for the six-gun she had at home, but there was nothing that would hold him off.

Eileen saw that he had every intention of hurting Amanda and knew she had to do something. She picked up the china bowl that had been on the table. She didn't know if she could knock him out with it, but she hoped she could slow him down long enough for them to escape.

"I'm not leaving here until I've paid you back for all the trouble you've caused me!"

"I don't know what you're talking about."

"Becky's gone, and it's all because of you!" He lunged at her.

Amanda tried to flee back into her small sleeping room, but his hand closed on her arm with vicious intent. He swung her around toward him and raised his hand to strike her.

It was then that Eileen struck, screaming loudly as she brought the bowl down on the back of his head. To her horror, the force of her blow shattered the bowl, but only stunned him. Blood flowed from a cut on his scalp, and he was cursing vilely as he turned back toward her, still holding tightly onto Amanda.

"I'm going to teach both of you a lesson, and then I'm going to track down Becky—"

Amanda fought with all her might to break free of him. She hit him as hard as she could, but he only gave her a vicious shake as he made a grab for Eileen.

Eileen proved too quick for him, though. She fled out the door, leaving him alone with Amanda. Once in the hall, she was terrified to leave and terrified to stay. She heard Amanda cry out and knew she had to go for help. She couldn't defeat the man by herself. He was too drunk and too mean.

Jack had lingered in the saloon until it was nearly time to take the women to dinner. He was just starting from the room when he overheard one steward talking to another.

"That Micah Jennings just found out about his wife." The man chuckled. "He's not a very happy man."

Jack interrupted immediately. "What did he find out? What happened?"

"When we docked, his wife took her things and left

the ship. When we sailed, she didn't return. He was a little angry, to say the least.''

"I'll bet," Jack said, frowning at the thought. He knew how drunk Micah had been when he'd left the saloon, and he knew the ugliness of the man's temper.

A sudden sense of urgency filled Jack and he hurried off toward Amanda's cabin without saying another word to the stewards. He found Eileen running blindly toward him when he entered the companionway.

"Jack—thank heaven! It's that man. He pushed his way into our cabin—"

Jack took her by the shoulders and looked down at her, seeing her bloodied lip and the stark look of terror in her eyes. "He hit you?" He was shocked.

"I don't care about me! He's alone with Amanda!"

"Go get the stewards," he ordered, then set her aside and went forward, intent on doing battle.

The look on Jack's face sent a shiver down Eileen's spine. She had never seen a man look so deadly or so fiercely determined. She rushed off to find the other men to help him.

Jack didn't even pause when he reached Amanda's cabin. With one shove, he threw the door wide. It crashed open, revealing Micah standing over Amanda where she was on the floor, her hair in disarray, her dress torn at the bodice. Micah was still holding her by the arm as he stood over her, his hand raised to strike her.

Jack's move was lightning-fast as he attacked. He launched himself bodily at Micah and knocked him away from Amanda. The two men rolled heavily across the floor in what little space there was, fighting and struggling for dominance. Amanda scrambled to get out of their way.

"This is the last time you're going to lay a hand on a woman! You want to fight, fight with someone your own size!" Jack growled as he landed a jarring blow to the other man's jaw.

Micah continued to battle back. His liquor-laden senses were slow to react, though. While the women had been no match for his brute strength, he could not overpower Jack.

With precise, hard-hitting punches, Jack battered him relentlessly, never giving him a second to regroup or rest. Blood covered Micah's face, but Jack didn't care. This man was a coward. He was the lowest type of man around, and Jack wanted to be sure he learned never to lay a hand on a woman in violence again.

"You don't hurt what is mine!" he snarled as he landed blow after punishing blow.

Determined to beat him into submission, Jack didn't stop as long as Micah kept fighting back. Only the arrival of the stewards, who ran into the room and pulled the opponents apart, stopped his attack.

Jack was panting and bloodied from the fight as he stood back and let the stewards drag the other man to his feet.

"I want him arrested—locked up. He broke into this cabin and attacked Miss Taylor and her traveling companion, Miss Hammond."

The stewards looked at the two women and saw their injuries.

"Is that true, Mr. Jennings?" one demanded.

They each had him by an arm, and he was hanging weakly between them.

"No . . . the women invited me. They wanted me in their room," he lied, his eyes gleaming with malice as he smiled a bloody smile at Amanda.

"Miss Taylor?" The steward looked to her for verification.

"That man pushed his way into the room and attacked first Eileen and then me. Mr. Logan saved our lives by showing up when he did. If it hadn't been for him, I don't know what that man would have done to us." She was trying to speak steadily and coherently, but she was trembling visibly. A bruise was already forming on her cheek, and a small trickle of blood was at the corner of her mouth. Her gown had been ripped, and she was holding it together over her breasts as best she could with shaking hands.

"Yes, ma'am."

"You lying bitch . . . You women are all alike! You're lying whores, all of you!"

Jack started forward to silence him once and for all, but the steward blocked his way. "We'll take care of him."

They started to drag the drunk away, and they were none too gentle in their handling of him.

"Don't worry, Miss Taylor, Miss Hammond. We'll make sure he doesn't cause you any more harm. He'll be locked up."

"Thank you," Amanda said in a voice that was barely audible.

When they left the room, Eileen quickly closed the door behind them and hurried to her side.

"Are you all right?" she asked, seeing how pale Amanda was and knowing how terrible the experience must have been for her.

"I don't know." Amanda answered truthfully, and then her knees started to buckle. She had never fainted before in her life, but she did now.

Jack was there. He had seen her distress and made his move the moment she swayed unsteadily on her feet. He swept her up into his arms and made his way to her small chamber. He gazed down at her. Her head lay on his shoulder, and she looked very fragile. Realizing how small and light she was and how very defenseless she'd been against Micah, a surge of protectiveness jolted through him. He wanted to protect her; he wanted to keep her safe from harm. And the desire had nothing to do with being her hired escort.

At the thought of her father and his duty to him, Jack grew angry with himself. He was supposed to keep her safe. He was supposed to make certain that nothing happened to her—and he'd failed. If he hadn't gotten there when he did, Micah might have killed her. The man had been that out of control. Thank God he'd overheard the stewards talking. There was no knowing what might have happened had he not headed for the cabin right then. He was disgusted with himself.

Jack gently laid Amanda upon her bed. The bodice of her gown fell apart then, and he was treated to a glimpse of pale-hued silken flesh where her breasts swelled above her chemise. He paused, his hands shaking, unable to look away from the beauty of her. But the memory of his failure returned, and he gave himself a fierce rebuke. He quickly drew her coverlet up over her as Eileen followed them into the room.

"Is she going to be all right?" she asked worriedly.

"I don't know. I'll go get the ship's doctor, just to make sure. Stay with her."

"I will." Eileen got a cool, damp cloth and pressed it to Amanda's forehead.

Jack strode from the cabin, a man with a mission. He returned a short time later with the doctor.

"Amanda's regained consciousness," Eileen told them as she let them in.

"I still want Dr. Phillips to examine her," Jack insisted. "That must have been a hard blow. Have him take a look at your face, too."

With Eileen to assist him, the doctor disappeared into Amanda's bedroom and shut the door behind them.

Alone, Jack stood in the outer room and waited. He was relieved that Amanda was awake, but he still wanted to hear from the doctor that she hadn't been seriously injured. Micah Jennings was a vicious man, and Jack was certain that he'd had every intention of doing her great bodily harm. The minutes that passed seemed to last for an eternity. Finally, the door to Amanda's room opened, and Dr. Phillips emerged.

"How is she?" he asked immediately.

"She's shaken, but she'll be fine."

"Be fine?" He didn't like the sound of that.

"There's some bruising. He managed to strike her twice before you saved her, but nothing's broken. She's in no danger. It's a good thing you got here when you did. You were a hero."

Jack nodded, but he sure didn't feel like a hero. The

whole thing should never have happened in the first place. He should have realized what Micah Jennings was capable of, and he should have been prepared.

"I told Miss Taylor to stay in bed for the rest of the day. She should be back to normal in no time."

"Thank you." Jack showed him from the cabin as Eileen came out to join him.

"Amanda's feeling much stronger now," Eileen told him, managing to smile at last. It had been a ghastly few hours.

"Good, and how are you?"

"My cheek is sore, but the doctor says I'm going to live."

"Is there anything else you need? Would you like me to have some food sent down for you?"

"That would be wonderful, and you should probably plan on sending breakfast down, too. I doubt either one of us will feel like leaving the cabin for a day or so."

He looked toward Amanda's closed door. He wanted to speak with her, but he knew it wouldn't be proper for him to see her so indisposed.

"Tell Amanda that I'll make certain Jennings is going to stay locked up until they hand him over to authorities at our next port of call. Ask her, too, if she wants to press charges against him. In the meantime, don't open this door to anyone but me."

"Don't worry. I've learned my lesson."

"I'm glad you're both all right," he told her, glancing one last time toward the closed bedroom door.

"Thank you for saving us. I don't know what we would have done without you." She looked up at him

103

as if he were the most wonderful man alive and on impulse drew him down to her so she could press a soft kiss on his cheek. "Good night."

Jack was startled by her kindness and actually felt himself blush. "Good night, Miss Hammond."

"I think, after all we've been through that it would be perfectly all right if you started calling me Eileen."

"Good night, Eileen." He smiled gently down at her.

He left the stateroom then. He was relieved that things had turned out as well as they had, but he was still furious with himself that the incident had happened at all. Amanda and Eileen had been in his care, and he'd failed to protect them.

It would not happen again.

Jack lay in bed, staring at the ceiling of his cabin. Sleep eluded him as images of what might have happened to Amanda haunted him. He muttered a vile curse, wanting Jennings to spend the rest of his days burning in hell, and all but threw himself from the bed.

Jack started to dress. He needed a drink badly. Dan had trusted him to keep his daughter safe, and he hadn't done it. The thought that he'd failed to recognize the possible danger unnerved him. This was the second time. Had he completely lost his ability to judge character? Not long ago, his judgment had been sharp. As a Ranger, he had been one of the best at instinctively knowing just when and where outlaws would strike. And then had come El Diablo. . . .

At the thought of his weakness for Elizabeth and how blind he'd been to what had been happening in

Del Fuego, Jack stalked toward the door. His word to Dan be damned! He was going to have a drink! He reached for the doorknob, then stopped. Raking a hand nervously through his hair, Jack swore again, and this time he cursed himself.

He turned back and sat down heavily in the one chair in the cabin. He stared bleakly around himself. The desire for a drink would not leave him, and neither would the doubts he had about himself. He thought of Amanda, of what a tigress she'd been smashing whiskey bottles when he'd first seen her and how the barkeep had even been a bit unsure if he could handle her or not. He thought of her true concern for Jennings's wife and how fiercely she'd tried to help her in spite of the woman's seeming indifference. He thought, too, of the look of defiance and bravery on her face when he'd charged into the room to save her from the other man. Amanda was a magnificent woman, and Dan should be proud of her. She hadn't cried when he'd gone to her. In fact, she'd held up very well until the last. . . . The memory of holding her, soft and helpless in his arms, touched something deep within him.

Jack suddenly realized the direction of his thoughts, and he scowled. Amanda Taylor was trouble. She had been since the first minute he'd laid eyes on her. He was taking her home to her daddy, and that was all.

Swearing under his breath again, he leaned back in the chair. He did not close his eyes to court sleep, though. He waited in silence for the coming of the dawn.

\* \* \*

Amanda woke early, before sunup, and lay in bed savoring the quiet of the moment. Her sleep had been fitful. She'd woken several times during the night after dreaming about the attack, but as she faced the new day, she felt strangely rested and at peace.

As she let her thoughts drift, Amanda realized that Jack was the reason she felt so safe. For all that she'd despised him for the way he'd treated her in Philadelphia, she had to admit now that without him, she would have come to serious harm at Jennings's hands.

Not that she wanted to give Jack any more credit than he was due. He was a man, after all. Had she been armed, she could have handled the drunken wifebeater herself, but Micah Jennings had caught her unprepared, and so she'd been helpless before him.

It greatly irritated Amanda to admit that he'd overpowered her. It didn't suit her nature to have to rely on anyone. Her father had raised her to be brave and smart, to ride and shoot with the best of the boys. Then she had gone back East and had become an independent woman. She could take care of herself—most of the time.

Amanda got up and went to look out her small porthole. As she watched the sunrise, she vowed then and there that such an incident would never happen to her again. From now on, she would always make sure she could take care of herself. She knew how to use a gun, and when Jack came to see her today, she would ask him to get her one. She never wanted to be helpless again.

\* \* \*

Jack accompanied the waiter who brought breakfast to Amanda's cabin that morning. He was pleased to find that both women were up and about when they arrived. When the waiter had gone, he turned to Amanda and got his first good look at her injury. His jaw tensed as he stared at her bruised and swollen cheek.

"It must hurt," he said tightly.

"Not so very much," she replied, wincing a little as she attempted a smile. "It would have been much worse if you hadn't arrived when you did. Thank you."

He was uncomfortable with her praise. She could have been killed while under his protection. "It should never have happened in the first place."

"I know, and you were right," she admitted. "If I hadn't tried to help his wife, he wouldn't have come after me."

Jack was pleased that she was finally seeing the error of her ways.

"I can't help but think how terrible it must have been for his wife Becky, though. He only had time to hit me once before you showed up. He could have beaten her for hours, and there was no one to come to rescue her."

Jack felt an uncomfortable stirring of conscience at the image of helpless terror her words evoked. "At least she was smart enough to get away from him while she could. I hope she's long gone, and he'll never be able to find her."

"You should have seen the look in his eyes when he was getting ready to hit me the second time."

Amanda shuddered. "He looked insane."

"Any man who would beat a woman is insane. He's locked up now, right where he should be, and I'll make sure that I see him ashore when we get to our next port, day after tomorrow. I spoke with the captain this morning about dealing with the authorities there. Do you want to press charges against Jennings? It would mean that we'd have to leave the ship and stay in town for a time."

"No, we need to get home to my father. His wife has had time to escape from him, so we'll just leave it at that."

"You're sure? The man hurt you and Miss Hammond—" Anger showed in Jack's eyes.

"But you saved us, and we're fine now."

"All right." He understood her need to put it all behind her.

"Thank you for all you've done, Jack. It's reassuring to know that you're watching over me."

"I intend to keep even closer watch now."

"Jack, I was wondering . . . Could you get me a gun to carry, just so something like this never happens again?"

"A gun?" He stared at her in disbelief. "What would you do with a gun?"

She gave him a look of disdain. "In case you've forgotten, I was raised in West Texas. By the time I was six, my papa had taught me how to shoot."

"You won't be needing any sidearm," he stated flatly. "I'll be watching you too carefully."

"If I'd had a weapon last night, though, I could

have taken care of Jennings myself and not had to rely on a man for my own well-being.''

Jack felt the sting of her words.

She went on smugly, ''An armed woman can be very dangerous, you know.''

Amanda had meant her remark to be light, but Jack's whole demeanor changed. The look in his eyes turned cold and his jaw tightened.

''I know all about armed women,'' he ground out. ''And they can be dangerous. But you won't be getting a gun from me. Nothing more is going to happen to you on the trip home. I guarantee it. And let me ask you one thing, little girl. Do you have any idea what it's like to take a human life?''

She was taken aback by his unexpected attack.

At her silence, he went on, ''I didn't think so. You haven't got what it takes.''

Amanda was surprised and angered by his condescending attitude. ''Well, if you won't give me a gun, then I'll just have to carry this knife with me for protection.'' She reached down to the table where the breakfast was set for them and picked up the sharpest knife there. ''This should do it.''

Jack stared at her in silence for a long moment as she stood before him with the knife in her hand.

''Stay here. Don't go out,'' he said harshly as his gaze went over her. ''I'll be back to check on you later.'' He turned and left them, shutting the door behind him.

''I don't think he was too pleased with your wanting to carry a weapon,'' Eileen said, staring after him, confused by the sudden change in him. It had been strange, almost chilling.

Amanda knew he seemed angry, but she didn't care. "He's probably just upset because I want to take care of myself. He'll come around." She looked down at the knife she still held. "This isn't a very good weapon, but it's better than nothing."

She slipped it carefully into the pocket of her gown. She would never be defenseless again.

Jack's expression was grim as he headed straight for the saloon. It might be late morning, but that wasn't going to stop him. He was going to have a drink, and he was going to have it now. The sight of Amanda standing there, the knife in her hand, had dealt him an almost physical blow. He needed to get away from the memories. He needed to escape. And he knew whiskey was his only salvation. If he had a drink, he could deal with his weaknesses. If he had a drink, he could face the life he was leading. If he had a drink.

"Whiskey, straight, and leave the bottle," he ordered as he strode up to the bar.

"You sure?" the barkeep asked, puzzled by his change in behavior. For days now, he'd been in the saloon and had not had any liquor to drink.

"What did I say?" Jack snarled as he turned a deadly gaze upon the barkeep.

"Just thought it was strange, that's all. You didn't touch anything yesterday, and now you're drinking today, and early, too."

"Don't worry about what I do or when I do it. Just

give me the damned bottle,'' Jack countered sharply.

The bartender set the liquor before him, and Jack paid him. He then took the bottle and glass and headed for a deserted table in the back. He wanted to get as far away as he could get from everything and everybody.

Jack uncorked the bottle and splashed a healthy portion in the tumbler. He stared at it for a minute as he remembered Dan's words to him. *I'm entrusting my daughter to your care. I want to know that I can count on you to stay sober while you're with her. . . .*

*While you're with her . . .* The words repeated in his mind and made Jack smile. Amanda damned sure wasn't in the bar with him right now, so he wasn't breaking his word to Dan.

Jack tossed down the whiskey. It burned, but he enjoyed the sensation. Soon, he would be able to forget everything. Soon, he could lose himself—if only for a little while.

He thought of Amanda and Eileen in the cabin and was glad that he'd told them to stay where they were. He would have just one more drink, then go up to his own cabin and sleep for a while. By the time he had to take them to dinner, he'd be back in control. For right now, though, he was going to allow himself a little peace.

# *Chapter Six*

Hours passed, and Amanda and Eileen realized it was getting late. They hadn't heard anything from Jack since he'd left in such a strange mood that morning. Dinner was already being served, yet they had had no word from him at all.

"You don't suppose something has happened to him, do you?" Eileen asked. "He hasn't been back to his cabin all day, and it isn't like him to say he's going to do something and then not do it. He is a man of his word."

They shared a puzzled look, trying to think of where he could have gone.

"I'll go see if I can find him. You wait here just in case he shows up," Amanda told Eileen.

"Are you sure you want to go up on deck alone? It's getting dark out."

"I'll be fine. Jennings is locked up, so there's really nothing to worry about. All I have to do is find out what happened to Jack. He probably got involved in a big poker game and forgot the time.''

Amanda left the cabin, not quite sure where to begin her search. She figured her first instinct was her best and made her way toward the men's saloon. As she neared the door, a steward came out and she stopped him.

''Excuse me, have you seen Mr. Logan? Is he in the saloon?''

''Yes, ma'am, he is. Would you like me to get him for you?''

''Please. I'll wait out on deck.''

Amanda went outside to stand at the rail to wait. When Jack didn't come out right away, she began to grow uncomfortable and she wondered where he was. She had just started back inside when he emerged and came toward her.

''Why, if it isn't little Miss Amanda Taylor, standing out here in the moonlight,'' he said in a low voice as he stared at her.

''You've been drinking!''

''Yes, I have, but I still haven't had enough.'' His words were slurred as he crossed the distance between them.

''You're disgusting!''

''Are you wishing you had your axe right now?'' He gave a drunken laugh.

''Oh, you—''

She started to walk away, to go back to her cabin, but he caught her by the wrist and stopped her. Jack stared down into the pale, beautiful face that had haunted him all day and saw the shadow of the bruise on her cheek. Every time he'd attempted to push the whiskey away from him, an image of her had floated before him, taunting him with her determination to be independent, yet teasing him with her vulnerability. And then there had been the moment with the knife. . . .

"I don't understand why you want to be so much like a man. As lovely as you are, you could have all the men in the world at your feet, trying to please you . . . begging for your favors."

"I want to be strong so I don't have to put up with men like you!" she snapped, trying to twist free of his grip.

Her defiance sparked something in Jack.

"You should be more feminine," he murmured, his gaze darkening as it settled on her mouth. Then, without thought, he drew her close.

Amanda knew she should fight him. She should try to get away, to resist him, but she hesitated. In that moment Jack sought her lips in a tender caress.

Amanda went still as his lips moved over hers. She was frightened, yet strangely breathless. Jack's kiss was a sensation unlike anything she'd ever known before. It was gentle, yet powerful. Demanding, yet tantalizing.

He pulled her closer to him, and she seemed to fit perfectly in his arms. And then he deepened the embrace, parting her lips to taste of her sweetness.

But at his bold invasion, Amanda tasted the whiskey he'd been drinking all day, and the power of it jarred her back to reality. This was Jack Logan! With all her might, she shoved against his chest. Jack was caught unaware by her sudden move and let her go.

She found herself free and glared up at him, her arms akimbo. "You're a horrible, terrible man!"

He grinned down at her. He thought she'd never looked prettier. "I've been called worse," he said.

"I'm sure you have!" she countered. "And you taste like whiskey!" She wiped her mouth with the back of her hand.

His grin grew lopsided. "And you, my dear, are one stubborn, hard-headed female. I feel sorry for your poor father. I don't know how he's going to handle you once I get you back to him. I wish him luck, because he's going to need it!"

"We can't get to San Rafael soon enough to suit me!"

"My sentiments exactly. It will be a pleasure to be rid of you," he drawled, watching her as she stormed off. Then, thinking better of letting her go alone, he followed her at a safe distance, wanting to make sure she reached her cabin without incident.

Amanda was still angry as she entered the stateroom.

"Did you find Jack?" Eileen asked, looking up from where she was sitting.

"Oh, I found him all right," she snapped.

"I can tell," the older woman said. "You must have had a wonderful visit."

Her sarcasm was not lost on Amanda, and she found herself smiling at Eileen.

"Wonderful doesn't even come close to describing

it," she began. "To begin with, he'd been in the bar and he was drunk!"

"Jack had been drinking?" The news surprised her.

"All day, from the look of him."

"I wonder why?" Eileen murmured.

"Why? Who knows why men drink? The point is, he was drunk and it was disgusting."

Eileen gave a motherly cluck of her tongue. "Now, Amanda, darling, you know that I appreciate your involvement with the suffragists, and I certainly understand some of the complaints of the temperance marchers. But sometimes things go on in life that you aren't aware of—things that might make a person turn to drink. Don't you remember how strangely Jack acted before he left us this morning? One minute, you were having a nice conversation and the next he'd walked out."

"You're right. So you think something that was said this morning upset him?"

"I'd bet on it—if I were a betting woman."

"I wonder what it was? I know he was angry about letting me have a gun, but I thought that was just the usual male reaction to my wanting to take care of myself."

"It could have been that or something entirely different."

"How do we find out?"

"I guess we don't until he tells us the reason, or someone else does. But remember, Amanda, one day or night of drinking does not make a man a drunk. Jack is certainly no Micah Jennings," she said in his defense.

"I suppose," Amanda grudgingly agreed, for it was true that there had been no violence in Jack tonight. She remembered how he'd come toward her, how he'd taken her in his arms. For a moment, she'd actually wanted to be in his embrace. She frowned, angered by the memory of her reaction to his touch. It wasn't violence that she'd had to fear from him, but the attraction she'd felt when he'd kissed her.

"You know, for all that you had this 'wonderful' encounter with Jack, did you remember to ask him about our dinner?"

Eileen's question interrupted Amanda's thoughts, and she was glad.

"No. I got so mad at him that I forgot. . . ."

Even as they spoke, a knock came at the door, and a waiter announced he had brought them dinner by order of Mr. Logan in the next cabin.

Eileen smiled at Amanda as she went to open the door. "At least Jack wasn't so drunk that he forgot we would be hungry. I told you he was a gentleman."

Amanda said nothing, but she was glad to have some dinner. Later, after they'd eaten, she went into her room to get ready for bed. As she stared at herself in the small mirror, Amanda wondered why Jack had said she needed to be more feminine. He'd said she was pretty—wasn't that enough? And he'd certainly had no compunction about kissing her. If he'd thought her less than a desirable female, why had he kissed her?

As she thought about it, Amanda grew irritated and defensive. She was certainly feminine enough! She wore the latest gowns and always styled her hair fashionably. But as she thought about it, it occurred to her that she had never had a real beau. She'd had male friends, but there had never been a man who'd sought her hand in marriage. Doubts stung her, and she grew even more annoyed.

Amanda climbed into bed, wondering where Jack was and if he would remember anything about their encounter the next morning. It was going to be interesting to see how he reacted to seeing her again. That thought made her smile.

She slept well that night.

And so did Jack—once he made it back to his cabin. He'd made sure Amanda reached her stateroom safely before he'd returned to the dining room to order dinner for the women. That done, he'd stopped by the bar again to retrieve what was left of his bottle of whiskey. Bottle in hand, he'd made his way slowly back to his room, more than ready to stretch out and get some much-needed rest. He lay down without bothering to undress, and after taking a few more swigs of the potent brew, he drifted off. His last thought as he fell into a deep, dreamless sleep was of a pale, dark-haired beauty whose kiss had stirred him more than he cared to admit.

Morning came with a vengeance as he stirred and came awake with the worst headache he could ever remember. He groaned out loud and rolled onto his side. It hurt even to open his eyes, but he did, just so he could look for his bottle and drown his pain in another blissful, liquor-induced haze. And then he remembered Amanda and Eileen, and he forced himself to sit up and face the new day.

The bottle he'd sought lay on the floor, empty. He'd done it justice, and he was glad the temptation of another drink wasn't right there before him. He stood up and made his way to look out his porthole. The light hurt his eyes, and he was sorry he'd made the effort. The sun was well up in the sky, and he knew it was time to see about the ladies' breakfast. Every movement was agony for him as he groped toward the washstand and tried to clean himself up. It had obviously been a long, hard night, though he remembered little of it.

Jack splashed water on his face, and the jolt of the cold water sobered him even more. He shivered and stared at himself bleary-eyed in the mirror. It wasn't a pretty sight—his eyes were red-rimmed and his color sallow. He growled at his own reflection as he picked up the razor and began contemplating just where to start. The unsteadiness of his hand gave him some pause, but he forged ahead.

It was just as he finished shaving that the fleeting memory of being on deck with Amanda in the moonlight returned to him. He tried to recall exactly what had happened between them, but his recollection was hazy. He definitely remembered that she had been angry with him for drinking and he'd taunted her about wishing she'd had her axe. Other parts of their conversation played in his thoughts, and then the remembrance of her in his arms, pressed against him, kissing him.

Jack frowned at nothing in particular as he wondered if that was a true memory or part of some wild dream he'd had while he was sleeping. He couldn't quite separate fact from fantasy, but he hesitated to believe that she really had responded to him as it seemed she had in his memory. He finished washing up and changed into clean clothes. He was as ready as he was ever going to be to face the world today, so he left his cabin to stop by Amanda's stateroom and see what the ladies wanted for breakfast.

"Good morning, Jack," Eileen greeted him as she answered the door. "Amanda, Jack's here."

"I came to see what you wanted to do about breakfast," he said, speaking softly. The less noise, the better it was for his throbbing head.

"I think we're feeling well enough to go to the dining room with you," Eileen told him.

"Why, Jack . . . You're not looking as if you feel too well this morning," Amanda said brightly as she came to join them. "Perhaps we should be bringing you breakfast in your stateroom this morning." His distress pleased her, and though she knew it was wrong to take pleasure in another's suffering, she believed this couldn't have happened to a more deserving man.

"No, I'll be fine."

"What's wrong? A little too much whiskey last night, or are you feeling like Eileen did on the first day of the trip? Is your stomach churning from sea-sickness?"

Jack hadn't even thought about his stomach until she mentioned it, and now he realized that the thought of eating wasn't particularly appealing. He looked at

Amanda, read her expression and knew she was enjoying every minute of his discomfort. Any doubts he'd had about whether the kiss between them had really happened or not were answered—it had. Why else would she be so happy that he was suffering?

"There's nothing wrong with Jack that a good cup of coffee won't cure," Eileen said, coming to his defense. "Shall we go? I'm starving."

"Of course," Amanda quickly agreed. "And I'm looking forward to a big breakfast today. I think eggs and toast and bacon sound wonderful."

Jack swallowed tightly and his stomach rebelled at the thought of such heavy food as he escorted them from the room.

The dining room was full of people, and the noise level was high. Everyone seemed intent on talking this morning, though Jack could not for the life of him figure out why. He ordered a full meal for the ladies, but only coffee for himself.

Amanda smiled when he did, and then, when a waiter passing behind them accidentally dropped his tray, sending everything crashing to the floor, she was hard pressed not to laugh out loud at the pained look on Jack's face.

"So you had a rough night, did you?" Eileen finally asked, seeing his misery.

Jack glanced at Amanda, but her expression revealed nothing. "I'm having a rougher morning," he answered with a pained smile that more closely resembled a grimace.

"It'll pass. Most things do," Eileen said, trying to be encouraging.

121

"Not fast enough," he growled.

"I understand completely," she said sympathetically. "My father often drank more than his share of
a bottle, so I know just what you're feeling. After
breakfast, why don't you go to your room and lie
down for a while? I'll bet you're more tired than anything right now. Amanda and I will be fine by ourselves, and we'll plan on dining with you again
tonight."

"That's a tempting suggestion."

"Then go ahead and do it. We'll see you later."

Jack excused himself from their company and disappeared from the dining room.

"He must have felt terrible last night," Eileen said
as she watched him go.

"And worse this morning."

Eileen glanced at her companion to find Amanda
smiling.


Cody and Luke left his father, Charles, and his
brother, Dan, watching over the Trinity ranch while
they made the trip to San Antonio to pay a visit to the
wounded Ranger. Jim's recovery was slow, but he felt
well enough to talk to them. He knew all about Cody
Jameson's reputation, and he also remembered how
Luke had gone undercover for the Rangers to help
bring down the El Diablo gang.

"I know Steve and Jack think highly of you both.
What can I help you with?"

"We're going after the Sheldons. What we need to
know is how you caught them the first time. I remember hearing about it when you brought them in. I think

everybody in West Texas felt like celebrating.''

"All the Rangers did, too. We were after them for months.''

"I know it was quite a feat putting them away. How did you do it?''

Jim's expression grew even more serious as he re-called the exhausting chase across the state. "A lot of hard riding, hard tracking, some praying and a little luck. Joe, Vic, Jack and me earned our pay on that one.''

"Was there one particular piece of information that led you to them? Did they have any relatives around who helped them? What about any weaknesses? Liquor or women?'' Cody began the litany of questions that would ultimately help her understand her prey. Once she understood them, she could anticipate their moves and catch them.

"They're the most savage bunch I've ever dealt with, and I've dealt with some scum in my time. The Sheldons didn't like to leave any witnesses when they robbed a bank or stage, so they killed everybody.''

"Nice guys.''

Jim nodded slowly as he remembered the bloody havoc they'd wreaked on their unsuspecting victims. "It was hell. They moved hard and fast when we were on their trail. Hank is the smartest of the brothers, but if you're looking for weaknesses, his was women. We finally got the clue we needed from a saloon girl. She'd been earning her keep and had heard them talking about their next job.''

"So Hank likes saloon girls.'' Cody smiled at this news.

Luke scowled. He knew exactly what his wife was thinking. Cody was an expert at disguise. Two of her favorite personas were Armita, a singer in a cantina, and Delilah, a working saloon girl. "What about Willy?"

"He's more or less a vicious fool," Jim told him. "His weakness is that he's not smart, but he makes up for it by being deadly. We managed to trap them because we caught them in the middle of the night in a whorehouse."

"How was the other brother, Kyle, killed?" Cody asked.

"He managed to get out of the building, but we had a man standing guard in the alley. There was a shoot-out in the street, and Kyle Sheldon lost." Jim smiled grimly at the memory. "We should have shot the other two and been done with it," he said angrily. "If we had, Vic and Joe would still be alive, and I wouldn't be lying here like this."

"They don't have any other family? Anybody who helps them on the sly?"

"Not that we were able to discover. As far as we were concerned, the three of them were enough. This world doesn't need any more Sheldons like them," he said fiercely and then fell back against his pillows.

Cody and Luke could see that Jim was nearly exhausted. "Is there anything else you can remember? Anything that might help us find them before they find Jack?"

He thought for a long moment, trying to remember the name of the woman Hank had been with when they'd caught him. "You might start looking for them in El Terrón. That was where we caught them. Rumor had it that the whore Hank was with that night was his favorite. Find her and talk to her. . . . Her name was Chica.''

"Thanks, Jim."

"No. Thank you. With both you and the Rangers looking for them, they won't be on the loose long.''

"We'd better let you rest now."

"I wish I was up to riding with you," he said, his gaze burning with a fervor to see justice done, once and for all. "Find them for me."

"We will," Cody told him confidently. "You just concentrate on getting better."

They wished him well and left.

"Are you sure you want to do this?" Luke asked Cody as they started making plans to ride for El Terrón.

"Yes. I think Armita will be getting a job singing at the saloon there. Who knows? Maybe she and Chica will become fast friends."

"Don't you mean become friends fast?"

Cody grinned at him. "Both. Chica may not know where Hank Sheldon is right now, but she might be able to give me a clue where to look next."

"In the meantime, let's just hope Steve gets word to Jack, so he'll be watching his back."

"All I have to do now is check in with Nate Thompson and see if he knows anything about them." Nate was the local sheriff and an old friend of her father's. He always helped her whenever he could, and usually his information was very accurate.

"While you talk to Nate, I'll pay a visit to a few

of the bars here in town and talk to some of the saloon girls. The Sheldons were here in San Antonio, so they might have done some loose talking while they were waiting for the chance to ambush Jim. I'll meet you in an hour at Nate's office.''

Sheriff Nate Thompson was always glad to see Cody. They visited for a while, speaking of family and mutual friends.

''I know you're not here in San Antonio just to see me. Does this have something to do with the Sheldons?''

''Papa always said you were the smartest sheriff in Texas,'' she said with a grin at his perceptiveness. ''And the answer is yes. I spoke with Steve Laughlin a few days ago, and Luke and I decided to go after them when we heard they were gunning for Jack.''

He nodded sagely. ''Jim Eskin was one very lucky man. They left him for dead. That was sloppy of them, and they're usually not sloppy.''

''Do you think they're getting overconfident?'' The possibility pleased her, for overconfidence led to mistakes.

''It's possible. I picked up their trail the morning after the shooting, and I stayed with it for nearly twenty miles before I lost it. The most I can tell you is that they headed west, and that isn't a whole lot of help. There's just a little bit of land in West Texas.''

Luke came in to announce that he'd had little success. He'd met only one saloon girl who remembered the two Sheldon brothers, but she'd told him that the two had been so secretive and hot-tempered that she and the other girls had avoided them. When they'd left that night, she hadn't known or wanted to know where they were going. She knew men like them could be deadly, so the farther away she stayed from them, the better.

They thanked Nate for his help as they mounted up.

"What are you two doing next?" Nate asked.

"We're heading for El Terrón. That's where Jim said Hank Sheldon had a special woman. We're going to see if we can find her. She just might be able to point us the right direction."

"Well, good luck to you. Is there any place I can wire you if I hear something?"

"No, but we'll keep in touch with you."

"Good luck."

As Cody and Luke headed from town, a familiar figure rode up to join them.

"Stalking Ghost!" Cody greeted her friend warmly. He had been her protector and helper ever since her father died. "You always seem to know when I need you."

He did not smile, but he was pleased. "You are hunting for the Sheldon gang," he stated simply.

"Yes." She quickly relayed everything that had happened and what they'd learned in San Antonio. "We need to let Steve know that we're going to El Terrón. Will you ride to Ranger Headquarters and tell him? I don't want to send that information by wire. When you see him, ask if he's heard anything about Jack."

Stalking Ghost nodded and then looked at Luke. "You will watch her for me?"

Luke met his gaze squarely. They both loved Cody

with all their hearts. ''I will see that she comes to no harm.''

Cody smiled. ''I'm glad I have the two of you to keep me out of trouble.''

''The problem is, sweetheart, you're the one constantly getting *us* into trouble,'' Luke told her.

''We're not going to get into trouble. We're going to bring in the gang and save Jack's life.''

Stalking Ghost looked at them and knew the Sheldons were facing their most determined adversaries ever. Once Cody took on a job, she did it. She would do what she'd vowed. And he would do all he could to help her.

''I will find you,'' he said, then he rode off to find the Ranger captain.

Cody and Luke headed west. The Sheldons were out there somewhere, and they were going to track them down.

# *Chapter Seven*

Amanda made certain she was never alone with Jack for the balance of the trip. It was difficult, though, for he was always close by, keeping watch and protecting her. No further mention was made of that fateful night when he'd been drunk or what had happened between them, and she was glad. The less said about it the better.

There were moments, however, when the memory of Jack's kiss would slip into Amanda's thoughts. Her cheeks would grow warm as she remembered being in his arms and the touch of his lips on hers. In annoyance, she always forced the betraying thoughts away, refusing to admit to herself that she'd found his embrace enjoyable.

Amanda was relieved as she stood on deck with Eileen and Jack watching Galveston come into view. Soon, she would be in San Rafael and Jack would be gone.

"You're almost home," Eileen said as she studied the Texas shore.

"Home," Amanda said quietly, thinking of her father and the confrontation to come. As soon as they reached San Rafael, she intended to have a serious talk with him about her future. She wanted to work with the suffragists, and in order to do that, she had to be back East. She just hoped that he would agree to her plan. He'd never refused her anything before now, so she didn't think he would be too upset once she explained everything to him. The only possibility that concerned her was that he would agree to let her go, but that he would hire Jack to escort her back. She would have to convince him that she and Eileen could make the trip just fine without him.

"Texas is lovely, Amanda. I had no idea it would be so beautiful here," Eileen told her.

"Galveston is lush. I love it, too, but it's a far cry from where we're heading."

"How much farther do we have to go? Will we reach San Rafael in another day or two?" Eileen asked hopefully. She knew Texas was big, but she didn't think it could be that much bigger than her home state.

"I wish that were true, but it will probably take us every bit of ten days, depending on the connections. And traveling isn't going to be as comfortable as the ship has been."

"Ten days?" Eileen was surprised. "Well, I wanted to see the Wild West, so here's my chance."

"We're going to see a lot of it, that's for sure. Especially once we're on the stage."

"Is the rest of Texas as pretty as this?"

Amanda smiled. "Sometimes beauty is in the eye of the beholder."

"In other words, I should wait and be surprised."

"If you like a lot of tall trees and green grass, you're going to be disappointed," Jack put in, thinking of the almost desolate landscape. "West Texas is beautiful, but in a powerful way. It's a rugged land and mostly dry. There are mesquite trees, but they're not the big shade trees you're used to back East."

"It sounds different, but wonderful. I'm looking forward to seeing it. What about Indians? Will I get to see any?" Eileen asked almost excitedly.

Both Amanda and Jack gave her startled looks.

"Why would you want to?" Amanda asked.

"I don't think you really want to see any Indians, at least not in West Texas," Jack told her. "If the Comanche are close enough that you can see them, it's a pretty sure bet that you won't be seeing much of anything else, ever again."

"Oh." Eileen looked frightened.

"The Comanche are deadly. They'll kill anyone who gets in their way. They're so bloodthirsty that sometimes they kill just for the pleasure of it," he explained. "You'll be lucky if you don't see any or hear of any while you're in Texas."

As the ship docked, they returned to their cabins to finish packing. They disembarked as soon as they were able and took rooms in one of the better Galveston hotels.

"I'm going to drop my things off in my room, and then I'll go check on the train schedule to see if we can leave for San Antonio tomorrow,'' Jack told them as he saw them to their room.

"Will we be dining here in the hotel tonight?'' Eileen asked as they unlocked their door.

"As far as I know. I'll check on you when I get back from the station and let you know about departure times. Do you need anything else before I go?''

"No, we'll be fine,'' Amanda told him as she disappeared into the hotel room. "We'll wait to hear from you.''

Jack left his things in his room, then stopped at the front desk on his way out to send a message to his sister Ellie. He wanted to let her know that he would be in town overnight and that he'd like her and Charles to come to the hotel and have dinner with them.

That done, Jack made his way to the railway station. He bought tickets for the train that left for San Antonio the following afternoon. Returning to the hotel, he went up to the front desk, hoping Ellie had responded to his letter already.

"No, sir. We've received no messages for you.''

"Thanks.'' He turned away, disappointed.

Jack headed upstairs. He still had an hour or two left before he had to take Amanda and Eileen out to dinner. He hoped to hear from Ellie before then. As he topped the stairs and started down the hall toward his room, he was surprised and elated to come face to face with his sister.

"Jack!'' Ellie cried as she spotted him. She had asked for his room number and had come upstairs to see him. When he hadn't answered her knock, she'd started back down to await his return in the lobby. She ran down the hall to him and launched herself into his arms. "I've missed you so! Where have you been?"

Jack enfolded his sister in a warm hug, twirling her around much as he'd done when they were young. "Around," he replied evasively as he held her tight.

"Well, you're here now, and that's all that matters. I've been worrying about you and missing you so much. Charles and the children have, too!" She reached up and kissed him on the cheek. "I love you, Jack Logan, and don't you ever forget it."

"I love you, too." He stood still and held her, his eyes closed as he enjoyed just being near her. She was a gentle woman, but one who was filled with fierce devotion and love. He knew her husband Charles was a very lucky man to have her.

Amanda and Eileen had heard a woman call Jack's name out in the hallway, and, curious, they opened their door just in time to see him take the pretty, petite, dark-haired woman in his arms and hug her close.

Amanda's expression didn't change as she watched them embrace. For some reason, it irked her to see him with another woman, especially one who so obviously adored him. When the woman told Jack without reservation that she loved him, Amanda wondered who she was.

Jack looked up just then to see Eileen and Amanda standing in their doorway. "Come with me, Ellie. I have two ladies I want you to meet."

"Oh, really?" Ellie said, surprised. Then added, teasingly, "*Two* ladies? One wasn't enough for you?"

He smiled at his sister lovingly as he took her hand

and drew her back down the hall toward Amanda and Eileen.

Amanda saw how easy he was with this woman and felt a surge of some foreign emotion. She supposed she could have identified it as jealousy, but that was ridiculous. She wasn't jealous of Jack. Why would she be? He meant nothing to her. She didn't care about him.

"Amanda Taylor, Miss Hammond, I'd like you to meet someone who's very special to me," he said as he brought Ellie to stand before them.

"Oh?" Amanda asked coolly, holding herself stiffly as she met the other woman's regard. She had to admit the young woman was attractive, and she certainly seemed at ease with Jack. Obviously, they'd known each other for a long time . . . maybe even intimately.

"This is Ellie"—he looked down at her proudly as he finished—"my sister."

"Your sister?" Eileen spoke up first, saving Amanda from embarrassing herself by stuttering in surprise at the news. "How delightful! How wonderful! Do you live here in Galveston, Ellie, or is it just Jack's good fortune that he ran into you today?"

"My husband Charles and I live here with our children. Jack sent a note to the house inviting us to join you for dinner tonight, but I won't hear of it. I insist that all three of you come home with me. In fact"— she looked up at him—"I want you all to come stay with us tonight."

"We couldn't do that," Amanda protested.

"I insist. In fact, I'll be insulted if you refuse.

We've got plenty of room, so let's get you checked out of here so we can go home.''

Amanda and Eileen looked to Jack, wondering what they should do.

''We'll gladly take you up on dinner, but are you sure you want us to stay the night?''

''I won't have it any other way,'' Ellie told them stubbornly. ''Now, let's get your things and go. How long are you going to be in town?'' She looked at Jack.

''Just tonight. We're booked on the train to San Antonio tomorrow.''

''Well, at least we've got the evening. There's so much I have to tell you. You've been away from me for too long.''

Amanda and Eileen quickly repacked their things, and they were on their way to Ellie's in no time. The trip was a short one, and as they drew to a stop before the house, both Amanda and Eileen were greatly impressed by her large, airy home.

''It's so nice getting to meet your family, Jack,'' Eileen said as they climbed out of the carriage. ''For some reason, I had the impression you didn't have any close relatives.''

''Ellie and Charles and their children are all I have left. My father and brothers died in the war, and my mother has passed away since. I lived here for a while with them, but my job as a Ranger kept me away most of the time.''

''That's the truth,'' Ellie put in. ''Even when he claimed he was living with us, he was rarely here. It

135

seemed he never had a dull moment when he was a Ranger.''

"Some day, you're going to have to tell me tales of what it's like to be a real Texas Ranger,'' Eileen said, her eyes aglow with excitement and interest. She thought that that vocation must be most intriguing.

"I'll do that,'' Jack promised. He was glad everything had worked out so he could spend time with Ellie and Charles. He was looking forward to his reunion with his niece, seven-year-old Kathleen, and his nephew, nine-year-old Ben.

"Uncle Jack's here!'' The shout of joy came from deep within the house, and seconds later the door flew open and two children raced outside.

Ellie, Amanda and Eileen watched as Jack hugged them in welcome.

"Come on, Uncle Jack! Papa's inside just waiting for you!'' They all but dragged him indoors.

Jack cast a look back over his shoulder toward the women.

"Go on,'' Ellie called. "I'll take care of Amanda and Miss Hammond.''

Amanda and Eileen were still smiling as Ellie turned to them.

"The kids just love Jack. He's so good with them.''

"Really.'' This surprised Amanda. If someone had told her that Jack had a softer side before that moment, she would never have believed it.

"He looks like he loves them very much,'' Eileen said, pleased to find that her estimation of Jack's character had been so accurate. She'd known he was a good-hearted man.

"So," Ellie asked, curious now that she was finally alone with Jack's two women. "How did you two come to be with Jack here in Galveston?"

"Jack was hired by my father to escort me back home to San Rafael from Philadelphia. Miss Hammond is my traveling companion."

"Oh . . . So that's where Jack's been. We hadn't heard from him in months and we were growing concerned," she said thoughtfully. "Well, let's go in and make you comfortable. Dinner will be within the hour. I'm sure after all the traveling you've done, you're ready for a home-cooked meal."

"It sounds wonderful," Eileen agreed.

Ellie's friendliness was genuine, and Amanda found herself liking the other woman.

It was nearly an hour later when they all gathered around the dining room table for the evening meal. The fare was delicious, the conversation intelligent and interesting. The children finally went to bed after dessert, leaving the grown-ups alone at last.

Amanda had watched Jack with his niece and nephew and had been amazed at how good he was with them. He truly seemed to like them and to like spending time with them. He answered their questions with patience and love, and even kissed little Kathleen good night before she went up to bed.

"Now that we're finally alone, I can tell you the news," Charles began when the children had gone.

"What news?" Jack asked, hearing his serious tone and wondering what was wrong.

"We had an unexpected visit from Steve Laughlin. He was looking for you."

"Steve was?" Jack was surprised. They hadn't talked since he'd quit the Rangers after El Diablo. "What did he want?"

"Who's Steve?" Amanda asked.

"Steve Laughlin was Jack's commanding officer when he was in the Rangers," Ellie explained.

"He came here to get word to you that the Sheldon gang have broken out of jail," Charles said.

Had he not been in mixed company, Jack would have sworn vilely.

"How did that happen?" he asked.

It had taken four Rangers to put that gang away several years before. The Sheldons were deadly—blood-thirsty, actually—and Jack had been relieved to see them in jail. They'd been sentenced to fifteen years, but now they were on the loose again.

"I don't know all the details. All Captain Laughlin told us was that they were gunning for the four Rangers who'd sent them to jail. Laughlin said that two of your friends—Joe Reynolds and Vic Everly—were shot down in cold blood."

"They're dead?"

"Yes."

Jack went still at this news. Joe and Vic had been good friends. They'd been through a lot together.

"They also ambushed a third Ranger, Jim Eskin. He lived, though, in spite of having two bullets in him. He's the one who identified his assailants for Steve, and he heard them say that they were coming after you next."

Amanda and Eileen glanced at Jack worriedly. "Is this gang as bad as they sound?"

"They're worse," Jack answered. He looked at Charles. "What did Steve want me to do?"

"He didn't say. I think he just wanted to make sure you were aware of the threat. He said to tell you to watch your back and be careful. The Rangers are trying to track them, but we haven't heard anything from him since he left."

Jack nodded. "As good as the Sheldons are at disappearing, it won't be easy to find them. It took us months to track them down the first time, and it's only going to be harder this time."

"What are you going to do?" Amanda asked.

"There's not much I can do but sit tight and keep an eye out. This gang is about as low as you can get. I wouldn't put anything past them, but the good news is they don't know where I am. I want to keep it that way."

"Are the Sheldons as bad as the El Diablo gang?" Ellie asked, fearing for her brother's safety.

Jack went still at the mention of El Diablo. "Almost."

"You are a very brave man, Jack Logan," Eileen put in as she listened to all they were saying. "The life of a Ranger is so challenging."

"And dangerous," Ellie added seriously, knowing how close her brother came to being killed not too long before. "I'm glad he quit the Rangers."

"You are?" Eileen was surprised. She thought Texas Rangers were men of honor and courage.

"I got tired of worrying about him. Jack, why don't you come back here once you've seen Amanda and

Miss Hammond to San Rafael? As long as you're with us, I'll know you're safe.''

Jack grinned at her. ''You're always trying to mother me, Ellie. Don't you realize I'm grown?''

''Yes, I know you're grown, but you're still my little brother. I'm never going to stop caring about you or worrying about you. So until the Sheldons are back in jail, I want you here where I can keep an eye on you myself.''

''Don't you think it would be better if I turned the tables on the Sheldons and went after them? Maybe it's time the hunters became the hunted.''

''No. I lived with the fear of you turning up dead for too long. And then this thing with El Diablo last year—'' Ellie shuddered visibly. ''I want to keep you safe and sound. You're the only brother I've got left, and I intend to keep you around for a while.''

''Yes, ma'am,'' Jack answered, but it was mostly just to change the topic. He already knew what he was going to do. He would see Amanda home to Dan, and then immediately set out to locate Steve. Between the two of them, they ought to be able to outsmart the Sheldons. He'd done it once. He could do it again.

The conversation drifted for a time, and then Jack and Charles went off into the study to speak of manly things. Eileen decided to go up to bed, but Amanda wasn't sleepy yet. Ellie's garden was magnificent, and Amanda asked if she could go for a walk there before retiring for the night.

Ellie went with her to keep her company. She'd noticed the way Amanda had watched Jack during dinner, and she wondered if there was more to their relationship than anyone had said.

"How long have you known my brother?" she asked when they were away from the house and no one could overhear them.

"Not long. I only met him for the first time when we were in Philadelphia. My father knew him in the war, though, and that's why he hired him to come after me."

"Is your father Dan Taylor?"

"Yes."

"I owe your father a lot for saving Jack's life the way he did," Ellie said, remembering her brother telling her about it when he'd returned from the war.

"Jack told me a little about it," Amanda said. She found herself wanting to know more about Jack, but she was not about to come right out and ask.

"He was so young when it all started. . . . He hasn't had an easy life. We lost everything in the war. All my other brothers and my father were killed. When we came to Texas, there was just Charles, my mother, Jack and me. We had a lot of hard years, but eventually things got better. Jack joined the Rangers, and he was doing well until he ran into El Diablo—"

She said the name with such loathing that it shocked Amanda.

"Who is El Diablo? You mentioned something about him earlier."

"Not him, Amanda, her."

Amanda frowned, confused. "I don't understand."

"Neither did a lot of folks until the truth came out, thanks to Jack. El Diablo was the leader of a murderous bunch of outlaws down around Del Fuego. Jack was there working on breaking up the gang when he was nearly killed by the outlaw leader.''

''But you just said El Diablo was a woman.''

''Exactly.''

Their eyes met as Amanda realized the import of what Ellie had just told her.

''What happened?''

''Jack was leading the investigation, and he had a man undercover in the gang. He was awaiting word from his source about their plans. What he didn't know at the time was that the infamous El Diablo was a woman—a very deadly woman. She stabbed him in the back and left him for dead in his hotel room. Luckily, he survived and was able to tell the others who she was and what she'd done.''

Amanda's eyes widened at her words. El Diablo had been a woman and she had attacked Jack with a knife! No wonder he'd gotten upset that morning on board the ship! She'd been bragging about armed women being dangerous and had even picked up a knife and told him she was going to carry it as a weapon! Amanda paled as she realized Eileen had been right in everything she'd said about Jack's reason for getting drunk that day.

''You look stunned.''

''I am. He mentioned in passing that something had happened that made him quit the Rangers, but he didn't elaborate. Now, I understand why. They got El Diablo, didn't they?'' She suddenly needed to know that the other woman had paid for hurting Jack.

"Yes, thank God. She's dead, and the rest of the gang's either dead or in jail."

"Good."

"I agree with you, but the last thing I want to do is worry about the Sheldons gunning for him. These next few weeks aren't going to be easy. Maybe you should tell him you've changed your mind and that you want to go back to Philadelphia. That would get him out of Texas for a while."

"Believe me, Ellie, your brother doesn't want to spend any more time with me than necessary. He can't wait to drop me off with my father."

Ellie laughed in complete understanding. "That's why I asked you how you came to be with my brother. Escorting females is a far cry from his usual work. I'm surprised he took the job."

"I think he's sorry he took it on, but we're almost back to San Rafael. He'll be rid of me soon, and then he can get back to his normal life." At her words, Amanda noticed a slight change in Ellie's expression—a darkening, a worry—and she assumed it had to do with the Sheldons.

"I hope he does get back to his normal life. That would be good for him. I hope he comes back here, too, as he said, but I get the feeling he just told me that to placate me. When Jack makes up his mind to do something, he does it. And if he's bound and determined to track down the Sheldons, nothing I can say will stop him. He believes in seeing justice done."

"I hope they find the Sheldons before we even get back to San Rafael. That way you won't have to worry about him."

"I do, too."

They shared a smile and started back inside. It was getting late.

Jack stood at the study window staring out into the night. He could just barely see Amanda and Ellie as they stood talking in the garden.

"What are you looking at?" Charles asked, from where he sat behind his desk.

"Ellie and Amanda decided to take a walk through the garden."

"She's a beautiful woman," his brother-in-law remarked.

"Of course, she is—she's my sister," Jack countered, turning back to Charles.

"I was talking about Amanda. How is it you've been reduced to hiring yourself out as an escort service?" he asked, humor shining in his eyes.

Jack told him of his connection to Dan Taylor. "He's a good man. I was glad to do it."

"Jack—" Charles paused, not quite sure how to bring up the subject that Steve Laughlin had told them about.

"What?" he looked up expectantly.

"When Steve was here, he told us some things—"

"Like what?"

"Like the way you've been living since you recovered from your wounds." Charles gave up trying to be polite and decided the best way to talk to Jack was straight out. "Steve said he got word that you'd turned into a drunk and were hiring out as a fast gun. He said it sounded like you had a death wish or something."

"Do I look like a drunk to you?" Jack tensed.

"I'm just telling you what he said."

"I know." Jack grimaced as he faced the truth about himself. He had had a death wish, and even now, he didn't care much one way or the other if he lived or died. Oh, sure, he loved his sister and her family, but he had no real reason to get out of bed in the morning, no real reason to go on. Before, his job as a Ranger had been his life, but after discovering how blind he'd been to Elizabeth's cunning, he hadn't trusted himself or his judgment anymore. Sometimes he thought he'd have been better off if she'd aimed truer with her knife.

"So, is it true?" Charles sensed Jack needed to talk, but he wasn't sure just how far he could push him.

"I spent a few months as a hired gun."

"What about all the drinking? You know drowning yourself in whiskey isn't going to make anything better."

"It sure as hell can help you sleep through the night, though," Jack countered angrily as he glared at his brother-in-law. "I know you're trying to help me, Charles, and I appreciate it. But I'm fine. I don't need any help. I'll finish off my job for Dan Taylor and then I'll look up Steve and see what I can do to help him find the Sheldons."

"That isn't what you told your sister." Charles was smiling.

"I know." Jack smiled back.

# *Chapter Eight*

Mona Taylor sat at the window watching the sun rise. The day she'd been waiting for had finally arrived. In just a few hours, all her dreams would come true. She smiled at the prospect.

She noticed then that the sky had a reddish tint to it, and she thought that was most telling. If things went as they were supposed to, it would be a very bloody day. A shiver of anticipation slid down her spine. Soon, very soon, it would be all hers.

Her thoughts drifted back to the time when the plan had been conceived. . . .

"I can't believe Dan and Asa haven't decided to sell the damned stage line yet!" she'd fumed to her son.

"They are stubborn, but they're not going to stop us." Ted smiled grimly. "If two robberies in a month didn't convince them to get out of the business, then we'll just have to apply a little more pressure."

"You can apply a whole lot more as far as I'm concerned. I've had enough of living here in the middle of nowhere!"

"What I don't understand, Mother, is why you married Asa Taylor in the first place."

Mona shot him a haughty look. "It seems you've forgotten the dire financial straits we were in eight years ago. I thought Asa had money. That's why I married him. I had no idea all of his worth was tied up in that stage and freight line with his brother."

"So you've found that eight years in West Texas is enough for anyone."

"One month in West Texas was enough, but I couldn't find a way to escape. But this idea you've come up with seems perfect . . . Or at least I thought it was until I listened to them talking last night. Dan and Asa are determined to fight back after the robberies. They're even adding an extra guard on some of the runs."

"They're not going to make this easy for us, are they? It would be so simple if they just sold out to Charles Johnson. He's waiting for the chance to buy the line. If they did, you'd have all the money you'd ever need. Of course, you'd still have to get it away from Asa."

"As tight as he is, I wonder if I'd even see a cent of it. He'd probably want to stay right here in San Rafael and hoard every penny."

Ted's expression had turned thoughtful, then cunning. "There is an easy way out of this, you know—a very simple way for us to take over everything."

"What? I'm willing to try anything at this point."

"Anything?" he had pressed.

"Anything," she'd repeated firmly.

"If something should happen to Asa—"

"If something should happen to Asa and Dan—" she'd added to his original deadly thought. "We'd still have to deal with Amanda, but as involved as she is back East, I'm sure it wouldn't be too difficult to convince her to sell out to Johnson."

"Then you approve of my idea."

"I think it's masterful, darling. Between the two of us, we'll take over for Amanda, sell the stage line to Johnson, send her her share of the money and head for New Orleans."

And now the day was finally here. They'd planned everything perfectly. Asa and Dan were going to ride together on the relay from San Rafael to Comanche Pass. The robbery would take place at the most remote location, and it had been made clear to the men working for them that there were to be no survivors.

Mona wondered if being a rich widow was going to be as wonderful as she hoped it would be. The thought was pleasant, and she was still smiling as she rose from her seat at the window and went to make herself breakfast. It was going to be a long day, waiting to hear the news, but she was sure she could pass the hours without too much trouble. The most important thing she had to remember was to be sure to act surprised and devastated when word came to her of the robbery and murders. She paused before a mirror to practice a tormented facial expression. Pleased with the devastated look she'd perfected, she smiled brightly and went on to the kitchen.

\* \* \*

Dan Taylor was watchful as he drove the stage through the rugged terrain. Asa sat at his side with his shotgun near at hand, keeping careful watch. The last months had been rough for them. The two robberies had left them nervous and unsure, but they were determined the payroll they were transporting that day would make it to its destination. They carried only one passenger on the leg to Comanche Pass, but that wasn't unusual. There weren't many travelers who wanted to go there, and Dan and Asa didn't blame them. It was a rough, wild town, and the salesman they were taking looked ill-prepared for what he was about to face.

Dan's handling of the four-horse team was masterful as they crossed a dry creek bed and started on the last leg of the journey. It was then that disaster struck. Shots rang out and horses whinnied in terror. Asa only had time to lift his shotgun to his shoulder when a gun blast ended his life.

"Asa!" Dan screamed his brother's name.

He crouched low and urged the team faster, trying to outrun their attackers, but it was hopeless. A bullet caught him in the shoulder, and he was thrown from the stage. Another shot hit him in the back. He lay, deathly still, face down in the dust.

The stage raced wildly on until one of the attackers managed to control the horses and stop them. One point-blank shot ended the life of the hapless salesman. Quiet once again reigned over the countryside.

"Well done, gentlemen," Ted said as he stripped off the mask he'd worn and surveyed the destruction that had been wrought. "Help yourselves to the payroll. You earned every cent."

"You ever need us again, just let us know," one of the gang told him as he shot the lock off the strong box and crowed over the money inside. The other outlaws ran to get their share.

"I think things are well in hand now. But your talents are appreciated." He turned his horse away and rode off, eager to let his mother know that all had gone as planned. Smoothly—very smoothly. Riches were soon to be theirs.

He did not look back as he headed for San Rafael. He felt no remorse over the shooting of his stepfather and step-uncle. Truth be told, he'd almost enjoyed shooting Dan in the back. He smiled as he imagined how fine life was going to be in New Orleans.

Isaac Moore glanced at his pocketwatch as he waited at the stage depot at Comanche Pass. Dan and Asa were riding together today, and if anybody could be depended on to make it on time, they could. He shook his head, troubled, and went back inside.

Isaac had worked for the Taylors for three years now, ever since he'd decided not to reenlist in the Tenth Cavalry and had gone looking for a better life. His life hadn't been much up until now. The son of slaves from Alabama, he'd been only ten when the war ended and he and his parents had left the South and headed west to start a new life. They'd migrated to Missouri, then on to Kansas. They'd lived there for a few years and had started a homestead, but then the sickness had come and both his parents had died.

Alone, with little to support himself, he'd traveled farther west and had ended up enlisting in the Tenth. He'd been posted to Fort Concho and had spent the last several years learning about the Southwest. He'd decided Texas was the place he wanted to be, and so when he'd had the chance, he'd left the cavalry and started out on his own. He wanted to settle down, and working for the Taylors seemed the way to do it.

He'd found true friends in Dan and Asa. They were men who judged others by merit and not skin color. After driving for them and proving his worth, he'd been put in charge of the station. He was proud of his promotion, but with it had come responsibility. And right now, it was his responsibility to find out what had happened to the stage. It wasn't like Dan and Asa to be late, and after all the trouble last month, he was not only worried, he was afraid.

Isaac waited the better part of an hour before he went looking for the other help.

"Shorty!" he called out to one of the men who tended the horses. "Saddle me up a mount. I'm going out to check on Dan and Asa."

"They that late?"

"Almost an hour, but I'm not taking any chances—not after those two robberies last month."

Shorty hurried to saddle a horse and then led the mount out to Isaac. He stopped by a hook on the wall where his holster hung and took it down. He handed it to Isaac.

"Here, wear this. There ain't no tellin' what you're gonna run into out there."

"Thanks," Isaac buckled on the gunbelt and settled

it low on his hips. He swung up in the saddle. "I'll be back. Real soon, I hope."

"Be careful."

The ride was hot, dry and quiet . . . too quiet for Isaac's taste. As mile after mile passed and he didn't run into the stage coming his way, his fear grew. He'd been out for almost two hours when he heard the sound of a horse whinnying. He spurred his mount to a gallop and raced over the low rise, where he came upon the scene of the carnage.

In horror, Isaac reined in and stared around in disbelief. The strongbox had been looted; the passenger was dead. He drew his gun and all but threw himself from the horse to look for Dan and Asa. He found Asa first and knew he was dead. Pain tore through him. This man had been his friend, and a robber's bullet had put an end to his life. He thought of his wife, Mona, and his son, Ted, and knew the news would devastate them. Grimly determined, he searched on, looking for some sign of Dan. He'd been the closest to Dan. He had been the one who'd trusted him and encouraged him.

And then he found him, lying facedown, unmoving in the dirt.

Isaac dropped to one knee beside him. He was certain Dan was dead. The bullet wound in his back looked lethal, and as bloodthirsty as the bandits had been, he was sure they'd wanted to make certain they'd left no witnesses. As he gently rolled his friend over to check him, he was shocked to hear Dan give a low groan.

"Dear God! Dan! You're alive!"

Dan didn't open his eyes, though, and Isaac could tell that he'd lost a lot of blood. He pressed his bandana against the most serious wound to staunch any blood flow. As carefully as he could, he lifted Dan and carried him to the stagecoach. He got him inside, along with the passenger and Asa, and then tied his own horse to the back of the stage before driving for town. He wanted to travel at breakneck speed, but he worried about tossing Dan around too much. When he got within range of Comanche Pass, he drew out the revolver and fired into the air.

Shorty heard the commotion, along with the rest of the folks in town, and they all came running.

"Get the doc! Call the sheriff! The stage was robbed!"

Everyone rushed to help as Isaac reined in the sweat-streaked horses.

"Dan's still alive, but he's in real bad shape! We gotta save him! Asa and the passenger are both dead," Isaac said as he jumped down to help lift his friend from the coach. He and Shorty carried him toward the doctor's office.

The doctor was as prepared as he could be for someone so seriously wounded. They brought Dan into the examining room and laid him face down on the table there, then left so the physician could tend to him.

Dr. Curtiss was careful as he cut away Dan's clothing to examine his wounds. The shoulder wound was not deadly. The bullet had passed clean through and so presented no mortal danger. The shot in his back, though, was far more complicated.

153

"Isaac! I need your help in here," the doctor called out.

Isaac had been waiting in the outer room talking with the sheriff from Comanche Pass, but at the doctor's call he quickly went to his aid. "What do you need?"

"I want you to hold him down. I've got to try to probe for the bullet. I have to get it out of there or he's a dead man for sure."

Isaac nodded and held Dan's shoulders down as the physician began to explore the ugly wound. Dan made no move and uttered no sound. Isaac said a heartfelt prayer that his friend would survive as he watched the doctor work on him.

"Damn . . ." Curtiss muttered.

"What is it? Did you get it?"

"No," he said angrily. "Not yet. It's in a very dangerous place. I have to be careful, because I don't know what damage has been done."

Wiping the sweat from his brow, he began to probe the wound again, hoping and praying that he could get the bullet out. Each minute seemed like an hour as he worked desperately to save the man's life. He had almost given up hope when he felt the deadly slug.

"I've got it!"

He knew it was nothing short of a miracle as he carefully worked the bullet from Dan's body. He dropped the slug into a metal dish nearby, then quickly applied pressure to the wound to stop the bleeding. It took him a few minutes more to cleanse and bandage the wound.

"Is he going to live?" Isaac asked worriedly.

"I don't know. We'll have to keep a close watch on him overnight."

Isaac nodded, but said nothing as he looked down at his unconscious friend. Dan's coloring was ashen, almost gray. If he hadn't seen the rise and fall of his chest, Isaac might have believed that he was already dead.

"I can stay with him, if you need me to."

"Thanks. We can take shifts."

Dr. Curtiss made Dan as comfortable as possible.

"I've got to send Shorty back to San Rafael to let everyone know what happened. Then I'll be back," Isaac told Curtiss.

"Fine. I appreciate the help." He settled in to watch over Dan.

Isaac found Shorty and the sheriff waiting outside the doc's office for some word of Dan's condition.

"How is he? Is he dead?" Shorty asked worriedly. He'd gotten a good look at Dan when Isaac brought him in, and he'd thought he wouldn't make it.

"He's still hanging on. I need you to ride to San Rafael and tell Asa's wife what happened."

"I'll leave right away."

The sheriff spoke up. "First thing in the morning, Isaac, I want you to show me where the holdup took place. We can ride out at first light."

"Yes, sir. I'll be glad to go with you just as soon as I know how Dan's doing."

"Good. I'll come back for you then. You say whoever robbed the stage got the payroll?"

"Yes, that's why both Dan and Asa were riding on

this trip. They were our best, and if our best can't stop them, I don't know who can.''

"Don't you worry. We'll find the miserable bastards.''

"I hope you do, Sheriff. I hope you do.''

Isaac saw Shorty off, then returned to Curtiss's office to watch and wait. It was going to be a long night, and he never stopped praying for his friend as the darkness settled over the land.

Shorty rode for San Rafael at breakneck speed. He made the trip in a little over six hours and arrived in town after midnight. He knew it was late, but he rushed straight to Asa Taylor's house to find his wife and son. He hated being the bearer of such horrible news, but there was no easy or pretty way to deliver this message. As he pounded on the door at the darkened house, he saw a lamp glow upstairs and knew that he'd roused them from sleep. A minute later the door was thrown open, and Shorty found himself face-to-face with both Mrs. Taylor and her son, Ted.

"Who the hell are you, and why are you pounding on our door in the middle of the night?" Ted demanded, glaring at the dirty, rough-looking man who stood on the porch.

"The name's Shorty, Mister. I work for the Taylors out of Comanche Pass—"

"Yes?"

"What's wrong? Has something happened?" Mona asked, stepping forward into the lamplight. She was clad in a modest dressing gown, and her hand was at her throat clutching the sides of the garment together.

"Yes, ma'am. I'm afraid I've got bad news for you."

"What is it?" Terror sounded in her tone as she leaned toward her son for strength.

"There was another robbery—"

"Asa . . . How's Asa?"

"Ma'am—" Shorty stopped, looking from the son's taut face to the wife's horrified expression.

"I'm sorry, ma'am. He was killed in the attack."

"Oh, my God . . ." She swayed and Ted caught her against him.

"Come in," he said curtly as he led his mother into the sitting room and helped her to the sofa.

Shorty followed nervously, his hat in his hands.

Ted sat down next to his mother, his arm around her, trying to calm her. "What happened? Has the law gone after them?"

"The law's going out in the morning. They can't track until then. Isaac was the one who found them. He went looking for the stage after they were late coming in."

"What about Dan? How is Dan? And the passengers?" Mona asked, her voice weak and shaky as she held tightly to her son.

"There was only one passenger and he was killed. Dan's alive, though, ma'am."

"He's alive!" They both almost shouted at the news.

Shorty understood their excitement. "It's a real miracle! He was shot twice, and it still don't look good for him. The doc worked on him and did what he could, but he doesn't know if he'll make it through the night or not.''

"I'd better ride for Comanche Pass," Ted said, his tone and expression serious.

"You might as well get a couple hours' rest, and I'll ride back with you at sunup. We'll make better time in daylight."

"All right."

"I want to go with you," Mona insisted. "I need to be with Asa . . . and Dan."

"Yes, ma'am. We'll all ride out at daybreak."

"Thank you, Shorty, for bringing us the news," Ted said as he rose to see him to the door.

"I just wish I hadn't had to come. Mr. Asa, he was a good friend to me. He never done anything mean to anybody. I don't know why they had to go and kill him—" Shorty's voice was choked as he expressed his sentiments. "I'll go get a room over at the hotel, and I'll be back at dawn."

"Thank you," Mona said softly, her eyes filled with tears of grief as she gazed at Shorty across the room.

"Yes, ma'am. I'm sorry, ma'am."

With that, he turned and left them. Ted closed the door softly behind him. He waited until he was certain that the man was out of earshot before he spoke.

"Son of a bitch!" he snarled. "I can't believe the bastard's still alive!"

"Well, at least I'm a widow!" she said, a note of hysterical laughter bubbling up. "Did I play my part well? Was I believable as the grieving wife?"

"Of course, Mother. I do believe you missed your calling. You're a born actress. You should have taken to the stage. He believed you were devastated.''

''Good. Let them all believe it. Tomorrow we'll make the trip into Comanche Pass and try to make certain that Dan doesn't live to come home.''

''With any luck, he'll be dead when we get there. That would save us a lot of trouble.''

''I can't believe he lived through it. I thought you said you shot him point blank in the back.''

''I did, but like Shorty said, he may not make it through the night.''

''Good.'' She was as pleased as she could be with the way things had gone. It certainly would have been better if both brothers had died, but this was close enough. Soon, very soon, she would have her wish and life would be worth living again.


Dan returned to consciousness slowly. He opened his eyes and stared around the dimly lighted room. He felt confused and panicky, for he didn't recognize his surroundings. He tried to get up, to go find somebody, but he couldn't. Pain wracked his shoulder at the effort, and with the pain came the memories.

''Asa,'' he groaned, as images of the robbery, haunted him.

Isaac had gone home to get a few hours' sleep, and Dr. Curtiss had taken over. He'd been dozing in a chair in the far corner of the room, but at the sound of Dan's voice, he came immediately awake. He turned up the lamp and hurried to him. ''Mr. Taylor?''

''Where am I?'' Dan managed weakly.

''You're in Comanche Pass. I'm Dr. Curtiss. They

brought you in this afternoon. The stage was attacked and robbed.''

"My brother . . . How's my brother?''

"We can talk about him later. Let's—''

"No! I need to know how he is.'' Dan drew upon all of his strength to demand an answer.

Curtiss could see the wild look in his eyes and knew there would be no lying to him or avoiding the truth. He already suspected the worst. "I'm sorry, Mr. Taylor. Your brother is dead.''

"No!'' It was a cry of denial from the depths of his soul.

The doctor said nothing, but stayed by his patient, wanting to ease his agony, but knowing he couldn't.

Dan closed his eyes against the pain of his loss. Asa . . . dead . . . The payroll gone. . . .

"Who found us?'' His words were a whisper.

"One of the men who works for you—Isaac. He suspected something was wrong when you were running late, and he went looking for the stage. He brought you in and got you to me in time to save your life.''

Dan gave a weak nod and moaned at the pain the movement caused. "Good man.''

"Mr. Taylor . . . Do you remember anything about the robbery or the shootings? Anything that might help the sheriff?'' He knew the sheriff would be riding out early in the morning and any help he could give him was desperately needed.

But as Curtiss asked the question, Dan's eyes closed and his head lolled to the side. Curtiss worried for a moment that he'd died, but when he checked, he found

Dan was still breathing. He was relieved and sat back in his chair to await further changes in his patient's condition.

"Where is he?" Mona asked as she entered the doctor's office. The ride from San Rafael had been long and rough, but she was relieved to be in Comanche Pass, at last.

"Hello, I'm Dr. Curtiss." He emerged from Dan's room to greet her.

Ted had followed her into the office and stepped forward to shake his hand. "I'm Ted Carroll, and this is my mother, Mona Taylor, Asa's wife. We just rode in from San Rafael. Shorty brought us the news late last night."

"Mr. Carroll," the doctor greeted him solemnly, shaking his hand. "Mrs. Taylor . . . I'm so sorry about your loss. When they brought your husband in yesterday, he was already gone."

Tears filled Mona's eyes as she clutched at Ted's arm for support. "Shorty told us what happened. I can't believe it. I can't believe any of this. Where is my husband? I have to see him."

"They took him on over to the undertaker's, ma'am. I'm sorry."

She choked back a sob. "And Dan . . . Is he any better?"

"He's about the same. He came out of it for a few minutes, but then lost consciousness again."

"Did he say anything? Anything at all that will help us find the ones who did this?" Ted asked quickly.

"No. He was too weak. He only asked about his brother."

"Asa . . ." Mona said his name in a strained voice.

"Can we see Dan?" Ted asked, putting an arm around his mother's shoulders. "Is he going to make it?"

"I don't know. Except for that minute or two of clarity last night, he's been unconscious. He could die at any time."

"How was he injured?" Mona asked.

"He was shot twice. Once in the shoulder, but that's not the wound I'm worried about. He was shot again in the back. I got the bullet out, but it's done a lot of damage. He'd lost a lot of blood, too, before they could get him in here."

The doctor led the way into the room where Dan lay.

Isaac was there, keeping vigil by his friend's side. He looked up at the sound of footsteps, and when he saw Ted and Mona, his gaze hardened. He had little use for the arrogant woman and even less for her son. Ted had only been back home for a month or so, but Isaac felt he was a troublemaker. There was nothing he could put his finger on. It was just a feeling he had about him, and through the years, he'd generally found out that his feelings were to be trusted.

"Hello, Isaac," Mona said softly, and then she gasped at the sight of Dan. His coloring was gray, and he barely seemed to be breathing. She buried her face against her son's shoulder.

"There, there, Mother."

"Oh . . . He looks so bad," she sobbed quietly.

Ted held her as he stared at Dan's inert form.

"I wish I could tell you that he is going to be better soon, but I just don't know yet," Curtiss said. "If the bullet had been an inch to the right, he'd have been killed instantly. He's very lucky to still be alive."

"We appreciate everything you've done," Ted told him.

Outwardly, he seemed truly upset over Dan's brush with death, but inwardly, he was cursing because his bullet had missed its mark.

"Is someone going to be staying with him every minute?" Mona asked, sounding concerned.

"I will be," Isaac vowed. "I'm not leaving his side until I know he's going to live."

"Thank you, Isaac," Ted told him.

"I need to see Asa," Mona said.

"I'll show you where the undertaker's parlor is," the doctor offered. "Your husband and the passenger are over there."

"That would be so kind of you."

"I'll let you know the moment there's any change in Mr. Taylor's condition. Will you be staying at the hotel?"

"Yes."

"We appreciate everything you've done," Ted said.

Dr. Curtiss gave them directions to the undertaker. Ted led his mother from his office and didn't say a word until he was certain they were far enough away so no one could hear.

"I hope the bastard dies of natural causes overnight," he muttered angrily under his breath.

"You're not the only one," she said in irritation.

163

"I was hoping they'd give us some time alone with Dan. A well-placed pillow could have taken care of everything in just a few minutes. But that Isaac was there, looking like a damned guard dog!"

"I know. I was thinking the same thing."

"What are we going to do?"

"Wait it out."

"Dan does looks terrible."

"Not terrible enough."

They entered the undertaking establishment and were taken by Robert Myers into the back room to view Asa's body. Mona cried over her husband in a display of what appeared to be true heartbreak.

"We've got to find the ones who did this! We have to! They're cold-blooded murderers!" she cried.

"We'll find them, Mother. I'm sure the law will do everything possible to make sure the right men are brought to justice."

Myers discussed how they wanted to handle the burial, and it was agreed that Asa's body would be transported back to San Rafael for internment. They left after making the necessary arrangements and checked into the hotel. They decided to rest before eating dinner and so retired to their rooms for the rest of the afternoon, waiting anxiously for word from the doctor on Dan's fate.

Dan groaned and came slowly awake. He was groggy and confused. Curtiss heard him stir and quickly went to him. It was almost sundown, and he was thrilled that his patient was coming around again.

"Mr. Taylor? Can you hear me?"

"Yeah," he said weakly.

"I'm Dr. Curtiss. You've been shot, and you're in my care here in Comanche Pass."

Dan gave a pained grunt in acknowledgment of the doctor's words as he struggled to make sense of all that had happened. He moved his head a bit and looked around. He saw Isaac sitting nearby and knew he was a true friend.

"How long?" he whispered hoarsely.

"The holdup was yesterday. Isaac, here, brought you to me last night."

"Thanks, Isaac." Dan gave a weak nod as he struggled to get more comfortable. "Doc—"

"What?"

"How bad am I?"

Curtiss smiled as he looked into his eyes and saw that he was aware of everything. He touched his arm. "The wound in your shoulder was clean, but the shot you took to the back was very serious. I had to dig the bullet out. If we can keep an infection from setting in, I think you'll make it."

"I can't stay down long. . . . I've got a stage and freight line to run."

"Don't worry about the line, Dan," Isaac spoke up, his tone emotional. "I'll take care of everything for you."

A tortured look crossed Dan's face. "Asa's . . . dead."

"I'm sorry about your brother," the doctor told him solemnly. "I wish I could have done something to help him, but it was too late when they brought him in. He had already passed away."

"I'm going to find the ones who did this! They're going to pay." The need for revenge filled Dan and gave him a reason to live.

"Right now, let's only worry about getting you well. You're very weak. It's going to be a while before you can be up and around again."

Dan looked at Curtiss, his gaze feverish with the need to avenge his brother's murder. "It doesn't matter if it takes me a month or a year. I'm going to find them."

"And I'll help you, Dan," Isaac added.

They shared a look of tragic understanding. Then Dan lay back on the bed and closed his eyes. He had to rest. He had to get better.

# *Chapter Nine*

Amanda stared out the window of the stage at the rugged hills of her native West Texas. Today they would reach San Rafael and she would be reunited with her father. Her mood was pensive as she anticipated seeing him again.

She looked up at Eileen sitting across from her. Her grandmother had done well in selecting the older woman to travel with her. Amanda hoped things worked out just as she'd planned, and they would soon be making the return trip together.

Watching Eileen now, Amanda smiled. Her traveling companion was such a dear. She was all but hanging out the window as she studied the Texas landscape. Seeing West Texas through the other woman's eyes had been enlightening for Amanda. She'd always thought it boring, but Eileen didn't. Eileen was intrigued and thrilled by the rugged terrain and distant vistas and had kept up a running dialogue filled with intelligent questions and astute observations about the countryside.

Beside Amanda, Jack sat in silence. Amanda cast a quick glance his way. His arms were folded across his chest, and his hat was pulled low over his eyes. She thought he might be napping, but she couldn't be sure. There was a lot about him she wasn't sure about.

Ever since Amanda had learned the truth about Jack's run-in with El Diablo, she'd been looking at him differently. It was no wonder he'd been so gruff and resentful of escorting her home. After the deadly outlaw, the last thing in the world he'd probably wanted to do was play chaperon for her. The trip was almost over now, though. Soon he would be free of her and able to go on his way.

To her dismay, Amanda suddenly realized she was going to miss him. *Oh, not a whole lot, but some,* she amended quickly. As much as she'd taken care never to be alone with him since that fateful night of the kiss, she had come to feel safe in his presence. He'd only kissed her because he'd been drinking and had wanted to put her in her place. She'd learned since talking to his sister that he was a fierce man, a man of dedication and determination. Not to mention that he was good-looking, too, in a rugged sort of way.

Amanda wouldn't go as far as saying that she'd grown fond of Jack, but she had come to respect him. Still, after he dropped her off with her father, she would never see him again, and for some reason, that bothered her.

Amanda remembered the threat of the Sheldon gang and wondered what Jack was going to do about it. His sister had predicted that he would go gunning for them. Amanda hoped he didn't. Not that she really cared what happened to him, but she certainly didn't want him to end up dead, and the Sheldons did sound vicious.

"I never knew what wide open spaces were before this trip," Eileen said happily, interrupting Amanda's thoughts.

"It's certainly different from Philadelphia, isn't it?" she responded, glad to be distracted from her troubling musings.

"I'll say. I'm really enjoying it. I'm glad you needed a companion, Amanda, dear. Remind me to thank your grandmother when I get home."

"I will, and I'm going to thank her, too. I'm so glad she hired you to travel with me."

"Everything did go rather well—except for my seasickness. And that awful encounter with Micah Jennings. Thank heaven our bruises have faded and no one can tell what happened."

"I know," Amanda agreed. The last thing she wanted to do was explain to her father how she'd managed to get a bruised face. It was going to be difficult enough as it was. She only hoped that Becky Jennings was faring as well as they were. "Let's just hope his wife had time enough to get far away from him."

"She should have had a good head start," Jack told them.

When he joined in the conversation so smoothly, it proved to Amanda that he really hadn't been asleep at all, but had been aware of everything going on around him. His ability to do that unnerved her even as it impressed her.

He went on, "The officials where we left him said that even though we didn't want to press charges, they'd keep him locked up for at least another day or two."

Jack had been glad to see Jennings behind bars. Every time he remembered how he'd come upon Jennings just as he'd been about to hit Amanda, he grew furious. The thought of anyone laying a hand on her enraged him. He had guarded her like a hawk for the balance of the trip.

*Not that she'd appreciated his vigilance.* Jack half smiled to himself as he glanced at Amanda beside him. She was looking out the window now, and he took advantage of the moment to study her profile. She was a beautiful woman, there was no denying that, and a spirited and intelligent one, too. Her father was going to have one heck of a time trying to control her.

Jack wasn't sure if Dan would permit Amanda to go back to Philadelphia or not. It would be interesting to see how she handled him, but he had no intention of sticking around long enough to find out. Even if she convinced her father to let her go, and his old friend asked him to make the trip back with her for double the money, he was going to refuse. He had a good excuse—he had to help Steve Laughlin recapture the Sheldon gang.

It occurred to Jack then that he would be done with Amanda that very day. Once he'd delivered her to Dan, he would never see her again. He told himself he was glad. She'd been nothing but a headache to him from the first. He would be thrilled to see the last of her. Then he could get on with his life.

"Look! There's San Rafael!" Amanda cried suddenly. "I'm home!" She hadn't expected to be so excited at seeing her hometown, but she was.

"How long have you been away, dear?" Eileen asked.

"Over six years now. I've come back for a visit every now and then, but mostly I've been living with my grandmother and going to school."

"And you plan to leave again as soon as you can?" Eileen asked.

"Yes. I've built my life in Philadelphia with my friends. They're counting on me to return and help them with the suffrage movement. We need to keep working. We can't ever give up."

"What if your father says no?" Jack inquired.

"He won't," Amanda answered automatically, and then noticed his expression. He looked smug, and it reminded her of that day on the dock when he'd accused her and Bethany of having been spoiled by their fathers.

"Are you sure?" Eileen wondered.

"Of course." Amanda sounded confident, but suddenly she realized that she had never even considered the possibility that her father might refuse to let her return. He'd always given her what she wanted, when she wanted it. She had no reason to believe that that would change just because she'd gotten expelled from school. Once she explained everything to him, she was sure he'd understand. Why wouldn't he want her to have the vote? Of course, he might still be angry about her not finishing school, but what did she need a college education for anyway? There was too much she could be doing to help the suffrage movement for her to waste her time sitting in classrooms listening to boring lectures on ancient Greece and Rome. No, the future for women was in the franchise, and she was going to be one of the leaders.

The stage drew to a stop at the station in town, and Jack climbed down first, then turned to help Eileen descend.

"Where's my father?" Amanda asked, craning her neck out the stage window. He should have been there waiting, but she could see no sign of him anywhere. They had sent a telegram from San Antonio letting him know when they'd be arriving, and she couldn't believe he wasn't there.

The possibility that he was so furious with her that he didn't want to see her until she got home brought her up short. She knew he was upset, but she hadn't considered that he might be that angry with her. She quieted in anticipation of the reunion to come.

"It doesn't look like he's here," Jack said as he saw Eileen safely out of the stage and then offered his hand to Amanda.

She took it distractedly and climbed down to stand in the dusty street. She looked in both directions for some sign of her father, but he was nowhere to be found. "I guess we'll just go on up to the house—"

"Amanda!"

Mona's cry came to her, and she looked up to see her Uncle Asa's wife hurrying toward her with a tall, handsome man at her side.

172

"Aunt Mona!" Amanda smiled and waved. She'd always liked the woman her uncle had married, but she wondered why she was the one coming to greet her.

"I'm so glad you're finally back! We've missed you so much," Mona said as she embraced her. When they broke apart, she made the introductions. "Amanda, this is my son, Ted Carroll. I don't know if you remember him or not?"

"Hello, Ted," she said, turning to Ted and smiling up at him. The smile he gave her in return was genuine and warm, and she decided that he had grown into a very attractive man. He was over six feet tall, with brown hair and friendly blue eyes. "It's nice to see you again. I remember meeting you the first year after your mother married Uncle Asa, but then you went away to school and I went back East."

"It's nice to see you, too," he replied.

"Where are my father and Uncle Asa? Didn't they come with you?" she asked, looking around anxiously, her eyes aglow at the thought of seeing them.

"Amanda, I . . ." Mona began, then hesitated.

"Did Papa have to drive today? Is that why he's not here to meet me?" She suddenly sensed that something very strange was going on. "Where's my father?" She looked from Mona to Ted expectantly.

Ted stepped toward her protectively. "Amanda, there's been trouble—"

"What kind of trouble?"

"Your father and Asa were making the run to Comanche Pass a little over a week ago when they were

173

attacked and robbed. Asa was killed and your father—''

''Oh,. God! How's Papa?'' She tensed, grabbing Ted's arm, fearing the worst. If he were dead—

''He was shot twice,'' Mona quickly explained. ''At first, we didn't know if he would survive or not. But he's pulled through and is recovering.''

''I have to see him.'' She had gone pale and was shaking. Her father was her stronghold. He was always there and had always taken care of her. He couldn't be hurt . . . He couldn't be. . . .

Amanda forgot everything else as she started off toward her house at a run.

''Amanda! Wait!'' Eileen called after her, but she didn't hear her and kept running.

''Ted, go after her. She's going to need you,'' Mona directed her son, and then she turned her attention to Jack and Miss Hammond. ''And you are?''

''I'm Eileen Hammond. Amanda's grandmother hired me to act as her companion on the trip back, and this is Mr. Taylor's friend Jack Logan. Mr. Taylor sent Mr. Logan to bring Amanda home. It looks as though we didn't get her back here a minute too soon.''

''I only wish it could be a happier homecoming,'' Mona said regretfully, her gaze following Amanda and Ted as they disappeared down the street.

''How is Dan?'' Jack asked, concerned about his friend.

''As I told Amanda, he's not doing well. It was very touch-and-go there for the first week. He seems stronger now, but you never know—''

''Is he able to have visitors?''

"I'm sure he'll want to see you if his strength holds up." She looked in the direction Amanda and Ted had gone. "I'd better go with them. Amanda's going to need my support. Come to the house as soon as you're ready. We'll be expecting you."

Mona gave them the address and left.

Jack was frowning as Eileen looked up at him.

"This is so terrible! How could this have happened?"

"The reason Dan hired me, the reason he couldn't go back East to get Amanda himself, was that there had been two robberies in the last few months," Jack explained.

"And things have only gotten worse."

Jack saw to their luggage and arranged for Amanda's and Eileen's to be taken to the Taylor house. Then he and Eileen followed the others.

"Papa—" Amanda said in a choked voice as she slipped into his semi-darkened bedroom.

Maria, their housekeeper and cook, had been keeping watch over him. She stood and went to Amanda. "It is good you are home. He has been wanting to see you."

"He looks so—"

Maria understood her reaction to the sight of her normally healthy, robust father so injured. "He's resting now."

"Papa . . . ?" Amanda said his name again, a little louder. When her father still didn't stir, she knew a moment of true terror. She thought he looked as if he

175

were dead. Tears burned in her eyes and her hands were shaking.

"Papa . . . It's me, Amanda. I'm home," she repeated, moving tentatively closer to his bedside.

Dan's eyes opened slowly and he stared up at his daughter. He managed a weak smile. "Amanda. . . ." It was barely a whisper. He slowly lifted one hand toward her.

She hurried to take his hand and knelt next to him, staring down at his pale features. His eyes were sunken and his cheeks hollow. He looked as if his life were draining away from him. "I'm sorry it took so long. . . . I didn't know you were hurt."

"I'm glad you're here," he said, gathering his strength to talk. Just seeing her again renewed him. "They wanted me to stay up in Comanche Pass until I was better, but I told them you were coming home. I had to be here."

"Don't worry, Papa. I'm back now. I'll take care of you. I'll take care of everything." Her tears were falling unheeded now. Her father had almost been killed, and she hadn't been here for him! Any thought she'd had about going back East disappeared. "Oh, Papa—"

"It's going to be all right, girl. The bastards, whoever they are, aren't going to beat me," he vowed angrily, then groaned in pain at having expended too much energy.

Amanda grew determined, too. Whoever had done this to her father was going to pay. She would see to it. "You don't have any idea who did this to you? Has the sheriff got any clues?"

"No, he doesn't know a damned thing," Dan said. "I sure as hell wish they'd found something out, but there was nothing at the scene of the robbery that was of any help to them."

"They can't just get away with this!" Anger filled her. Her uncle had been killed, and her father had been grievously wounded.

"The sheriff says he'll get them, but that it's going to take time."

"Is the line still running?" she asked, knowing what was most important to her father, and knowing she couldn't let him down. The Taylor Stage and Freight Line was her father's life. She would do whatever she had to do to keep it going.

"Ted came back home, and he's been helping Isaac run it. It's been tough, but Isaac's doing as good a job as he can, considering the circumstances."

"Well, there's no need for them to worry anymore. I'm going to be running the stage line from now on," she declared, wiping away her tears as she began to focus on what she needed to do.

"You?" Her father looked at her and frowned.

"Who better than me? I grew up around Taylor Stage and Freight. I know everything there is to know about the operation. You don't have to worry at all, Papa. I'm taking over, and I'll keep everything running until you're back on your feet."

"I don't know if that's a good idea, Amanda," he cautioned. "You're just a girl, and whoever these men are, they're deadly."

Amanda had expected this argument. She'd been hearing it from him all her life. "Isaac will help me, and, as you said, Ted's back. Things will be fine, you'll see.''

Dan wanted to argue with her. She couldn't possibly take charge of such a big operation. But he didn't have the strength.

''I'll let you rest for now. We'll talk more later when you're feeling stronger,'' she promised as she leaned close to him and pressed a kiss to his cheek.

Dan watched her walk from the room, and he knew he had to do something to protect her. If he and Asa couldn't stop the robberies, how could she? ''Send Jack in,'' he called out hoarsely.

''I will, and you take it easy and don't worry. I want you healthy again as soon as possible.''

Amanda stepped into the hall and closed the bedroom door behind her. Her heart was pounding, and she was trembling. She had just told her father that she was going to take over the day-to-day running of Taylor Stage and Freight. She swallowed nervously as she leaned weakly back against his door. Doubts assailed her as she wondered if she could do it. But even as she feared the unknown that lay ahead of her, she knew in her heart that she was as smart as any man, and she did have a background in the business.

Pushing herself away from the door, Amanda squared her shoulders and stiffened her spine. She was Amanda Taylor. She had marched with the suffragists and smashed up saloons with the temperance protesters. This was her stage line, and she was damned well going to run it!

With Isaac's help and Ted willing to work, too, she could do it. She knew she could. She would prove to them all just how capable a woman could be, handling what was supposedly a man's job.

She started off down the hall and met Mona and Ted on their way to find her.

"How is he?" Mona asked, concern showing in her expression.

"Very weak," Amanda said. "I've never seen him in such bad shape."

Ted automatically went to her and put a supporting arm around her shoulders. "We're here to help you in any way we can, Amanda."

"Thank you." She managed to smile at him. "From what Papa told me, you've already helped him a lot. I appreciate it."

"We're family," Mona said, smiling sympathetically. "If there's anything you need, anything at all, you only have to ask."

"You're both wonderful."

"Shall we go into the parlor and talk for a few minutes? Catch up on everything?"

"Yes, I'd like that. I especially want you to tell me what's been happening with the line, Ted," she said, gathering her thoughts and getting ready to take control. "Is Isaac here in town? I'd like to speak to you both at the same time."

"Since your father was shot, Isaac moved here to San Rafael to take charge and to be near your father. He's been with him almost every minute. He's very dedicated to him."

"Papa cares a lot about him. They're good friends."

"I'll go get him for you. I know he's eager to see you."

"Good. Mona, I'll meet you in the parlor after I find Jack. My father wants to see him," Amanda said with authority, glad to have something to do to distract herself. All she really wanted to do was sit down and cry, but there was no time for that. Her father was alive and recovering. Right now, she had to be strong for him. She had to be the son he'd never had. She had a stage line to run.

Mona watched Amanda disappear downstairs, then looked at her son. The expression in her eyes was hard. "I thought she was going to be a sweet, young thing who'd be easy to control."

"Calm down, Mother," Ted chided. "She'll be fine. She's probably still in shock right now. All we have to do is explain to her how terrible things have been, how bad business has gotten, and then convince her to sell the stage line."

"Do you really believe it will be that simple?"

"We're going to find out."

"If Dan's recovering, there's no way she's going to sell."

"I suppose we'll just have to convince both of them that it's the wise thing to do, won't we?" He strode off after Amanda, intent on locating Isaac.

Amanda was coming downstairs just as Jack and Eileen entered the house.

"I'm glad you're here," she told them. "My father was asking for you, Jack. He wants to see you. He's upstairs in the last bedroom on the right."

"How are you? Are you all right?" Jack asked as he went to her where she stood at the foot of the steps.

She looked pale, shaken and almost fragile. He was tempted to take her in his arms and comfort her, but he stopped himself.

"I'm fine. It's just my father—" she said, lifting her tortured gaze to Jack's. "It's so hard seeing him this way."

"Did you ask him about going back East?"

"No," she answered sharply, glancing back up the stairs. "I can't even think about leaving him the way things are right now. He needs me here, with him."

Jack nodded, knowing how much it had cost her to give up her dream. "I'd better go see what he wants."

"Thanks."

Jack started up the steps just as Ted and Mona appeared at the top. He nodded as he passed them and continued on his way down the hall.

Eileen went to Amanda and slipped an arm around her waist. "Honey, you look exhausted. Let's go in here and sit down." She led her into the parlor.

Ted left the house in search of Isaac while Mona went to join Amanda and Eileen.

Jack knocked softly on Dan's bedroom door. "Dan?"

"Come on in, Jack," Dan called out, glad his friend had come to see him.

Jack entered quietly. "I'm sorry about your brother. What happened? Was it the same gang as before?"

"I don't know," his old friend said wearily. "Pull up a chair so we can talk."

Jack did, settling in close to the bedside. He understood Amanda's reaction to her father's condition. Dan looked as if he were at death's doorstep.

181

"Thanks for bringing my little girl home to me."

"She's not such a little girl anymore," Jack said ruefully.

"She always will be to me," her father said softly. "Your money's there in the top drawer of my bureau." He nodded toward the bureau.

"Thank you."

"Did you have any trouble with her?"

"No, everything went smoothly." Jack did not want to burden Dan with the news that his daughter was involved in the temperance protest or tell him about the ugly encounter with Jennings aboard ship. Everything had turned out all right in the end, so there was no need to bother him with the details.

"Good . . . good." Dan sighed in relief. "She can be a handful sometimes."

"We made it just fine."

"Jack . . . There's something I've got to ask you."

"What?" Jack waited, unsure of what was to come.

"When Amanda was in here just now . . . She said she was going to take care of me and the stage line. She plans on taking over and running the line herself."

"She can't be serious?"

"She is. Jack . . . whoever's been robbing the line isn't going to stop until they're caught and put behind bars. I can't let Amanda get mixed up in all this. It's too dangerous."

"It sounds like she already is."

"What if something were to happen to her?" He gave Jack a tormented look. "I need you, Jack. I need you to stay here and keep an eye on her for me."

"Dan, Amanda doesn't want anything to do with

me. I'm sure she's thrilled at the thought that after today, she'll never have to see me again. She's quite the independent woman, and she's made it perfectly clear that she doesn't want a man taking care of her.''

''I don't care what she wants. I've got to know that she's safe.'' Somehow, Dan garnered enough strength to lever himself up on an elbow and look straight at Jack. ''Tell her I hired you on as a driver. With Asa dead and me laid up, we need all the help I can get. You know how to handle a team, but better yet, you're a dead shot. Pretend to be working for the line, but in reality be her bodyguard. Protect her, Jack. Keep her safe for me, until I'm well enough to take care of her myself.''

Jack wanted to leave. He wanted to get away from Amanda. He was tempted to tell Dan about the Sheldon gang, how they were gunning for him and how he needed to go after them, but he didn't. The thought of Amanda in danger disturbed him. Instead of refusing, he nodded tightly. ''All right. I'll do it, but she isn't going to be happy about it.''

''I don't care if Amanda's happy or not. I just want her to stay alive.'' He lay back heavily and let his eyes shut as exhaustion washed over him. ''Thanks, Jack. I'll make it up to you one of these days.''

''You don't have to make anything up to me. We just have to convince Amanda that you really hired me to work for the line.''

''I'll handle Amanda. You just keep an eye out for trouble and make sure nothing happens to her.''

''You got any idea who's behind this?''

"If I did, I'd have taken care of them myself," Dan said with a fierceness that belied his weakened condition. "I'm counting on you. Amanda's my life."

"I'll take care of her, Dan," Jack promised.

"Thanks."

Downstairs in the parlor, Amanda spoke with Isaac and Ted as Mona and Eileen listened.

"I've just talked with my father, and I told him that I was going to take over the day-to-day operations of the stage line."

"Amanda, that's ridiculous," Mona said, drawing a challenging look from Amanda.

"Why, Mona?" she asked. "Because I'm female?"

"Well . . . Yes. I mean, Amanda, dear, you've been away back East at school. Why should you trouble yourself with all this, when you have Ted and Isaac to run the place for you? Things seem to be going along all right for them," she pointed out.

" 'All right' isn't good enough for me. My father is the majority owner of Taylor Stage and Freight. As his daughter, I am assuming control until such time as he's recovered enough to return to his duties running the line himself."

Mona was in shock and gave her a disapproving glare. Ted kept his expression carefully benign.

Isaac was smiling broadly at her. She was her father's daughter. "Welcome home, Miss Amanda," he said, proud of her courage in taking on such a big job. "Where do you want to start?"

"I'll get settled in tonight and meet with you early tomorrow morning. You can tell me then exactly how we're running and the general status of things.'' She looked at Ted. ''Can you meet us here at seven-thirty?''

''I'll be here—but Amanda, do you really think this is a good idea?'' He glanced over at his mother. ''With your father so weak, Mother and I had been discussing the possibility of selling the line. Charles Johnson has been trying to buy your father out for the last year, and we were thinking this would be the time to take him up on his offer.''

She was shocked by his suggestion. ''Taylor Stage and Freight is my father's life. It was Asa's life, too.'' She fixed Mona with a steady regard. ''They built this business from scratch. Neither one of them would ever have considered selling out, and I won't either.''

''If you feel that strongly about it, all right. I just thought that you might want to sell while we could still get a good price for it.''

''Taylor Stage and Freight Line is not for sale, so meet me here at seven-thirty, and we'll plan what we're going to do to increase security and keep the stages running smoothly and on time.''

''Yes, ma'am,'' Isaac said, glad that she was proving to be decisive and determined. He'd missed working with Dan and Asa. Ted tried to help, but he had little idea of what he was doing, and that made things twice as hard. ''I'll be here.''

''Thanks, Isaac.'' She smiled warmly at him as he left.

''I'll see you then,'' Ted said, rising to go.

Mona went to his side, and Amanda walked them to the foyer.

"Mona, I don't know if I had the chance to tell you how sorry I am about Uncle Asa," Amanda said, taking her hands in hers. "This can't be easy for you."

"You have no idea," Mona responded. "I just thank heaven that Ted's been here for me." She looked at her son with pride. "He's been such a big help."

"I'm glad you're here, too, Ted," Amanda said, gazing up at him. "I don't know what Papa would have done without you and Isaac these last few weeks."

"I was glad to help. Your Uncle Asa was always good to me, and if I can do anything to make things easier for you, just let me know."

"I will, believe me."

"Good night, Amanda," Mona said, kissing her on the cheek as she started from the house.

"Good night," Ted said as he leaned down to kiss her cheek, too.

"I'll see you tomorrow." Amanda had been surprised by Ted's kiss, but also a little pleased by it. She watched him from the doorway until they had gone from sight.

# *Chapter Ten*

"So you're going to see him tomorrow, are you?" Jack's already bad mood had darkened as he'd stood at the top of the steps and watched Ted kiss Amanda. There was something about the man he didn't like. Ted was too smooth, too friendly, too nice—and too attentive to Amanda. He was going to have to keep an eye on him.

Amanda had been unaware of Jack's presence, and she was startled by his remark. "Not that it's any of your business, but yes, I'm meeting with Ted and Isaac in the morning to discuss business."

"Well, you might as well include me in your little meeting," he said.

"Why should I? You're leaving. You've done what my father hired you to do. You escorted me home, and now you're free to go."

"Afraid not." Jack grinned wickedly at her shocked expression. "I've got a new job."

"What are you talking about?"

"You're looking at Taylor Stage and Freight Line's newest hand. Your father just hired me on. He said with your uncle dead and him laid up, he needed someone who could handle a team and a gun, and I fit the bill."

Amanda couldn't believe it. "Well, I've taken over the running of the line in my father's absence and that makes me the boss. I say you're not hired!"

"Sorry, darling. You can't unhire me," Jack drawled. "Your father may be weak right now, but he's still the owner. He's the one who took me on, and he's the only one I answer to."

"We'll just have to see about that," she declared tightly, glaring at him as he gave her a mocking smile.

"I told him how much you were going to enjoy having me around for a while longer."

Amanda turned her back on him and stalked into the parlor.

"Good night, Amanda," Jack called before he let himself out of the house. "I'll be staying at the hotel, just in case you need me for anything."

"I won't," she answered back.

Eileen had been waiting for her in the parlor, and she was smiling as Amanda came in. "Did I just hear Jack say that your father has hired him and he is staying on for a while?"

"Yes."

"That's wonderful."

"You may think so, but I don't."

"If anyone can help straighten things out around here, Jack can," Eileen said with confidence.

"What makes you think that?" She glanced at Eileen.

"Why, he's a Ranger, my dear."

"An ex-Ranger," Amanda corrected, and then teased, "And I think you're just glad he's staying on because you've secretly fallen in love with him."

"I'm afraid Jack might think I'm just a little too old for him." Eileen was grinning mischievously. "But you, on the other hand—"

"Jack Logan is obnoxious and arrogant! I'd never fall in love with someone like him! Why, I can't believe my father hired him to stay on and help with the line!"

"But as Jack just said, he is good with a gun, and judging from the looks of things, you need someone like that right now."

Amanda knew Eileen was right, but it didn't make her feel any better. She'd thought that after today Jack would be gone from her life, and once he was, she would never again be reminded of how disturbing his embrace had been. But now she was going to be stuck with him for what looked like weeks on end until her father had improved enough to go back to work!

The thought of working so closely with Jack was enough to make Amanda pray even harder for a miracle cure for her father. She glanced out the parlor door toward the stairs and wondered if her father was feeling any better yet.

"What are you thinking, Amanda?" Eileen asked. "You look like you're up to something."

Amanda grinned and looked a little embarrassed. "I was just wishing that my father was cured and that he would come walking into the room right now so I wouldn't be caught up in all this. But I don't think that's going to happen, no matter how hard I pray."

Eileen went to her and gave her a supportive hug. "You've been through a lot in the last few hours. Earlier today, you thought everything was going to be simple, and now your whole world has been turned upside down."

Amanda sighed heavily, not realizing until that moment how upset she really was. "He could have been killed in that robbery. . . . Thank God he's alive."

"And that's all that matters. I was thinking, Amanda—instead of my hurrying back to Philadelphia, why don't I stay on here for a while and help you? I know you have Maria working here in the house, but I've done some nursing in my time. I'd be more than willing to help out until your father's back on his feet."

Amanda brightened at the prospect. "You wouldn't mind staying on?"

"No, not at all. In fact, I'd enjoy helping you."

"I have plenty of room here at the house, if you'd like to stay with us."

"That would be fine. Thank you for the offer."

"Let's see about getting your things put away; then we'll talk to Maria and see what needs to be done."

Jack was scowling as he headed for the only hotel in San Rafael. He was tempted to stop off at a saloon and have a drink, but he controlled the urge. Drinking might have eased his mood for a little while, but it wouldn't change anything. Come tomorrow morning, he'd still be here, working for Dan and dealing with Amanda.

Jack wasn't happy with the way things had turned out, but there had been no other way to handle things. The Taylor Stage and Freight Line was in trouble. By taking over, Amanda had put herself in danger. He would guard her from harm, but he wondered if he could keep her safe from herself. Something about Ted Carroll troubled him, and he was going to keep an eye on him, especially when he was around Amanda.

He thought of Steve Laughlin and the Sheldon gang, and wondered how things were going in his old boss's efforts to track down the escaped outlaws. He stopped at the telegraph office to send a wire to Steve in care of Ranger headquarters. He wanted to let his friend know where he was and what he was doing. There hadn't been any point before because he'd been on the move, but it looked as if he was going to be staying in one place for a while now. If Steve needed him, at least now he'd know where to find him.

Jack claimed his bags from where he'd left them at the depot and checked into the hotel. His room was small and clean, and that was all he needed.

Jack headed to the sheriff's office next to find out what was being done about tracking down the robbers. It proved a wasted effort, for little was known. Whoever had murdered Asa and the passenger had gotten clean away. The news troubled Jack. He wondered just who these men were that they could disappear without a trace. He ate a solitary meal in the dining room and then retired for the night.

\* \* \*

Amanda and Eileen had a late dinner together and then made their way upstairs. Amanda made sure that Eileen was comfortable in her room, then stopped in to check on her father before going on to bed. He was sleeping, so she drew a chair up next to the bed and just sat with him for a while. She hadn't been in the room long when he stirred and awoke.

"Amanda?" he said softly, as he opened his eyes to find her there.

"Yes, Papa. It's me."

"I thought I'd dreamed that you were back."

"No, it wasn't a dream. I'm here. I just came in now to say good night."

"I missed you. I'm glad you're home."

"I'm glad I am, too."

"Did you talk to Jack? I hired him to help you out with things."

She gritted her teeth as she answered him. "He told me. Are you sure we need him? I think I could do fine with just Isaac and Ted helping me."

"Jack's a good man, and he's a fast gun. You're going to need someone like him. Isaac knows how use a pistol, but Ted—" He let the thought drift off, not wanting to say anything bad about him. Mona and Ted had been a great help to him in the last few weeks, always checking on him and worrying about him. He knew they both meant well.

"Don't you like Ted? I thought he seemed nice."

"He is. He's just not used to life out here. He'll come around, I guess."

"I'm meeting with the three of them in the morning to arrange the schedule for the next few weeks."

"Don't do anything foolish. Make sure there's someone good with a gun going on every run. I want those outlaws stopped, and once we catch them, I want them to pay for what they've done."

"I'm sure the sheriff's working on it. You get some sleep now, and I'll let you know how the meeting goes in the morning."

Dan nodded, wearied by the effort he'd expended talking. His eyes drifted shut. Amanda stayed a little longer, making sure he was comfortable, then kissed him gently on the cheek and slipped from his room.

Amanda entered her own bedroom and, for the first time that day, really felt as if she were home. Things were just as she'd left them after her last visit. That happy time seemed so long ago now. She started to get ready for bed and had just finished unbuttoning her dress when she caught sight of herself in the mirror over her dressing table. Amanda paused to stare at her reflection.

Earlier that day, she had had her future all planned out. She'd known exactly what she wanted to do and how she wanted to do it. The biggest problem she'd faced had been how to convince her father to let her go back East again to work for women's rights.

Amanda gave a slow shake of her head. The woman who stared back at her in the mirror was not the same innocent young girl who'd stepped off the stage that afternoon. The woman who returned her regard in the reflection had grown up fast. Heavy responsibility rested on her shoulders. She had nearly lost her father to a murderous gunman, and he was still not completely out of danger. Her dreams of suffrage and marching for women's rights seemed somehow frivolous now. There was no time for protesting. She was going to have to prove that she could do everything she said she could. She had to keep the Taylor Stage and Freight Line running.

Amanda turned away from the mirror, uncertain and a little frightened. She told herself there was no time to be afraid. She had a job to do and she was going to do it. It was time for her to get some rest. She had a meeting at seven-thirty in the morning, and she wanted to be at her best.

"We want Armita!" a drunken cowboy shouted from the bar.

"Where the hell is she tonight?" another demanded of the barkeep.

"She likes to keep you waiting. It makes you appreciate her more," Cal, the bartender, said as he served them another round of drinks. "She'll be along."

"I been here over an hour already, and she ain't come down yet."

"She's worth the wait," Cal told them. "Since she's been here, my business has really picked up."

"Where did she come from?"

"She wouldn't say, and I didn't ask. She wants to be mysterious, I guess, and it sure is working. Look at the crowd in here tonight." He was proud that the Silverado was packed.

"Armita sure is a good-looker."

"Yeah, but she don't mess with anybody. That's probably why you all want her so bad," Cal remarked.

"One of us'll get her eventually. You'll see," the drunk said with a confidence born of liquor.

"You want to take any bets on that?" the barkeep asked with a smile. When he'd hired the hot little singer, she had told him straight out that she didn't whore. She was an entertainer, that was all.

The cowboys mumbled something drunkenly just as Armita appeared at the top of the steps. The piano player saw her and struck a chord. The saloon went suddenly silent as all the men looked up at her. To a man they thought she was beautiful. With her raven tresses and flashing eyes, she was a cowboy's dream.

Cody stood at the top of the steps in her disguise as Armita. With her hair dyed black and her skin darkened, she looked every bit the sultry, seductive temptress. Her gaze swept over the crowd below, but she was disappointed, for she saw no signs of the elusive Chica. The Silverado was the saloon the Sheldons had frequented the night the Rangers had caught up with them. In the days that Cody had worked there, though, she had never heard anyone mention Chica.

Determined to ask some pointed questions about the missing woman this night, Cody signaled the piano player to begin her first song. She started down the steps with a sensuous sway as she serenaded the men.

An hour later, Cody had finished her first act for the night and was making the rounds of the tables, flirting outrageously with all the customers. A big, burly cowboy named Harlen snared her around the waist and hauled her onto his lap.

"You sure you only want to make your livin' by singin'?" Harlen asked, his words slurred.

He groped at her, wanting her. Armita was beautiful, and he had a powerful hunger for her. Before he could blink, Cody had drawn her knife from where she kept it strapped to her thigh.

"Keep your hands to yourself," she said in a dangerous tone. "I would hate to send you home to your wife with a body part missing."

"I ain't got no wife!" he bellowed, red in the face.

Cody stood up and stepped away from him. "And you never will have one if I cut you up a bit. Armita is not a whore. Armita is a singer. I will sing for you. That is all."

"Yeah, but you're a pretty little thing." The fact that she was so wild and dangerous excited Harlen even more.

"So are the other girls who work here. Surely you would enjoy one of them. Or maybe Chica? I have heard of her, and it is said that she knows how to please a man."

"Chica? Who'd want her now?" he said in disgust.

Cody was surprised by his words. "I do not understand. I had heard she is very beautiful and very good to her men."

"She was, until ol' Hank found out about the other men she was layin' and put it to her."

She pretended ignorance. "I had not heard that there was trouble."

"Put that knife away and come sit on my lap again, and I will tell you what happens to a woman when she plays the whore for too many men."

Cody made quite a display of re-strapping her knife to her thigh. She lowered her skirts in a deliberately controlled but sexy move and smiled at him. The drunk was enthralled by the look she gave him, even as he was cautioned. She then moved sinuously back to stand right before him.

"We will talk, nothing more. I do not play the whore for any man. Tell me of Chica."

"She was a looker, all right."

"Was?" Cody suddenly feared the other woman was dead.

"She was Hank's woman, but when the Rangers caught him, she thought he would never come back."

"And he did?"

"He did. He found her with another man right after he broke out of jail."

She shuddered deliberately. "How is the other man?"

Harlen laughed at her question. "Better off than Chica. Hank just killed him."

"What did he do to his woman?"

"She ain't nobody's woman no more. He cut her up so bad, ain't no man ever gonna want her again."

"I think perhaps Chica should have carried a knife of her own. Then he would have been the one no woman would ever have wanted again."

"You're a feisty little thing, but even you wouldn't be no match for Hank Sheldon. He's the most deadly man I ever run into. He done shot a dog out front of the saloon one day, just 'cause it wagged its tail at him."

"This man is your friend?"

"Hell, no! I stay as far away from him and his brother as I can."

"I have not heard of them before."

"Well, you'll probably be hearin' more of them. Since they broke out of jail they've been back here twice."

"And Chica? What of her?"

"Who cares?" he said, shrugging as he took a drink. "No man would want her now."

"Men like this Sheldon you just spoke of are dangerous. You will warn me if he comes back, won't you?"

"You bet I will. I'll just tell him you're my woman. That way he won't mess with you."

Cody knew Harlen was no match for Hank Sheldon. Hank would shoot him down just like the dog he'd killed if it would get him something he wanted. She played along with his false bravado anyway. "Because of you, I feel safe now. You are a good man. I will sing this next song just for you."

Cody signaled the piano player to strike up a tune. She moved away from Harlen, singing of a lost love.

For all that she was playing the seductress, her mind was racing, going over the information Harlen had just given her. She could bide her time there in the bar in the hope that the Sheldons would show up again, or she could go looking for Chica to see if the woman knew anything more of the brothers' whereabouts. If he had hurt her as badly as Harlen had said, Chica might just be willing to tell her where she could find them. It was worth a try.

Cody looked around the room and spied Luke where he sat in the back at a table by himself, nursing a drink. She made her way through the crowd of men and ended up standing before him.

"You look lonely, cowboy. Shall I keep you company for a while?"

"I love beautiful women," he said with a slight smile. "Have a seat."

"No, I think I would prefer to sit on your lap. I enjoyed my visit with Harlen that way."

"Well, don't let me stop you." He pushed his chair back and welcomed her against him.

"Make this look good," she whispered.

Luke nuzzled at her neck while she mockingly attempted to ward off his caresses. "What did you find out?" he murmured.

"They've been here twice since they broke out. Hank caught his woman with another man and evidently hurt her pretty bad. She's no longer a working girl."

"What do you want to do?" he asked, enjoying the game they were playing.

Cody pushed him away and looked indignant. "I want to find Chica. She may be more than willing to help us now."

"I'll see what I can do."

"I'm going to slap you."

"That's better than using your knife on me."

She followed through on her threat and slapped him as she stood up in anger. "You would do well to learn from Harlen. He was a gentleman," she said loudly enough for the others to hear.

Luke just rubbed his cheek. He had to admit that

# Bobbi Smith

Cody played Armita with style. She certainly had
every man in the Silverado panting after her, himself
included. He smiled crookedly as he watched her walk
away from him. It was good to know she was his.

# *Chapter Eleven*

"What are you doing here, Logan?" Ted asked, as Jack walked into the parlor the next morning a few minutes before seven-thirty. His presence there was an unpleasant surprise to Ted, and he wondered what the other man was up to.

"I'm here for the meeting with Amanda," Jack told him as he casually took a seat on the sofa.

"Why? I thought you would be leaving now that you've brought her home."

"I did, too, but when I talked with Dan yesterday, he hired me on. I thought I'd better show up today and hear what our new boss lady has to say."

Ted wasn't pleased with the news. Logan had a reputation as a fast gun, and he'd heard all about his years as a Ranger. The last thing he and his mother needed was an ex-Ranger sniffing around.

"Suit yourself," he said with as much indifference

as he could muster. "Whatever we do, it isn't going to be easy."

Isaac and Amanda entered the room together.

"Good morning, Ted, Jack," she said in an authoritative tone. "Isaac arrived a little early, so we've already made up the schedules for the week. Ted, you'll be driving the noon stage today, and Isaac will ride along with you as shotgun. I spoke with my father last night after you all had gone, and he insisted that each stage have an armed guard. We want to make sure no one else is ever again injured while traveling on the Taylor Stage and Freight Line. Can you be ready to ride with Isaac by noon, Ted?"

"If you need me, I'll be ready."

She smiled at him warmly. "Thank you. Everything else looks smooth for the rest of the day. We've got a freight shipment due in sometime this afternoon, but that shouldn't be any trouble. The driver who's bringing it in is scheduled to take it on to Eagle Rock. Do you have any questions?"

Jack was glad that she hadn't sent him on the run with Ted. He had strict instructions from Dan to stay with her, and that would have been hard to explain without revealing the real purpose of his being there. "When are you going to need me?" he asked as the other men rose to leave.

It was on the tip of Amanda's tongue to say "never," but she controlled herself. "I'll let you know."

"I'll be waiting."

*   *   *

Isaac and Ted pulled out of town right on time, and Amanda finally allowed herself to relax for a while. The peace didn't last long, though. Less than an hour later, the freight wagon of lumber that was bound for Eagle Rock arrived. Amanda went out to meet the driver.

"Good job," she praised him. "You're right on schedule."

"Who are you?" Dave Wilson asked as he climbed down from the driver's seat. He looked around. "Where's Isaac?"

"Isaac's out on a run right now. I'm Amanda Taylor. I'll be taking over managing the stage line until my father's able to come back to work."

"You're going to run the line?" He stared at her, making no effort to hide the disgust he was feeling.

"That's right."

"Well, lady, you're going to have to find yourself another driver."

"What?"

"I quit."

She was shocked. "Why? This load has to get to Eagle Rock on time."

"You're the new boss. You figure it out."

"I need your help. I want to keep the line running as close to normal as possible. You can't just quit."

"Sorry, but I just did. I ain't working for no woman."

Amanda bristled at his stupidity. "Mr. Wilson, you are an employee—"

"Who just quit. Find yourself another driver. I

heard about all the trouble, and I don't trust no damned woman to keep things going right.''

''What if there was a bonus involved for delivering this load on time?''

''No, thanks.'' He turned his back on her and walked away.

Amanda hadn't sworn often in her young life, but she did then as she watched him go. She tried to figure out what to do. With Isaac and Ted gone, it was up to her to see that the lumber got delivered.

Returning home, Amanda dug through her clothes to find what she was looking for. When she found the trousers in the back of her closet, she shed her ladylike daygown and button shoes. In the blink of an eye, she transformed herself into the girl she'd been, growing up in West Texas. Even so, though she was wearing men's pants, boots, a long-sleeved shirt and a leather vest, there was no mistaking her for a male. The pants fit almost too perfectly, showing off the fullness of her curves and the long, slender length of her legs. Amanda knew she would draw looks when she went back to the station, but she didn't care. She had neither the time nor the patience to worry about it. The lumber had to be delivered, and she was going to do it.

Stopping at her father's room, Amanda peeked in to see if he was awake. She was pleased to see that Eileen had already been in, for the window shade was up and sunlight brightened his chamber.

''Papa?''

He was propped up in bed by several pillows and had glanced up when she knocked softly at the door. ''Amanda . . . This Miss Hammond of yours is a wonder. Your grandmother certainly chose well when she picked her to travel with you.''

"Like her, do you?'' She entered the room and crossed to the bed.

"Very much, but from the look of you, we've got more to talk about than Miss Hammond. What are you doing dressed like that?''

"I'm going to make the freight run to Eagle Rock.''

"Like hell you are,'' he said with more energy than he'd had since being shot.

"I have to,'' she countered just as stubbornly. "The driver just quit on me and the lumber has to be delivered.''

"I won't have it.''

"Papa, I don't want to fight about this. The lumber has to get to Eagle Rock and I'm doing the driving.''

"You can wait for Isaac and Ted to get back.''

"I can't. This load is supposed to be delivered by late tomorrow, and as the person responsible, I intend to see that it gets there.''

"If I could just get out of this bed—''

She kissed his cheek. "Don't worry, Papa. I'll make the trip and be back as soon as I can.''

"Take Jack with you for protection.''

"I don't need Jack with me.''

"You heard me, Amanda. I don't want you on the road alone. What if something happened to you? What if the wagon broke down?''

"Then I'd ride for help. I'll be fine.''

"You'll take Jack with you, or I'll get out of this bed and make the trip myself. You can send for him or I'll do it. It doesn't matter which one of us does it, as long as he's on the wagon with you when you ride out of town.''

Amanda knew her father was bull-headed enough to do just what he said if she didn't obey his wishes. ''Yes, sir.''

''That's more like it.'' He settled back on the pillows.

''Are you going to be all right while I'm gone?''

''I have Miss Hammond and Maria to take care of me. I'll be fine. You just make sure you stick close to Jack. You'll be safe as long as you're with him.''

''Papa, I don't need Jack Logan to keep me safe. I can take care of myself. In fact, I was just going to ask you where my gun is. I want to take it with me.''

''It's in the locked compartment of my gun case. Take a rifle, too.''

''I will, Papa, and I'll see you when I get back.''

He watched as she walked from the room, and he had to admit he was proud of her. He didn't know many women who were brave enough to take on what she had. For all that she had the knowledge and the courage to attempt to run the line without him, though, she was still a female in a man's world, and that could be very dangerous.

Dan hoped Jack upheld his part of the bargain and kept a close watch over her. He didn't want anything to happen to Amanda. She was too precious to him.

Amanda unlocked her father's gun case and took out her gun and holster. The weapon felt strange when she strapped it on, but she knew she would have to get used to it. She wasn't about to ride off into the wilds unarmed. She selected a rifle and took all the ammunition she needed. That done, she sought out Eileen and Maria and explained to them what had happened.

"I should be back within three days. The hard part is going to be getting there. The trip back without the load should be easy."

"Is Jack riding with you?" Eileen asked, wanting to make sure she'd be protected.

"Father has insisted on his going, though I don't know why. I could handle it on my own," she told her.

"I'm sure you could, but why take chances? It's far better for you to be safe. Have you told him yet?"

"No. I'm on my way there right now. I hope he can be ready to ride within the hour."

"Be careful. We'll be worrying about you, but with Jack along, I'm sure you'll do fine."

"I'm glad you have such a high opinion of him."

"I do, but I also have a very high opinion of you. Do you realize how brave you are? Why, some of those friends you have back East wouldn't even recognize you now, let alone believe what you're undertaking."

Amanda glowed under Eileen's praise as she looked down at her clothing a bit self-consciously. "I suppose I would shock some of them, but there are others who actually took to wearing bloomers every chance they got."

"Well, those are hardly bloomers you've got on." Eileen eyed her figure, which looked anything but boyish in the boyish garb.

"When I was young, Papa used to let me wear

boys' clothes all the time to play in. For the work I have to do, these clothes are the only thing that's practical. I could hardly drive a team in a daygown.''

"I agree with you. Just be careful and hurry back. I know your father will be worrying the whole time you're gone.''

"I'll be back, and Eileen—thanks for staying and taking care of my father." Amanda gave her a hug, then grabbed a pair of leather work gloves and left the house. She had a lot of work to do and very little time.

"You Jack Logan?" a little boy who was about ten years old asked as he came up to Jack at the poker table in the saloon.

"Who wants to know?"

"Miz Taylor sent me over here to give this note to Jack Logan. She said he'd look like you—tall, dark-haired, kinda mean-looking—so that's why I thought you was him.''

"I am," Jack told him, trying not to smile at the boy's recital of Amanda's description. "You guessed right. What can I do for you?''

"Nothing. Miz Taylor just said to give you this." He thrust the one-page missive at him and darted from the saloon. His mama had told him all about the evils of drinking and gambling, and he didn't want to stay in there too long.

Jack gave his fellow poker players an apologetic look. "Excuse me for just a minute.''

He unfolded the letter and read it quickly.

"Gentlemen, I'm afraid I have some business to attend to. Thank you for an enjoyable game.''

# GET YOUR 4 FREE BOOKS
## NOW—A $21.96 Value!

*Mail the Free Book
Certificate
Today!*

# Get Four Books Totally FREE – A $21.96 Value!

▼ Tear Here and Mail Your FREE Book Card Today! ▼

PLEASE RUSH
MY FOUR FREE
BOOKS TO ME
RIGHT AWAY!

**Leisure Romance Book Club**
P.O. Box 6613
Edison, NJ 08818-6613

AFFIX
STAMP
HERE

They watched him leave and wondered what had come up to drag him away from the table. It had to be important. They'd been playing some pretty serious poker before the interruption.

Jack went straight to the stage office to seek out Amanda. As he entered, he saw her for the first time in her working clothes. His gaze was riveted upon her. He'd always known she was beautiful, but he'd had no idea just how perfect her figure was until this moment. The trousers she wore hugged her hips as if they were a second skin, and his gaze grew warm as he traced a visual path over her. Heat filled him against his wishes, and he was forced to look away from the sight of her so dressed.

"Amanda, what do you mean, you're driving the wagon?"

"I mean just that," she said, turning on him. She put her hands on her hips as she glared at him across the room. It had been difficult enough facing her father about this trip; the last thing she wanted to do was argue with Jack. The job had to be done, so she was going to do it. There was nobody else. "I'll be driving, and my father insists that you come along as shotgun. How soon can you be ready to leave?"

Jack could tell just from the way she was standing before him so challengingly that there would be no talking her out of going. He could see, too, that she was wearing a gun and holster. For some reason, he thought it looked almost sexy on her. It certainly made handling her even more of a challenge, that was for sure. "I'll be set in less than half an hour. I'll meet you back here. Is the team ready?"

"I've got the stable hands harnessing them up this very minute. I'll be ready to ride when you are." She met his gaze levelly, daring him to say more.

"Nice gun," Jack said. Then he turned and walked away.

He went back to his room to pack the few things he needed and to get his own sidearm and rifle. When he returned to the freight wagon, Amanda was already in the driver's seat, leather driving gloves on, reins in hand, ready to roll. She had her own rifle propped in the driver's box next to her.

He stared up at her. She'd donned a Stetson and looked every inch the cowgirl. He'd seen her in day dresses and evening gowns, but he'd never thought she looked more lovely than she did now. She looked wild, as if she needed to be tamed. He wondered if he was man enough for the job.

When he realized the direction of his thoughts, Jack berated himself. She was Dan's daughter. He was her protector. He would keep his mind on business and off the thought of how great she looked in the form-fitting trousers.

Jack was scowling as he climbed up to sit next to her, his rifle in hand.

"You ready?" she asked, casting him a sidelong glance and wondering why he looked so angry.

"As I'll ever be," he answered, sounding annoyed.

Amanda slapped the reins against the team's backs, and they were off, heading for Eagle Rock. With any luck, it would be a smooth, uneventful trip.

\* \* \*

The going was slow and rough, and it was after dark when they reached the first way station.

"Who the hell are you, and where's Dave?" Wes Bayless asked as he stood before his house, rifle in hand, eyeing Amanda and Jack. They were late in arriving, and he'd been worrying, what with all the trouble that had been going on. Now, seeing two strangers bringing in the load, he was cautious.

"Dave quit and left at San Rafael. I'm Amanda Taylor, Dan's daughter. We didn't have another driver available, so I decided to take this run. This is Jack Logan. He's riding shotgun for me."

Wes eyed her in the light coming from his cabin. "I'll be damned. So you're little Amanda? If this don't beat all." He laughed loudly. "Dan done told me all about you lotsa times, but I never thought I'd meet you driving a freight wagon. Come on in, honey. My missus has got a meal all ready and waiting. She's been keeping it warm for you."

"Thanks, Wes." Amanda jumped down. Every inch of her body was aching. She'd forgotten just how rough riding on a freight wagon could be. She stretched wearily. "I'll see to the mules and be right with you."

"There's no need for you to do that. Me and Jack, we'll take care of them. You go ahead on inside."

Amanda was grateful for his help, and she smiled at him as she made her way indoors. It had been a very long day.

"I heard Wes say you were Amanda Taylor," the woman inside told her. "It's nice to meet you. I'm

Charity Bayless, Wes's wife. Come on in and get something to eat. You must be tired.''

"Just a little, but tomorrow's going to be a lot rougher. We'll have to head out right at dawn.''

"Well, we'll get you up and going in plenty of time, don't you worry none. You can wash up over there.'' She pointed to a washstand.

Amanda quickly washed the trail dust from herself and then sat down at the table. Charity put a plate of steaming stew before her, along with a thick slice of hot, fresh bread. It smelled delicious. Amanda hadn't realized until then just how hungry she was. She smothered the bread in butter and took a big bite. It tasted as good as it smelled, and she thought she was in heaven.

It occurred to her then just how much her life had changed in the last few weeks, and she found herself smiling.

"Do you like it?'' Charity asked.

"It's wonderful. You're a marvelous cook.''

"Why, thanks.''

"I was just sitting here thinking about how much my life has changed in the last few weeks. Not so long ago, I would have been attending the theater with my grandmother or shopping or going out to a fancy ball in Philadelphia. And now here I am, back in West Texas, right where I started from.''

"Your life before sounds like a dream. Did you like it? Shopping and going to the theater? The only shopping I get to do is in San Rafael, and there isn't much there to choose from. I've never been to a real theater.''

"It was different," Amanda admitted. "And I did enjoy it, but somehow, being back here feels right."

"You're home."

"Yes, I'm home."

The men came inside just then.

"Something sure smells good in here," Jack said as he was shown where to get cleaned up.

As soon as he'd finished washing, Charity served him a hot meal, too.

"So you didn't have any trouble between San Rafael and here?" Wes asked when he sat down at the table with them.

"No, things went smoothly. We're not carrying any cash, so I figure it's a pretty safe trip for us," Amanda told them.

"I hope you're right. We've done had enough trouble. I wish the law would find the ones causing it, but it don't seem like they're doing much. It's been weeks now."

"I checked with the sheriff in San Rafael the other day," Jack said. "And he didn't have anything new to go on. He said it seemed like they all just vanished into thin air."

"Somebody out there knows something. They're just not talking," Wes said.

"Well, I'm going to make sure they find the men who killed my uncle and shot my father. They can't just get away with it. Somehow, we've got to figure this out."

"I just say thank God your father wasn't killed," Charity said.

"Me, too. I didn't even know about it until I got back here."

"It must have been quite a shock to you," Wes said.

"It was, but the good news is that he's improving. With any luck, he'll be back on the job in a month or so."

"What will you do when he's better? Surely, you don't intend to keep working as a driver all the time," Charity asked.

"I don't know," she answered thoughtfully. "I really haven't had much time to think about it. Right now, all I care about is making sure Taylor Stage and Freight stays in business. And if I have to drive to do that, I will."

"Dan's lucky to have you," Wes said.

She smiled at him. "Thanks. I aim to make him proud."

Jack saw the gleam of happiness in Amanda's eyes when Wes complimented her, and he realized how much this really meant to her. For a while, he'd thought that she might just be playing at it, but it seemed she really did want to keep things running to the best of her ability. Not many women could do what she was doing.

Amanda had impressed him that afternoon on the drive. It had been hot and dusty, but she'd never complained. She'd handled the team well, and she'd listened and learned the few times he'd offered her advice.

"What about you, Jack?" Wes said. "How'd you come to be working for Taylor Lines?"

"I'm a friend of Dan's and Amanda's." As he said that, Amanda gave him a quick look, but he just kept on talking. "They needed some extra help right now, so I volunteered. I'm handy with a gun, so I'll be riding shotgun mostly, just in case there is any trouble."

"It sure can't hurt to be prepared," Wes agreed.

They talked a little longer, and then Charity could tell that Amanda was ready to go to bed for the night.

"We were expecting just Dave to show up, so we really only got the one extra bed there." She pointed toward a small, uncomfortable-looking cot in the far corner of the main room. "Will that be good enough for you, Amanda?"

"That'll be fine, but what about Jack?"

"I'll just bed down out in the stable," he said. He'd noticed that the place was small, and he'd figured he'd be camping out that night.

"Let me get you some blankets," Charity offered, and she disappeared into her own bedroom. She came back in a few minutes with some bedclothes for Jack. "You all get some sleep now, and we'll get you up before dawn so you can have some breakfast before you have to leave. It's a long trip into Eagle Rock. You're gonna want a big breakfast."

"Thanks, Charity."

Jack left then, and when Charity and Wes went into their room and bedded down, Amanda quickly changed into her nightgown and slipped into bed. As she lay in the strange bed, thinking of all that had happened that day, her thoughts lingered on Jack's words—*I'm a friend of Dan's and Amanda's.*

It surprised her to learn that Jack thought of himself as her friend. Funny, but she'd certainly never thought of him that way. He'd always been her adversary, preventing her from doing what she'd wanted to do, keeping her out of trouble, to his way of thinking. He'd saved her from being arrested, he'd saved her from being beaten, and now he was riding shotgun for her. ·

Jack didn't have to work for the stage line. Amanda knew how worried he was about the Sheldon gang and how much he'd wanted to track them down. She wondered what her father had said to him to get him to stay on. She wondered, too, why he had stayed if what he'd said all along was really true—that he couldn't wait to get away from her.

Sleep came easily to Amanda, for she was exhausted. Hers was a dreamless rest. She awoke early and rose at the sound of someone moving around outside the cabin.

Amanda dressed quickly and crept to the window to look out. She knew it wasn't Charity or Wes outside—their bedroom door was still closed—and she worried it might be trouble. To her surprise, she found it was Jack.

Jack was standing near the water pump, clad only in his pants and boots. He was in the middle of washing up, and she watched him in fascination. The only light was from the lamp he'd carried with him, and his broad chest and muscular shoulders were gilded by the golden glow. Her gaze went over him, lingering on the smooth planes of his hard-muscled torso. He looked much like a statue of Adonis she'd seen once in a museum in Philadelphia. He looked . . . beautiful.

*What was she thinking? Jack? Beautiful?* Amanda shook her head, but she did not look away. It was almost as if she was hypnotized by the sight of him— so powerful, so lean, so strong.

And then he turned slightly, and she saw for the first time the scar.

Amanda gasped. The lasting reminder of the near-deadly knife wound gleamed white against Jack's tanned skin, marring that solid expanse. She stared in horror at the scar, knowing just by its location that the wound should have killed Jack. It was a miracle that he was still alive.

And a woman had done that to him.

She thought back over the conversations they'd had and remembered the night on board the ship when they'd been at dinner. He'd told her then how he didn't trust women, how he'd learned the hard way that women weren't always what they seemed. She understood better now what he'd meant, and she also understood why he felt that way. He'd been betrayed . . . and it had almost proven fatal.

Amanda wondered what kind of relationship he'd had with El Diablo before the night she attacked him. She wondered if they'd known each other or if the outlaw had just come after him because he'd known too much. Being a woman, it would have been easy to insinuate herself into his room. But to catch Jack so completely unawares . . . That would have taken careful planning on her part.

Anger filled Amanda at the thought of the vicious murderer and the way she had deliberately plotted to kill Jack. She was glad that El Diablo was dead. She might have been tempted to shoot her herself, if she had still been alive. Amanda remembered Jack telling her that she didn't have what it took to kill somebody, but she knew it wouldn't have bothered her at all to be the one who put El Diablo six feet under.

She moved quietly away from the window for fear that Jack might catch her watching him. As she sat back down on her bed to await the sunrise and the start of the new day, Amanda made a promise to herself to start practicing with her handgun as soon as she got the chance. She not only wanted to be able to protect herself—she wanted to be able to protect those she cared about.

Amanda didn't delve too deeply into that thought and its connection to Jack. She just waited for the others to rise so they could have breakfast and get under way. They had a long day of travel ahead of them.

# *Chapter Twelve*

An hour later, Amanda and Jack had eaten Charity's delicious breakfast and were loaded up and on their way to Eagle Rock. The good news was that it was cloudy, and the bad news was that it was cloudy. Not that it rained much in West Texas, but a good gully-washer might cause them some problems today, for they had to cross the Brazos on the way.

Normally, the Brazos was low and slow-flowing, its water muddy and red. If there was a downpour anywhere around, though, the river could become a dangerous, raging torrent. That would definitely slow them down, and they didn't need that. They just wanted to get to Eagle Rock and make their delivery as soon as they could.

Luck wasn't with them, though. Late in the morning the skies darkened and finally opened up.

"Stop here," Jack told Amanda as they reached the top of a low rise. He could see the river in the distance,

but he doubted there was time for them to cross before
the current got too strong.

"You don't think we can make it if we hurry?"

"Do you want to risk losing the load?"

"You're right. Better a little late than washed
away."

Lightning lit up the sky and thunder boomed around
them. It wasn't going to be just a quick shower, Jack
could tell.

"Come on! We'd better get in back! At least there's
some protection there," he told her as he jumped
down.

Jack quickly tied up the team and then ran around
back and lifted the canvas tarp that covered their load.

"Climb in!"

He gave Amanda a boost up and climbed in after
her. It wasn't comfortable, but it beat the heck out of
sitting in the pouring rain. He dropped the tarp to
shield them from the downpour.

"It isn't supposed to rain much in West Texas,"
Amanda complained.

"We're just lucky, I guess."

"I'm not feeling very lucky. I'm just feeling wet."
She'd gotten soaked in the short time it had taken to
tie up the mules and run around to the back of the
wagon.

"You'll dry out," Jack said with a grin, but it was
then that he noticed how her soaked blouse was clinging to her breasts. His mouth went dry. He swallowed
tightly and forced his gaze away.

Amanda got as comfortable as she could, bracing
herself against a stack of lumber, but it wasn't easy.

Even though it was warm, sitting around in damp clothes didn't make for comfort. Soon, she began to shiver.

"You're cold?"

"Yes." She thought about moving closer to him to stay warm, but realized that she didn't want to get too close to him. She remembered all too clearly the way he'd looked with his shirt off. It was better if she kept a physical distance between them.

"Do you want me to get your dry clothes for you? Then you could change."

"You wouldn't look?"

"I'm a gentleman, remember? I would never take advantage of a young lady. Just ask Miss Hammond. She'll tell you how wonderful I am."

"Well, Miss Hammond's not here to keep an eye on things."

"Do you need keeping an eye on? I thought that was why I was here."

"Yes, but who's keeping an eye on you?"

He grinned at her wickedly, then turned serious. "If you're really that cold, I'll get your things."

"Thanks."

Jack jumped out in the pouring rain and hurried to get her small traveling bag out of the driver's box. While he was gone, Amanda unbuckled her gunbelt and laid it aside.

"Here," he said as he climbed back in with her, "and don't worry. I'll turn my back to give you your privacy. I promise I won't look. Not that I'm not tempted, mind you." He shifted so his back was to her and he was looking away.

Amanda paused at his words. "But on the ship, you told me I should be *more* feminine."

"I was angry when I said that," he said.

"What did you have to be angry about?" she demanded. "You were the one who'd been bullying me."

"I was angry because I had to keep you out of trouble and get you home to your father in one piece, and you seemed determined to do everything in your power to make that difficult for me."

"I was just doing what I thought was right." She quickly started to change her clothes.

"I know, and I hope things did turn out all right for Becky Jennings. At least, we know she escaped her husband and had enough time to save herself. She would never have dared to make the move without your goading."

"Do you really think so?"

"Yes."

She couldn't believe it. Jack was telling her that he was glad she'd done something that had gotten her into trouble. "I'm sorry I caused you so much trouble."

"I'm beginning to think it's your middle name."

She laughed. It was a throaty sound, a sensual sound, and Jack reacted instinctively to it. He almost swore out loud at the heat that rose in his body.

Amanda stared at him as he sat with his back to her. She remembered the scar and wanted desperately to reach out and touch him. He seemed so distant from her, though, even though he was right there.

"Jack—" she began tentatively.

"What? Are you done changing yet?" He sounded impatient.

The rain was beating a staccato rhythm on the canvas above them. Thunder was rumbling in the distance. A sense of timelessness overcame the moment.

Jack knew Amanda was sitting right there within arm's reach. He knew how her damp blouse was caressing her and how her pants fit so perfectly across her hips. He wanted to touch her, to hold her. He also knew he couldn't.

"I'm almost done, but I wanted to ask you something else." She paused.

Jack didn't say anything as he waited for her to go on.

"Jack," Amanda said quietly, "why don't you like me?"

The question startled him. "Like you?"

"Yes. I heard you tell Wes and Charity that you were my friend, but all you've ever wanted to do was get me back here so you could be rid of me."

"Playing escort isn't what I'm good at."

"What are you good at?"

Her question hit the very heart of his dilemma. "I was a good Ranger once."

"But not anymore? Not since El Diablo?"

"A lot has changed since then."

"What happened? Your sister told me a little about what happened to you when we were in Galveston. How did El Diablo manage to catch you unawares?"

"She managed because I was a fool," he answered tightly. "I thought Elizabeth was a beautiful, warm, wonderful woman, but in truth, she was a cold-blooded killer.''

She heard the bitterness in his voice. ''But how were you to know?''

''It was all there. I just wasn't looking for it. She lied to me about everything, and I believed her.''

''Did you love her, Jack?''

There was a long silence again. ''I thought I did, but I found out a lot about love with Elizabeth.''

Amanda could sense the tension in him as they spoke of the outlaw. ''What happened after she stabbed you?''

''She fled out of town with her brother. She was tracked down and brought in later.''

''Did she hang?''

He gave a harsh laugh. ''No. One of the wives of one of the men she'd seduced and then murdered shot her before she could stand trial.''

''Too bad,'' Amanda said fiercely. ''I wish she'd been hanged. Shooting was too good for her.''

''You didn't even know her,'' Jack said, surprised by the anger in her tone.

''No, but she almost killed you.''

''In some ways, I think she did kill me,'' he admitted in a low voice.

His words tore at her heart, and Amanda couldn't help herself. She reached out to touch him, her hand covering the place on his back where she'd seen the scar. ''I'm sorry.''

Jack stiffened at her unexpected touch. It had been a long time since anyone had touched him with gentleness. He knew he should move away. He needed to distance himself from her. He needed to get away from her sweetness. He reminded himself that he was there to protect her, not take advantage of her. He was her bodyguard. He shouldn't even be thinking about turning to her. But her touch was an invitation he could not refuse.

Jack faced Amanda. She knelt before him and lifted a hand to touch his cheek. He turned his head and pressed a kiss to her palm before gathering her close. She bent to him, her lips seeking his in a gentle caress.

The passion that simple kiss evoked between them was neither gentle nor tender. The unspoken desire that had filled Jack for days surged through him. He crushed her to his chest as his mouth covered hers in a hungry exchange.

This time, as he deepened the kiss, Amanda did not try to push him away or end the embrace as she had on the ship. Instead, she welcomed him, reveling in his nearness.

They were pressed together, thigh to thigh, hip to hip, the softness of her breasts full against his chest. Jack's hands moved restlessly over her, caressing her back, then moving lower. Needing her nearer, he cupped her hips and brought her against him.

At this intimate touch, sensations unlike anything Amanda had ever known pulsed through her. She wanted to be as close to him as she could. He was heat and excitement and passion. She gave a low moan in her throat as she linked her arms around his neck and eagerly kissed him back.

Jack slipped his hands around to unbutton her blouse and seek the silken beauty of her breasts. When he touched her for the first time, she gasped in delight at his bold caress. He pressed his lips to her throat and then moved lower to explore the sweet flesh he'd just exposed.

Amanda trembled at the caress of his lips upon her. She had never known such ecstasy. She instinctively arched her back, offering herself to him.

Jack lay down, bringing Amanda on top of him. They fit perfectly together, as if they were meant to be one. At the thought, he groaned low.

"Amanda. . . ." He said her name as he drew her down for a kiss.

"Don't say anything," she whispered, not wanting to think, only wanting to feel.

At her words, so innocently spoken, cold, hard memories suddenly intruded on Jack. They were memories he would have preferred to forget forever— memories of the night Elizabeth had come to him, the way she'd entreated, *Don't say a word*, when he'd made love to her.

The similarity of the phrases stopped him just as he was about to strip away Amanda's clothing and claim her for his own. He was jarred back to reality, suddenly remembering with all-too-painful clarity just who he was and what he was doing there.

And he wasn't there to make love to Amanda.

He was there to keep her from harm.

He went still, and holding himself under iron control, he shifted away from her to sit up.

"Jack?" Amanda had been lost in the wonder of his loving, and now suddenly he had distanced himself from her. She didn't understand and felt bereft. She wanted to be back in his arms, holding him, kissing him. She reached out to him, hoping he would come back to her.

"No, Amanda. Don't." His voice was harsh.

"But Jack—" The haze of sensual awareness he'd created was shattered by his cold rebuff.

Jack knew he had to put an end to this now. He was deliberately sarcastic as he said, "Look, little girl, I work for your father. What we were doing here isn't part of my job."

Amanda was stunned by his rejection. She had thought that he cared for her. She had thought that he'd wanted to kiss her as much as she'd wanted to kiss him. "You know, Jack, maybe you were right. Maybe El Diablo did kill something inside you. Maybe El Diablo killed your heart."

She twisted away, not wanting to look at him anymore. It hurt too much. She quickly rebuttoned her blouse, strapped her gunbelt back on and prayed for the rain to stop so they could get under way again.

When she glanced back a moment later, Jack had left the freighter.

Jack had never been more glad to see a storm end than he was that one. Sitting under a freight wagon waiting for the rain to stop had not been his idea of a pleasant pastime, and neither was making this trip alone with Amanda. His mood was as vile as his clothes were wet, and his clothes were going to dry a lot sooner than his mood was going to improve. He wanted to be in a bar somewhere, drunk. He wanted to be riding with Laughlin trying to find the Sheldons.

He wanted to be anywhere but where he was.

The rain let up completely, and Jack climbed out from his poor excuse for a shelter to check on the team. The mules had weathered the storm without any problems, so Jack walked down toward the Brazos to get a better look at how it was running. It was flowing high and fast right then, but with any luck it would fall back in a few hours and they could be on their way. At least, he hoped it would only be a few hours. The possibility of being forced to spend an entire night alone with Amanda on the trail unnerved him.

"What do you think?"

Her voice surprised Jack. Her nearness angered him even more, for it proved to him just how distracted he was. He hadn't even heard her walk up, and he was glad she wasn't one of the Sheldons.

"We should still be able to make it into Eagle Rock today." He didn't even turn around to look at her as he spoke. "But we're not going anywhere for a while."

Amanda stared at his back, expecting him to say more. When he didn't, she returned to the wagon. It was going to be a long wait for the river to go down.

Amanda was thrilled when Eagle Rock came into view late that same day. It wasn't a moment too soon as far as she was concerned. Every inch of every mile since they'd started out again after the rain had been hellish. They'd had to battle not only the mud, but the threat of possible quicksand, too.

Other than to make a few comments on the condition of the road, Jack hadn't spoken to her since they'd been on the move again, and that had been fine with her. He'd said it all when he'd left her in the wagon.

They delivered the load in town, then spent the night at the small hotel there. Amanda skipped dinner, just so she could avoid being with Jack. They started home at first light and arrived in San Rafael at dusk.

Her home town had never looked better to her than it did as they drove in. Amanda couldn't wait to get back home and see how her father was doing. She said little to Jack as they arrived at the station and left the wagon and team with the hands who were working that night. Jack was still in the stable when she left, and she didn't care. It didn't matter to her if she never spoke to him or saw him again.

Eileen met her at the door. "Thank heaven you're back!"

"Why? Is something wrong?" She could tell her friend was deeply troubled.

"Yes. Your father's taken a turn for the worse. He's developed a fever."

Amanda turned her worried gaze toward the stairs. "How bad is he?"

"I just checked on him a few minutes ago, and he seemed to be resting peacefully for now. But the doctor was here earlier and said he'd done everything that could be done to bring the fever down. He said it's just a matter of having to wait and see if your father has the strength to fight it off."

"Of course he does," Amanda stated immediately. "I've got to go see him."

Eileen said nothing more as Amanda hurried up the stairs. She would give her a few minutes alone with her father and then follow to make sure they were both all right.

Amanda's heart was in her throat as she all but ran down the hall to her father's room. He couldn't be worse! He couldn't be! He'd been getting better when she'd left him. She would never have gone away if she'd thought he was going to get worse.

She paused outside his door to collect herself. Her hands were trembling. She clasped them together to steady herself as she quietly opened the door and looked in. Dan was lying motionless on his bed. His face was flushed from the heat of the fever. Amanda crept forward, not wanting to disturb him if he was asleep.

"You're back," he said in a hoarse voice as he became aware of her moving toward him.

"I thought you were sleeping."

"No, just resting. I've missed you. How did your trip go?"

He sounded so weak that Amanda had to fight desperately not to cry. Here he was seriously ill, and all he was worried about was the stage line.

"Jack and I did just fine. We got caught in a storm and were a little late getting into Eagle Rock, but we still kept close to schedule."

"Good . . . good."

"The doctor says you're going to be just fine," she lied, wanting to cheer him.

"I hope so . . . but this fever . . ."

"I'm back home now, so I can help take care of you. We'll have you up and around in no time."

He gave her a fading smile that unnerved her as his eyes closed. "I just feel so tired."

She kissed him lightly on the cheek and left him. When she'd made it to the hall and had closed the door behind her, she knew true desolation. She had thought he looked bad the first day she'd gotten back from Philadelphia, but today he really was worse. He had lost weight and the ravages of his injuries were showing in his drawn features.

Amanda stood in the hall breathing deeply, trying to steady herself. She wasn't going to give in to the tears that threatened. She had to be strong.

Making her way slowly back downstairs, she found Eileen in the hall just about to come up after her.

"How was he?"

"Not good. He's so weak, and he looks awful," she answered honestly. "I can't believe that he's gotten so much worse in just two days."

"I know. It's a terrible thing. There's little we can do but pray that he pulls through. Can I get you anything? Are you hungry?"

"I would like something to eat, but first I'd like a bath."

"I'll see to it. Go on up to your room."

"Thanks, Eileen. I don't know what I'd do without you."

"I'm glad you don't have to find out."

"Me, too."

Half an hour later, Amanda was feeling a little refreshed. She'd taken a warm bath and changed into clean clothes. After eating a light meal, she slipped outside to stand on the front porch and enjoy the peace and quiet.

It was a dark night. Clouds blocked the nearly full moon from shedding its silvery light over the land. Her thoughts were as dark as the night as she stared off across the silent landscape.

It had been a hellish few days. First, she'd made a fool out of herself with Jack. The humiliation she suffered was great. It hurt to realize that she would have given herself to him, and yet he had put her from him. Then, she had come home to find that her father's condition was deteriorating. It was almost more than she could bear.

Guilt ate at her. She should never have left her father. She should have stayed at home with him. Maybe if she'd stayed at home, he would be doing better instead of going downhill as he was.

Tears threatened, but she fought against giving in to them. She felt it would be a sign of weakness on her part if she cried. Things were bad, but she could handle the situation. She wanted to be a man's equal, so she'd better be ready to shoulder a man's responsibilities.

Amanda had been standing there for only a few minutes when she saw a man approaching. It wasn't until he drew closer that she recognized Ted.

"Amanda?" He said her name quietly as he saw her on the porch. "What are you doing standing outside all by yourself?"

"I was just enjoying the night. How did your trip with Isaac go?"

"We just got back, so I thought I'd come here to

check on your father. How's he doing? Is he up to talking to me?''

"He's not doing well tonight. He's developed a fever.''

"Is it serious?''

"As weak as he is, it could be very serious.''

"I'm sorry. Things are awfully tough for you right now. I wish I had something good to tell you.''

She heard hesitation in his voice. "Is something bothering you?''

"Well, yes.'' He came to stand before her on the porch and leaned back against an upright post. "Mike, one of our drivers out of Comanche Pass, quit while we were there.''

"Another one?''

"Another one,'' he confirmed regretfully.

This news was the final straw to Amanda. She had put up with Jack's rejection. She had learned her father's condition was deteriorating, and now another driver had just quit. Tears welled up in her eyes, and she could no longer deny them.

"Amanda—'' Ted was shocked to see that she was crying. He took a step toward her. "I'm sorry.''

"So am I.''

Ted was gentle as he took her in his arms. Though he held her tenderly, he was secretly pleased with what had happened. He couldn't have planned a better way to get some time alone with her. Here she was in his arms, crying on his shoulder, needing his support. It was perfect.

"I'm sorry,'' Amanda managed brokenly as she tried to pull herself together. It was so comforting to have Ted to turn to, and tonight she needed that.

"It's going to be all right, you know," he reassured her.

She drew a shuddering breath. "I hope so. It's been such a bad day. First, learning that my father's worse, and now another driver's quit—"

"I'm here to help you, Amanda. We'll work it out. Don't worry."

Amanda felt stronger and drew back to look up at Ted. She'd known he was nice, but she'd never realized just how nice. "Thank you."

"I'm glad I could help," he said softly. Gazing down at her in the darkness, he could see how lovely she was. He drew her closer and kissed her.

Amanda was tentative at first, a little surprised by his forwardness, but then she relaxed and accepted his embrace. Memories of Jack's heated kisses seared her as Ted's lips met hers. Jack's kiss had left her wanting more of him . . . needing more. Ted's kiss was gentle and not overly demanding. It was . . . nice. There was no rush of wild passion, no desperate desire. When at last he ended the embrace and released her, she was not bereft as she had been when Jack had let her go.

And that bothered her.

This was Ted. She liked him. He was a nice man, a gentle man. He treated her with respect and seemed to genuinely care about her as a person. Why, then, wasn't she responding to him as wildly as she'd responded to Jack?

"Amanda, you are so beautiful," he said softly as he sought her lips again.

This kiss was more demanding as he allowed himself more freedom with her. When at last they broke apart, he apologized for his boldness.

"I'm sorry, Amanda. I shouldn't have—"

"Don't apologize, Ted. There's nothing to be sorry for," she told him as she touched his arm.

He drew her back, close into the circle of his arms, and she rested lightly against him. His touch was warm, but it evoked no rapturous response from her.

"I know things have been difficult for you lately, and I want to support you in any way I can," Ted said.

"You have, more than you'll ever know."

"Is there anything else I can do for you? Or my mother can do?"

"All I need or want is for my father to get better soon. That's all that really matters."

"That would be wonderful," he agreed. "I was on my way up to see him. That's why I came over tonight."

"He was sleeping when I left him. It would probably be best if we just let him rest."

"I'll come back in the morning."

"I'll be looking forward to it."

"See you then." He kissed her once more, and then moved away. "Good night."

"Good night, Ted."

He was smiling to himself as he disappeared into the night. Things were going very well indeed.

Amanda watched him go.

"That was very touching," Jack drawled, speaking up from where he'd been standing in the darkness watching her with Ted.

# *Chapter Thirteen*

"How dare you spy on me!" Amanda gasped in outrage at the sound of his voice so near.

"I'd hardly call it spying when you're standing right outside in front of God and everybody," Jack countered harshly.

"I hardly think everybody was watching."

"I was."

"You must lead a very boring life, if you don't have anything better to do than watch me," she snapped.

"I didn't come here to discuss my life. I came here to see your father," he answered flatly, trying to control the fury that was still raging inside him. The power of his reaction to the sight of her in the other man's arms surprised him.

"If you were listening, you heard me tell Ted how my father was, so you can go ahead and leave."

"I'm afraid I missed the more serious parts of your discussion. How is he?"

She glared at Jack, seeing his confident, knowing expression and almost hating him for it. "He's not doing very well. He's developed a fever."

"Has the doctor seen him?"

"Yes, and Eileen says he's doing all he can."

Jack nodded. "I need to speak with him, but I'll come back tomorrow. Maybe he'll be feeling better by then."

Amanda didn't respond as he walked away. She was just glad to see him go. The last thing she needed or wanted was to be around Jack.

Jack was furious. Just the day before, Amanda had been in his arms, and now she'd turned to Ted. Images of her kissing the other man would not go away, and Jack grew angrier with every step he took.

The sounds of a piano player's raucous tune drew him, and he crossed the street to enter the saloon. It had been a damned long time since he'd had a drink, and tonight, by God, he was going to remedy that. He ordered a bottle and a glass and went to sit at a table in the back where no one would bother him.

Jack opened the bottle of whiskey and started to pour out a healthy portion. Then he stopped, cursing himself, as he stared at the amber liquid that could grant him peace—at least for a little while.

The last time he'd been driven to drink was when Amanda had evoked memories of El Diablo. But this time . . . This time, it was Amanda who was affecting him.

Yesterday, it had taken all of his considerable will power to deny himself the joy of making love to her in the back of the freight wagon. He had been aching with desire when he left her. He had stopped because he was there to protect her, not because he didn't want her.

The knowledge that he desired Amanda startled him. After Elizabeth, he'd sworn he would never allow himself to care for another female again. But somehow, his little suffragist had shattered the ice that had encased his heart, just as surely as she'd smashed those bottles back in The Palace in Philadelphia.

Jack scowled at the bottle of liquor on the table before him. For all those long months after El Diablo, he had drunk himself into a stupor to forget Elizabeth and her deadly betrayal. He no longer felt that frantic desperation that had driven him to lose himself in whiskey. He had healed . . . in his body and in his mind.

The realization amazed Jack. At one time, he had longed for death. He had thought he would never recover, but as he stared at the powerful liquor, he knew he no longer needed its oblivion. He could deal with his life again.

And then he thought of Amanda in Ted's arms, and he swore under his breath.

"Damn it!" In irritation, he shoved the glass and whiskey away from him.

"Oooh, you look like you need some cheering up," a sultry, feminine voice said.

Jack glanced over his shoulder to see a buxom, raven-haired bar girl watching him with interest. "You in the mood to do the cheering?"

"You bet, handsome," she told him. Tall, dark and

handsome was what she liked, and he was perfect. She'd been eyeing him since he'd walked into the saloon, and she'd already told the other girls working there that he was hers if he was so inclined.

Jack's black mood needed relieving, and since he was swearing off liquor, the thought of a warm and willing woman was tempting. "What's your name?"

"Susie," she answered as she slid into the chair next to him. "What's yours?"

"I'm Jack."

She smiled at him, liking the intensity she sensed in him. She rested a hand on his knee and leaned closer so he had an unobstructed view of her cleavage. "It's nice to meet you, Jack. Pour me a drink?"

She pushed her glass toward him and he obliged.

"You can have the whole bottle if you want it."

"Thanks. I like generous men. You ready to go upstairs, or do you want to drink some more?"

"Let's go on upstairs. I'm done drinking."

"Come on, sugar," she said, rising. She picked up her glass and slipped an arm around his waist. "I'm going to show you a good time when we're alone."

Jack didn't say a word. He got the bottle and walked with her up the steps and into the bedroom she used for her customers.

The bed was rumpled and the room smelled of whiskey and stale perfume. Jack knew if he'd been drunk, it wouldn't have bothered him, but sober as he was, it tempered any thoughts he'd had of making mindless love. Still, he wanted to put the memory of Amanda and Ted from him. He wanted to seek his pleasure with a willing woman who knew what he needed and wanted, and gave it to him without question. There would be no recriminations with Susie. There would be no regrets.

Susie was unaware of his mood as she began to undress enticingly before him. She knew the cowboys liked her a lot, and she expected this one to be no exception. She'd learned early in life how to please a man, and she made good use of her talent.

Jack placed the bottle of whiskey on the small dresser. He stood just inside the closed door, watching as Susie slipped out of her dress and stood before him clad only in her corset and stockings. She did have a lush figure, and, had he been so disposed, he would have appreciated the fullness of her bosom and her rounded hips.

But even as he watched Susie moving seductively in front of him, another woman controlled his thoughts. In his mind's eye he saw only Amanda as she'd looked in his arms the other day, her eyes heavy-lidded with newly awakened desire, her cheeks flushed from the passion he had aroused in her.

The intrusive memory made him frown.

"Did I do something wrong?" Susie asked, wondering why he looked so fierce.

"No," he answered uncomfortably.

She went to him and linked her arms around his neck, pulling him down for a hot, wet kiss. Jack accepted her kiss. She was a pretty girl under all her make up, and he was a man who'd been a long time without a woman. He should have responded hungrily to what she was offering. He should have stripped off what was left of her clothes and enjoyed himself with her on the rumpled bed. A few years ago, nothing would have bothered him or stopped him.

But that was before Amanda.

Susie ended the kiss and took his hand, wanting him to get into bed so they could get real serious real fast. "Come on, honey. Time's a-wastin'."

"Susie—"

The tone of his voice was strange, and when he resisted her efforts to draw him to the bedside, she looked back at him, confused.

"This isn't going to work," he admitted.

"What?" She was shocked. He was one gorgeous man, and she wanted him all for herself. "Did I do something wrong?" she asked, fearing that she'd somehow angered him. He'd seemed so eager when they were downstairs.

"No. You're just the wrong woman, that's all."

"I don't understand," she told him.

"Neither do I," he mused.

"You don't want me?"

"You're a good-looking woman, Susie, and a man would be crazy not to want you. But there's another woman—"

Slowly she began to understand. "You're in love with somebody?"

The possibility jarred him. "I don't know if I'd go that far—"

"Why else would you turn down a very willing, hot-blooded woman who was standing right before you, practically naked?"

Jack realized how ridiculous his situation was, and

he gave her a lopsided grin. "I'm sorry, Susie. I have to get out of here."

She pouted as she moved back to stand right in front of him. "Are you sure? I know how to show cowboys a good time."

"I'm sure you do, but I'm not going to be one of them."

"Too bad," she said in a sultry voice.

"I have to go."

She stood on tiptoe and pressed her lips to his. "Your woman's lucky to have a man like you."

"One of these days I'll get around to telling her you said so." He did not respond to her kiss, but put her from him. He dug some money out of his pocket and pressed it into her hand. "Take the rest of the night off."

She looked down at the generous amount he'd given her and smiled even more broadly. "I will. You sure you don't want another kiss before you go? A girl likes to earn her money."

"No, Susie, but thanks. There's only one woman I want to kiss right now, and she's not here."

She stuffed the money down her cleavage. "Well, Jack, thanks for an interesting night."

"Good night." With that, he was gone from the room.

Susie was surprised by what had happened, but fell back upon the bed to rest for a while. Later, when she went downstairs, she told the other girls how generous he'd been with his money and how much she'd enjoyed being with him. And it wasn't a lie.

Jack left the saloon, greatly irritated with himself.

He'd gone in there to get drunk and had decided not to drink. He'd planned on enjoying the services of one of the working girls and had talked himself out of that too. It seemed a wasted night.

Jack returned to his room at the hotel and went to bed. He lay there sleepless, trying to understand what he was feeling, and finally came to accept that there was only one woman he wanted—Amanda.

And wanting her was only going to cause him trouble, lots of trouble.

Jack found himself smiling into the darkness. Amanda was one amazing female.

Cody approached the shabby little house cautiously. It had taken her a few days of discreet questioning, but she had finally managed to find out where Chica was living now. After her violent run-in with Hank Sheldon, Chica had moved in with her widowed, elderly mother in this home on the outskirts of town.

Cody hadn't been able to get much information out of the other girls at the saloon. As popular as Chica had been with the men, the girls had been glad to see her go. The only point they'd made when speaking of her was to emphasize how they knew she would never be back. Cody had asked one of them how she could be so sure, and the girl had just laughed and said, "If you ever see her, you will know."

She knocked on the door and waited.

"Who is it?" a muffled voice called from inside.

"My name is Armita. I am here to speak with Chica."

"Go away!"

"I mean no harm. I just wanted to talk with Chica about Hank Sheldon."

There was a long silence, and then the door was pulled open just a little bit. Cody could see only a part of a woman's face in the crack of the open door.

"I mean you no harm. I only want to talk."

"Hasn't Hank done enough to me?" Chica was nearly hysterical.

"I'm here because I need your help. Is there some place where we could speak in private?"

"Why?"

"Because I'm trying to save someone's life, and you're the only one who can help me."

The door opened a little wider and Cody got her first look at Hank Sheldon's handiwork. Chica's face had been cut to shreds. Hank had obviously tortured her, and he had also made sure she could never again earn her living as a saloon girl. The wounds were still red and raw and inflamed. Cody knew she had to be in great pain.

"Did he do this to you?"

Chica nodded.

"I'm sorry."

"It would have been better if he had killed me. Now—" She shrugged.

"May I come in?"

The other woman eyed her again. Then, sensing no threat in her, Chica let Cody enter the room. It was sparsely furnished. Her mother sat in the far corner and did not speak as Cody and Chica sat down at the table together.

"What do you want with me?"

"I am going to tell you the complete truth. There is only one other person in El Terrón who knows what I am about to reveal to you. I am trusting you because unless we trust each other, there can be no justice."

"I don't understand."

"My real name is Cody, not Armita. I am a bounty hunter, and I'm after the Sheldon brothers."

"Why are you here?" Chica asked, trembling visibly. "Can't you see what he's already done to me?"

Cody reached out and touched her hand. "I'm here because I want to make sure he never hurts anyone ever again."

"If he finds out—"

"Who will tell him?"

Their eyes met. Cody did not smile, but met Chica's gaze directly. She wanted Chica to have confidence in her. She did not want her to be afraid.

"Why are you doing this? For the money?"

"The bounty is a good one, I won't deny that, but my reason for going after the Sheldons is purely personal. They're out to kill a friend of mine, and I intend to make sure that doesn't happen."

"Why should I help you?"

"I want to make you an offer, Chica. I will give you half of the bounty I earn on them, if you can tell me where I can find them right now. I don't have time to wait here for them to return. A man's life is at stake. It's a lot of money. Your share would be five thousand dollars."

"That much?" She was shocked, and her eyes narrowed as she considered the offer. "But what if I tell you where you can find him and then you don't capture him? What if Hank finds out that I told you? What he did to me before would be child's play compared to what he'd do to me then.''

"There's always that possibility—but, Chica, do you want to spend the rest of your life living in terror of Hank Sheldon? If you don't help me, he may never be caught. Then, for the rest of your life, you'll be looking over your shoulder, fearing that he might be somewhere nearby, just waiting to hurt you again.''

Chica was silent; then she glanced over to the corner where her elderly mother sat quietly, watching and listening. She spoke to her mother in Spanish, explaining all that was transpiring, and the old woman answered quickly.

"My mother says I must tell you everything about Hank, and I know she is right. Am I wrong to trust you?''

"No. You have my word that I will give you half the bounty on the Sheldons as soon as I receive it.''

She nodded. "I will tell you.''

"Thank you. You won't regret it.''

"The only thing I regret in my life is that I ever met Hank Sheldon in the first place.''

"Where is he now? Is he traveling with his brother?''

"Yes. They are always together. There are only two other towns where they hide out—Rock Water and Del Cuero.''

Cody nodded. She'd heard of both towns and knew of their reputations as hellholes. "Thank you. Do you know which one they would most likely go to?''

"No. They have friends in both places who would

help them. You say they are out to kill your friend?''

''Yes.''

''Then I wish you luck. They are evil men who will stop at nothing to get what they want.''

''Thank you for your help. I will send word to you as soon as I have them in custody.''

''I hope you are as good at your job as you seem.''

''I always do my best.''

Again their gazes met and locked.

''Vaya con Dios,'' Chica said. ''You will need all the help you can get.''

''I will take all the help God can give me.''

Cody left her and returned to the Silverado. She acted the part of Armita as she entered the saloon, smiling and flirting with the customers, but her thoughts were far away. She had much to do and little time. First, she had to find Luke, so she could arrange to meet him and tell him everything she'd learned.

As she made her way through the saloon, she finally caught sight of her husband sitting at one of the quieter tables in the back. She was anxious to head out of town after the Sheldons.

''It is good to see you,'' Cody told Luke with a big smile as she came to stand beside him.

''Armita . . . You're looking as gorgeous as ever today,'' Luke said for the benefit of any other customers who might be listening to their conversation.

''I think I am ready to quit my job in this place.''

''You are?'' Luke asked, playing along.

''Yes, this town is too quiet for Armita. I want a more exciting life. I think I will travel to Rock Water.

I have heard that there is much to be learned in that town.''

"Would you like an escort, pretty lady? Traveling alone might prove dangerous for a woman like you."

She eyed him, a bold appraisal. "You look like a man who could keep up with me. I'll meet you at the stables in an hour."

"I'll be waiting for you."

A little over an hour later they were riding for Rock Water.

Cody quickly told him everything she'd learned from Chica.

"Well, I hope Chica is reliable . . ." Luke began.

"She is," Cody interrupted. "I believe every word she told me. She has every reason to hate Hank Sheldon now."

"What did he do to her?"

"He cut her up. She used to be a beautiful woman, I hear, but now she won't go out in public. It's tragic. She lives in constant terror that he might come back."

"How did you get her to help you?"

"I told her the truth."

"And?" Luke prodded, knowing his wife would use any inducement necessary to get what she wanted.

"And I promised her half the bounty. She deserves it," Cody said sadly, thinking of Chica's wounds and the pain she must be suffering. When she gazed at Luke, the look in her eyes was one of fierce determination. "We're going to do this—for Jack and for Chica."

They rode hard for Rock Water.

# Chapter Fourteen

Amanda was up early to check on her father. He seemed a little less feverish, and, with Eileen's assistance, she helped him to have breakfast.

"What do you think?" Amanda asked Eileen when they'd left him to rest again.

"He is better this morning. Certainly he's not as flushed as he was yesterday."

"I was really worried last night." Amanda looked at her friend. "I don't know what I'd do if anything happened to him."

Eileen tried to reassure her. "He's going to be all right eventually. His injuries were serious, though, so it's going to be a slow recovery for him. It's hard for him, because he's a man used to doing what he wants to do when he wants to do it."

Amanda smiled at that characterization of her father. "You know him very well already."

"It didn't take long to figure out how frustrated he

was being incapacitated this way. We just have to keep him occupied so he doesn't have time to realize how weak he is. He needs his rest more than anything.''

''Both Ted and Jack want to speak with him today.''

''That will be fine as long as we don't have to wake him to do it. I'm sure he'll appreciate the visits. How is Jack? I was so surprised when I learned that he was staying on. I'd thought for sure he'd go after the Sheldons as soon as we got here.''

''I did, too, but my father convinced him to stay.''

''Well, I'm glad he did,'' Eileen said with conviction. ''I feel much better about things knowing that Jack is here, don't you?'' She slanted Amanda a sidelong glance, wanting to see her reaction.

''Frankly, I wish he was gone.'' Amanda's expression remained neutral and betrayed nothing of what she was feeling.

''But don't you need him? I mean, since Jack was a Ranger, I'm sure he's very good with a gun.''

''The stage line needs him, but I don't. I have Isaac . . . and Ted . . . to help me.''

''You and I both know that Jack is twice the man Ted is. Why, I'd trust Jack with my life.''

Amanda wanted to contradict her, but didn't. She knew that in Eileen's opinion Jack could do no wrong. ''You're right. He is good with a gun, but starting today, I'm going to do some target shooting myself.''

''Why, when you have Jack?''

''Because there are going to be times when I'll be on my own. Jack isn't always going to be hovering around, and I want to be prepared. I don't ever want to be trapped and helpless again the way I was with Micah Jennings.''

"I admire you so much,'' Eileen said.

"You do?'' She was surprised.

"Oh, yes. You're smart and resourceful and brave. You are so determined to succeed. I don't think you will ever let anything stop you, once you set your mind to accomplishing something.''

"Thanks.''

"You're welcome, but remember, I'm not saying that just to make you feel good. I only tell the truth.''

They shared a look of understanding, then smiled at each other. They were just starting down the steps when Ted knocked at the front door.

"Ted's here,'' Amanda said. "I'll let him in.''

She was pleased that he was there, for his presence would distract her from thoughts of Jack. She definitely didn't want to be thinking about Jack.

Eileen watched her hurry down the steps to let Ted in and wondered why Amanda was so glad to see him.

"Good morning, Amanda. You look lovely,'' Ted greeted her smoothly as she let him in.

"Why, thank you. Come on in.''

"Good morning,'' he said to Eileen.

"Hello, Ted.''

He turned back to Amanda. "Is your father up to seeing me this morning?''

"He's resting right now. But you could stay and join us for breakfast. After we eat, we can see if he's awake and up to it. Will you breakfast with us?''

"I'd like that,'' he said, his gaze warm upon Amanda.

"I'll tell Maria we need to set another place," Eileen offered. She was smiling, but there was something about Ted that set her teeth on edge. She couldn't quite say what it was. Maybe he was too nice, too concerned. Eileen told herself she was being too hard on the man and went off to the kitchen.

The meal was a cordial one. Ted told Amanda of how he'd been away at school until a few months before. He encouraged her to talk about her activities in Philadelphia. He was very interested in the women's movement and complimented her on her involvement.

"You are an extraordinary woman, Amanda Taylor."

She blushed prettily at his compliment.

"And here you are, back in West Texas after living all those years in the East. The change must be hard on you, and now you've given up your own dreams just to help your father."

Amanda hadn't considered her staying in San Rafael a sacrifice. Truth be told, she hadn't thought much about the suffragist movement since learning what had happened to her father. She realized as they talked about it that she still had to write a letter to Bethany and tell her what was going on. She knew for a fact that she wouldn't be going back to Philadelphia any time soon and vowed to post a letter to her friend later that day.

"It's not so much that I've given up my dreams," she said, "as I've just—postponed them."

"Admirable. You are a woman ahead of her times. Look how well you're doing with the stage line."

"I don't know if that's true, especially after what

you told me last night about another driver quitting.''

"It's got to get better soon. The sheriff's bound to come up with something.''

"I hope so. I just have to keep the line running until the sheriff makes some arrests.''

"I wish he'd find the culprits soon," Ted said. "I don't understand how they can disappear so completely.''

"Neither do I.''

"Shall I go look in on your father and see if he's up to a visit?" Eileen offered as she finished her meal. She'd been watching Ted with Amanda. He was handsome, articulate and certainly seemed to like her, and that was good, for they would be working closely together until Dan recovered.

"Please," Amanda answered.

Ted was thrilled when the older woman left him alone with Amanda. He'd been thinking about her all night and wondering what he should do next.

The original plan he and his mother had conceived to get rid of Asa and Dan had failed, but now he knew there were other ways to get what they wanted. Since Dan was shot, Ted had had the opportunity to get a good look at the books. He'd learned what a truly lucrative enterprise Taylor Stage and Freight was. With this knowledge, a new plan had come to him overnight, and it all centered on Amanda. If he controlled Amanda, he ultimately controlled the line. He had to woo her and win her.

True, Ted hadn't spoken to his mother yet. But since her only motivation was to get money so she could get out of San Rafael, he knew she would be happy with whatever he did—just as long as it met her needs. And his plan would, for once he'd taken over, he would send his mother happily on her way with generous funding to keep her in the style she longed for. If he married Amanda, he would be the new owner of Taylor Stage and Freight Lines, and that would make him very successful.

"I'm glad we're finally alone," he said. "I wanted to apologize again for last night. I hope I wasn't too bold."

Amanda smiled at him. "No, Ted. There's no need to apologize."

He smiled back at her, his expression relieved, as if he truly had been worried that he'd offended her. "I'm glad."

He would court her just as any Eastern gentleman would, and she would be his—along with the stage line. Ted was most pleased with his cunning.

"Ted? Dan's awake and says he'd like to talk to you," Eileen announced as she came back downstairs.

"Thanks." He looked at Amanda. "Will I see you later?"

"Of course. In fact, if you like, I'll wait for you, and we can go over to the office together."

"Fine. I'd like that."

It was late afternoon when Amanda finally got away from the stage office. She had passed a very busy day. Ted had been working by her side for most of it, and she was coming to enjoy his company and his intelligent conversation. He was unthreatening, agreeable and interested in her activities in Philadelphia—a far cry from Jack Logan.

After putting Isaac in charge, Amanda went straight home. She checked on her father and found that he was doing much better. Relieved, she went downstairs and got her gunbelt out. She had just started to strap it on when Eileen found her.

"Are you going out to practice?" Eileen asked.

"Yes, there's a safe place out back. It's about three-quarters of a mile from the house. I'll be far enough away that the noise won't bother Papa."

"You be careful."

"I will."

"Maybe one of these days you can teach me how to shoot. Then I could ride shotgun on the stages with you, too," Eileen told her with a grin.

"You let me know when you want to start learning, and I'll teach you. I was a pretty decent shot as a kid. I just hope I haven't lost my touch." She checked her sidearm and slid it into the holster. "I hope I'm just out of practice."

"Well, no matter what, you've still got Jack around for protection."

Amanda's expression turned serious. "That's exactly the problem. I don't want to have to rely on Jack or any other man for anything. If I can run this business, I can certainly learn to protect myself. All it will take is a little target shooting."

"I'll be worrying about you."

Amanda grinned wickedly as she patted her sidearm. "No need to worry, ma'am. I've got my trusty six-gun."

"It's my nature to worry about those I care for, especially when guns are involved," Eileen told her.

"Yes, ma'am," Amanda teased as she headed out the door.

Jack had already been at work at the stage office when Ted and Amanda arrived together that morning. She had come into the office, laughing happily at something Ted had said and gazing up at him as if he were the most wonderful man in the world. Jack wasn't scheduled to ride out with Amanda until the next afternoon, so he'd deliberately taken jobs that kept him busy and away from her and Ted all day.

It was near dark when Jack finally finished all his work. He went to his room and cleaned up before heading over to the Taylor house to speak with Dan.

As he neared the house, though, Jack heard the sound of gunfire in the distance. Fearing trouble, he headed in the direction of the shots. He was careful not to make any noise as he approached the area, for he had no idea who might be out there shooting.

Jack made his way carefully through the mesquite trees and emerged in a clearing to find Amanda, her six-gun in hand, taking careful aim at a line of bottles she'd set up in the distance. He watched in silence as she concentrated on her target and fired the shot. Her hand jerked. The shot went wide. It wasn't even close.

"Damn!" Amanda muttered, greatly irritated with herself. If she'd been firing at an attacker, he would have been unscathed and she, most probably, would be dead right now.

"I thought ladies didn't cuss," Jack observed.

She gasped and turned to find him smiling wryly at her. She was suddenly nervous, surprised by his intrusion.

"I'm not that kind of lady," she said, sliding her gun back in her holster.

"My mistake," he drawled. "What are you trying to do? Practice up for your next temperance march, when you'll be carrying guns instead of axes?"

"I needed some target practice," she announced. "It's been a long time since I've had to use my gun."

"I hope it will be a long time before you have to use it again." He nodded toward the bottles. "But if you want to practice, go ahead and draw again. Let me watch. Maybe I can help you."

She drew the gun, aimed and fired. Again her shot went wide.

Jack went to stand next to her. In one smooth move, he drew his own gun, fired and blasted away one of the bottles. He slid his gun back into his holster in a slick move and smiled down at her.

"Show-off," she muttered resentfully as she went to set another bottle in its place.

"Do you want some advice?" he offered as she marched determinedly back to where he stood.

It was in her mind to tell him what he could do with his advice, but she knew he was a gunman and she did want to learn. "All right. Tell me. What am I doing wrong?"

Jack tried to think of the best way to explain the techniques, but decided it would be easier to demonstrate. "Let me show you."

Jack moved to stand behind her. He felt her stiffen

257

as his hand covered hers. "When you draw, make it a slow, smooth motion, not jerky, but steady. And then shoot from the hip."

He guided her hand over the gun grip and helped her draw and fire. The shot shattered a bottle.

"Like this?" She repeated the move with his help and shot the second target.

"See how easy it is? It should feel right when you do it. Your gun should feel like it's a part of your body. Let's do it one more time."

His words, spoken so close to her ear, sent a shiver down her spine. It was difficult enough to concentrate with him standing directly behind her. His big body was warm and powerful, and as he fitted himself to her to help her draw, it was all she could do to keep from trembling from the force of her reaction to his nearness.

Damn him!

Amanda wanted to lean back against him, to rest her head on his strong shoulder and let herself enjoy the hard-muscled circle of his arms around her.

Something about Jack deeply disturbed her, and not in a way she liked to be disturbed. She was a woman who was used to being in control of her senses. She was logical and intelligent and independent. She didn't need this kind of distraction. She didn't need Jack Logan!

"I'll try it on my own this time," she declared fiercely, needing to fight the attraction she felt for him.

"Are you sure you can do it alone?" Jack asked as he stepped away from her.

"I'm going to try."

Amanda took a deep breath and drew and fired. Her shot was closer than before, but she still could not hit the target.

"It looks like you need another lesson." He went to her and put his arms around her again.

"It's almost dark."

"Then we'd better hurry."

He felt her tremble.

"But before, you said to do it slow."

"Shall I show you again?"

"Yes." Her words were soft and inviting.

Jack knew the lesson he was about to teach Amanda had nothing to do with guns. He forgot about her sidearm; he forgot about the bottles. All he knew was that Amanda was in his arms, pressed against him, and the scent of her perfume was intoxicating.

"Amanda—" He said her name in a low voice as he turned her to face him.

With a gentle hand, Jack cupped her cheek and lifted her face so she was looking at him. He saw the confusion in her gaze and smiled at her.

Amanda saw the heat of desire in Jack's eyes, and her heartbeat quickened in response. She knew he was going to kiss her, and she knew that she wanted his kiss. When Ted had held her in his arms the night before, it had been nice. But now, in Jack's embrace, she knew the true meaning of excitement.

Jack moved slowly to kiss her, and Amanda was lost as his mouth settled over hers in a possessive, passionate exchange. Any and all logical thought vanished before the persuasive ecstasy of his embrace. Her world narrowed to the deepening shadows of night, the cool of the evening—and Jack. She moaned low in her throat as she looped her arms around his neck and clung to him.

"Amanda." He said her name in a voice hoarse with passion.

She drew back to look up at him, but didn't speak. He could see that she felt the same thing he did.

"I was teaching you how to—"

She cut him off with a soft kiss. "There's only thing I want you to teach me, Jack Logan, and it has nothing to do with guns."

As he watched, she stepped away from him and slowly, almost sensuously, unbuckled her gunbelt and laid it aside. Without a word, she went back into his arms and lifted her lips to his.

At her unspoken surrender, any restraint Jack had had over himself was gone. He kissed her hungrily, then sought the sweetness of her throat as he lifted her up in his arms and laid her upon the soft grass. Locked in each other's arms, they came together in ecstasy's splendor.

With each touch, each kiss, their passion grew. Jack helped her slip off her blouse, and she reached for him, working at the buttons on his shirt. She was as eager for this closeness as he was. When at last they came together without the barrier of their clothing between them, she reveled in the heat of his hard body against her.

The spark that had ignited the fire of their need had now become a raging inferno. Jack caressed her, wanting to pleasure her, wanting to show her the beauty of loving. Her flesh was silken beneath his touch. He longed to bury himself in the hot depths of her, to claim her for his own and brand her forever with his love.

Amanda had never known such ecstasy. There were no thoughts of right or wrong as she gave herself over to his loving. She wanted—no, needed—to be with him. She longed to lose herself in his arms, to kiss him and hold him and love him. He was all hot, hard, dangerous male, and she wanted to surrender all of her innocence to him even as she wanted to conquer him with her softness.

When Jack moved over her to make her his, she stilled and looked up at him. Her expression was passionate, yet fearful, as she faced the unknown for the first time.

Jack braced himself on his forearms above her as he slowly, sensuously fitted himself to her.

"If you want me to stop, Amanda, tell me now."

She lifted her arms to him in welcome, and he pressed his strength home, seeking the silken depths of her. The proof of her innocence stopped him. He almost drew back for fear that he was hurting her, but she held him more tightly than ever and shifted her hips to accept him more fully. At her move, Jack could no longer deny the need that drove him. He pressed deeply forward, claiming her virginity, making her his own.

The pain of his possession was sharp. Amanda quieted as she adjusted to the sensation, so foreign to her. She was unsure and a bit timid at the intimacy.

Jack understood her reaction. He remained unmoving as he kissed her. It was a tender kiss at first, but the passion that smoldered within them ignited again. Soon Amanda forgot everything but the glory of being one with Jack. His touch aroused a spiraling desire within her that left her aching for more. She began to move with him, matching his rhythm, learning how to please him.

Amanda's eager response was almost Jack's undoing. He sought the peak of pleasure, taking her with him, wanting her to know the rapture that could be theirs. And then the beauty of it burst around them, enveloping them in a sweet rapture that left them clinging together.

They lay on the soft bed of grass, their desperate need for each other sated. As their wild passion eased, they slowly became aware of their surroundings and the magnitude of what had just happened between them.

Jack recovered his sanity first, and he couldn't believe what he'd done. He had just made love to Amanda.

Silently, he berated himself. He was disgusted with his lack of control. He knew he wouldn't blame Dan if his friend came after him with a gun or a horsewhip. Amanda had been a virgin.

"Amanda." He said her name quietly as he shifted away from her.

"Hmmm?" she asked languidly, still caught up in the afterglow of love. She reached for him, wanting him back in her arms.

"Amanda, I'm sorry. This won't ever happen again."

"What?" She opened her eyes to look at him in confusion.

"I never meant for this to happen. I took advantage of your innocence."

His words jarred her from the blissful haze that had surrounded her to the harshness of reality—she had just made love to Jack Logan.

"I am my own woman. You did not take advantage of me," she ground out. "So there's no need for any guilt on your part."

Suddenly, the warmth she'd been feeling was gone, and she was chilled in body and soul. She snatched up her clothes and began to dress.

Jack was caught totally off guard by her harsh reaction. "Amanda, I—"

"Don't say it. What happened here was obviously a mistake. It might be wise, the next time you see me taking target practice, to cut a wide path around me. You're a bigger target than my bottles, and I might not have as much trouble hitting you."

With that she snatched up her gunbelt and stalked away into the darkness that now covered the land.

Jack knew he'd been a fool to give in to his desire for her. But as he watched her walk away, he thought she was the most magnificent woman he'd ever seen.

# Chapter Fifteen

Amanda was furious with herself as she stomped back toward the house. She was grateful for the cover of darkness, so no one could see how agitated she was. Jack Logan had been driving her crazy since the first day they'd met, and she didn't understand how she could have given herself to him so easily. One kiss and she'd all but thrown herself at him.

Her weakness was disgusting. . . . It was horrible that she had so little self control. But his kiss had been exciting. And loving him had been wonderful. . . .

Stopping in the night, Amanda faced the truth. She'd given herself to Jack because it had been exactly what she'd wanted to do. Ted's kiss had been nice. Jack's kiss was devastating. He had only to touch her, and she was his.

Amanda stared off into the darkness, thinking of Jack, of how he'd rescued her from the bar in Philadelphia and saved her from Micah Jennings. She remembered his kiss on the ship and how close they'd come to making love in the back of the freight wagon. She thought of tonight and how she'd reacted when he'd put his arms around her to help her draw her gun, and the truth came to her.

As irritating and arrogant and demanding as Jack was . . .

She loved him.

The knowledge frightened Amanda. She tried to deny it, but the memory of his loving could not be banished. Her knees went weak as she recalled how wonderful it had been to be with him. She had never known that loving someone could be so beautiful. It had been ecstasy. She wanted him still—all of him— and yet he'd told her it would never happen again.

Her anger turned to despair. He'd apologized. He'd said he was sorry that they'd made love. He'd said that he'd taken advantage of her innocence.

She might love him, but he obviously didn't love her.

A great heaviness settled in her heart. Their coming together had meant nothing to Jack.

Amanda waited a minute longer to collect her thoughts. She smoothed her hair into a semblance of order and brushed off her clothes. She wanted to make sure she looked normal when she returned to the house. As eagle-eyed as Eileen was, it would be hard to put something past her. When she'd finally gathered her wits about her, Amanda went on inside.

"There you are. I was getting worried about you," Eileen told her as she met her at the door.

"I ran into Jack and we talked for a while," she explained, deciding not to lie.

"Is he coming up to see your father?"

"No. We had words, so he went on back to his hotel, I guess."

"I do wish you and Jack could get along better. He's such a fine young man."

Amanda was in no mood to listen to Eileen sing his praises. "He's all yours, Eileen. Why don't you marry him and run off with him? Then I wouldn't have to put up with him anymore."

Eileen smiled brightly at the thought. "If he'd have me, I'd go with him in a minute, but I think the fact that I'm old enough to be his mother might put him off a bit."

Amanda caught a glimpse of the beauty Eileen was once as a young girl. "Were you ever married?"

"No"—Eileen sighed—"but I was in love once, oh so many years ago."

"What happened?"

"He was a sailor on a merchant ship that went down in a storm," she said simply.

Even after all the years that had passed, Amanda could still hear the pain in Eileen's voice as she spoke of it. "I'm sorry. What was his name?"

"His name was Andrew—Andrew Copeland." She paused. It had been so long since she'd allowed herself to think of him. "We were young . . . so very young. I believe I was seventeen and he was twenty. We were engaged, and he promised we would be married after his next trip. But he never made it back. The ship was lost somewhere off the coast of France. There were no survivors.''

Amanda went to Eileen and put an arm around her. ''I wish there was some way to turn the clock back and shanghai him before he sailed on that last trip.''

''So do I. I've wished that a thousand times over the years. He was such a good man . . . handsome, too. I have a small portrait of him.''

''Could I see it?''

Eileen opened the locket she wore on a long gold chain around her neck. Inside there was a tiny oil painting of a very handsome young man. He had blond hair and dark eyes, and Amanda could easily understand how her friend had loved him.

''He was very handsome, your Andrew.''

''I know. There were many girls chasing him, but he loved me. It's that thought that's sustained me all these years. I know, some day, we will be together again. It won't be in this lifetime, but I know he's waiting for me in heaven.''

''That is so beautiful.''

Eileen smiled a sweet-sad smile as she closed the locket. ''That's why I keep prodding you toward Jack. I sense something there between the two of you. I've seen the way he looks at you when you don't know he's looking, and I've seen the way you react to him. He's a wonderful man, who's been through a lot. You could do a lot worse, you know.''

Amanda laughed at Eileen's matchmaking. ''I could?''

''Of course, just look at Ted—not that he isn't nice

and all," she amended, "but next to a man like our Jack—"

" 'Our' Jack?"

Eileen gave her a sly look. "I'm fond of him, and you are too, if you'd just admit it."

"Oh, sure, I'm fond of him the way I'm fond of rattlesnakes," Amanda said.

"Just because he keeps you out of trouble is no reason to be angry with him. That's his job, you know. That's what your father hired him to do."

Eileen's use of the phrase "that's his job" reminded Amanda of Jack's words in the back of the freight wagon, and her irritation grew. "Papa hired him to bring me safely home, and then he hired him on as a worker for the stage line."

"I overheard one of their recent conversations by accident," Eileen replied. "Your father specifically hired Jack to guard you and keep you safe."

"That's ridiculous. Jack said—" She stopped at the look Eileen gave her. She had been angry with Jack when she'd come into the house, and now, if possible, she was even angrier. "I don't believe this!"

"It's true. Your father was worried about you, what with the robberies and all, and he wants Jack to make sure you're guarded all the time."

"But I don't need protecting! I'm even carrying my own gun now!" She dropped her hand to the revolver on her hip.

"Well, darling, you have to learn that you cannot teach an old dog new tricks. Your father is a man of the old school who believes that women should be cherished, guarded and protected. You are his precious daughter, and since he can't take care of you himself, he's having Jack do it."

"I should have realized something was going on when Jack said he was staying."

"Don't be angry with Jack. He obviously cares about what happens to you. If he didn't, he would have gone after the Sheldons as soon as he'd turned you over to your father."

Amanda didn't believe there was anything heroic about Jack's decision to stay. "I am sure that Jack doesn't care about me the way you think he does, Eileen. I'm sure money had a lot to do with his decision to stay on."

"Maybe, maybe not, but just remember how I lost my Andrew. I don't want you to lose something precious, too."

Amanda almost snorted at Eileen's use of the word precious. There was nothing the least precious about Jack Logan to her way of thinking.

"We'll see," Amanda replied evasively. She'd done all the talking about Jack that she wanted to do for one night. "I'm going to go take a bath and get cleaned up."

"Do you want dinner? I ate about half an hour ago."

"Could you just bring up something on a tray for me in my room? I'm tired and I think I'll go to bed after I get cleaned up and tell Papa good night."

"I'll have your food up to you in a few minutes."

"Thanks."

Amanda started up the steps, feeling suddenly very tired. She needed some quiet time alone to think about all that had happened and to try to figure out what to do. The story of Eileen's lost love stayed with her through the night.

Jack quickly threw on his clothes and returned to town. He had wanted to speak to Dan that night, but knew it would have to wait. He was in no condition to have an intelligent conversation with him. He thought about stopping by the bar, but chose to return to the hotel directly. After eating a quick meal there, he went up to his room and stretched out on the bed. He didn't have to be anywhere or see anyone until the following morning, so he knew he could relax.

There was nothing relaxed about his thoughts, though, as he lay there going over in detail all that had happened with Amanda. He hadn't meant to make love to her. Not that he regretted it—loving her had been magnificent, but it shouldn't have happened. He'd known from the beginning how she felt about him. Her parting words had certainly conveyed the full depth of her affection—or lack of affection—for him.

He swore silently to himself, wondering what he was going to do. Logic told him to leave, head out first thing tomorrow. But his promise to Dan held him in San Rafael. Of course, if Dan learned what had happened between him and Amanda, Dan would personally run him out of town on a rail.

Jack wondered how he'd gotten himself into this mess. And the answer came to him, as visions of Amanda played in his mind. He saw Amanda smashing liquor bottles in the bar and standing up to the outraged barkeep. He saw Amanda trying to help the abused woman and then suffering abuse herself at Jennings's hands. He saw Amanda surrendering to him as they made love on the bed of grass only hours before. She was unlike any woman he'd ever known. There was no deceit in Amanda. She said what she thought and did what she believed best, no matter what the consequences. She was a rare woman, indeed.

And he loved her.

Jack had no idea what he was going to do about it, and he knew he had to come up with something fast. They were scheduled to make a run to Comanche Pass together the following afternoon, and somehow they would have to work this thing out between them by then.

*He loved Amanda....*

The thought made him smile and then frown. He'd been in some difficult situations before, but this one topped them all.

It was going to be a very interesting trip.

Amanda was up before dawn. She'd tossed and turned for most of the night thinking of Jack. It was sweet that Eileen believed he was there because he cared about her, but she knew different. Jack had told her that it was his job, and he'd told her that he was sorry they'd made love. It didn't get much plainer than that—Jack didn't care about her. She had thrown herself at him, he'd taken what she'd freely offered and he'd regretted it later.

It was for that very reason that Amanda knew what she had to do. She had to leave. She had to get away from Jack. She needed time to pull herself together.

She needed time to become strong again, because right then, remembering Jack's lovemaking, she didn't feel strong. She felt only devastation and pain and anger at herself for her own weakness.

And so, she was dressing in her work clothes and strapping on her gun to get ready to ride. Isaac and Ted were scheduled to go to Las Brisas at five-thirty this morning. Instead, she would go. One of them would have to stay behind and go with Jack this afternoon. She didn't care if they complained or not. She was the boss, and it was her decision. She wanted to be long gone before Jack Logan even got out of bed.

Amanda left a brief note for her father and one for Eileen, too, so they wouldn't worry. She quietly crept from the house, not wanting to disturb anyone. She wanted to get away as quickly and as quietly as she could.

Isaac and Ted were already at the office getting ready to leave. They were both surprised to see her.

"What are you doing here so early?" Ted asked. He was pleased because he thought perhaps she'd come down just to say good-bye to him.

"I've decided that I prefer to make the morning run today, so one of you will have to stay behind and ride this afternoon with Jack," she explained quickly, not giving either of them the chance to argue or question her decision.

"I'll take it," Ted said quickly, glancing over at Isaac.

"Are you sure this is a good idea?" Isaac asked. Dan had told him about how he'd hired Jack to guard Amanda, and he wanted to abide by Dan's wishes. He knew for a fact that Ted was not that good a shot.

"It's a fine idea," Amanda stated firmly. "Ted can do the driving, and I'll ride shotgun."

Isaac saw the look in her eye. She was running the place, but he still didn't like it. "But your father—"

"Put me in charge. I'm taking the morning run."

"Well, I guess I'll go get me some more sleep," Isaac agreed, reluctantly.

"I didn't inform Jack of my change in plans, but it shouldn't make any difference to him."

"I'll tell him when he shows up."

"You ready?" She looked at Ted.

"If you are. We're right on schedule."

"Good."

They climbed aboard. Amanda took up her position as shotgun while Ted picked up the reins and urged the team out of San Rafael. They were carrying three passengers, mail and a small payroll. Amanda expected it to be an uneventful trip.

Isaac watched them go. He had misgivings about the two of them riding together, but as she'd said, she was the boss. True, she was a decent shot and could handle a team, but Ted had yet to distinguish himself as a good driver. Isaac hoped that everything went smoothly, but somehow something didn't feel right.

He waited until sunup and then sought out Jack. He wanted to talk to him about what had transpired.

"Yeah, who is it?" Jack called out as someone knocked at his hotel room door just after dawn.

"It's Isaac."

Jack got up immediately and pulled on his pants.

For Isaac to seek him out, something had to be wrong with the stage line—and that meant Amanda could be in trouble. When he'd finished fastening his pants, he threw on a shirt and didn't bother to button it as he opened the door to let Isaac in.

"What's wrong? Has the five-thirty run gone out yet?"

"They left on time."

"They?" Jack closed the door behind Isaac and motioned for him to sit in the only chair. He settled on the edge of his bed.

"That's why I came to see you. Miss Amanda showed up just in time to ride out with Ted. She said I should work the afternoon stage with you."

"I see," Jack muttered and then swore under his breath. He'd hurt her so badly the night before that all she wanted to do was get away from him. He was tempted to go after them, to bring her back so he could keep an eye on her, but he decided not to. By her actions, she'd made it perfectly clear that she wanted nothing more to do with him.

Still, the thought of her riding with Ted set Jack's nerves on edge. He would have felt much better if she'd gone with Isaac. He trusted and liked Isaac. He was confident of his ability to handle trouble. Ted, however, was a different story. Jack didn't want Amanda anywhere near Ted, but he could hardly go after her and drag her back as he'd dragged her out of The Palace. He would have to be patient and bide his time, and that didn't sit well with him.

"I've been thinking," Isaac began, unsure of how

to voice his suspicions, but knowing he had to talk to someone. "Things around here were going real good until Ted showed up."

"I don't understand." Jack frowned as he glanced over at Isaac.

"I mean, it just seems a real strange coincidence to me that there hadn't been a robbery around here in years, and then Ted comes back to live with his mother and Asa, and the next thing we know all hell breaks loose."

"Are you saying the robberies didn't start until after he'd returned?"

"That's right. He'd been back about a month when the first one happened."

"Did he ever say anything or do anything to arouse your suspicions?"

"No. Nothing. That's what's bothering me. He seems all right, but there's just something about him—"

"I know what you mean. Something doesn't ring true."

"I keep thinking . . . he and his mother were the ones who benefited the most from Asa's death, but I can't imagine a woman as nice as Miss Mona being involved in anything like that."

The mention of Mona's possible involvement sharpened Jack's interest. "Never underestimate women. It could mean the death of you. Did you hear about El Diablo?"

"Just that the gang was brought in."

"Well, El Diablo was a woman. She was running the whole thing, and she was as deadly and vicious as they come. Keep an eye on Mona, and the next time Ted drives, I'll ride shotgun with him.''

"That's a great idea. Dan and Asa worked hard to make this line a success. I want things to straighten out for Dan. I don't want Taylor Stage and Freight going under.''

"Neither do I," Jack agreed. "When are Amanda and Ted due back?''

"Early tomorrow afternoon.''

"I guess we'll just have to wait and see how things go. You'll be ready for our trip later?''

"I'll be ready whenever you are.''

"I'll come to the office in another hour or so.''

"See you then.''

Isaac had only just departed when another knock sounded at Jack's door. He expected it to be Isaac again, and he wondered what the other man had forgotten to tell him. He opened the door without pause and was shocked to find himself facing Stalking Ghost.

"Stalking Ghost! Come in!" He welcomed him, truly glad to see him. "Did Cody and Luke come with you?''

"No. I came alone to find you.''

"Why? Has something happened to Cody or Luke?" Jack asked.

"No," Stalking Ghost answered. "I came here to you to let you know what has happened. Your Captain Laughlin came to see Luke and Cody to find out if they knew where you were. He told them how the Sheldons had broken out of jail and were after you.''

"Cody didn't . . . ?" Jack immediately knew what Cody Jameson Majors would do.

Stalking Ghost nodded. "Once Captain Laughlin had gone, Cody convinced Luke that the bounty was too good to pass up."

"I hope to hell she doesn't go getting herself killed."

"Cody is the best at what she does. She will find them," Stalking Ghost said with complete confidence.

Jack knew that was true. That was the reason he'd hired her to help him bring down the El Diablo gang. "I know, but the Sheldons are almost as dangerous as El Diablo was."

"That's why she wants them behind bars again. She sent me to tell Laughlin that she and Luke were going after the gang. When I found him to give him the message, he told me that he had gotten a message from you and that you were here. That is why I have come—to make sure that you are well. Have you seen or heard anything of the Sheldons yet?"

"Nothing, and I hope it stays that way. I'm here working for the stage line as a favor for an old friend." He quickly explained what was happening with the robberies and how he was scheduled to ride out that afternoon. "Are you staying here or going after Cody and Luke?"

"I will be near," he answered obliquely.

Amanda was trying to relax and enjoy the trip with Ted, but it wasn't proving to be as easy as she'd thought it would be. No matter how hard she tried not to think of Jack, he was constantly in her thoughts. She almost felt like screaming in frustration at being unable to banish her memories of him . . . memories of his kiss, his smile, his touch, the heat of his body against hers. . . . With an effort, she controlled her desire to scream. Not that she wouldn't have felt better, but she didn't want to frighten the passengers or have Ted question her sanity.

"You're scowling," Ted remarked, noticing her dark expression. "Is something wrong?"

"No, I was just thinking about the robberies and wondering why the sheriff can't find anything out. The first robbery was on this very run, wasn't it?"

"That's right. It was just up ahead a ways where the road narrows and the terrain is rocky."

She nodded. "Good choice on the robbers' part. It's next to impossible to track anybody over rock."

"Whoever they are, they know what they're doing. Let's just hope they've moved on. We don't need any more trouble. Things are bad enough as they are now, with all the drivers quitting."

"That's the truth."

"My mother still talks about seeing if your father will sell out, but I don't know if that's a good decision or not. I got a look at the books and there's definitely money to be made here, if everything calms down."

"I doubt my father would ever sell. It's been his whole life. It means too much to him. With your help and Isaac's, I can handle most of the business until he's recovered and can take over again."

"But what if the robberies continue even then?"

"The law's going to have to catch the robbers," she said fervently. "They murdered Uncle Asa and that passenger. We can't let them get away with that. The outlaws will make a mistake, and when they do, they'll be caught. I'm almost tempted to send for the Rangers, but I'm going to give the sheriff another week or two to see if he comes up with any new leads.''

''The sheriff's a good man. If there's anything out there, he'll find it,'' Ted said. He really thought the man was just shy of being an idiot, but that was fine with him. It made things much easier.

''I hope you're right.''

Amanda tightened her grip on her rifle as they neared the site of the first robbery. She felt uneasy and tried to dismiss the feeling, telling herself she was on edge because she was upset about Jack.

''How good are you at driving?'' she asked, her gaze sweeping over the surrounding landscape

''I'm learning on the job,'' Ted told her with an easy smile meant to ingratiate himself and impress her with his confidence. ''Isaac taught me on our first trip together over a month ago, and I've been doing the driving ever since.''

''I'm serious about this, Ted. If something were to happen, would you be able to control the team?''

He realized then that she was questioning his ability, and it infuriated him. ''Don't worry, Amanda.'' He managed to sound easygoing, despite his anger. ''I'll take care of you.''

She was just starting to set him straight, to tell him that she didn't need taking care of, when shots rang out around her.

# *Chapter Sixteen*

Amanda shouldered her rifle and fired. These murdering thieves had killed her uncle and seriously wounded her father, but she was going to make damned sure they didn't kill her—at least not without some payback.

"Faster, Ted! Get the team going!" she shouted as she kept shooting.

The outlaws were showing no sign of giving up, despite Amanda's accurate return fire.

Ted slapped the reins as hard as he could and the horses jolted forward. He caught a glimpse of the outlaws as they came riding down out of the rocks, firing continually in their direction. Amanda ran out of ammunition in her rifle and tossed it aside. She braced herself and drew her revolver.

"Get down!" Ted yelled at her. "Are you trying to get yourself killed?"

"Just keep this stage moving!" she returned, never letting up in her firing.

And then the bullet struck her.

Ted was horrified when she cried out and collapsed beside him on the driver's bench.

"Amanda? Dear God—" He urged the team onward as he drew his own revolver and tried to fire back at the oncoming attackers.

One of the male passengers was armed, and he, too, was firing out of the stage window. Ted heard shouts of pain and managed a quick glance back to see that two of the outlaws had fallen and the rest had stopped their pursuit. He kept going at a frantic pace until he was certain they were safely away. He didn't slow the team until he was in the open where they couldn't be ambushed again.

"I need help up here!" he shouted as he took Amanda in his arms and climbed down. It was difficult, but he made it. Carrying her gently, he laid her on the grass at the side of the road to see to her injury.

"Oh, my God," a woman's voice cried from inside the stage as she saw Amanda. "They've killed her!"

Ted feared the worst. Blood was streaming from a wound on Amanda's head. He brushed her hair back from her face, not knowing what to expect. Relief flooded through him when he discovered the bullet had only grazed her forehead.

"She's still alive!" he called back to the others as he quickly took his handkerchief and pressed it to the wound.

Ted was thankful that she wasn't dead. His whole

point in setting up the fake robbery attempt today was to make himself look good. Isaac was supposed to have been along. If things had gone as originally planned, Isaac would have seen how well he'd handled things and been impressed with his courage and ability. He'd always felt the other man had suspicions about him, and today's plan had been contrived to convince him otherwise. When Amanda had decided to take Isaac's place, Ted hadn't been worried. Either way, if things had gone according to plan, he would have come out looking like a hero. No one was supposed to have been injured.

But now . . .

"Shall we take her inside the stage with us? There's nothing you can do for her out here," offered the man who'd helped fight off the outlaws as he came to kneel beside Ted.

"Yes. We'll have to head back to town. She needs a doctor right away."

"What about the outlaws?" the passenger asked, fearful that they might be waiting for them.

"They're long gone by now. We'll be safe."

"Will she live?"

"I hope so." Ted sounded suitably anguished as he lifted Amanda and carried her to the stage. With great care, he laid her inside. The passengers all did what they could to make her comfortable.

The trip back to San Rafael was the longest Ted had ever made. Each mile seemed a hundred, and he wondered if the town was ever going to come into sight. When finally they reached the outskirts, he heard the cry go up in the streets that something was wrong, the stage was back. He didn't even stop at the depot, but drove straight to the doctor's office.

"Help! There's been a shooting!"

Dr. Clayborne heard his call and came running out of the office.

"Oh, my God! It's Amanda Taylor! Bring her in here!" he directed as he saw Ted carrying her from the stage. "What happened?"

"There was another robbery attempt, but I managed to get away from them. She was riding shotgun and a bullet grazed her head," Ted explained as he laid her on the examining table.

Dr. Clayborne took a quick look at her wound. "Thank God, it only grazed her. Another inch over, and she'd be dead."

"Is Amanda going to live?"

"I'll know more after I examine her. I can't tell right away with this kind of wound. Was anyone else injured?"

"No, I managed to outrun them, and then I brought her straight back here."

"You'd better go tell Dan what's happened. This is going to hit him hard, but I want him here at his daughter's side," Dr. Clayborne directed.

Ted nodded and hurried off to get Dan. He rushed to the Taylor house and pounded on the door.

Eileen had no idea why someone would be knocking so loudly at the door. She hurried to answer it.

"Dear God! Ted, there's blood all over you!" Eileen cried.

"I have to see Dan," he told her gruffly, walking past her.

"What is it? Why are you back? Where's Amanda?"

He ignored her questions as he took the steps two at a time. He knocked on Dan's bedroom door and opened it at his call to come in.

"There's been some trouble," he said solemnly as he entered the room. He was shocked to find that Jack was with Dan.

At the sight of Ted, so bloodied, Jack was immediately on his feet.

"Amanda—" Jack's tone was deadly as he moved toward Ted. "Where's Amanda?"

"There was a robbery attempt. She was shot."

"You son-of-a-bitch!"

Ted had no time to defend himself as Jack hit him with all the power of a man in the grip of uncontrollable fury. Jack felt no satisfaction when Ted dropped to the floor before him, his nose broken and bleeding.

"Where is she?" Jack demanded, standing over him, his fists still clenched.

"You bastard! You broke my nose, and I saved the damned payroll!" Ted cried miserably, blood streaming from his nose.

"I don't give a damn about the money," Dan snarled. "Where's my daughter?"

"She's at Dr. Clayborne's office."

Eileen had followed him upstairs, fearful of just such news, and she rushed to Dan's side.

"I have to go to her," Dan said, a frantic look in his eyes.

"I know. Let me help you get up and get dressed."

"How bad is she?" Jack hadn't moved, but remained standing threateningly over the fallen Ted. It wouldn't have bothered him at all to continue to pummel the fool.

"It was a head wound."

"Oh, God." At this news, Jack knew pain so deep and so cutting that he was surprised he was still standing. His jaw tightened as he fought for control. Amanda was his and she'd been shot! She might even be dead.

"Dan's ready to go, if you can help us, Jack," Eileen told him as she kept a supporting arm around the older man.

Jack went quickly to their aid. They quit the room, leaving Ted behind. It was slow going to Dr. Clayborne's office. Dan was weak, but his iron-willed determination drove him on. He had to get to his daughter. She might be dying. They arrived at the office to find that the physician was still in the examining room with Amanda.

Eileen and Jack helped Dan to sit in one of the chairs, and then she sat next to him. Jack could not sit down. He paced the waiting room like a caged wild animal.

"I should have gone after her this morning. I shouldn't have left her alone with Ted—"

"This is no time for that, Jack," Eileen said soothingly.

"I don't understand why Amanda went off like that," Dan said miserably. "The reason I hired you was just so something like this wouldn't happen. And here she took off on her own . . . with Ted." He added the last in complete disgust.

Jack knew exactly why Amanda had done it. She'd done it to get away from him.

Guilt filled Jack, along with a driving need for revenge. Whoever had shot Amanda was as good as dead. Once he knew she was going to be all right, he was going after the outlaws, and he wouldn't come back until he'd found them.

Ted arrived at the office a short time later with his mother, and Mona hurried to her brother-in-law's side.

"Dan . . . I'm so sorry about what happened. How is Amanda?" Mona asked.

"The doctor's still in there with her." He nodded toward the closed door.

"This is so tragic," Mona went on, casting a sad glance toward the examining room. "If only we'd sold the stage line after Asa was murdered, none of this would have happened. You should have listened to me, Dan. It isn't worth it. None of this is worth it."

Dan glared at her, barely in control of his temper. "Amanda was on that stage because she wanted to be, Mona, not because anyone forced her to go. She cares as much for Taylor Stage and Freight as I do. She wants the line to continue. She doesn't want to just cut and run."

"When will you see that it's just not worth it? You've already lost your brother. Will it take losing your daughter, too, before you realize just how foolish you're being?" she persisted.

When she and Ted had originally made their plan, she'd thought they would be out of West Texas in a matter of a few short weeks. After the botched robbery that left Dan injured but alive, everything had changed. Now Ted was talking as if he wanted to stay on and keep his hand in the till, so to speak. While Mona didn't care what her son did, she did want to make sure that she got what was coming to her and she didn't intend to wait much longer to get it.

"I think that's quite enough." Eileen spoke up with an air of authority that surprised everyone. She knew it was none of her business and she should keep her mouth shut, but she couldn't help it. She'd understood when Andrew had sailed that last time that the sea was his love. Nothing could have stopped him from going. And so it was with Dan and Amanda. They loved the stage line.

"I beg your pardon?" Mona was aghast that Eileen had spoken to her that way. "Why are you here? You aren't even family."

Eileen had expected her to counterattack, but she'd never expected the defense that came her way.

"No, she's not family. She's better than family. She's my friend," Dan said. "Family, you don't get to pick," he said pointedly as he sliced an angry look at Ted. "Friends, you do."

"Well, I never," Mona huffed.

"That's right, Mona. You never have understood what all this means to the Taylors, and I'm coming to believe that you never will," Dan said tightly. "Taylor Stage and Freight is not for sale, and it never will be."

Mona thought about getting up and leaving, but knew that would prove her insensitivity. She had to remain and find out about Amanda's condition. She had to play the role of the concerned aunt. "I am only worrying about Amanda. She's such a sweet young girl, and to have this happen to her—''

Jack was standing alone, apart from the others, silently praying that Amanda would recover. He had only been half-listening to their conversation. He knew they were angry, but he didn't care about them. Nothing mattered except Amanda. She had to be all right. She had to be.

The door to the examining room opened and Dr. Clayborne came out. Jack started to go to him. His gaze was riveted on the doctor's face, trying to read his expression. He needed to know. He had to know. And then Jack realized that he wasn't a relative and so had no right to ask how she was. He hung back, watching and waiting for the doctor to say the words he so desperately needed to hear.

"Dan?" Dr. Clayborne went straight to the older man.

Dan got slowly, painfully, to his feet. He saw the doctor's serious expression and feared the worst. "What is it? How's my Amanda?"

"It was so close," he said quietly. "She's a very lucky young woman."

"She's going to be all right?" Dan asked, his eyes widening in hope.

"Yes, she'll be fine. She's going to be groggy for a day or two, and certainly she'll have a headache for a while. But she's in no mortal danger. In fact, if you move her carefully, you can take her home."

"Oh, thank you, doctor," Dan said, clasping his hand in a warm, hard grip. "Thank you. Can I see her now?"

"Of course. Come on in." He helped him into the examining room and closed the door behind them to give them privacy.

Dan went to where Amanda lay on the examining table and gazed down at her with tears in his eyes. "Thank God, you're going to be all right."

"Papa—" Amanda's voice was soft and filled with pain. "I'm sorry."

"You have nothing to be sorry for."

She looked up at him. "Yes, I do. Eileen told me last night how you'd hired Jack to take care of me, and that just made me all the more determined to prove I didn't need him guarding me. But Papa, I was wrong."

"It doesn't matter. All that matters is that you're alive, and you're going to be fine."

"I did shoot two of them," she managed with a weary smile.

"That's my girl. Good shooting," he said with as much enthusiasm as he could muster under the circumstances.

"What about the payroll? Did they get the strongbox?"

"No. I have to admit, Ted did do a good job. One of the passengers was armed, so between the passenger and Ted, they saved the stage. He got you back here as quickly as he could."

She tried to nod, but it hurt too much to move her head. "I'm sorry I worried you, Papa."

Dan's tears began to fall, and he made no effort to resist them. "Sweetheart, I just want you happy and well. Don't worry about another thing."

"Yes, Papa." She paused, wondering where Jack was and how angry he was with her. "Does Jack know what happened?"

Since she knew how he felt about her after last night, Amanda assumed that he wouldn't care. She thought he'd probably gone ahead with Isaac on the run to Comanche Pass.

"Of course he knows!" Her father wondered how she could doubt that. "He's furious."

"I can imagine," she said more to herself.

"Jack was with me at the house when Ted came to tell me you were injured. Jack was less than patient with Ted—"

"I don't understand." She frowned painfully as she looked at her father.

"He hit him."

"Jack hit Ted?"

"I think he broke his nose."

"Oh, my . . ."

"I have to tell you, I was angry with Ted, too. When I think of how you might have been killed . . . I don't even care that he brought in the payroll untouched. I would have preferred that you had come back untouched."

"So you really did hire Jack to guard me."

"Yes, I did. You're the most precious thing in the world to me. Everything I do is for you, and I want you to be safe and happy."

"Thank you, Papa." It was wonderful to be loved this way—unconditionally and completely. Her father was a rare and gentle man, and she loved him very much. "I love you."

"I love you, too, sweetheart. The doctor said we can take you home now if you feel up to being moved."

"I'd like that, Papa."

"I'll tell him. You just rest easy. He said it would be best if you just stay in bed for a few days until you're all better."

"Right now, that sounds like great advice," she said weakly. "But what about the stage line?"

"Don't you worry about the line. We'll take care of it. You just get better."

Eileen went to Jack as soon as Dan had gone in to see Amanda.

"Don't you worry. She's going to be all right. She's a fighter." She patted his arm reassuringly.

"She is that." Jack looked down at Eileen and had to smile at her. It was a tight smile, but one that let her know how much he appreciated her. Just by standing next to him, she had given him the strength he needed to stay in control.

While he'd been waiting, he'd been silently planning what he would do once he knew Amanda's exact condition. A few hours before, he would never have guessed that he would be so glad to have Stalking Ghost in town, but now he was. There wasn't a better tracker in the state of Texas. Between the two of them, the outlaws who'd done this didn't stand a chance. He was going to hunt them down and see them pay. They would not get away this time.

Mona and Ted had been talking between themselves in low tones.

Ted looked over at Jack, taking care to keep his expression one of concern for Amanda, and told him, "Once we're sure she's out of danger, I'll go over to the sheriff's office. I'm sure he'll want to know the details. Do you want to come with me?"

"No. You're the one who saved the payroll. You talk to him. I'm going to be busy."

"Doing what?" Ted demanded, believing that the running of the line had fallen to him now that Amanda was injured. As terrible as Amanda's being shot was, he was rather pleased with the way things were working out.

Jack fixed him with a cold stare. "I'm going after the men who did this."

"That's what the sheriff's for," Ted protested.

"I don't have time to wait for the sheriff. He's still trying to find out who killed your stepfather," he sneered.

"And you think you can do better?"

"I know I can."

Eileen was listening to the interchange between the two, and her heart swelled with pride as she gazed up at Jack. The man who stood before her was a man of confidence and determination. He was a man to be reckoned with, and she knew that if anybody could bring the outlaws in, Jack could. "You'll do it. I know you will."

"I think I'm going outside for a while. You want to come?" Jack invited her.

"I'd like that. Will you call us when Dan comes out?"

"Of course," Mona said haughtily. She was glad to

see the two of them go. Now she could have some time to talk to Ted alone.

Once Eileen and Jack were outside, Eileen motioned for him to stoop down a bit. Jack thought she was going to whisper something to him, but instead she pressed a sweet kiss on his cheek.

"What was that for?" he asked, surprised by her gesture of tenderness.

"I'm glad you hit Ted," she whispered. "If you'd been the one riding with her, Amanda would never have been hurt."

His gaze darkened at the thought. "But I wasn't with her. This is all my fault. I could have gone after her this morning when I'd found out that she'd gone out with Ted, but I didn't."

Eileen touched his arm again. "That was her decision. If you had known what she was going to do, you would never have let her get away with it. That's why she did what she did. Amanda wanted to prove to herself that she didn't need you, that she was perfectly capable of taking care of herself."

"But she wasn't."

"And I think she knows that now, too. Sometimes, people just have to learn things the hard way." She paused, seeing the anguish in his expression. "Jack?"

"What?" He turned to face her.

"She's going to be fine. You'll see."

Jack looked down at the woman who seemed to know him so well, and he managed a gentle smile. "I love you, Eileen Hammond." It wasn't often in life that one met a woman like her. A woman who was so kind and filled with love that she glowed. He'd been blessed to know two—his mother and now Eileen. "You're an angel."

"You know, Amanda said I should run off with you, since I'm so crazy about you, but I told her I was too old for you."

"You're not too old," he told her with a grin. "I'm just not the marrying kind."

"So, I guess this means there's no hope that you might change your mind?" She looked disappointed, even as her eyes were twinkling with mischief.

"I can't." He pretended disappointment to go along with her teasing. "Not that the offer's not tempting, but once I find out for sure just how Amanda's doing, I'm going after the men who did this."

"What about the sheriff?"

"What about him? He's useless. He hasn't even solved Asa's murder yet. No, once I know she's going to recover, I'm going to send a wire to my captain, Steve Laughlin, and tell him I'm taking my old job back."

"Ranger Jack Logan," Eileen breathed. "I like the sound of that. Amanda will be proud of you."

Jack gave a harsh laugh at her words. "Hardly. Amanda doesn't care if she ever sees me again. The last thing she said to me last night was something about not coming around when she was target shooting, because I was a bigger target than her bottles and she wouldn't have any trouble hitting me!"

"She does have a way with words." Eileen frowned. She'd known that Amanda was irritated with him last night, but she hadn't thought it was this bad. Somehow, deep inside her, she'd always thought they would eventually fall in love. They seemed so perfect for each other.

"And she does care for Ted," Jack continued.

"No, she doesn't. He's just a friend to her."

"I'd like to believe that, but I saw her kissing him the other night."

"She kissed Ted?" Eileen was shocked. "Oh, my . . . I didn't think it had gone that far between them. He's not half the man you are." She glanced up at Jack and saw a flicker of sadness in his expression, before it was quickly disguised. "I'm sorry."

"I'm just glad she's alive," he said after a long, quiet moment.

"So am I."

They stood together in companionable silence, offering up their prayers of thanks for Amanda's survival, until Mona's call drew them back inside.

Dan had emerged from the examining room and was speaking to the doctor as they went back indoors.

"Does Amanda want to stay here for the night or return home?" the doctor asked.

"She wants to go home."

"I'll have my carriage brought around for you."

"Jack?" Dan looked at his friend, totally ignoring Ted and Mona. "Will you carry Amanda out to the carriage for me?"

He nodded and followed Dan back into the room. At the sight of Amanda lying on the table, looking so fragile, her forehead swathed in a bandage, pain tore at Jack. The knowledge was awful. *Amanda could have been killed. . . .*

Dan went to her and was explaining what they were

going to do. "Amanda, Jack's going to carry you out to the carriage so we can take you home."

She looked Jack's way and was startled by his stony expression. His gaze seemed cold. She wasn't sure what he was thinking or feeling as he came toward her.

"Couldn't Ted do it?" she asked, looking quickly, almost nervously from Jack to her father.

Jack said nothing at her request for the other man, but kept his expression emotionless. He merely lifted her gently into his arms and started to follow Dan from the room. He didn't trust himself to speak.

Amanda had been terrified of being in Jack's arms again, and rightfully so—for his touch was her heaven and her hell. Obviously, from his cold expression, he didn't care what happened to her. He was just annoyed that she'd gone out without him and had gotten herself in trouble. When he picked her up and cradled her against his chest, tears filled Amanda's eyes and she began to cry. She didn't make a sound, though, as her tears fell freely. It felt so right being held by him. All she wanted to do was rest her aching head against the strength of his shoulder and never move again for as long as she lived. But it couldn't be. . . .

She might love him . . .

But he didn't love her.

Amanda sighed and gave in to the desire to nestle against him. She felt his arms tighten around her and figured he was just afraid he was going to drop her on the way out to the carriage. When he placed her carefully on the seat next to Dan, who'd already climbed into the vehicle, she felt suddenly lost and alone. So very alone.

"I'll meet you at the house," Jack told them, for there wouldn't be room for him to join them in the carriage once Eileen had climbed in.

"Thanks," Dan said.

Jack helped Eileen up into the conveyance, then started off walking toward the house.

Dan helped Eileen to settle in, then glanced at Amanda to make sure she was comfortable. It was then that he saw her tears. He was instantly worried. "Is something wrong? Should I call the doctor?"

"My head just hurts, that's all," she said in a quiet voice, but her gaze was on the solitary figure of a man who strode the streets of San Rafael.

# *Chapter Seventeen*

Jack reached the house just a few minutes after the carriage to find that Dan was waiting for his help. Without needing to be asked, Jack lifted Amanda from the vehicle, and with Eileen directing, he carried her upstairs to her bedroom. Eileen had hurried ahead of him to turn back the covers on Amanda's bed while Dan remained downstairs.

Jack crossed the room with Amanda. As he laid her carefully down on the wide softness, he saw how pale she was and knew she was in pain.

When Amanda didn't say anything to him and took great care not to make eye contact with him, he understood. Her earlier request for Ted's help had said it all. She didn't love him, but that didn't change the way he felt—he loved her.

It had been his job to keep her safe. He had failed in that, but he would not fail now. A deadly, driving anger filled him. He was going to find the men responsible for this, and they were going to suffer the consequences of their actions.

"Dan is waiting for you downstairs," Eileen told him in a soft voice. "He wants to talk with you."

Jack was glad for the distraction. He turned and left the room. There was no point in staying with her. Ted was the man she really cared for, not him.

Jack found Dan sitting behind his desk in the room he used as a study.

"Thank you for your help, Jack," Dan said, motioning him toward a chair. "Sit down."

"Are you feeling strong enough to stay out of bed?"

"I have to be," he answered simply. Strain showed in his features, but so did his iron will and steely self-control.

"Where did Ted and Mona go?"

"I told them I'd speak with them tomorrow. There was no need for them to come here. There's nothing they could do right now anyway. Ted was planning to go by the sheriff's office and fill him in on whatever the passengers forgot to tell him. I'm sure the sheriff will want to get started after them at sunup."

"He'll be wasting his time."

"Why?"

"Because I'm leaving tonight."

"You're what? But I need you here," Dan protested. "Where are you going?"

"I'm going after the bastards who tried to kill Amanda," Jack said tersely, the fire of his fury burning in his eyes. "And I'm going to bring them in."

"What are you going to do that the sheriff can't?"

"Find them," Jack said with confidence. "Now that I know Amanda's going to recover and you're well enough to be up for a while each day, you won't miss me."

"But what about the line?"

"You've got Isaac and Ted. They can keep things moving until I get back."

"Jack, I . . . I wish I was strong enough to go with you. You can't imagine how useless this makes me feel to have to stay here and let you be the one to avenge my brother's death and my daughter's attempted murder."

"Oh, yes, I can." He remembered all too well when he'd sent Cody and Luke off to track down El Diablo after he'd been stabbed. "But you're needed here. Amanda needs you, and the stage line needs you."

Dan was resigned to staying behind, but it didn't sit well with him. "Is there anything I can do to help you?"

Jack thought of Amanda, of how he wanted to hold her and kiss her and tell her everything would be all right, but he knew he couldn't. Their coming together had been a moment of weakness for the two of them. It had meant the world to him, and he would treasure the memory always. But he was realistic enough to know that she didn't love him—she never had and never would.

"Yes, just take care of Amanda. Make sure she gets well."

Dan was surprised by his words and by the flash of pain he thought he saw for just a moment in Jack's eyes before his friend rose and walked toward the door.

"You take care, and hurry back. We'll be waiting for you."

Jack knew Dan would be waiting, but he doubted Amanda would be. He nodded and left without saying more.

Dan heard the sound of the front door as it closed behind his friend, and for some reason, it sounded solemn and final to him.

*Captain Steve Laughlin,*

*I've decided to go back to work. I am tracking the outlaws responsible for the Taylor Stage and Freight Line robberies. If you need to get a message to me, contact me through the stage line in San Rafael.*

*Jack Logan*

Jack finished writing the message, then double-checked it.

"It's ready. Go ahead and send it to Captain Laughlin in care of Ranger headquarters. If you get any messages back for me, just take them over to Dan Taylor and leave them with him," he told the telegraph operator.

"Yes, sir, Ranger Logan, sir," the operator said with a grin as he read the letter before sending it. "I hope you get those outlaws. We've had enough killing and maiming around here. San Rafael used to be a quiet, safe place to live."

"It's going to be that way again real soon."

"Thanks."

Jack walked from the telegraph office. It was nearly dark, but he didn't care. He went back to his room at the hotel and got his bedroll and rifle. He was almost ready to ride, but there was one more thing he had to do. Jack dug down in his saddle bags and took out the small wrapped article buried deep in the bottom. With infinite care, he unwrapped his Ranger badge. He stared at it for a long moment, judging the weight of it in his hand, knowing the dedication that went with wearing it. There were no more doubts in his heart and soul; there were no more fears. Texas Ranger Jack Logan was back.

Jack pinned on the badge and quit the room.

His next stop was at Mona Taylor's house to see Ted.

"I need to talk to you," he said flatly when the other man answered his knock at the door.

"What about?" Ted said defensively. His nose was swollen and it looked as though he would have two black eyes in the morning.

"I want the details of what happened during the robbery."

"You're not planning on going after the outlaws yourself, are you? I've already told the sheriff everything," Ted argued, seeing the Ranger badge Jack was wearing.

"In case you haven't figured it out by now, the sheriff isn't having much luck solving anything lately. I don't intend to wait around while these killers get away. I'm bringing them in myself. Now, where did the ambush take place?"

Ted was angry, but he gave the location of the attempted robbery and a few of the details. He was careful not to give him anything too specific. The last thing he needed was Jack stirring up trouble.

Ted had heard the talk about Jack in the saloon. Rumor had it that Jack used to be a damned good Ranger. He hoped it wasn't true. Ted was glad that the men he'd hired were professionals. They knew when to lie low, and he hoped they were doing that right now.

"That's all you remember?"

"There wasn't a lot of time to take notes," Ted said scathingly. "I was driving the team and Amanda was doing the shooting."

Jack nodded, keeping a tight rein on his anger. He walked away without looking back.

Jack headed for the stage line's stable, where he kept his horse. He was not surprised when Stalking Ghost appeared while he was saddling his mount.

"I was hoping you were nearby, keeping track of me," Jack said by way of greeting.

"You are riding out tonight?"

"Yes. Did you hear about the stage?" At the Indian's nod, he went on, "I'm going to find the robbers and bring them in. Can you go with me?"

"I will meet you at the edge of town." Stalking Ghost slipped away into the night.

Isaac had been working late. When he saw Jack go into the stable, he sought him out. He was surprised to find him saddling up. "You're leaving?"

Jack turned toward him, and Isaac caught sight of his badge.

"I'm going to track down the men who shot Amanda."

"Good," Isaac replied with fervor. "And I'm glad you're back to being a Ranger again. Dan said you were a good one."

He shrugged off the praise. "I do my job."

"Well, this job ain't going to be easy, but you'll do it. I was just thinking about something tonight, though—"

"What's that?"

"I'm just wondering if the ones we're looking for aren't right here in San Rafael under our noses."

Jack's gaze narrowed as he glanced at Isaac. "What are you talking about?"

"Ain't it strange how good shots like Asa and Dan can't fight these men off, but Ted can outrun them and outfight them single-handedly after Amanda was wounded? Asa's dead, Dan's wounded, Amanda is almost killed, and yet Ted comes back untouched, bragging about how he saved the payroll." He shook his head in amazement. "It sure seems strange to me."

Jack knew Isaac was right. "Keep an eye on him for me. If you see him talking to any strangers, let me know. There are a number of men involved in this, and we need to get them all."

"I will."

"Good. I'll be back as soon as I can. I appreciate all your help. Dan's lucky to have you."

"He's my friend."

Jack swung up in the saddle. He lifted his hand in farewell to Isaac, then rode off to meet Stalking Ghost. As he made his way out of town, he passed the Taylor house. His gaze was drawn to Amanda's window. It was dark in her room.

He hoped she was resting peacefully. She'd been through a lot that day. He wanted her to recover quickly. He wanted to see Amanda laughing again. He wanted her to be arguing with him. He even wanted to see her smashing liquor bottles again.

At the thought of bottles, he remembered their target-shooting lesson and what had happened when he'd taken her in his arms.

Jack deliberately forced those memories from him, though it wasn't easy. He concentrated, instead, on the conversation he'd just had with Isaac. Everything the other man had said to him about Ted was reasonable. If there was a connection to Ted in all this, he would find it.

Jack glanced one last time at Amanda's window. She might think that she cared for Ted, but if he turned out to be the one behind all the stage line's troubles, that would change. For right now, though, all he could do was track down the would-be robbers. If they had a connection to Ted, he would uncover it later.

Grimly determined in his pursuit, motivated by a fury that would not be tempered, Jack met Stalking Ghost at the edge of town, and, together, they rode for the scene of the robbery.

Amanda had not been able to rest, in spite of the exhaustion that claimed her. She was lying in bed, staring about her darkened room with haunted eyes. The entire day had been horrible. Everything had gone wrong, desperately wrong, and she didn't know what she was going to do about it.

She realized now that she'd made a terrible mistake riding out with Ted that morning. Though he was a nice man, Ted was not Jack. Eileen was right. If she'd been on a run with Jack and the attack had come, no doubt he would have saved both her and the payroll.

A lone tear traced a path down Amanda's cheek as she remembered Jack's arms around her as she'd been trying to take target practice. Loving him had been beautiful and exciting. She loved Jack Logan. She loved his strength . . . his intelligence . . . his touch.

But he didn't love her. There could never be a future for them.

It devastated her to think that he didn't want her. There was no denying it, though. He'd made it perfectly clear that he'd been sorry about what had happened between them.

The sound of a lone rider slowly passing by the house drew her attention. She wondered who it could be at this time of night, and, painfully, she got up from her bed to look out the window. She was moving slowly, but as she reached the window she caught a glimpse of the man and recognized Jack immediately. She wondered where he was going.

Behind her, the bedroom door opened quietly, and her father and Eileen peeked in.

"Amanda! What are you doing out of bed?" Eileen asked, rushing to her side for fear that she might collapse from weakness.

"We were just coming to check on you and make sure you were resting comfortably. I had no idea you would be up moving around,'' Dan added, frowning at her foolishness. He quickly lit her bedside lamp so they could see better. ''The doctor said you should stay in bed for at least two days.''

''Yes, Papa,'' she said meekly as she allowed them to help her back to bed.

''Why did you get up?'' Eileen asked as she busied herself straightening her covers.

''I heard a rider outside and went to look. It was Jack, Eileen, and he was riding out of town. Where is he going? Isn't he staying here to help you with the line, Papa?'' She looked between the two of them, desperate for answers to her questions.

''No, sweetheart,'' Dan began to explain, ''Jack and I talked earlier this evening, and he's decided to go back to work as a Ranger.''

''He's leaving forever?'' she said, shocked.

''He's going off to find the ones who shot you. He'll be back when he's got them in custody. He's determined to bring them in himself.''

''And he'll do it, too,'' Eileen told her with certainty.

''But what if something happens to him?''

''It won't.'' Eileen was firm. ''Jack's the best. You know it as well as I do. When that man makes up his mind to do something, he does it. He'll find them, Amanda, and he'll be back.''

Amanda drew a shuddering breath as she lay weakly back on her pillow. ''I hope he's careful. They're dangerous . . . and the Sheldons are still out there looking for him, too.''

''The Sheldons?'' Dan asked, frowning.

Amanda quickly explained about the outlaws who'd broken out of jail and were hunting for Jack. "He's got to watch his back. He's got to be careful."

"Jack will be. He's a professional. He doesn't take chances," Dan assured her. He pressed a soft kiss to his daughter's forehead. "Now, you get some sleep."

"I'll try."

They turned the lamp back down and left her alone again. When they were in the hall, they shared a knowing look.

"I think she cares more for our Jack than she'll admit."

"And I think he feels the same way."

"We'll just have to let nature take its course, I guess," Eileen remarked, wondering if there was any way to help Amanda recognize her feelings for Jack.

"That's the safest way, but sometimes it's the slowest way, too."

"We'll see what happens."

"Let's just pray everything goes well for him."

"I will."

Back in her room, Amanda lay staring out the window at the starry sky. She wondered if Jack was looking at the same stars. She wondered, too, if he thought of her at all.

Sleep finally claimed her, and she rested.

Dawn found Jack and Stalking Ghost poring over the scene of the attack. Stalking Ghost located the outlaws' trail right away, and they rode off in pursuit of the attackers. The going was slow, for the gang had deliberately chosen to ride over the worst terrain so it would provide the best cover for them.

But Stalking Ghost enjoyed a challenge. Working together, they never lost the tracks completely and made good time in the hunt. The outlaws were heading north, and the only town in that direction was Del Cuero, a hard two days' ride ahead. It had a reputation for being wild and deadly, and no doubt the gang could hide out there and feel safe.

Jack planned to change all that. They kept moving at a steady, ground-eating pace as they trailed the outlaws. Their days of freedom were numbered.

Pete and Mick sat at the table in the back of the Gold Nugget Saloon in Del Cuero, nursing their drinks and their foul moods. The fake robbery attempt on the stage was supposed to have been easy, but from the minute they'd fired the first shot, there had been nothing easy about it.

"Damn," Pete swore as he tried to move his injured arm. He'd been shot in the shoulder, and even now, after three days, he was still in considerable pain. Of course, he was much better off than Rich and Merle. They were dead. "If I ever get my hands on Carroll—"

"You'll have to drag me off of him, because I'll be there before you," Mick told him. He had seen his friends killed and had almost been wounded himself. "I kept thinking he'd send some word to us to let us know what went wrong, but he ain't done nothing."

"Good thing he paid us up front, but he still didn't pay me enough to take a bullet for him."

"He didn't pay Rich or Merle enough either," Mick added. "I hope there wasn't trouble back in San Rafael. Surely, if there had been, we would have heard by now."

"Whatever happened, I guess he just wants us to lay low for a while."

"I don't mind laying low, but if he comes up with any more ideas like this last one, I'm moving on."

"I think we should move on now. What with only the two of us left standing, there ain't a lot we can do, and I don't want to bring anybody new in on this."

"I'm with you on that. Let's give it a few more days and see what we hear from Ted. Then we'll see what we're doing next."

It was late afternoon and the streets of Del Cuero were busy as Jack rode in alone. His pace was slow and his manner cautious. He was wearing his Ranger badge and had his hat pulled down low over his eyes. He looked dangerous, like the kind of man you didn't want to anger, and more than a few heads turned to watch him as he rode silently by.

Jack and Stalking Ghost hadn't been sure exactly who they were after until they'd found the graves late the first day out. Once Jack had identified the remains of Merle Jones and Rich Lavel, he'd known the other two they were tracking. It had to be Pete Martin and Mick Humes.

Jack remembered the four men from his early years as a Ranger. They had been only small-time thieves then, so it looked as though they'd graduated to more exciting endeavors now.

One thing troubled Jack, though, and that was that none of them was smart enough to have coordinated all the robberies. He was anxious to catch up with them, but he had to be careful about shooting first and asking questions later. He would have liked nothing better than to gun them down on sight. He wanted revenge for Amanda, Asa, and Dan, but he knew if Martin and Humes were dead, they wouldn't be able to tell him who the boss was, and he wanted the man—or woman—behind it all.

Jack reined in at the stable and moved through the building, casually checking the horses there. He found the stallion with the partially broken shoe boarded there. Their luck had held.

"Can I help you?" Harry, the stable owner, asked in a gruff, threatening voice as he came up behind Jack. He wondered what this stranger was doing in his stable, looking over his horses.

Jack slowly turned to face him. "I'm just checking a few things out here."

"You're a Ranger?" the big, burly man's eyes widened as he saw Jack's badge.

"That's right. Jack Logan's the name. Do you know who owns this horse?"

Harry was suddenly nervous. His beady eyes shifted from the horse to Jack and back. He knew damn good and well that it was Pete Martin's mount. "Why're you asking?"

"I've been tracking a horse with a broken shoe just like this one all the way from the scene of a stage robbery near San Rafael. Thought I might have a talk

311

with its owner." He spoke in easy tones, but there was no mistaking the steel behind his words.

Harry looked at the Ranger badge again and knew it was time to cut and run. You didn't mess with the Texas Rangers. Everyone knew they could ride like Mexicans, track like Indians, shoot like the Tennesseans and fight like the devil. He didn't want to get on the wrong side of them. "That particular horse belongs to Pete Martin."

Jack knew he was telling the truth. "Any idea where I might find Mr. Martin?"

"He and his partner, Mick Humes, have rooms over at the Gold Nugget. It's just down the street."

"Thanks."

"Can I see to your horse for you?" Harry offered.

"No, I don't plan on staying in town long enough to use your facilities, but thanks for the offer."

"Don't mention it."

With that, Jack mounted up and rode down the street to the saloon. He dismounted with careful deliberation and walked into the bar.

It was a quiet time at the Gold Nugget. Only one girl and the barkeep were working, and there were just a few customers partaking of the saloon's hospitality. Jack surveyed the patrons in a single glance and knew Humes and Martin weren't among them.

He glanced up at the balcony that ran across the width of the room. The doors to the rented rooms opened onto it and would give anyone coming out a clear view of all that was transpiring below.

Jack went to the bar and ordered a drink. He nursed it, enjoying the bite of the liquor.

"What brings you to town?" Jim, the barkeep, asked, trying to make conversation.

"Just trying to catch up with a few friends. Heard that they were staying here and thought I'd see if I could find them."

The barkeep worked at polishing the bar in front of him as he spoke. "Who you looking for?"

"Two men—Pete Martin and Mick Humes. You wouldn't happen to know which rooms they're stayin' in, would you?"

Jim looked decidedly uncomfortable, but knew he had no choice. He had heard what Rangers could do to a place if something upset them, so he decided to tell the truth. "They're both upstairs. Humes is in number five; Martin's in eight."

"I appreciate it."

The bartender only grunted, disgusted with being put in such a position. He moved away, not wanting to be anywhere close when the inevitable happened.

As Jack finished his drink, his thoughts were on Amanda. He remembered how pale and fragile she'd looked after being shot, and a cold and ruthless determination filled him. He started up the steps after the men who'd almost killed Amanda. They had murdered Asa, wounded Dan and robbed the stage line numerous times. It was time to see them put away.

He approached room five first. He drew his gun, then knocked on the door.

"Who is it?" Mick called out in a slurred voice.

Jack didn't respond. He knocked again, and stepped back and to the side to wait for his quarry to physically answer the door.

Mick was irritated that someone was playing games with him. He was still half-drunk from what he'd imbibed earlier that day, and he was in no mood to put up with anything or anyone. He didn't even think about picking up his gun as he stumbled drunkenly from his bed to open the door.

"What the hell do you want?" he roared angrily as he opened the portal to find himself staring down the barrel of Jack's gun. "What the—"

"You're under arrest for—"

Jack got no further. Mick turned and dove toward the table beside his bed where he'd left his sidearm. Jack was too fast for him. He fired, his shot taking the wanted man in the shoulder. Mick gave a scream of pain as he collapsed on the floor in agony. Jack moved into the room and picked up Mick's gun, then went back to the doorway to watch for Pete.

Just down the hall, Pete had heard the sound of the gunfire and grabbed his revolver. He ran from his room to find Jack standing in the hall, a gun in each hand.

"Hello, Martin. I see you're still working with your old partner, Humes, here."

"What the hell . . . ?"

"Hell's where you're going if you try to use that gun," Jack said in a cold voice. "Just put it down on the floor and kick it aside. I'd hate for any accidents to happen."

"Who are you? What do you want?"

"The name's Logan, Ranger Jack Logan, and I'm here to arrest the two of you for the murder of Asa Taylor and the wounding of Amanda and Dan Taylor."

# *Chapter Eighteen*

"We never killed nobody!" Pete shouted after he'd done what Jack had ordered him to do and kicked his gun away.

"I guess we'll have to let a jury decide that." Jack had expected them to lie and claim they were innocent.

"I'm telling you, Logan—we didn't do it!"

Jack gestured him toward Mick's room with his gun. Pete moved quickly. As he entered the room, he was shocked to see an Indian climb through the window. He looked back at the Ranger, thinking he would be surprised, too, but Jack just tossed the Indian two pairs of handcuffs.

"Restrain them, Stalking Ghost," Jack told him.

Pete watched as Stalking Ghost handcuffed the wounded Mick and then came toward him. He was tempted to run, to try to fight his way out of there, but knew there was no escape. He knew he wouldn't make it to the door.

Once Jack was certain that the two outlaws wouldn't be causing any more trouble, he holstered his gun and set Mick's aside. He went to the wounded man and examined his shoulder.

"He's going to have to see a doctor before we can ride for San Rafael."

"I'll get him."

Just as Stalking Ghost started from the room, the sheriff of Del Cuero, Ken Barnes, came running into the saloon. The patrons told him the shooting had happened upstairs. He took the steps two at a time, ready for trouble.

"The sheriff is here," Stalking Ghost told Jack.

Jack moved to the doorway to greet the lawman as Stalking Ghost continued on his way to get the doctor. "I'm Ranger Logan, and I'm taking Pete Martin and Mick Humes in for robbery and murder."

"Sheriff," Pete pleaded. "I keep telling him we didn't kill nobody, but he won't listen!"

"You know for sure you got the right ones?"

"Tracked them all the way here."

Barnes nodded. He knew how good the Rangers were. "You need any help taking them back or do you want to use the jail until you're ready to go?"

"Thanks. If you could lock up Martin for me until the doctor's had a chance to patch up Humes, I'd appreciate it."

"No problem." The sheriff marched Pete from the room. "I'll be waiting to hear from you."

Jack helped Mick onto his bed after the sheriff and Pete had gone.

"You bastard!" Mick swore as pain jolted through him with each move he made.

Jack's regard was deadly. "You keep talking like that, you'll be making the trip to San Rafael without seeing the doctor. It wouldn't trouble me in the least, and it might keep you from trying anything."

"Pete told you we didn't kill nobody. Why don't you believe us?"

"Why should I?"

"Because there's more to this than just stage robberies," he said earnestly.

Jack eyed him suspiciously. "My information places you and your partner at the scene of the robbery near San Rafael less than a week ago. Why should I believe there's more to it than that?"

"Because there is."

"That's what they all say," Jack replied disparagingly. "Look, Humes, I've already found the bodies of your other two partners where you buried them on the way here."

He walked over to the small dresser where Mick had left his saddlebags. He opened them and pulled out a stack of bills, still banded, that had been part of the payroll from the earlier robbery.

"And this just proves it all. This money was part of that take, and whoever robbed the stage a few weeks ago murdered Asa Taylor and severely injured Dan Taylor. One of you also shot and nearly killed Amanda Taylor during this last attempt."

Mick was nervous. He knew things looked bad, but he also knew he hadn't done any killing. "The money proves the robbery part, all right, but I'm telling you, we didn't kill anybody.''

"If you didn't, who did?" Jack waited tensely for his answer.

Just then Stalking Ghost returned with the doctor, and he was forced to wait for his answer. The physician made quick work of treating the wound. The bullet had passed through, so the wound was relatively clean. He bound his patient up tightly and pronounced him fit enough to ride. Jack paid the man for his time. Stalking Ghost went downstairs when the doctor departed, leaving Jack alone with Mick.

"You were about to answer my question."

"What's in it for me?"

"I think you should be more concerned about what's going to happen to you if you don't tell me." Jack was in no mood to negotiate. He had won.

"All right . . . All right . . . We were in on it from the start . . . all four of us. But something went wrong the other day. He'd told us the robbery was supposed to be a fake. He wanted us to make the attempt, but then let ourselves be driven back by his return fire."

"*His return fire—*" Jack repeated Mick's words as Isaac's suspicions were confirmed.

"Ted Carroll. He hired us to disrupt the stage line's business. He wanted to take it over and sell it off. He even rode with us that time when the one owner was killed and the other one was wounded. He's the one who wanted them dead. He did the shooting, but he didn't do a very good job. And then with this fake attempt . . . I don't know what the hell he was thinking, setting that up. He said he wanted us to make him look good, but it was no game to whoever was riding shotgun. He meant business.''

"That was no man. That was Amanda Taylor," Jack ground out.

"The shotgun was a woman?" Mick was completely shocked.

"That's right.''

He shook his head in disbelief. "She's the one who shot Merle. Ted should have warned us that things had changed. After Merle got shot, we decided to even the score a bit.''

At that moment, if Jack had had his gun in his hand, he could easily have administered his own brand of justice and saved himself a long trip back to San Rafael. But he was glad he was under control. He wanted Ted Carroll behind bars, and he would need Humes and Martin to testify against him to do it. "You'll testify to Carroll's involvement?''

"Damn right I will. All this was his idea. I ain't gonna hang for the likes of him. He should get what's coming to him.''

"He will." Jack's words were hard.

Mick wasn't a man given to fear, but the look in the Ranger's eye and the tone of his voice sent a shiver of apprehension through him. He was glad he wasn't Ted Carroll.

Jack called Stalking Ghost back up to the room and left him with Mick, while he went to talk to Pete at the sheriff's office. Pete told him almost exactly the same things Mick had, and he was glad. They had had no time to make up a story, so this version was the truth.

It was a truth Jack was going to be glad to deliver to Dan.

They saddled up their horses and started off for San Rafael. Jack wanted to get back as quickly as he could. He wanted Ted revealed for what he was.

It was the fourth day after the robbery, and Amanda was finally feeling well enough to be up and around. Still, Dan had forbidden her to go back to work just yet. He wanted to make sure she was completely well before she returned to the office.

"I wish Papa would let me go back to work," Amanda complained as she sat in the parlor with Eileen, doing nothing of consequence. "I'm not used to being idle for this long."

"It's for the best, dear. He understands how much you like to keep busy, and he's afraid you'll over-do if you go back too soon."

"Over-doing would be far preferable to under-doing," she retorted.

"You must be feeling better. You're starting to argue with me." Eileen smiled at Amanda, quite pleased at her show of spirit.

"There are times when I get a little dizzy, but other than that I really do feel fine."

"Good. When I remember how terrible you looked right after the shooting . . . Jack and I were so afraid that you were going to die. Thank heaven, you're fine now. I wonder how Jack is doing, though. There's been no word from him since he left."

"He was going to come back here, wasn't he?"

"That's what I understood. But he did say he wasn't

coming back until he'd found the men who'd shot you.''

''That could take months. Look at the trouble the sheriff's had finding the robbers. Maybe Jack will never find them.''

''Oh, I don't know. He was going back to work as a Ranger, and I get the feeling that Rangers never give up. He'll find them and he'll bring them in. He said he would and he will.''

A knock at the door drew Eileen to answer it.

''Why, Ted. This is a surprise,'' she said. ''Can I help you with anything?''

''Actually, I'm here to see Amanda. Dan had mentioned that she was feeling a little better, so I thought I'd drop by and visit for a while.''

''Ted?'' Amanda heard his voice and came out of the parlor.

''Hello, Amanda,'' he said, his gaze warm upon her. She looked fully recovered, and he was glad.

''Come in,'' Amanda invited him, noticing how the swelling had gone down around his nose.

''You're looking much better,'' he said.

''Thanks.''

They walked into the parlor and sat on the sofa.

Ted was pleased when Eileen left them alone to talk. Things had been going smoothly for him since the fake robbery. As long as Jack didn't catch up with Humes and the others, everything was going to be fine.

''How have you been?'' Amanda asked him.

''We've been working hard,'' he told her. ''I've been helping your father as much as I can, and things seem to be going all right, for now.''

"I appreciate your standing by him. I know it means a lot to him to have someone he can rely on."

"I'm glad to do it." He smiled at her, feeling very confident. The way things were looking, all he had to do was get Amanda to the altar and the stage line would ultimately be his. He was relatively certain that with just a little courting, she would fall right into his arms.

"With any luck, I can be back working with you soon."

"You're feeling that much better?"

"Yes, I am. In fact, I'm almost ready to argue with my father and convince him to let me go back to work."

"There's no need for you to hurry back," he said quickly. "Take all the time you need. We're doing fine right now."

"Are you sure? With Jack gone, I was worried."

"What does Jack have to do with anything? He was only riding shotgun for us."

"He was the best gun we had," she said defensively.

"I don't know why you care about him. All along you said he was only in this for the money."

Ted's well-chosen reminder stung. Amanda was quiet for a moment, trying to think of the right way to phrase what she wanted to say. Then she answered, "I guess I care because he's proved himself to be a true friend."

"I'm glad you said a 'friend,' " Ted said silkily.

"Why?" She was puzzled.

"Because for a moment, I was afraid you were thinking of him in another way."

"And what if I was?"

"Well, I can tell you, he's not the man for you."

"Why?"

Ted had been waiting for quite a while to feed her this information. He leaned toward her as he answered, "I was down in the saloon one night last week, and one of the girls was talking about Jack. She was bragging about how much he'd paid her for her services that night."

Amanda paled at his statement. *Last week . . . Just last week she and Jack had been together. . . . They had made love last week. . . .* And Jack had been with one of the saloon girls at almost the very same time.

"Do saloon girls really do that? Do they really brag about the men they consort with?"

"Of course. They're proud of their accomplishments, but I didn't bring that up to upset you. I just wanted you to know what kind of man you're dealing with."

Amanda looked at Ted and saw that his expression was sympathetic. She was devastated by this news about Jack and the saloon girl. As her gaze met Ted's, she could sense that he wanted to kiss her, so she leaned slightly toward him to encourage him. She wanted to prove to herself that she could enjoy his kiss, that he could excite her the way that Jack did.

Ted needed no further encouragement. He slipped an arm around her and drew her closer to him as his mouth moved over hers.

Amanda wanted to be thrilled by his embrace, especially after this devastating news he'd just brought her about Jack and the saloon girl. But Ted's kiss evoked no wild, mindless response in her. No matter how she pretended, Ted was not Jack. Disappointment filled her as he ended the kiss and she drew away.

Ted was completely unaware of her thoughts. He thought things were going magnificently. He thought she was very close to being in love with him.

"Amanda . . . You are so special to me," he told her, looking into her eyes.

She was caught off guard by his unexpected display of devotion, and she only managed a smile.

"I am so thankful that you've recovered. You can't imagine how frantic I was that day when you were shot."

"I appreciate all you did for me, Ted," Amanda reassured him.

"I just wish it had never happened. I never want anything to happen to you," he said. "I want you safe and happy."

Amanda felt trapped by the intensity of his gaze and words. "Well, I'm safe now, and I'll be very happy once Jack gets back with the robbers."

Ted grew angry at her mentioning Jack again. He was about to say something when Eileen entered the room.

"Were you talking about Jack, Amanda? Has there been any word yet?"

"No, nothing yet. I was just telling Ted that I'll be happy again once I know the gang is behind bars."

"That we will," Eileen agreed.

"I hope Jack is as good as you think he is." Ted

ground his teeth at their confidence in Jack. If the gang was caught and brought in, he would be in trouble.

"He is," Eileen said. "If they're anywhere in Texas, he'll catch them."

When the older woman settled in to chat with them, Ted knew he had to leave. He'd wanted time alone with Amanda, and luckily he'd gotten at least a few minutes with her. He rose, said his good-byes and went back to the stage office.

"You look quite thoughtful, Amanda. What's on your mind?" Eileen asked when he'd gone.

"I don't know. I like Ted. I truly do, but . . ." She sighed, trying to put into words what she was feeling.

"But he's just not the man for you?"

"I suppose that's it. He's nice, but lately, it seems he wants to be more than friends . . . and I don't know if that's possible."

"I understand completely. After my Andrew died . . . Well, no other man could ever measure up to him. The right man for you is out there, Amanda."

"If I even need a 'right man,' " she said quickly, angry at the news Ted had brought her about Jack. "You've been happy by yourself, haven't you?"

Eileen looked sad for a moment, then managed to smile. "Yes. I've lived a wonderful life. But sometimes, I allow myself to dream of what it would have been like had Andrew returned to me. It would have been so special to have a family of my own . . . children and grandchildren." She paused, realizing she sounded a bit maudlin. "I'm sorry. Yes, you can be happy alone. You just have to make up your mind that you're going to enjoy every minute of every day and live life to the fullest. Then everything else falls into place.''

"Then that's what I'm going to do. Once Papa lets me out of this house.''

"Shall we play cards?'' Eileen suggested. "I'm not very good, but it does help to pass the time.''

"Let's. Maybe we can figure out how to play poker.'' She shot her friend a wicked look. "If Papa won't let me go back to work, maybe I'll start up a gaming parlor here.''

"Believe me when I tell you that he'd much rather have you at the stage office.''

"That's what I thought.'' She grinned devilishly. "Maybe I'll bring up the gaming parlor idea at dinner tonight.''

"And be back to work tomorrow.''

"Exactly.''


Ted was about to retire for the night when Mona called out to him from in the parlor.

"What have you heard about the Ranger?''

"Nothing, absolutely nothing. I wish to hell I did know something, but we haven't heard a thing.''

"Are you sure the men you hired are smart enough to avoid Logan?''

"I hope so. They've been at it for years and have never been caught.''

"No one was ever killed before, though.''

"No, but that doesn't matter. They're going to know that the law will be after them for a while, so if they've got any brains at all, they'll stay out of sight.''

"I hope you're right, but they've never had the Rangers after them before."

"I know. It's going to be a long wait, until we hear something." He was tense at the thought that Jack just might find the outlaws and bring them in.

"You don't think we should cut and run, do you? There's a little bit of money left in Asa's account. I could take that and we could disappear."

"And look guilty? I don't run."

"Wise men know when to cut their losses."

"I'm not losing," he declared hotly. "Amanda's almost mine. It's just a matter of a few more weeks, and I'll propose. Then everything will fall into place. I'll take over the entire stage line and we'll both be set for life."

"All right. I'm trusting in your judgment, Ted. You'd better not be wrong."

"Mother, when have I ever been wrong?" He gave her a dismissive glance.

Mona watched him walk from the room, her gaze narrowing as she went over what she knew. They had never considered a Ranger getting involved. Things were not going well, and she had an uneasy feeling about it. Her instincts told her to get out of San Rafael as soon as possible.

Hank Sheldon was really enjoying himself with the girl named Nina. She was young and pretty and knew what he wanted, and he liked that in a woman. She didn't waste time talking. She just pleasured him, and that was what a woman was supposed to do.

They'd been up in her room at the saloon for most

of the night, and he wasn't a happy man when his brother started pounding on the door.

"What the hell does he want?" he snarled as he stopped making love to the willing Nina.

"Ignore him," she murmured, moving against him to help him forget his brother.

Hank buried his face in her breasts for a moment, enjoying the bounteous fare, but Willy would not go away. With a groan, Hank put Nina from him and stood up.

"This better damned well be important." He pulled on his pants.

Nina started to cover herself, but he grabbed her wrist.

"No. Leave the covers just like that. I like to see you naked."

"But your brother—" She glanced toward the door.

"If he thinks you're pretty enough, he may want to try you, too." He gave a derisive laugh at her ludicrous modesty as he caressed her breast one more time before going to answer the door. She was a whore. Since Chica's betrayal, he would treat them all alike from now on.

"Hank! You in there?" Willy was shouting. He didn't care if his brother was with a woman. He had something important to show him.

"What the hell do you want?" Hank demanded as he threw the door open.

"I gotta talk to you, man," Willy told him, and then he caught a glimpse of the nude woman on Hank's bed and realized his brother had not just been sleeping, he'd been busy—real busy.

"I got company."

"I don't care. You're gonna want to see this right now." Willy was ogling Nina and trying to concentrate on what he had to tell Hank.

"What?"

"Read this!" He shoved a page of the Rock Water newspaper into his brother's hands, all the while gazing hungrily at the woman who was giving him an inviting look from where she lay posing on the bed.

*"Del Cuero. Mick Humes and Pete Martin were arrested today by Texas Ranger Jack Logan for a series of armed stage robberies and murder in San Rafael. Ranger Logan is taking them back to San Rafael for trial."* Hank looked up at his brother. "Son of a bitch . . . We found him! How old is the paper?"

"It's two days old. He's got a head start on us."

"It don't matter. All that matters is we know where he is. He's in San Rafael, and real soon he's gonna be six feet under."

They shared a look of mutual bloodlust.

"You done with that?" Willy asked, pointing toward Nina.

"Yeah. You go ahead and help yourself. I'm going downstairs for a celebration drink."

Willy advanced into the room. He started to undress as his brother finished throwing on his clothes.

"Hank?" Nina looked at her lover, wondering what he was doing.

"I've got business to tend to, and so do you, sweetheart. This is my little brother. You take care of him nice and good now, you hear?"

"But Hank . . . It's you I want."

He walked to the side of the bed and dragged her up to him. He kissed her savagely and pawed at her breasts before almost throwing her from him. "You're just like all the others, Nina. You say you want me, but the minute I'm gone, you'll have somebody else between your legs."

Nina felt tears burn in her eyes. His touch had been painful. "And you are just like all the other men. The minute you are gone, you will find another woman to warm your bed."

"That's right, and don't forget that. It'll save you a lot of trouble. Now, take care of Willy here. I think he likes you a lot."

Hank left the room chuckling. It had been a very good day, and tomorrow promised to be even better. He knew where Jack Logan was. His revenge was almost complete.

When he'd closed the door behind him, Willy threw off his clothes and went to Nina. She cowered before him, still frightened by the unexpected violence she'd sensed in Hank. Willy liked her fear. It made him feel powerful. He grabbed her by the wrists and threw her back on the bed, falling heavily on top of her. He had no time for foreplay. He knew what he wanted, and he took it, roughly. It didn't matter that she was crying and begging him not to hurt her. After all, she was only a whore.

An hour later, Willy went downstairs to find Hank. Hank was at the bar, enjoying his whiskey. Willy ordered a shot, too, and took a deep drink.

"When do you want to ride for San Rafael?" Willy asked.

"First light. The sooner I get there, the happier I'm gonna be. We got him now. After all these weeks of searching, we finally got him."

"We ain't got him yet. I'm not gonna be happy about this until I see him lying dead in the dirt."

Hank smiled tightly at him as he drew his revolver and spun the chamber with practiced ease. "Don't worry. Jack Logan is ours. He ain't getting away from us. One way or the other, within the week, Logan is a dead man."

# Chapter Nineteen

It had taken an extra day for Jack and Stalking Ghost to make the return trip to San Rafael with their prisoners because Mick's injuries had slowed their pace. But Jack was feeling real good as they rode into town on that third day and headed straight for the sheriff's office.

"Do you think the lawman will be there?" Stalking Ghost asked.

"Yeah. He wasn't able to find the gang before now, so I doubt he's wasting much energy still trying to find them."

As they reined in before the jail, Jack's prediction proved true. Sheriff Riley was sitting at his desk, studying some wanted posters. He looked up only when they walked in.

"What the . . . ?"

"Afternoon, Sheriff. I tracked down the men who shot Amanda and attempted to rob the stage."

332

"But how? Where were they? I took a posse out, but we lost the tracks on the rocks about ten miles away from the scene of the robbery."

"I had good help," Jack said, casting an appreciative glance toward Stalking Ghost. "We caught up to them in Del Cuero. They've confessed to the robberies and had a few other things to tell me that I think you'll find interesting."

"Well, bring them on in and we'll lock them up right now." Riley hurried around his desk to get the keys.

They locked Mick and Pete in a jail cell.

"What's the additional information you said they had?" the lawman asked once they were secure.

"You boys want to tell the good sheriff all you know?" Jack prodded.

They looked resentful and didn't answer at first, knowing things were going to get real exciting once the truth was out.

"We can try you for murder, you know. I found the money in your possession, and I tracked you the entire distance. What's it going to be? Do you want to talk to the sheriff or the judge?"

"All right, all right . . . We'll tell you everything."

Pete and Mick exchanged looks, and then Pete started talking.

"It's like we was telling Ranger Logan. We did the robberies, but we didn't do no killing. The man who hired us is the one who shot Asa Taylor dead and shot Dan Taylor in the back. He would have gotten away with it, too, if they'd both died."

"Who is he?" Riley demanded, outraged that there

was a sinister plot behind all the robberies.

"Ted Carroll. He's the one who planned it all with his mother. They thought with both Taylor men dead, the stage line would be theirs."

"And it would have been, if he'd been a better shot," Jack said. "Thank God, he wasn't."

"It was Carroll? All this time, it was him?" Riley was shocked. "But he's family!"

"That's right. I'd like to take Ted and Mona Carroll into custody right away. They might try to leave town if they get word that I'm back and that I've brought in these two."

"Of course. I'll go with you."

Riley checked his sidearm and grabbed a rifle out of the gun case. He put his deputy in charge of keeping an eye on the prisoners, and they started off to find Ted.

"It's three o'clock. They should both be at the stage office," Jack told him.

They made their way across town to the depot. Jack spotted Isaac by the stable and only nodded in response to his surprised wave. He didn't want to take the chance of alerting Ted to his presence. He saw Isaac frown, and he knew the other man understood that something important was about to happen.

"Jack!" Dan looked up as the door opened. He was thrilled to see Jack enter the office followed by Sheriff Riley. "You're back already! Did you find them?"

Jack's gaze swept the office, looking for Ted, but he saw no sign of him. Only Dan was there. "Yes, I found them, and after today, you're not going to be having any more trouble."

"Who were they? Where are they?"

"I brought two of them in, and they're locked up right now over at the jail. Two were killed during the last robbery attempt, and there are two more we've come to arrest."

"Two more?" Dan was shocked.

Jack's gaze was solemn as he met Dan's. "Where's Ted? And Mona? Have you seen them today?"

"Yes, but—why do you want Ted?" Dan was staring at him, trying to come to grips with the implications of Jack's question.

Jack went to his friend. "The two I brought in are Mick Humes and Pete Martin. They were recruited by Ted, along with two other men, to harass the stage line. He wanted you and Asa dead so he could take over. Ted was the one who shot you in the back. When you lived through the attack, he had to come up with a new plan, so he set up this last robbery as a fake to make himself look good. I guess he realized that Isaac had some doubts about him, and he wanted to come out of it a hero. His plan was to win your confidence and convince you and Amanda to either sell out or give it to him to run. Either way, he and Mona would come out of this with a lot of money."

"The bastard!" Dan was seething. "He killed his own stepfather."

"And he tried to kill you. He's the reason Amanda was wounded."

"I'm going to kill him—" Dan rose from behind his desk, grabbing for the gun he kept in the top drawer.

"No, Dan." Jack reached out and stilled his arm.

"Leave the gun here. Let the law handle this. Ted will get what's coming to him."

"You're damned right he will!" Dan was still not very strong, and he was shaking from the power of his fury. "And so will Mona!"

"Where is Ted?"

"He's taken to making regular stops by the house to visit Amanda. He should be there with her right now."

"Let's go."

Dan called out to Isaac to take charge of the office, and the other man hurried inside.

"Is it what we thought?" Isaac asked Jack.

"You were right. It was Ted the whole time."

"You suspected him?" Dan looked at Isaac in surprise, but with renewed respect.

"It sure seemed strange to me that all this trouble started up right after he got here, and how on that last robbery, he managed to outrun them when you and Asa couldn't. I know how that man drives, and there's no way he's a better driver than you are. I told Jack what I thought before he left to track the gang. Looks like my hunch was right." He was glad that he'd recognized the danger, but sorry that he hadn't figured it out sooner.

"We're going to arrest him now. He won't be causing any more trouble," the sheriff said.

"Be careful," Isaac cautioned. "He's going to be like a cornered animal. There ain't no telling what he might try to do."

"We will."

The three men left the stage office and hurried to

the Taylor home. Dan didn't hesitate but opened the door and walked in with Jack and Sheriff Riley following behind.

Amanda was in the parlor with Ted, enjoying what had become his ritual afternoon visit. Today, Ted had brought her a small bouquet. She knew he was actively courting her, but even though she would have liked to be able to care for him, it wasn't to be. No matter how illogical, her heart still belonged to Jack.

"Papa?" she said when Dan came into the parlor. "What are you doing home so early? Aren't you feeling well?" she asked, rising from the sofa to meet him. She was surprised to find Jack and the sheriff in the front hall, too. "But why are . . . ?"

"Ted?" Dan forged ahead to confront the man responsible for his brother's death.

"Yes, Dan?" Ted stood up, wondering what he wanted with him. He'd been relaxed, playing the ardent suitor, and he was caught off guard by Jack stepping into the room behind Dan. He struggled to keep his panic from showing. "Jack . . . You're back. Did you catch up with them? What did you find out?"

"Jack found out exactly who was responsible for all the trouble around here. Jack found out exactly who shot Asa and me during the robbery, and who was responsible for Amanda's being wounded."

"That's wonderful! Who was it? Did you lock them up?"

"You low-life, son of a bitch!" Dan started to swing at him.

Ted was ready. He moved quickly, darting out of

his way, and drew the derringer he kept in his pocket. "Stay back—all of you."

"Ted—what are you doing?" Amanda was staring at him aghast, trying to figure out what was going on.

"Amanda, get behind us," Jack ordered. "Ted here, along with his mother, has been running the gang that's been robbing the stage line."

"Ted!" She looked at him and finally saw the evil gleam in his eyes. "This can't be true!"

"Oh, but it is, my dear. And things would have worked out just fine, if your father had died in the damned robbery! But once he started to recover I had to change my plans to sell the stage line. That's where you came in."

"Me?" Amanda repeated.

"Oh, yes. I had planned to pay you off, but once you came back here to live, I decided to marry into the money. I was almost there, too."

Amanda's temper was hot as she glared at him. She didn't care if he was holding a gun or not. He had killed her uncle and seriously wounded her father. He deserved to rot in hell. "You overestimate your attractiveness, Ted. I had no intention of becoming involved with you. I've never cared for you other than as a friend."

"That's not what your kisses said."

She laughed at him disparagingly. "I don't care for you, Ted, and I never would have married you. Not when I love someone else!"

"Someone else?" Her words did the damage she'd hoped they would.

Jack was surprised by Amanda's declaration. He

had thought Ted was the man she loved, but he had no time to worry about it at that moment. "Drop the gun, Ted, and surrender. You're not going anywhere. There are three of us here who are planning to stop you."

"Four!" Amanda said.

"I can take some of you with me!" Ted declared.

"Don't be stupid," Sheriff Riley told him. "Just put down the gun and come with us."

Ted was furious. All of his plans, all of his dreams, destroyed . . . He knew then, if he was going to kill one of them, it was going to be Jack. He must be the one Amanda loved. Well, let her go on loving a corpse.

"The hell with all of you!" Ted shouted as he lifted the gun to fire.

Suddenly, seemingly out of nowhere, a dining room chair came sliding across the floor toward him, catching him unaware and forcing him to jump back. In that instant, as he lost his balance, Jack made his move. He tackled Ted, throwing him to the floor. The derringer went off, but the shot went wild.

Jack held nothing back as he throttled Ted soundly. The fight was over almost before it had begun. Jack knelt over Ted, ready to hit him, until he realized the man was already unconscious. In disgust, Jack released the hold he had on his shirt and let him drop back to the floor.

"Here's your man, Sheriff."

Riley hurried to cuff the prisoner.

Jack slowly got to his feet. He glanced toward the

front hall and smiled at Eileen, who was peeking around the corner.

"You just saved our lives. I told you you were an angel," he said.

"I was so afraid for you."

"You were wonderful." Jack went to her and gave her a hug.

Eileen sagged weakly against him. Dan saw her nervous distress and hurried to her side.

"Let me help you sit down." He put an arm around her waist and led her to a chair nearby.

"Thank you, Dan. I saw that man holding the gun on you, and I knew I had to do something."

"You were terrific," Amanda told her. "And you're getting very good at coming to the rescue—what with Jennings on the boat and now Ted."

"What happened on the boat?" her father asked. They'd told him the trip was uneventful.

"Oh . . . nothing." Eileen tried to brush it off as unimportant.

Dan glanced from Jack to Amanda, but they feigned innocent looks. Riley dragged the slowly reviving Ted to his feet and shoved him toward the door.

"Let's leave him at the jail and go after Mona."

"I'm coming with you," Dan declared, and neither man would deny him.

"So am I," Amanda said, following them.

"Amanda, I don't think—" her father started, but then he saw the look in her eyes and recognized it as the stubbornness that matched his own. "All right, but be careful and stay with me." He looked over at Eileen. "Will you be all right here by yourself?"

"Maria is here. I'll be fine," she told Dan with a smile.

"We'll be back," Dan said.

As Eileen watched him walk out of the room, she suddenly realized what a handsome, vital man he was, and her pulse quickened. She hoped everything went smoothly with Mona, for she was eager for Dan to come back.

They took Ted straight to the jail and locked him in with Mick and Pete.

"He looks damned good behind bars," Dan said as he stared at the man who'd killed his brother. "I hope he stays there for a long time."

"He will. Don't worry," the sheriff assured him.

They made their way to Mona's house.

"We're looking for Mrs. Taylor," Sheriff Riley told Mona's maid when she answered the door.

"She's not here."

"Do you know when she'll be back?"

"No, sir."

Dan had been standing back, trying to control his fury, but this was the last straw. He knew in his gut that Mona was in that house, and he was going to drag her out of it.

"Get out of the way," he ordered the sheriff. "This is my brother's home and I'm going to take a look around."

He and Amanda stalked into the house, sending the maid scurrying.

"I'll check upstairs," Amanda said as she started up the steps.

"Wait. I'm going with you." Jack was immediately

by her side. She was unarmed and possibly confronting a desperate woman. He would not let her go alone.

Riley went with Dan as they searched the main floor.

Amanda and Jack entered separate bedrooms, looking under beds and in closets.

Jack had a sense that she was there, close. His instincts were screaming a warning. Pausing in the doorway of the next bedroom, he looked around for some sign that she might be hiding there. The only sign that something might be amiss was the hairbrush on the floor next to the dressing table. He strode across the room and stooped down to pick up the brush.

In that moment, Mona made her move. She'd been caught upstairs when she'd seen them coming toward the house, and she'd called down to her servant to tell them that she wasn't home. Desperate for a weapon and almost out of time to hide, she grabbed up the small hunting knife that had been Asa's and hid in the closet in her bedroom. But Jack was in her room now, searching for her and there was no escape unless she attacked.

Opening the closet door quietly while his back was to her, Mona raised the knife and started toward him. If she could kill Jack, it might give her time to slip out the back way and get to a horse.

"Jack!"

Amanda's call came just as Jack sensed a movement behind him. He turned and faced the horror of his nightmare. Mona was charging at him, a blade gleaming in her hand, a look of crazed hatred in her eyes as she raised her arm to stab him.

He met her attack face-on, grabbing her wrist and violently twisting the knife from her hand.

"Damn you!" Mona shrieked, struggling against him.

Amanda ran in and grabbed up the knife. Mona was powerful in her fury, but Jack finally subdued her just as the others came running into the room.

"Mona!" Dan said in disgust as he came to stand before her.

"I hate you, Dan Taylor!" she snarled at him as she fought against Jack's dominating hold. "Ted and I had it all figured out. . . . Everything was going to work out perfectly. . . . Asa would be dead and you, too. But damn you! You didn't die!"

"No, I didn't," Dan said without emotion.

"I hope you go to hell!"

His regard was cold. "The feeling is mutual, Mona." He turned away from the sight of her still struggling to escape from Jack's iron grip. "Let's go home, Amanda."

Amanda rushed to his side, and together they headed toward home. Their hearts were heavy with the knowledge of the betrayal that had devastated their family.

"Let's get her to the jail," Jack said.

He didn't trust Mona and refused to ease his hold on her for even an instant. She was as deadly and as vicious as any rattler. If he let his guard down for even a moment, he was certain she would find a way to strike out at them. He'd learned his lesson from El Diablo. He would never make the same mistake again.

"You got her?" Riley asked.

"I've got her."

As they left the house, Jack glanced down the street to where Amanda walked with her father. He realized that in all the excitement, he hadn't had time to thank her for warning him about Mona.

It was nearly an hour later when Jack finally left the sheriff's office. Riley had everything under control. The circuit judge would be there in two weeks, and the trials would be held then.

Peace reigned once again in San Rafael. It was a good feeling.

Jack stopped at the stage office to fill Isaac in on all that had happened. That done, he debated with himself whether he should go back to his hotel or go check on Dan.

The memory of Amanda's declaration to Ted that she loved someone else left Jack puzzled. He wondered if she'd really meant it or if it had just been a ruse to make Ted angry so that he'd make a mistake. Jack had to talk to Amanda and find out, for now that the stage line was back in business, he would be leaving soon. He had to find Steve and hunt down the Sheldons before they ambushed him. Before he rode out, though, he would see Amanda. Loving her as he did, he needed to know the truth of her feelings for him.

Eileen saw him coming to the door, and she called out to Dan and Amanda, "Jack's here!"

She hurried to let him in.

"Are Dan and Amanda all right?" he asked as he entered the house.

"They're as fine as they can be," she told him.

Dan had come to the door of the parlor to greet him. "Come on in, Jack. We're about to have dinner. Will you join us?"

"I really just came over to say good-bye," he began.

"Good-bye? Where are you going?"

"Now that everything is safe here, I've got to head out and see about locating the Sheldons."

"You haven't heard any more about them?"

"Not a word, and that bothers me. They're out there somewhere gunning for me, and I don't like being the hunted. I'd much rather be the hunter."

They walked into the parlor where Amanda was sitting.

"Jack's planning on leaving us, Amanda," Dan said as they entered the room. "He's going after the Sheldons."

Amanda met Jack's gaze across the room. "I knew you would. I'm just surprised that you stayed as long as you did."

"Dan needed me. I couldn't let him down."

"And you didn't. I don't know what we would have done without you."

"I was just glad I could help."

"Will you stay for dinner?" Dan prodded.

"All right."

"Good," Eileen said from behind them. "I'll have Maria set an extra place."

The meal was at once a celebration and a time of mourning. Though Asa was dead, at least the ones responsible were now in custody and justice would be served.

"I could sure use your help around here, if you want to change your mind and stay," Dan was saying as they finished the meal.

"If I didn't have the Sheldons to worry about, I might stick around, but I don't want to risk their showing up in San Rafael and causing more trouble. Two friends of mine, Luke Majors and his wife, Cody, sometimes work as bounty hunters. They're out tracking them now, so I plan to ride out with Stalking Ghost first thing in the morning. If I can catch up with Cody and Luke, I'll be able to find out what's going on."

"I hope they've already caught them," Eileen said. She was worried about Jack and wanted him to be safe.

"That would be nice," Jack agreed, but he knew he wouldn't be that lucky. "The way things have been going lately, though, I doubt it."

"But look at how quickly you found the robbers, and the sheriff had been looking for them for weeks," Amanda put in.

"That was just good tracking," Jack said as he looked across the table at her.

"Maybe your luck is changing," she said earnestly.

"I'd like to think so—"

For one searing moment, their gazes met and locked. Though it was only for an instant, it seemed an eternity to them.

Amanda was remembering everything Eileen had told her about her Andrew—about how he'd gone away and never came back. She wondered if she could let Jack go without telling him the truth of her love for him.

Jack was mesmerized by the intensity of the look in Amanda's eyes. He remembered her words to Ted— *Not when I love someone else.*

Still, Jack knew he had to find the Sheldons and put them away where they belonged.

The sound of Dan's voice jarred them both back to reality.

"Well, I'm feeling a little weak after all this excitement. I think I'd better lie down for a while," he said.

Amanda tore her gaze from Jack's and noticed how pale and drawn her father looked. "I'll help you upstairs," she said, quickly going to his side as he started to get up from the table.

"And I'd better be going," Jack announced as he, too, stood.

"Will we see you again before you go?" Dan asked.

"No. I'll be heading out at dawn."

"You be careful and let us know how you are," Eileen said, her heart breaking at the thought that he was leaving.

"I will," he promised her as he went to shake hands with Dan.

"We'll miss you," Amanda said simply.

Jack looked her way, and again their gazes met. His went over her carefully, storing away the memory of her beauty to carry with him.

"Good bye, Amanda." His words were quiet, reflecting none of the searing emotions that filled him at the thought of never seeing her again.

Amanda ached to tell Jack how much she wanted him to stay, but he had already turned and was walking from the room. She watched him leave the house and wondered if she could bear to let him go.

# Chapter Twenty

Much later that evening, Amanda sat on the porch alone. The night was quiet. It was dark, too, as dark as her mood. She longed for a distraction, anything to take her thoughts from Jack, but there was none. There was just the all-enveloping loneliness and her memories of Jack's loving.

Amanda got up and moved to stand at the porch railing. She stared up at the night sky, but did not see the stars that shone there. Instead, she saw only infinite emptiness. She saw a reflection of her life without Jack.

She smiled ruefully at the truth of her feelings. He had matched her toe-to-toe since that night at The Palace. She had met her match, and her match was Jack Logan.

A soul-weary sigh wracked her. It did little good to stand there and profess her love for him to herself.

She knew the way she felt, but Jack didn't, and he was leaving San Rafael in just a few hours.

All that Eileen had told her about her lost-at-sea fiancé continued to haunt her. Could she let Jack go without telling him that she loved him? He might not care. He might laugh at her and dismiss her claims of devotion as nonsense. But then, there was always the chance, however slight, that it might make a difference, that he might truly care in return.

Tormented, Amanda started back inside. She meant to go up to her room to bed, but she knew she wouldn't sleep, not with Jack leaving at dawn. Unable to decide what to do, she was doing nothing, and that was totally foreign to her personality. Usually, she would act on her impulses, but then, she'd never been in love before.

As she started up the stairs, Amanda was startled to see Eileen come out of the kitchen.

"I didn't know you were still up," Amanda told her.

"I couldn't sleep. It was such an eventful day—"

"I know. That's why I was sitting outside. I knew I wouldn't be able to sleep, so I thought a breath of fresh air would help."

"Did it?"

"No, not really. I keep thinking about Jack."

Eileen smiled knowingly. "I don't want him to go. I've truly come to care about him."

"He is a good man."

"Who's had a very hard life. Things don't come easily to him."

"You were right about him being a good Ranger. I

still can't believe that he found Ted's men so quickly.''

"He's very good at what he does. Look how he got you back here all safe and sound.''

Amanda smiled, her first smile in hours. "He certainly earned his money.''

"And I doubt he would have traded the adventure for anything.''

"I don't know about that. I tend to think that he would rather have been out tracking down the Sheldons than staying here, guarding me.''

"Tracking the Sheldons would probably have been easier.''

They shared a smile.

"I hope he finds them soon.''

"I do, too. Then maybe he'll come back here to us.''

"I don't know, Eileen. As a Ranger, he'll have to travel all the time, won't he? He wouldn't want to come back here.''

"Not unless he knew there was something worth coming back to. Did you ever tell him how you felt?''

"I wasn't really sure until just lately, and now it's too late. He's leaving.''

Eileen looked sad. "I'm sorry. You're both so perfect for each other. I thought surely you would see it.''

"We were too busy being at cross purposes to allow ourselves to fall in love. I don't think he feels for me what I feel for him.''

"I wouldn't be too sure about that. You didn't see him when you were brought back wounded. I did.''

Amanda looked at her, surprised. "What happened?"

"Well, first, you know he hit Ted. Then, when we were waiting at Dr. Clayborne's office, he was like a caged animal. He cares about you Amanda... deeply."

Amanda's eyes misted at the thought that Jack truly did care for her. "I didn't know—"

"I don't know what's kept you apart, but don't you think it's time you straightened it out? He'll be leaving in just a few hours. If you really love him, then go to him now and tell him," Eileen urged. "Don't miss your chance at happiness. How would you feel if you never had the chance to tell him you loved him?"

Amanda hesitated only a minute more. Then, impulsively, she hugged Eileen. "Thank you."

"Go to him and talk to him. At least then you'll know the truth of how he feels."

Amanda cast a look up the stairs, worrying about her father.

"Don't worry. He's sleeping like a baby. Go!"

Amanda hurried from the house and went straight to the hotel. There was no one in the small lobby except the night clerk. Amanda didn't even stop, for she knew Jack's room number. The clerk eyed her strangely. It was highly unusual for a woman like Amanda Taylor to pay a night visit to anyone. He wondered what was going on.

Amanda made her way to Jack's room and didn't hesitate before knocking. She was afraid that if she took the time to think about what she was doing, she would change her mind, and she couldn't do that. She knocked at the door and waited.

Jack was lying in bed, staring at the ceiling, counting the hours until sunrise. He would be leaving San Rafael forever. There was no reason to come back. There were no ties to bind him here. No reason to stay.

The knock at the door took Jack by surprise. He thought it was either Stalking Ghost or Isaac coming to bring him news. Pulling on his pants, he raked a hand through his hair as he went to open the door. He expected one of his friends. He was startled to find Amanda standing in the hall.

"Amanda! What are you doing here?"

"I need to talk to you, Jack."

"What's wrong? Has your father taken ill?"

"No, this has nothing to do with Papa."

"Then, why . . . ?"

"May I come in?"

Disconcerted, he stepped back. "Of course."

She moved past him, her head held high. He watched her cross the room to stand near the window. He tried to gauge her mood, but she gave nothing away. He closed the door and faced her.

"What's wrong, Amanda?"

"Nothing is wrong, Jack. It's just that I—" She looked over at him. He was so tall and handsome. It was all she could do to stay where she was and concentrate on what she had to say to him. Remembering Eileen's story of her beloved Andrew, Amanda couldn't deny her feelings any longer. "Jack . . . I needed to see you one more time before you left. I couldn't let you go without telling you—"

"Telling me what?" He had no idea what she was about to say.

"I love you," she said simply, defying the nervousness that had threatened to hold her mute.

Jack stood stock-still for a moment. "You love me . . . ?"

"I know you probably think this is crazy," she went on quickly, nervously. "I did myself for a long time, but I realized I couldn't let you go without telling you how I feel about you."

Jack crossed the room toward her, his gaze never leaving her. "Amanda—"

She lifted her eyes to his as he neared her, and in that moment she knew she'd done the right thing. The truth of his feelings shone in his regard. He loved her as she loved him.

"I love you, too, Amanda," Jack said softly. "But I thought Ted was the man you wanted."

"Is that why you went to the saloon girl?" She knew it was stupid to bring it up, but she had to know the truth.

"Who told you about Susie?" He was shocked.

"Ted did. He heard her bragging about what a great time she had with you the night you went to her."

Jack chuckled as he took Amanda into his arms. "She had a great time because she didn't have to do anything for her money."

"I don't understand." She drew back to look up at him.

"It's true I went to the saloon the night I saw you kiss Ted. I had intended to get good and drunk. But as I was sitting there with a full bottle of whiskey, I realized that I was back in control of my life again, and that I didn't need to get drunk. I had almost decided to get up and leave when Susie walked over to me and propositioned me. I said yes and went upstairs with her because I thought you were in love with Ted.''

Amanda stiffened in his arms at the thought of him with another woman. He stroked her back in a soothing motion as he went on to tell her the end of the story.

''But when I got upstairs alone with Susie, I realized it was all wrong. I didn't want to make love to her. You were the only woman I wanted, the only woman I needed. . . . I paid her, but I told her that I wasn't interested—that she should take the money and take the night off. I'm sure that's what she was doing when she bragged about what a wonderful time she had with me.''

Amanda looked up at him, seeing the look of total honesty in his expression. ''You didn't make love to her?''

''No, I didn't, Amanda. I told her what I'm about to tell you—there is only one woman I want, and she wasn't the woman.'' Jack lifted a hand to cup her cheek. Softly, tenderly, he said, ''You are.''

He stopped talking then, and showed her how much he loved her. His kiss was a gentle caress of exquisite devotion. He cradled her to his heart, loving her, adoring her, never wanting to be separated from her. Loving her as he did, though, he put her from him.

''You'd better go home now.''

''Why?''

"Being here with me this way isn't going to do a thing for your reputation."

She smiled coyly, her gaze upon him. "Then I guess you'll just have to marry me to protect me."

He chuckled at her brazenness. "Are all the suffragists as determined and outspoken as you are?"

"Some are worse," she said with a grin. "You'll have to meet my Philadelphia friends some day."

"I'd like that. We could go there on our honeymoon."

"You'll marry me?"

"I suppose it would be more proper if I asked you, what do you think?"

She controlled her excitement and waited as he drew her back into the circle of his arms.

"Amanda Taylor, will you do me the honor of becoming my wife?"

"Yes, Jack. Oh, yes!"

She threw her arms around his neck and returned his kiss fully.

"You should go now," Jack said in a tight voice as he tried to control himself.

"I should," she said in a sultry voice that held much promise, "but I'm not going to."

"Good," he growled, his mouth claiming hers in a passionate exchange.

"I love you, Jack!"

It was a flaming kiss that made them both forget everything but the wonder of their need for each other. They came together in a blaze of glory.

Jack took infinite care as he helped her undress. His every caress and kiss told her all she needed to know about the depth of his love for her. When, at last, Amanda lay unclothed on the bed, she lifted her arms to him in silent invitation. He came to her and she sighed in welcome. She had wanted this moment ... longed for this moment. Jack loved her and she loved him. They would be married.

Jack moved over her, and his body was a searing brand against her. Amanda surrendered to the fire of his need, giving herself up to his knowing caresses. Lost in the mindlessness of their passion, they sought only to please each other. Each touch, each kiss stoked their desire higher and higher.

There was no shyness in Amanda this time. In Jack's arms, she'd found her heaven. She never wanted to be parted from him. As he claimed her for his own, she clasped him to her. She held him to her heart as they rocked together in the age-old rhythm. Rapture burst upon them in a moment of blissful perfection. Clinging together, they soared to the heights of ecstasy. Conquering and surrendering. Love's victory was theirs.

Limbs entwined, their hearts beating as one, they savored the intimate aftermath of their union with gentle touches and soft kisses.

Slowly, reality returned. Dawn would be coming soon. Soon, Jack knew he would have to ride out of San Rafael.

"I don't want you to go," Amanda said quietly as she lay cradled in his arms. She had splayed one hand across his chest and loved the feeling of the power of his heartbeat beneath her fingers. "Forget the Sheldons. Let your friends find them. Stay here with me."

There was nothing Jack wanted more than to stay with Amanda, loving her and cherishing her for the rest of his life, but there could be no hiding from the threat of the Sheldons. Until they were caught, everyone around him was in danger. He rose to press a soft kiss on her lips. "I love you, Amanda. But I have to make sure the Sheldons are caught."

"There's nothing I can say or do to change your mind?" She lifted one hand to caress his cheek, and he pressed a kiss to her palm.

Pain shone in his eyes as he looked down at her. "I don't want to leave you. God knows I don't, but these men are killers who will stop at nothing to get me. I want to find them before they find me."

They said no more, but came together again, desperate to love, to have these memories to sustain them when he left.

The dark hours of the night began to fade, and Jack drew away from her.

"It's almost light, Amanda."

"I know. If I had my way, dawn would never come, and we could stay here forever."

He kissed her one last time, then left the bed to dress. It was with a heavy heart that he forced himself to leave her, but he knew it was the only way for them to have a future.

"I'll take you home before I go. I want to make sure you're safe. And as soon as I get back, we'll be married."

"I'll be waiting."

"I'll hurry back."

She rose and dressed. Jack took her in his arms and

358

held her quietly for a long moment. When at last they broke apart, Amanda had tears in her eyes as she gazed up at him.

"You'll be careful?"

He nodded solemnly. The depth of her emotions touched him. It strengthened him to know that she would be waiting for him.

Jack had gathered his things and strapped on his gun. Amanda watched him quietly and saw the intensity and courage that made him such an effective Ranger. When he turned to look at her, her heart swelled with pride. Jack Logan would soon be her husband. She loved him.

They slipped quietly from the hotel. When they reached her house, he kissed her one last time and watched until she was safely inside.

Determination settled over him as he turned away, grimly ready to finish what the Sheldons had started. He did not know that Amanda was watching him go from the window or that she was praying that he would be safe.

Amanda turned away from the window and was surprised to find Eileen watching her from the top of the steps.

"He's still going?" the older woman asked as she came downstairs.

"Yes . . . But we're going to be married as soon as he gets back."

"That's wonderful!" Eileen went to her and hugged her. "Your father will be thrilled. He thinks the world of Jack."

"So do I." Amanda sighed. "I love him so much, Eileen. I couldn't bear it if something happened to him."

Eileen gave her a sympathetic look. "I know, but nothing is going to happen to our Jack. He's the best. He's going to hunt down those Sheldons and get back here as quickly as he can."

"Do you think he'll be back by noon?" Amanda asked, forcing a smile.

"As good as he is, anything is possible." Eileen laughed. "He'll be back. You've given him something to live for. Nothing will stop him from returning to you."

"I hope you're right."

Eileen hoped she was, too. Jack had told them how dangerous the Sheldons were. With all her heart, she prayed that they were caught soon. She loved Amanda like a daughter and wanted her to have the happiness with Jack that she herself had never had with Andrew. She slipped an arm around Amanda's waist.

"Do you want to go to bed or shall we have a very early breakfast and start planning your wedding?"

"Let's have breakfast," Amanda said, smiling. She knew Eileen was trying to distract her and she was glad for her efforts. "I can't wait to tell Papa."

They walked into the kitchen, looking toward the future.

Rock Water turned out to be every bit as decadent as Cody and Luke had heard. Cody was quickly hired on as Armita at the saloon. She always went into these situations not quite knowing what to expect. In El Terrón it had taken a long time to find out what she needed to know, but this time she was surprised and pleased by the looseness of the talk. She supposed it was because most everyone in town was on the wrong side of the law that no one cared who talked. Alice and Nina were filling Armita in on the clientele.

"Nina, when are your two favorite customers coming back?" Alice asked her sarcastically.

"Never, I hope," the girl spat.

"From the look on your face, Alice is teasing you about them being your favorites. Who are they? Maybe I should watch out for them, so I can avoid them," Cody said.

"Their names were Hank and Willy. They were brothers. I don't know their last name and I don't care."

Cody was careful to keep her reaction hidden, but she tensed at the mention of the first names. It had to be the Sheldons. There couldn't be two other brothers in the same area with the same names. "What did they do that was so horrible?"

Nina shivered visibly. "The one named Hank seemed nice enough at first, but I was wrong. They were mean and ugly—both of them."

"You were lucky they left then," Cody remarked, wanting to lead with that question.

"Yes, but I feel sorry for the man they are after."

"They were after a man? Were they lawmen?"

Nina laughed coldly at her. "No, the one they were after—he was the lawman. A Ranger named Logan."

"How did they find out where he was? Rangers usually keep on the move, don't they?"

She shrugged. "All I know is that they read something in the newspaper about how this Ranger had arrested a gang in Del Cuero and was heading back to San Rafael."

"If they are as mean as you say, I wouldn't want to be that Logan right now, and I really wouldn't want to be one of the girls in San Rafael," Cody said.

"Me either. I hope they never come back here."

A few men drifted into the saloon then, and Nina and Alice went to see to their needs. Armita got ready to put on another show. Luke hadn't come in yet, but when he did, she'd warn him to be ready to ride at midnight. They had to get to San Rafael fast. The Sheldons were closing in on Jack.

The following day at the saloon everyone wondered what had happened to the beautiful Armita. She had disappeared without a trace.

# *Chapter Twenty-one*

"I heard some interesting news today," Jenny said almost snidely as she came to stand by Susie at the bar.

"What?" Susie was always eager to hear gossip.

"I was in the dry goods store and I heard two women talking. You know, that Amanda Taylor and the old lady who lives with her."

"Yes. So?"

"So, it just turns out that your precious Jack Logan is getting married."

"What?"

"That's right. For all that you said he showed you a real good time that night, I guess you didn't please him enough. He's marrying the Taylor girl just as soon as he gets back to town."

"I didn't even know he'd left," Susie said with a shrug.

"I thought you liked him." Jenny had hoped to upset her. She was jealous of Susie because all the customers seemed to like her best.

"I do like him, but I didn't want to marry him. Amanda Taylor is a lucky girl."

"I'll say," Jenny agreed.

"Where did Jack go, do you know?"

"They were talking about it, but all I heard them say was that he had some Ranger business to take care of."

"That's right. I heard he'd gone back to work for the Rangers. I heard he was real good at his job, too."

"He must be. Look at how quickly he brought in the ones responsible for robbing the stage."

"I don't know what kind of a life it's gonna be for his wife, being married to a Ranger."

"Not much of one, I'd think. I sure wouldn't want to be married to a Texas Ranger. It's a dangerous job."

They started to talk of other things, unaware of the two trail-dusty, unshaven men standing just a short distance from them at the bar.

"That marriage is going to be a short one, if they have time to get married at all," Hank said to his brother with a smile.

"Sometimes we just get lucky," Willy said, feeling very good about being in San Rafael. "He may be gone right now, but his intended is here and we know he'll be back. All we have to do is lay low and wait for him to walk right into our trap."

"Shall we spend the night here and check out Miss Amanda Taylor in the morning?"

"That sounds like a plan to me."

"I think I'll get a shave and a bath and a woman while I'm here," Hank said.

"Enjoy. I'm just going to drink."

Hank had one more whiskey and then snared Susie around the waist and kissed her. "You know how to show me a good time?"

"I sure do, honey," she cooed.

"Good. Get me a bath up to one of the rooms, and I'll let you wash my back."

"Is that all you're going to let me wash?" she asked, giving him a hot look.

"Woman, you can wash whatever you want on me. The night is yours."

"I think I'm going to enjoy you, cowboy." She took his hand and led him upstairs.

Willy just watched them go and shook his head. He knew what Hank was thinking. From the conversation they'd overheard, Logan had bedded Susie, and now Hank wanted her. It wouldn't surprise him in the least if Hank went after the Taylor girl after they'd taken care of Logan. That might just be worth watching.

He ordered another whiskey.

When Hank emerged from Susie's room the next morning, he found his brother sleeping at one of the tables. He kicked his chair to wake him.

"Let's go. I want to check on that Taylor woman. Susie mentioned that she works at the stage office some days. So we can walk past there and get a look at her. I want to see what kind of taste Logan has in women."

Willy stood up, still groggy from all the liquor he'd drunk. He was half-staggering as he followed his brother from the saloon. They were careful not to draw any attention to themselves as they moved through town. They walked past the stage office and saw the dark-haired beauty through the window. Once they'd moved far enough away, Hank just had to remark on her.

"He's got fine taste in women," he told his brother. "I wouldn't mind sampling some of that."

"You wouldn't mind samplin' some of anything that wears skirts."

Hank grinned a leering grin at him. "Some meat is better quality. She's a looker."

"And that's all you're gonna do—just look. We're here for Logan, nothing else."

"We'd better ride out of town and find us a campsite. If he's off running with the Rangers, it may be a while before he comes back. Somebody'll start wondering about us if we stay in town too long, and we don't need that."

They picked up supplies at the general store and left San Rafael that morning. They would check back in a day or two to see if Logan had turned up. Patience was the answer to finding him, and they would wait as long as they had to.

Cody and Luke had some planning to do before they could ride into San Rafael. It took them an extra day to put their new disguises together, but finally Sister Mary's Salvation Show rolled down the main street. Cody was dressed in a high-necked, long-sleeved black gown, and Luke was dressed in a black suit and tie. They looked solemn and holy and ready to convert the entire town. The wagon they were driving was painted with revival slogans—*Repent And Be Saved! The End Is Near!* Cody hoped the last one was particularly true. She wanted the end to be near. She wanted the Sheldons back in custody.

As they passed through town, Cody reined in at every corner. Luke jumped down and nailed up handbills proclaiming the news that they were in town and that their revival would start the following night and run for five straight nights.

Cody hoped five nights would be all it would take to locate the Sheldons. They were here somewhere. She could feel it. All she had to do was flush them out and trap them. As Sister Mary, she would have far greater access around town than she would have had as Armita, and, having enlisted Luke's help as a preacher, she was ready. With her gun hidden in the cut-out middle of her Bible, she could minister to the needs of both the poor in spirit with her preaching and the poor in morals with her gun.

Sheriff Riley saw the wagon coming and called out a greeting.

"Hello, Sheriff. I must say you have a beautiful town here," Cody said as she reined in before him.

"Why, thank you. It's a quiet place, and we like to keep it that way."

"You must have a lot of law-biding, God-fearing people in San Rafael."

"Sure do."

"It's no wonder, being named after Saint Raphael and all. We're going to enjoy our visit. It should be a profitable one for you and for us."

"I hope so. Anyone preaching the good news is always welcome here."

"Any suggestions where we might set up our tent?" Luke asked.

"Right on the outskirts of town up ahead will be fine. You should draw a good crowd."

"We plan to do our best to deliver our message," Cody added. "Repent and be saved! The end is near!"

"Will you both be preaching?"

"Yes. I'm Sister Mary and this is my partner, Luke. When he's preaching he goes by Brother Luke," she said earnestly. "His speeches are inspiring."

"Well, good luck to you. I'll be looking forward to hearing you. When will you be starting?"

"Tomorrow night. Eight o'clock."

"I'll be there."

They rode to the site the sheriff had suggested and began to set up their tent. They had an entire day to get the word out around town that Sister Mary's Salvation Show had arrived—and to locate the Taylor Stage and Freight Line's office and find out where Jack was.

It was late afternoon when Cody and Luke entered the office of Taylor Stage and Freight. Dan and Amanda were both working.

"Can we help you?" Dan asked, studying the somberly dressed pair.

"Hello, I'm Luke Majors and I'm—"

"You're Jack's friends," Amanda said, smiling brightly. "He told us about you. You must be Cody."

"Jack told you about us?" Cody was surprised.

"Oh, yes. He mentioned that you were bounty hunters," Dan said.

"Is he here?" Luke wanted to know. "We need to talk to him."

"No," Amanda told him. "He and Stalking Ghost rode out a few days ago to look for you. He wanted to learn what you'd found out about the Sheldons."

Cody and Luke exchanged glances, and then Cody quickly explained the situation. "We've been trailing the Sheldons, and they're here, somewhere close. They know that Jack made an arrest in Del Cuero and brought the men back to San Rafael for trial."

Luke asked, "Have you seen any strangers around town in the last few days?"

"I haven't noticed anyone," Dan said thoughtfully.

"Well, keep an eye out. I've got the wanted poster right here, so you'll have an idea of who to look for." Cody pulled the paper out and unfolded it for them to see.

Both Amanda and Dan studied it carefully.

"They're ugly. I won't miss them if I see them," Amanda said.

"Good, but be careful if you do see them. They're deadly and they know about Jack's connection to the stage line."

"Jack and I are going to be married."

Cody smiled brightly at her. "I'm so happy for you. Jack's a wonderful man."

"So what are your plans?" Dan asked.

"I'm Sister Mary. We're here as Sister Mary's Salvation Show. We're both preachers and we're holding a revival meeting that will begin tomorrow night."

"So we should call you Sister Mary in public."

"Please. Our hope is to somehow draw the Sheldons out into the open so we can catch them."

"If you need anything, anything at all, just let us know. We want to see them caught, too."

"All we ask is that you keep our identities a secret and let us know immediately if you see or hear anything."

"We will. I hope you find them soon," Amanda told them. "Do you have plans for dinner tonight? Would you like to come to our house?"

"Thank you. We'd love to."

Several hours later, they were all gathered around the dining room table at the Taylor home. Dinner had been delicious, and now they were taking the time to talk. Amanda and Dan had told them how Jack had come to be working for Taylor Stage and Freight. Luke had told them of Jack's background and then they had both filled in the details of the near tragedy with El Diablo.

"So he's back with the Rangers again," Luke said with satisfaction. "That's good. Last we'd heard of him was what Steve Laughlin told us when he came out to the ranch looking for him. It looks like meeting up with you, Amanda, straightened him out."

"Amanda is quite a woman," Eileen said. "I don't think Jack has ever met anyone like her before."

At their curious looks, she went on.

"Amanda is involved in the woman's movement. She's a suffragist."

"You are?" Cody looked at her with even greater respect. "That must be exciting."

"Occasionally it is, but mostly it's an uphill battle."

"But one worth the effort."

"I think so, but I haven't had much time to deal with it since I've been back home."

"Tell Cody what you were doing when you first met Jack," Eileen encouraged her. "Tell her about The Palace. She'll enjoy that story."

"The Palace?" Dan interrupted, a curious look on his face. "Exactly what is The Palace?"

Amanda smiled sheepishly at her father. "A saloon in Philadelphia."

"Your grandmother let you go into a saloon?" he roared.

"Grandmother didn't know. I told her I was spending the night with a friend. It wasn't a lie. I was planning to—after we marched on The Palace."

"You marched on a saloon?" Cody was amazed.

Amanda nodded. "I was involved with the temperance marchers, too. We went into The Palace that night and smashed up liquor bottles using axes."

"You what!" Dan was shocked.

"Don't worry. Jack got me out of there just in time. I didn't get arrested, but some of my friends did."

"Amanda—" he began in a stern voice.

"Papa," she said with dignity, "a man who drank there regularly had gotten drunk and beaten his wife to death. That's why we attacked it."

"No wonder your grandmother wanted you to come home," he said, finally coming to understand what his mother-in-law had meant when she'd said that Amanda was out of control.

"It wasn't that outrageous," she argued. "It was important."

"What did Jack say when he found you there?" Luke had to know.

"He wasn't altogether pleased," she said mildly.

"I'll bet," Dan remarked drolly. "Here I promised him that you were a sweet young thing who just needed an escort home."

Amanda couldn't help smiling. "The first time he saw me, I was smashing whiskey bottles with an axe."

"You're kidding." Cody couldn't believe it. Amanda looked like such a lady—but then, she realized, she herself looked like a lady most of the time, too, and she was a bounty hunter.

"No, he had to take my axe away from me and carry me out of the saloon over his shoulder."

"He did?" Luke laughed at the image her description conjured up.

"At first, I thought I'd been kidnapped. It wasn't until he had me away from the saloon that he told me who he was and what he was doing there."

"I'm sure he won your heart that very first night," Cody teased.

"Hah! I thought he was high-handed and arrogant. I didn't want anything to do with him, and I think the feeling was mutual. But now, I can't wait until the Sheldons are locked up again so we can be married."

"We'll do everything we can to speed up your wedding date," Luke assured her.

"I'm counting on you. I just wonder where he is now. I wish I knew."

\* \* \*

Jack and Stalking Ghost made it to Del Cuero on the second day of travel and decided to spend the night there. Jack was in the Gold Nugget having a drink when Sheriff Barnes came in.

"Logan, I heard you were in town again. Good to see you . . . unless you're here on business?"

"No, just passing through," Jack said, smiling at the lawman.

"Things have been quiet since your last visit, but I have to tell you, you've been the talk of the town. People were excited to know that the county was safe for clean-living folks again. Why the Daily News ran an article about you making the arrests, and I think the Rock Water paper picked it up, too."

Jack stilled at this news. He hadn't thought that the arrests would be publicized. "The newspaper reports . . . Did they use names and dates?"

"Yeah, it was a good write-up about you."

Jack tensed. An article like that was the equivalent of sending up a smoke signal, telling the world where he'd been, and if the Sheldons saw it, it would be an open invitation for them to descend on San Rafael. "Thanks for telling me. I'm glad things are peaceful for you now."

"So are we."

They talked for a few more minutes; then Barnes thanked him again and left. Jack stared at his half-full glass of whiskey and knew there was no time to finish it. If the Sheldons had heard about the arrests, they were on their way to San Rafael right now—if they weren't there already.

Jack pushed his chair away from the table and stood

up. He would find Stalking Ghost and let him know that they would be heading back first thing in the morning. Amanda was in San Rafael unprotected. As vicious as the Sheldons could be, he wouldn't put anything past them. If they found out about his connection to Amanda, they might hurt her just to take revenge on him. He had to get back there right away.

Hank and Willy rode into town quietly after dark. They'd stayed away from San Rafael for a few days, lying low, wanting to give Jack time to return. The thought of whiskey and women, though, had driven Hank to ride back in tonight. He was ready for some action. As they reined in before the bar, he noticed the torches at the far end of the street.

"What the hell's going on down there?"

"I don't know, and I don't care," Willy told him. "I just want to get a drink. Your Susie will probably know."

They entered the saloon to find it crowded, and they had to stand at the far end of the bar to get a drink.

Hank asked the barkeep what the tent and torches were all about, and he told him.

"Traveling salvation show. It's been going on for a few nights already now."

"It certainly ain't hurt your business none," Hank chuckled, looking around at the hard-drinking crowd.

"Nah, if anything, them preachers just make us sinners want to sin more," the barkeep drawled.

"They any good?"

He shrugged. "I listened to them for a while the

first night. The woman calls herself Sister Mary and the man calls himself Brother Luke.''

"They didn't convince you to repent and clean up your life? Give up sinning and all that?"

"They were good, but I figure I'm too far gone to be saved." He chuckled. " 'Course if I was going to be saved, I'd sure want that Sister Mary to do the saving. She is one nice looking woman—if she wasn't so damned serious about sinning and going to hell.''

"She's that good?"

"She's worth listening to. Why don't you have a whiskey or two and then go give it a listen? It'll probably sound better to you after you've had a few. Besides, you're not going to miss anything. The revival usually goes on for a couple of hours.''

"Sounds good to me. Fill it up again," Hank said as he shoved his glass across the bar.

The bartender did as he'd directed.

"Where's the lovely Susie tonight?" Hank wondered as his gaze skimmed over the room looking for her.

"Oh, she's around. Just keep an eye out. She'll turn up.''

He and Willy enjoyed two more drinks before Susie approached them.

"Evening, Hank . . . Willy. Good to see you back in town.''

"It's good to see you, too. But I want to see even more of you.''

"I like the way you think," she said in a deep voice, looking up at Hank hungrily. He'd paid her nicely the last time he was there.

"Let's go."

"What about the revival?" Willy asked.

"Go take a look and let me know. As good as I'm feeling tonight, this ain't gonna take long."

Susie rubbed against him as they started upstairs to take care of business. Willy had another drink, then left the bar to see what was going on down at the tent.

"Say Amen!" Cody called out to the crowd gathered under her tent.

Amanda and Eileen were sitting in the very front row, enjoying her show. Dan had attended the night before and had decided to stay home and rest tonight.

"Amen!" they shouted in return.

"Do you believe in salvation?"

"We do!"

"Do you believe in the Lord's Commandments?"

"We do!"

"Then live those Commandments, brothers and sisters! Every day of your lives, live the Lord's Commandments!"

"Amen!"

"Do unto others as you would have them do unto you!"

"We hear you!"

"Love one another!"

Willy had been standing in the back of the crowd, but slowly made his toward the front. When Sister Mary called out for them to "love one another," he couldn't resist.

"Hey, Sister, come on down here, and I'll follow that Commandment! You can love me all you want!"

His tone was lewd and drew groans and disgusted looks from the others at the revival.

Cody couldn't see him clearly from where she stood on the stage, but she wondered if maybe—

"Brother, I will come to you, if it will save your immortal soul," she said, descending from the stage and making her way through the crowd toward him.

Luke took over on the stage. He wasn't quite sure what his wife was up to, but then, that wasn't unusual. "Let us pray that Sister Mary may convert this man's soul. Let us pray that he will be saved tonight!"

"Amen!" The crowd was really getting in the mood of the prayer meeting now.

Amanda and Eileen turned in their seats to watch as Cody, carrying her Bible, walked toward the loud-mouthed man. He was obviously some crude fool who just wanted to disrupt things, but Amanda was sure Cody could handle him. Certainly if he gave her any real trouble, Luke was very close, not to mention all the men who were there because they truly wanted to be. As Amanda stared at the sinner, though, she went still and grabbed Eileen's arm in a nervous grip.

"What is it?" Eileen asked, wondering at the sudden change in her.

"Look at him!" she said in a low voice.

Eileen did, and then glanced back at Amanda. "Do you think . . . ?"

"The resemblance is there."

Cody approached the would-be troublemaker. "What is your name, friend? Tell us, so we can pray for your soul."

"To hell with this. My soul's just fine." The man's

tone was ugly as he started to turn away.

"But, friend, we are here to help you. We want to see you reach the Promised Land. We want to see you glorified in the Spirit!"

"I'm glorified in the spirit all right," he laughed at her. "The spirit is called whiskey, and I glorify it every chance I get."

" 'Be ye not drunk with wine, but be ye filled with the Spirit!' " she exhorted him.

"I like drunk with wine better," he said nastily as she came to stand before him.

Cody stared up at him long and hard. All the on-lookers thought it was just Sister Mary trying to win him over. But Cody was studying his rough-hewn features carefully and identifying him as Willy Sheldon.

"If you will not repent and change your ways, at least tell your brothers and sisters gathered here to-night your name, so we can pray for your immortal soul."

"These ain't my brothers and sisters. The only brother I got left alive is back at the saloon, mounting some whore." He started back in the direction of the saloon.

This man was Willy Sheldon. There was no doubt in Cody's mind, and from what he'd just revealed, Hank was nearby, too.

Cody's mind was racing as she tried to figure out the best way to entrap them. She couldn't just stop her revival and run off to the saloon to take them into custody. She could try to take Willy right now—she had her gun close—but the tent was crowded and, as drunk as he was, Willy just might be stupid enough to try to shoot it out with her. There had to be a better way. The hardest part of her job was over. She'd located the Sheldons, and Jack was still alive.

"We should pray for your brother, too," she said quickly, following him. "He is a lost man."

Willy chuckled lasciviously, but didn't stop walking. "Hank ain't lost right now. He knows exactly what he's doing and who he's doing it with. See ya later, sister. Good luck saving souls—you're going to need it. But if you ever decide to give it up, I can find something else for you to do for a living."

Luke was busy speaking to the crowd while trying to keep an eye on his wife. It was impossible to see what she was up to, and he wondered why she was bothering with the drunk.

Amanda and Eileen exchanged looks. "We've got to help her. That was Willy Sheldon!"

"What can we do?"

Amanda thought for a moment and remembered The Palace saloon. "Come on! I know exactly what will work!"

# Chapter Twenty-two

Cody watched until Willy had re-entered the saloon; then she cast a quick glance toward the stage. She needed to alert Luke to the Sheldons' presence, but he was continuing to preach to the crowd, unaware of her discovery. Amanda and Eileen approached her just then.

"Sister Mary!" Amanda called out as she and Eileen marched up to her. "Do you agree that demon liquor is the bane of our existence?"

Cody's eyes lit as she quickly guessed Amanda's strategy, and she reminded herself to be sure to thank Amanda when this was over. "Liquor is the root of all men's evils!" she agreed.

"Down with demon liquor!" Eileen shouted, and in that moment, Amanda and Eileen held up the axes they'd just grabbed from a nearby store.

"Let's drive that evil influence from our midst!" Amanda urged, goading the crowd to action.

"Let's march on the den of drunkards—the saloon of sinners—the garden of the godless!" Cody called out.

"Amen!" Eileen echoed enthusiastically.

"Let's bring these degenerate men to their knees. Only then, when they've been humbled, will they learn the saving grace of God's love!" Cody preached.

A roar of approval was growing through the crowd.

"Sister Mary! What's happened?" Luke called from the stage.

"We are marching on the saloon to save the sinners there!"

Cody started off in the lead, her Bible clutched firmly in hand. Willy and Hank Sheldon were inside the bar, and she was going to nail them. Amanda and Eileen followed right behind her, proudly holding their axes.

"Down with demon liquor!" Eileen shouted, grinning at Amanda. Then she whispered, "Since I've known you, my life has become so exciting!"

Amanda chuckled at her friend. "I'm glad you're enjoying this."

"I won't really be enjoying myself until the Sheldons are locked up and our Jack is safe, but I'm going to do everything I can to help!"

"Maybe you missed your calling. *You* should have been a Ranger."

"The first female Texas Ranger? If only I were a few years younger," Eileen mused, finding the idea most intriguing.

The crowd behind them grew as Luke hurried down from the stage. He tried to catch up with Cody, not wanting her to face whatever was going to happen alone, but as he came down the steps, the townspeople gathered around him to ask him questions. It took him a few moments to be able to break free and follow his wife.

They looked like a straggling parade as Sister Mary led the revivalists though the center of San Rafael. Wanting to stay in disguise, Cody burst into strains of "Onward Christian Soldiers." Amanda and Eileen picked up the tune, and soon a rough but vocal chorus was singing along with them.

Cody reached the swinging doors of the saloon and didn't even pause. She marched straight in and confronted the patrons.

"Repent of your evil ways and be saved!" she shouted, holding her Bible high.

"What the hell?" The bartender was shocked by this mainly female invasion.

Cody ignored him as she let her gaze sweep the room, looking for both Hank and Willy. She spotted only Willy, standing at the far end of the bar.

"We've come to save you from the evils of liquor and sin!" Amanda announced, and with one easy swing of her axe, she cleared a large portion of the bar and sent customers scurrying for safety.

"Down with demon liquor!" Eileen followed Amanda's example and smashed a bottle of whiskey on a nearby table.

"Get out of here!" the barkeep thundered as the bar began to fill up with more and more of their followers.

Upstairs, Hank and Susie had just finished enjoying

themselves and were coming out of the room as the excitement broke out below.

"What's going on?" he asked, peering down over the railing.

"It's crazy!" Susie said. "There's that Sister Mary from the Salvation Show, and she's busting up the bar!"

Hank muttered a few curses at being so disturbed. He'd just wanted to have a few drinks and enjoy himself. He went on downstairs to get a good look at the stupid woman who'd dared to invade the saloon. As he reached the main floor, he noticed that the Taylor girl was with her. In fact, she was one of the two females who were wielding axes, breaking liquor bottles.

"Why the hell aren't you doing something?" Hank demanded of the barkeep. "Stop them, damn it! They're wrecking the place!"

"They're ladies—" the barkeep said impotently as he watched them smashing more glasses.

Cody had maneuvered herself closer to Willy, under the pretense of wanting to save his soul.

"Brother, pray with me," she said, getting ready to open her Bible.

"Get away from me, woman!"

"But, friend, you came to us. Your soul is obviously yearning for salvation." She glanced toward Luke to see if he was closing in on Hank. He was, and she knew it was time to make their move. She didn't want to wait until things got too chaotic. It might prove too dangerous then.

"I don't give a damn about salvation. Go find yourself another sinner to save."

"But you're the one I want to deliver," Cody said as she slipped her hand inside the Bible. Coolly, calmly, she drew her revolver out and pointed it at Willy. She kept it low, where no one else could see it. "Let's go. I want you to walk right out of here like nothing is happening." Her tone changed. It was cold, hard and business-like.

Willy stared at her gun and grinned a drunken grin at her. "I didn't know preachers converted by force these days."

"I'm not converting you, Sheldon." She used his name. "I'm arresting you. My name's not Sister Mary. It's Cody Jameson Majors, and you're under arrest. Now move, before I put a hole in you right where you stand. The reward's payable dead or alive."

Willy was furious. He didn't like women much to begin with, and this bitch had caught him off guard. He wanted to hit her, to take the gun from her and use it on her. He almost tried, but decided against it. He'd heard of Cody Jameson before and knew she could handle the weapon. Glancing over at Hank, he saw his brother duck as he dodged flying glass from another destroyed bottle of liquor. Willy wanted to get his attention, but he had no time. Cody motioned for him to start moving.

"And make sure to keep your hands away from your sides. I'd hate to accidentally shoot you because I thought you were going for your gun."

Willy swore loudly as he passed her. He hadn't

given up. He was going to watch and wait for the chance to break free.

Amanda and Eileen were wreaking havoc in the saloon. Amanda was watching Cody, and when she saw her get her man, she wanted to cheer. Instead, she smashed another table full of glasses and bottles to keep everyone distracted. She'd recognized Hank when he'd come down the stairs, and she turned now, wanting to see if Luke was closing in on him. To her surprise, Hank was standing close to her, scowling as he watched her smash the liquor. Luke was caught up in the crush and was trying to shoulder his way through the crowd toward them.

It happened quickly.

Willy shouted out in warning to Hank. "It's a trap, Hank! Watch out! They're bounty hunters!"

Cody's reaction was swift. She pistol-whipped Willy from behind, driving him to his knees. In an instant, she had his hands bound behind him.

Hank heard his warning, saw Luke coming and immediately drew his gun.

People started screaming as they realized something other than a revival was going on. Some customers ran for the door.

Hank knew a shoot-out wouldn't work. He needed a shield—someone he could use for a hostage as he made his getaway—and the Taylor girl was perfect. He grabbed Amanda just as she realized his intentions. She tried to swing the axe at him, but he fended her attack off and tore the axe from her grip.

"Let me go!" She started kicking and screaming in earnest, until he brought his gun up for her to see.

"Shut up or I'll shoot you right now. I know you're Logan's woman. It won't bother me to kill you. In fact, I just might enjoy it!"

His hands on her were bruising, and Amanda knew real terror. This was nothing like when Jack had carried her out of The Palace. This was a real kidnapping.

She lifted her gaze toward Luke. He was standing within six feet of them, his gun drawn, his expression deadly.

"Let her go, Sheldon," Luke ordered.

Hank smiled evilly. "You're not getting your bounty this time. Willy!"

"Yeah," his brother answered groggily as he slowly staggered to his feet.

"Let's get out of here. I've got the Taylor woman."

Willy shook his head to clear it. When he saw what his brother had done, he grinned. "Untie me. You ain't that good that you can outsmart the Sheldons."

Cody did not yield to his threat. She did not lower her gun, but cocked it instead. "You're not getting out of here, Willy. Tell your brother to let Amanda Taylor go, or I'll shoot you right where you stand."

"Hank—" Willy was suddenly believing again all the stories he'd heard about Cody Jameson. "Hank, this is Cody Jameson. She's says she'll shoot me unless—"

"I heard her," Hank snarled. He was a survivor. His own safety and well-being had always come first with him, and he was trying to figure out just how to get himself out of there in one piece. He'd let Willy take care of Willy, and he'd get himself out of town.

He could always come back later and break him out of jail, if need be.

Hank held his gun to Amanda's head as he slowly moved toward the swinging doors. He was careful to keep his back to the wall.

"Untie and let him go," he ordered, knowing Cody wouldn't do it, but trying to threaten her anyway.

"I'm not giving your brother anything but a fast trip to jail," she returned. "You shoot Amanda Taylor, and I'll make sure you're both dead before she hits the ground."

Amanda was trembling and helpless as she listened to them. She longed for Jack. If Jack were there, she would be safe. Jack would save her. But Jack was gone. There would be no rescue.

Eileen, too, was standing off to the side. She was armed with her axe, but she knew she could do nothing to stop this. Luke and Cody were their only hope. She prayed desperately for help.

Luke was trapped. He kept hoping for a clear shot at Hank, but the outlaw was too cunning.

Hank dragged Amanda with him as he kept shifting his position, moving around the tables and people. The way he was holding her, with his gun at her head, kept Luke from taking his best shot. Cool heads prevailed at times like these, so he kept steely control over his desire to put Hank Sheldon six feet under. He kept his gun ready, waiting for the opportunity to save Amanda.

"You're not going to get out of town, Sheldon," Luke said in a low, threatening voice.

"Watch me."

All eyes were on him as he backed slowly toward the swinging doors.

Jack and Stalking Ghost rode straight for the Taylor house when they reached San Rafael. Jack all but threw himself from his horse and ran up the steps to pound on the door.

"Jack?" Dan was surprised to see him.

"Is Amanda here?" He wanted to make sure she was safe.

"No, not right now. She's in town with Eileen." He frowned. "What are you doing back so soon? Were the Sheldons caught already?"

"No. We got to Del Cuero and found out that the news about my bringing in Humes and Martin had spread around the county. If the Sheldons were close, they would have heard it and headed here looking for me. Have you seen any sign of them?"

"Not yet, but your friends Cody and Luke are here. They came into town just after you left."

"Are they still here?"

"Yes. In fact, that's where Amanda and Eileen went. They're at Sister Mary's Traveling Salvation Show."

*Sister Mary* . . . He remembered the stories of how Cody had tracked the El Diablo Gang. "Thanks, Dan. I'll be back."

He turned and hurried back to where Stalking Ghost was waiting for him. He mounted up.

"Sister Mary's in town," was all he had to say.

They found the tent relatively deserted.

"Where is everybody?" Jack asked the few towns-people who'd lingered behind.

"Down at the saloon," one lady told him. "Sister Mary led the way there. She wanted to rid the town of liquor. Some of the ladies who went with her were even carrying axes!"

Jack swore low under his breath. It had to be Amanda and Eileen. But why would they attack the saloon? Unless . . .

"The Sheldons must be down there," he said, look-ing at Stalking Ghost.

"I will go around back."

Stalking Ghost disappeared as Jack reined in and tied up his horse. On foot, he headed for the saloon. There were people milling around out in front talking in hushed excitement.

Jack made his way to the doors and looked inside to see Luke leveling his gun on Hank Sheldon, who was backing straight toward him. To Jack's horror, he could see that Hank had Amanda in his grasp and was holding a gun to her temple.

Rage filled him. He wanted to shoot Hank right then and there, but he dared not endanger Amanda. It took all of his iron-willed self-control to wait for the perfect opportunity.

"Hank!" Willy squawked from where Cody had him under the gun. "What are you doing? You can't leave me here!"

Hank didn't say a word. He just kept the gun on Amanda and his attention on Luke. He was getting out of there. He was not going back to jail. He had almost reached the doors. Once he was out of the saloon, he would quickly throw Amanda Taylor across his horse in front of him and ride out of town. Nobody would dare try to stop him as long as he had her with him.

Hank prided himself on being smart. He'd break Willy out later. Nothing was going to happen to Willy, but Logan's woman—now that was another story. He was going to enjoy having her all to himself. He smiled grimly and tightened his hold on Amanda as he felt the swinging doors at his back.

"Don't you worry none, little lady," he said in a low voice. "I'm going to take real good care of you. You won't even have the chance to miss your Ranger boyfriend."

"That's right," Jack said in a lethal voice as he stepped behind Hank, his gun digging into his spine. "Because her Ranger boyfriend is right here."

"Hank! Look out behind you!" It was Willy's shout that broke the stalemate.

Willy threw himself at Cody, going for her gun. Because she was a woman, he believed he could over-power her. But he'd never dealt with Cody Jameson Majors before. Cody fired instinctively at his attack. Her shot was deadly and accurate.

Willy Sheldon would never kill again.

In the same moment as Willy's attack, Hank turned. He threw Amanda aside bodily, ready to shoot Logan.

Two shots were fired, but neither came from Hank Sheldon's gun.

Jack's and Luke's shots hit the outlaw. When the smoke cleared, Hank lay dead at Jack's feet.

"Jack! You came!" Amanda got to her feet and launched herself into his arms.

Jack wrapped her in the strength of his loving embrace as Luke hurried to check Hank and make sure he wouldn't be hurting anyone ever again.

"Thank God I got here when I did," Jack groaned, holding her close. He gazed down at her, knowing he couldn't have gone on if anything had happened to her.

"I love you, Jack," she sighed, drawing him to her for a kiss.

Cody came to kneel beside Luke as he checked Hank over.

"He's dead?"

"Yes."

"Good shooting," she complimented both of them. "Amanda, are you all right?"

Amanda turned in Jack's arms to look down at her. "Now that Jack's here, I'm fine. Where's Eileen?"

"I'm here," she called out, hurrying to join them. "Thank God our Jack showed up."

"He does always seem to rescue us at just the right moment, doesn't he?" Amanda said, looking up at him with glowing eyes.

"That's what Texas Rangers are supposed to do, isn't it?" Eileen asked, a teasing look in her eyes.

Jack smiled at them. "You know, it would be nice if just once in a while, you two could stay out of trouble."

"Eileen and I realized that that was Willy Sheldon who'd come down to the tent to cause trouble. We had to do something to help Cody."

"And you did a fine job," Cody agreed as she stood up. "Your idea of marching on the saloon was brilliant. We couldn't have brought them in without you."

Eileen beamed. "I suppose we have to take you home and tell your father now, don't we, Amanda?"

She looked guilty. "Maybe we could wait a day or two before we tell him. I really don't want to upset him."

"Don't worry," Eileen said. "I'll handle it."

Stalking Ghost joined them then. He'd entered the saloon from the back entrance and had just made it to the main room when the shooting erupted.

"All is well," he said, looking at the two dead outlaws.

"All is well," Jack agreed. He drew his future bride to his side, just needing to make sure she was safe.

Sheriff Riley came running up then, for someone had gone to get him at the jail. "What happened?"

Jack explained all that had happened. "Luke and Cody Majors just brought in the Sheldon brothers. The bounty goes to them. I'll wire Steve Laughlin at Ranger Headquarters and let him know that the Sheldons are no longer a threat."

As Sheriff Riley took over, Amanda, Eileen and Jack headed for home. Cody and Luke agreed to come to the Taylor home as soon as they'd taken care of the salvation show.

It was several hours later that Amanda stood on the front porch with Jack, gazing up at the stars.

"I'm glad you're back safe and sound," Amanda told him as she stood before him, leaning back against his chest. "When Sheldon was dragging me out of the bar, all I wanted was for you to come and rescue me."

"I'm glad I could oblige," he told her. He was thrilled to be holding her and never wanted to let her go.

"Your friends Luke and Cody are wonderful. I could have used Cody back in Philadelphia."

Jack chuckled. "She is amazing. She and Luke are perfect for each other."

"Just like us?" Amanda asked, turning in his embrace and lifting her arms to loop them around his neck.

"Just like us," he agreed.

He kissed her then as he held her to his heart. It was a kiss of passion and devotion. It was a kiss that told her he was hers for all time.

They were perfect for each other.

# *Epilogue*

*Five Months Later*

The bride was beautiful as she stood at the altar before the priest with her groom beside her. Her white dress was full and flowing. Her veil was a sheer, elegant work of lace and seed pearls. Her groom was as handsome as she was lovely. Everyone in attendance at the wedding knew they were going to live happily ever after.

"I now pronounce you man and wife," the priest intoned. "You may kiss your bride."

She turned to her new husband and smiled almost shyly. They were married. They were man and wife. She had thought the day might never come, but it had.

"I love you," she whispered.

He only smiled and took her in his arms. Her heartbeat quickened and her pulse raced at being in his embrace. As his lips moved over hers, she gave herself into his safekeeping. They were finally married.

Everyone in the church looked on rapturously as they shared the couple's first kiss as husband and wife. It was so romantic.

"Isn't it wonderful?" Amanda sighed as she stood in the first pew with Jack, smiling blissfully at the sight of her father kissing Eileen.

"Very," Jack agreed. He slipped an arm around his own wife's shoulders and hugged her to him. "She's almost as beautiful a bride as you were four months ago."

She looked up at him, all the love she felt for him shining in her eyes. "Why, thank you."

"I'm only telling you the truth."

"I guess this makes us the old married couple now."

"That sounds good to me," Jack said. "I'm enjoying married life."

"I worried about that at first. I know you were so used to traveling with the Rangers all the time, and I didn't know if you could be happy living in one place."

"I'm happy living wherever you are," he told her. "Especially now that my son's on the way." He let his gaze drop to her slightly rounded stomach.

"Your daughter," she corrected.

"We'll see." He laughed. "Well, it's a good thing that I'm going to be around."

"I'm glad Papa gave you a full partnership in Taylor Stage and Freight when we got married."

"I am, too, and I promise you, Amanda, I'm going

to do everything in my power to make sure it stays as successful as it was when your uncle Asa was alive.''

''I know that, and so does Papa.''

''Did I tell you I picked up a letter from Cody and Luke at the post office earlier this morning?''

''No. How are they?''

He grinned. ''I don't think they're going to be doing any bounty hunting for a while.''

''Why not? Is something wrong?''

''No, something's very right. Cody is expecting their first baby just about the same time we're expecting ours.''

They smiled at the thought of their dear friends sharing the same joy that they were—soon they, too, would be parents.

Dismissed with a blessing by the priest, Eileen and Dan turned and started back down the aisle. Amanda and Jack and the rest of the wedding guests followed.

As Amanda and Jack left the cool, dark haven of the church and stepped out into the brilliant sunlight, they knew the future was going to be as bright and beautiful as that sunny day.

They would live happily ever after.

**Christmas means more than just puppy love.**

### "SHAKESPEARE AND THE THREE KINGS"
**Victoria Alexander**

Requiring a trainer for his three inherited dogs, Oliver Stanhope meets D. K. Lawrence, and is in for the Christmas surprise—and love—of his life.

### "ATHENA'S CHRISTMAS TAIL" Nina Coombs

Mercy wants her marriage to be a match of the heart—and with the help of her very determined dog, Athena, she finds just the right magic of the holiday season.

### "AWAY IN A SHELTER" Annie Kimberlin

A dedicated volunteer, Camille Campbell still doesn't want to be stuck in an animal shelter on Christmas Eve—especially with a handsome helper whose touch leaves her starry-eyed.

### "MR. WRIGHT'S CHRISTMAS ANGEL"
**Miriam Raftery**

When Joy's daughter asks Santa for a father, she knows she's in trouble—until a trip to Alaska takes them on a journey into the arms of Nicholas Wright and his amazing dog.

___52235-7                              $5.99 US/$6.99 CAN

# THE LADY'S HAND
## BOBBI SMITH
### Author of *Lady Deception*

Cool-headed and ravishingly beautiful, Brandy O'Neal knows how to hold her own with the riverboat gamblers on *The Pride of New Orleans*. But she meets her match in Rafe Morgan when she bets everything she has on three queens and discovers that the wealthy plantation owner has a far from gentlemanly notion of how she shall make good on her wager.

Disillusioned with romance, Rafe wants a child of his own to care for, without the complications of a woman to break his heart. Now a full house has given him just the opportunity he is looking for—he will force the lovely cardsharp to marry him and give him a child before he sets her free. But a firecracker-hot wedding night and a glimpse into Brandy's tender heart soon make Rafe realize he's luckier than he ever imagined when he wins the lady's hand.

\_4116-2                                          $5.99 US/$6.99 CAN

**Dorchester Publishing Co., Inc.**
**P.O. Box 6640**
**Wayne, PA 19087-8640**

Please add $1.75 for shipping and handling for the first book and $.50 for each book thereafter. NY, NYC, and PA residents, please add appropriate sales tax. No cash, stamps, or C.O.D.s. All orders shipped within 6 weeks via postal service book rate. Canadian orders require $2.00 extra postage and must be paid in U.S. dollars through a U.S. banking facility.

Name_____

Address_____

City_____ State_____ Zip_____

I have enclosed $_____ in payment for the checked book(s).

Payment <u>must</u> accompany all orders. ❏ Please send a free catalog.

# ATTENTION ROMANCE CUSTOMERS!

## SPECIAL TOLL-FREE NUMBER
### 1-800-481-9191

*Call Monday through Friday*
**12 noon to 10 p.m.**
**Eastern Time**
*Get a free catalogue,*
*join the Romance Book Club,*
*and order books using your*
*Visa, MasterCard,*
*or Discover®*

Leisure
Books

Love
Spell